TEMPTING HEATHER

Glen Innes Series

K.J Margaret Austin

EBOOK ISBN - 13 978-1-7635142-6-3
PAPERBACK ISBN - 13 978-1-7635142-7-0
HARDCOVER ISBN - 13 978-1-7635142-8-7

Cover design by: Roo Binary
Library of Congress Control Number: 2018675309
Printed in the United States of America

Craig & Kris - Thank you for letting me pick your brains about the wonderful, Aussie sport - Polocrosse. I hope I've done it justice.

To my brothers friends who have been waiting, very patiently, for Heath and Nate's story - enjoy ladies.

CONTENTS

'PROLOGUE'

Glancing around the crowded chapel with a sense of detachment, Heather Ross ignored the pitying looks, the whispers hushed behind hands. Her entire focus centred on the two open wooden caskets, tucked side-by-side on top the raised platform, a harsh statement of her place in life now. Orphaned. Alone.

Drawing in a shaky breath, Heather ran her hands down the length of her Dutch braids. Pulling the ends over her shoulders so they sat against her chest, the thick weight comforting.

Her mother had loved Heather's thick, dark hair, and for the first fifteen years of Heather's life, she never left the house without her mum first weaving it all into an intricate braid.

When mum had suddenly died late one cold, wet night, Heather's first thought had been: who will braid my hair every morning before school now?

Enter Oma and Opa; Heather's maternal grandparents, the only remaining relatives Heather had—her father's parents having long since passed away when Heather was only a few days old.

It had never been a question of them taking Heather in, their love and feelings of loss for their beloved daughter and son-in-law encompassing Heather. She'd been able to breath for the first time since finding out about the *accident, only now...*

Crashing back to Earth to the tinkling sound of glass hitting tiles, Heather glanced dazedly down at the broken pieces at her feet, a faceless being hovering around her saying words she couldn't understand.

She let herself be shifted away from the sharp mess and folded into her grandparents' soft lounge, distantly recognizing that they were no longer at the chapel but back at home.

Unaware of the trip from one place to another, Heather clenched her hands in her lap, staring sightlessly out at the crowd of adults milling around her grandparents' lounge room.

Oma would have been in her element—she loved entertaining—and Opa would have been in the corner, arguing energetically with his two friends.

Friends who stood too silent and grave now.

Friends who hadn't been able to look at Heather, their sorrow such that they had only wrapped their arms around her once in a tight embrace.

There wasn't enough air in the room. On her feet and moving through the kitchen to the back door before she was consciously aware of anything, Heather ignored the people calling her name.

Slamming out into the cold, crisp winter air, her legs carried her only as far as the top step leading from the veranda to the backyard. Folding in on herself, knees tucked to her chest, even the cold wood beneath her couldn't penetrate the emptiness she felt.

The dry washing blowing gently in the breeze was a cruel taunt—Oma had hung that load out to dry what only felt like seconds ago.

"Heath?"

Josh's voice spurred Heather into action. Surging to her feet, she hurried down the stairs and into the outside laundry room, grabbing the washing basket and peg bucket in each hand.

At the clothesline she started removing each garment, folding it neatly to set in the basket, and dropping the peg back into the bucket with a 'clack' against the others.

"Heath—you don't have to do that now—" Jackson's voice, soft and cajoling, moved closer. "Let someone else—"

"Oma would be so disappointed in me for leaving them out here," Heather interrupted, her tone brisk. "It's my responsibility to bring the washing in. It rained yesterday, Jesus, they've had an extra rinse cycle and everything."

Suddenly there were hands on her shoulders, spinning her gently from her self-appointed task, turning her till she faced three of her best friends. Josh Hart, his dark gaze stormy with anger and helplessness, his handsome face pale. Oliver Lawson, his too-tall body and too-wide shoulders spaced awkwardly to the side. And finally, Jackson Hart—the younger of the Hart twins, often overlooked for being the quieter of the two. It was his hands which cupped Heather's shoulders now, his eyes twisted with a pain that echoed hers.

Jackson had his own brand of heartbreak—his girlfriend and Heather's heart-sister having disappeared along with her family only twenty-four hours earlier.

"Why does everyone keep leaving, Jacko?" Heather asked, her words choking her. "Why does everyone keep leaving?"

Pulling her in for a tight hug, Jackson let her sob into his chest as he rubbed her back. "I dunno, Heath. But I'm not going anywhere."

"We're not going anywhere," Oliver murmured, adding his hand to Heather's back.

Jackson glanced at Josh who still stood silently apart from the group, and knew by his twins expression that Josh was holding on through sheer force of will.

Finally, Josh moved, and though he didn't add his voice to theirs in the promise they'd made, he rested his hand against the back of Heather's head firmly.

Life wasn't ever going to be the same again for them now—too much had happened in the last few weeks— but whatever the future did hold, they'd face it head-on: together.

'CHAPTER ONE'

"You look like a fairy princess!" Bastien announced in his high, squeaky voice, his gaze bright with excitement and interest as he stared up at his mother.

Smiling, Heather settled the veil a little more firmly into Faith's hair, adding her voice to the murmured agreements from the women in the room. "Couldn't have said it better myself, Bas-man."

"I'm so happy for you, Fay!" Ella Ives, one of Faith's bridesmaids, sniffed and then shifted on her feet fanning her face. Her rounded stomach from a surprise pregnancy, lovingly displayed by the dresses Faith had picked.

"Sorry," the woman muttered as she dabbed at her eyes, chin lifting she glared up at the roof, "damn hormones!"

Laughing, Faith whirled towards Ella and wrapped the woman up in a hard hug, ignoring her mother Sinead's half-hearted warning about wrinkling the dress.

"Don't apologise. I know how hard it is growing a person." Leaning back, she then sent a loving look at her small daughter, cradled protectively in Maria's arms.

Harmony Deirdre Hart had made her entrance into the world three months back, and was the light, alongside her big brother Bastien, in her parents' eyes.

She was also spoilt rotten by absolutely everyone

around her.

But she was an easy baby to love; with those famously wide green Hart eyes, her mother's small features, and almost no hair.

"Bald little alien," Heather whispered affectionately, running her finger down the length of Harmony's soft cheek. The little girl shifted slightly towards the soft caress, before settling back into deep slumber.

A weight resting on her shoulder, and glancing down at Faith's slightly smaller frame, Heather smiled. "God only hopes the hair comes in at some point—pretty as she is, I'm not sure that'll be enough if she's that bald kid through school."

"We'll buy her wigs," Faith replied sagely, her tone overflowing with contentment.

A soft knock at the door pulled everyone's attention away, and when Sinead bade the newcomer enter, Samuel smiled sheepishly as he stood framed in the doorway.

Weathered features creasing into a wide smile, he merely surveyed the room for a moment. "Wow. I must have stumbled up to Heaven's gates surely, for this cannot be a room of women, but rather a room full of angels."

Standing, Maria smiled and moved towards him while the others in the room giggled. "You, Samuel Hart, are an incorrigible flirt."

Accepting his smallest and newest granddaughter, Samuel pressed a soft kiss against the sleeping infant's forehead, would have replied had Constance not elbowed her way into the room at that second.

"What is everyone doing!" Constance demanded, colour high on her cheekbones as she pushed a strand of that distinctive dark, red hair out of narrowed eyes.

"Relax," Heather murmured, catching up a crystal wineglass filled with expensive champagne. She pressed the cool glass into Constance's fingers. "Everything is running on time."

Just as the rim of the glass touched her lips, Constance redirected, "Wait—I can't drink this. I haven't expressed any milk for Leo."

Sighing, Heather accepted the drink back and watched as Constance marched around the room, ordering everyone around like the tiny general she was.

She'd taken on the Maid of Honour role quite seriously, her friendship with Faith having blossomed into something deep and binding the past year.

Sipping the champagne herself, Heather eased into one of the deep lounge chairs, surveying the room with a critical eye.

Maria and Sinead stood with Samuel between them, dressed up to the nines and clucking down at the sleeping face of their newest grandchild.

To the side, Grace and Bastien were watching something on her iPhone with rapt attention. Every so often they'd both descend into fits of loud laughter.

Isla was furiously typing away at a laptop which she balanced on her knee, simultaneously picking pieces of fruit off the tray immediately to the right of her on the table. The whole time she showcased her multitasking skills, holding a conversation with Deirdre who sat across from her.

Constance and Hope looked to be in a serious conversation, while Faith sat in front of the mirror, gazing dreamily at her own reflection.

The air was perfumed with the aroma of roses and

lavender, and the soft light filtering in through the wide-open windows also allowed for the sound from outdoors to mingle with the soft buzz of conversation.

The wedding party on the bride's side had spent the night at the pub, but you'd be forgiven in believing the experience was anything less than five stars.

The renovations had completed five months prior, and the establishment was wholly unrecognisable. The detailing and finishes to such degree that Heather knew, without asking, Nathaniel had stood and personally overseen every single touch.

At least that narrative fit her personal view of the man: controlling to a capital C, with OCD tendencies and a possessive streak a mile wide.

Thinking about Nathaniel inevitably brought warmth to her lower extremities. Finishing her champagne in a very unladylike gulp, Heather stood and moved towards the table.

Smiling, Deirdre took her empty glass and offered another. Accepting with a quiet 'thanks', Heather tried to glance down at what Isla was doing on the computer. "You're working?" Heather asked, incredulous.

"Sadly, yes." Sparing her a single, distracted look, Isla snatched Heather's glass and drained it quickly. Shoving back her long, cascading ringlets with a huff she declared, "Shit's just falling apart back in Perth without me."

Eyebrows high, Heather took the empty glass back and shared a look with Deirdre, who smiled with a short shrug. "Is it really that bad?"

Sighing, Isla slumped. "Maybe?"

Tipping her head slightly, Heather slapped her open palm against her thigh—a nervous habit—before asking, "Nathaniel in trouble?"

"No. He's in the process of acquiring a new chain of hotels on the West Coast—a failing chain of hotels, I'll add. Why? I have no idea. I've told him that company is just haemorrhaging money, but you know what he's like. Won't be told no, especially once he sets his mind to an idea."

Reading the implication in her tone, Heather smiled. "He still on you about moving here?"

"Yes, and I just cannot wrap my head around it!" Isla growled in frustration. "He needs me over there, especially since he spends most of his time here. If I leave, everything will fall apart over there." As if realising maybe she'd said too much, Isla glanced at Heather with open shock. "I'm sorry—that. I shouldn't have—"

"It's fine," Heather shrugged and popped a strawberry into her mouth. "You obviously need to download. I'm pretty good at listening."

"No, I know you are. That's not—" Sighing in frustration, Isla closed the lid on her laptop and returned the device to the bag at her feet. "You know Nate—he's successful but not the cutthroat-successful the media likes to portray him as. He's pursuing this chain because an 'old buddy' of his father's approached him with the merger idea, but I don't think it's in Nate's best interest. He's doing it out of some misguided sense of responsibility, which is what old mate was counting on."

Nibbling on her lower lip, Heather fought and lost the battle to not care. Returning Isla's smile and waving off the woman's subdued apology, she watched as the small woman then moved to Faith's side.

Reaching for the inner pocket Faith had insisted all the bridesmaid dresses have, she pulled out her smartphone and tapped on the screen.

Pulling up her messages, she found the thread with Nathaniel's name and typed out a new message:

Heather: Have you got a second?
Nathaniel: For you, *Tesoro*, always.
Heather: Meet me downstairs by the bar.
Nathaniel: I'll be the one wearing a suit.
Heather: You're always wearing a suit.
Nathaniel: Fine. Then I'll be the one down there who's butt-naked, hard, and ready for your attention.

Closing the screen of her phone, Heather cleared her throat and glanced around the room once more. Everyone was busy doing their own thing, and she highly doubted they'd notice her leaving.

Nonetheless, she sidled over to Grace and leaned down to whisper, "Gracie, if anyone asks, I've gone to the bathroom."

"By bathroom do you mean, 'I've gone to rip the clothes from a hot Italian's muscled body, to fuck his brains out against the wall' bathroom?"

"Jesus," Heather whispered, her face heating, "you have a filthy mouth."

Smiling wickedly, Grace turned her head slightly to face Heather, Bastien still fully engrossed in the colourful show that played on her phone.

"If I had a man who looked like that—and looked at me like I was his favourite flavour of gelato—I'd have zero willpower. My clothes would literally melt off. That's all I'm saying."

Deciding she'd be better off not answering, Heather

slipped out into the hallway. Gathering the silk of her rust gown in one hand, she took the length of the floor with quick steps.

Down the grand stairs restored to their natural wood finish, her hand resting on the banister for balance in her high heels, Heather swept into the quiet bar with a sigh.

As was the case with the rest of the establishment, the bar had been lovingly restored with an attention to detail and care—interior darkened slightly, but with enough light spilling through the large floor-to-roof windows that Heather spotted Nathaniel immediately.

Seated in the far corner on a comfortable-looking sofa chair, he was in fact dressed in a pair of simple jeans and a T-shirt, one ankle resting on his opposite knee, hand cradling a glass half-filled with amber liquid.

At her entrance he'd lifted his attention from the book which lay open in his lap, the heat of his gaze as it lazily traversed the length of her body making her shift restlessly.

Snapping the book shut and tossing it to the low coffee table in front of him, Nathaniel tipped his chin back, swallowing the contents of his glass, which disappeared to the floor at his side.

Gaze dark and unfathomable, he shifted, settling heavily into his chair as he watched Heather stalk his way, her hips swaying provocatively with each step.

Nathaniel had never met another woman so unashamedly beautiful—the fact that she didn't have the faintest idea titillating in a way he didn't care to examine.

All his life Nathaniel had beautiful women throw themselves at him. Often it was due to his own looks—

he wasn't naïve to what his face and body did to a woman.

However, usually it was his name and money that attracted them; he had the kind of disposable income most couldn't even dream of.

Heather was different. Heather was unique.

Dark chocolate hair, thick and luxurious, worn loose today and styled, fell in waves down the length of her back. Her tight curves, encased in a rust floor-length silk gown with spaghetti straps.

Those spaghetti straps. Already Nathaniel could envision sliding those flimsy straps off her shoulder. He knew the back swooped low and offered to the small of her back a tantalising expanse of smooth flesh.

Would she be wearing a bra beneath the gown or was the silk kissing naked skin...?

Fingers snapping in front of his nose awoke fast reflexes, and reaching out his hand wrapped around silky, warm skin. With a firm hold on her wrist, Nathaniel tugged sharply, tumbling Heather into his lap.

Her gasp he instantly made his own by covering her lips with his, taking advantage to dip his tongue past her defences and take her mouth for his own.

"Fucking ambrosia," Nathaniel purred, finally releasing her mouth once she'd gone boneless against him. "You tempt me, *Tesoro*. God knows how you tempt me."

"I didn't come down here to tempt you, Nate," Heather muttered, releasing a shaky breath.

"You breathing is temptation enough," Nathaniel argued, burying his face into the crook of her neck. Inhaling, he tortured himself further by running one hand up the length of her leg.

Gathering the silky material he found there, he had shifted his hand underneath the fabric and to the inside of her thigh, just shy of his goal, when Heather clamped her own hand down on his.

Smiling against her skin, Nathaniel expelled a breath and leaned back, leaving his hand exactly where it was but giving her his full attention.

Those eyes.

The windows into her soul, which when turned his way drove every single thought from his head bar one.

One day she'd be his. Unequivocally and unapologetically his. And he planned on drowning in her eyes then.

"I have something serious I want to discuss with you."

"Yes," Nathaniel answered immediately. "I accepted your proposal to a dinner date—my only stipulation, you let me pick the restaurant."

Those eyes wide with surprise, he couldn't help his amusement as she spluttered, "No. No—that's not. A date? Seriously, Nate, that's all you can think about right now?"

"Oh no, *Tesoro*. All I can think about right now is finding out exactly what you have on underneath this gown, and whether or not I might be allowed to run my tongue up your—"

Clapping her hands over his mouth, Heather blew out a frustrated breath. "Would you just calm down a damn minute, you over-sexed Italian stallion."

With his mouth covered, Nathaniel was unable to respond to her jab. Instead, he fluttered his fingers on the warm skin of her inner thigh.

Her legs flexed, and her lashes lowered to half-mast as she sucked in a small breath, her tone full of warning.

"Nate."

After a moment, he nodded, and once she'd removed her hand, said, "Fine, *Tesoro*. What do you want to discuss?"

For a long moment, she studied him. Then, slowly, she removed her grip on his hand, seemingly happy to ignore his proprietary hold for the moment.

"I was talking with Isla before. She's concerned, you know."

His turn to sigh, Nathaniel rubbed his thumb along the soft skin of her upper thigh contemplatively. "Don't I know it."

"Her fears aren't unfounded, Nate."

"I know."

"If you know, what are you doing?"

Sighing again, Nathaniel tipped his head all the way back and glanced up at the intricate roof, thinking his answer through in that slow way of his.

Having grown accustomed to his long silences, Heather waited patiently, rewarded when he finally returned his gaze to hers and said simply,

"Because I know I can turn it around. I've done it before, I can do it again."

"The difference this time is you want to move Isla here to Glen Innes, where she's noticed you spend a lot of time. She's worried with the two big players out of Perth, there'll be no one to stay on top of things over there."

As he sat there frowning, Heather smothered her smile, knowing he hadn't thought of it like that—her assumptions confirmed when he nodded briskly.

"I hadn't considered that."

"Maybe it's why Isla is still so vocal in her determination

to stay in WA and not move here," Heather continued, smoothing her hand over the length of his shoulders—so broad and strong and utterly oblivious sometimes.

"Then I will just have to have a word with my brother. It is time he returns from gallivanting around the world, and takes an active role in the business."

Shocked, Heather gripped his chin and pulled his attention to her. "You have a brother?"

"Yes. Younger by fifteen months."

"You've never once mentioned him." Heather felt something settle low in her stomach—something that felt too much like hurt for her peace of mind.

Coiling her muscles to stand and put some much-needed space between them, Nathaniel prevented the move by tightening his hand on her thigh.

"Heather, look at me."

Complying simply because he never used her name, she met the deep brown of his gaze, knew her face gave too much away when his expression softened.

"*Tesoro*, so much of our courtship is spent dancing around your tough topics, I forget when I come up against some of my own."

"Your brother is a tough topic?" Heather asked, relaxing slightly when he made a low noise of assent. "We don't have to—"

"He is my half-brother. My father had an affair when I was still a baby, with his receptionist at the time. She had a child—Matteo. The whole matter is almost too ironic to swallow. My mother has since forgiven the indiscretion, and Matteo is a part of our life in the very best sense of the word. But always unspoken is the knowledge of his illegitimacy, and my father's affair."

Quiet for a long moment, Heather finally admitted, "I

wish I had a brother or a sister—someone to share the death of our parents and later my grandparents with. I'd have appreciated the support of not going through the darkness alone."

Gathering her close, Nathaniel pressed a kiss against her hair. "Oh, *Tesoro*, I'm sorry."

"Not your fault, Nate. These things happen sometimes. I'm glad you have Matteo."

Determined to shake free the melancholy of their conversation, Nathaniel pressed his lips more firmly against her hair, nudged her slightly till her face lifted and he could capture her lips.

Stroking his fingers along her inner thigh, Nathaniel moved his caress down the column of her throat, leaning her back against the arm he braced on the armrest.

"Just a taste," Nathaniel cajoled as he lifted his hand free of her skirt, and slid it up her body to her breast. "Just a peek."

"Persistent," Heather moaned, arching into his hand.

She hadn't said no, Nathaniel reasoned, so moving his hand up further he plucked at one of the straps, sliding it down her skin to bare her breast—then paused.

Laughing now at the confusion in his expression, Heather glanced down at her own breast, covered by a cleverly designed stick-on bra which was surprisingly supportive.

Thwarted, Nathaniel didn't resist as Heather straightened and then lifted from his lap. Sighing dramatically, he spread his hands in a 'what are you gonna do' gesture and smiled.

"I'll see you at the wedding?" Heather couldn't resist asking.

Nodding, Nathaniel stopped her walking away by gripping her waist, pulling her between his legs, which he spread to accommodate her.

"Spend the night with me?"

She wanted to say yes. She wanted to melt back into his arms and ask him to finish what he'd started.

"I have to be up early," Heather murmured, tangling her hands in the thick, inky black strands of hair which sat untidily atop his head.

Shrugging, Nathaniel kissed the inside of her wrist and leaned back. "Another time then."

Unable to answer because she couldn't definitively argue that there wouldn't be another time, Heather turned on her heel and quietly left the room.

Behind her, the easy smile Nathaniel had fixed in place dropped, and he sighed. Reaching once more for the empty glass, and bottle of whiskey, he refilled his glass with a scowl.

Patience, he reminded himself—one of his better qualities, and one he relied on now. He'd make it past those walls one day.

Patience.

'CHAPTER TWO'

Pulling into her usual parking spot by the front gate the next morning, Heather tucked her head into her hat while sliding her phone into her back pocket.

The sun barely peeking above the trees ensured that very few others would be up and about, so deciding against heading into the kitchen, Heather made for her office.

The large figure sprawled out on her old sofa made her pause in the doorway. Quickly regaining her equilibrium, she sat on the coffee table and cleared her throat.

"Ollie? Oliver Lawson, what are you doing here on my sofa?"

A rumble of noise, accompanied by one bloodshot blue eye briefly meeting hers, preceded the big man rolling over with a sigh.

Clucking her tongue, Heather surveyed him for a second. Then, feeling mischievous, she reached out and firmly set her fingers into the dip of his waist.

As she knew it would, she only had to twitch her fingers, and Oliver was swinging back around to push her hand away. His sharp bark of laughter was immediately accompanied by a groan, as he pressed his hands against his eyes.

"Damnit, woman. Let me sleep!"

The blanket he'd found slipped enough that Heather was given an unimpaired view of his shirtless chest, and she'd have to be at death's door not to appreciate the sight.

Sighing, Heather cupped her chin in her hand. "Not that I'm complaining—a woman could get used to this kinda view—but what the hell are you doing here?"

Colour flagged his cheekbones and, pulling the throw back up his body, Oliver rubbed his eyes. "I was too drunk to drive home."

"So why aren't you inside? In one of the rooms?"

"Isla's in there."

"Isla's in there," Heather repeated, curious now. She poked his side. "Spill. What's the deal with you two?"

"What's the deal with you and Nate?" Oliver grouched back.

"Well, we have a mutually beneficial friends-with-benefits thing going on, so whenever either of us gets the itch we—"

"I don't need a blow-by-blow account, Heath," Oliver interrupted, his tone dry. "Friends-with-benefits surprisingly covered it."

Chuckling, Heather waited a long minute before pressing, "Isla?"

"I don't know." Scrubbing large hands down his face, he then let them settle in his lap, sitting up fully. "I can't figure her out. Every time we see each other—" He paused, thinking through his words. "Well, things happen. But she won't answer my calls or texts, doesn't acknowledge that anything happened. She blows hot and cold and I can't keep up."

"Have you told her this?"

"I've tried." Oliver met her gaze and shrugged. "She

doesn't want to talk about serious stuff though."

Patting her thighs reflectively, Heather wasn't sure what to say—knew her expression gave her away by the way Oliver's shoulders dropped.

"Why have women gotta be so complicated?" Oliver asked finally, his tone and the smile on his face forced.

Reaching out to pat his knee, Heather shrugged.

"Because we'd be no fun if we were predictable?"

"Cop out." Oliver muttered, his smile a little more genuine.

Slapping her thighs, Heather stood. "Well, since you're here, wanna help me work some of the horses?"

Groaning, Oliver laughed. "No, Heath! It feels like a band is using my skull as a practice room. I want to go back to sleep for another eight hours at least."

"No way, Jose. No time for lazy-bones here. Besides, did you know Happi and Annabelle are coming in later this morning? Passing through on their way to a competition down in Armidale."

Perking up, Oliver straightened once more. "Happi? No kidding, that's awesome. I was really glad to hear about his recovery and return home."

Unacknowledged between them that it had all happened during the time Oliver hadn't felt capable of being at Emersons—his unrequited love for Constance not something he'd got over easily.

Tipping her head consideringly, Heather tried to recall the exact moment Oliver had returned to the farm, remembered that it had been around the time of Constance's baby shower.

A baby shower Isla had been in attendance for.

"Wow, Mary really went all out," Heather commented, shoving a chocolate-covered strawberry into her mouth. At

her side, Constance smiled, the expression shaky.

Using a paper napkin to quickly wipe chocolate from her fingertips, Heather reached out, catching Constance's cold fingers in a tight grip.

"Hey, it's okay."

"It's not." Constance's voice wobbled, her eyes filling with tears as she stared across the room at Josh and Oliver. "I feel like if I hadn't come here, they'd have been just fine. Instead, Ollie can't even be in the same room as me half the time—" Hiccupping, Constance dashed away tears. "Why am I crying?"

"Because you're growing a baby and hormones are a bitch?" Heather wrapped her arm around Constance's shoulder and squeezed. "Oliver will be alright, you'll see. And I highly doubt Josh's life would have been 'just fine' without you. He's crazy about you, and we both know it."

A shift in the air preceding the scent of lavender, and then there was Isla—her gaze alight with concern as she asked, "What's wrong? Connie, you okay?"

Sniffing, Constance managed a trembling smile. "Yeah, just drama and hormones—you know."

"I noticed." Isla slid a glance towards Oliver, observing the stiff set of his very wide shoulders.

Curious, Heather studied the tiny woman, reminded of the handful of times she'd seen Isla and Oliver together—their chemistry explosive though both parties seemed inclined to ignore it.

"Alright." Heather rubbed Constance's back soothingly with one hand, while reaching out for the tray of chocolate strawberries. "Here, eat these. You know you want to."

Laughing, Constance accepted the tray and plucked up one of the treats, raising the delicacy in a toast, to which Heather and Isla lifted their glasses.

"If I'm gonna help out here this morning, I need you to step outta the room."

"Step out of my office? Why?" Heather demanded, shaking the memory free and returning to reality.

"Because I gotta get dressed, Heath."

Wiggling her eyebrows Heather teased, "You nekked?"

"No!" Oliver flapped his hands at her, holding the blanket against his chest as something curious, and warm slide down and settle in Heather's stomach.

"You're kidding, right? I've seen you naked—we used to swim every summer at the billabong in nothing but the skin on our backs—"

"It's different now," Oliver muttered.

"Yeah. 'Cause you're not naked now, you're just shirtless, you prude."

"Heath, c'mon."

"Fine. I mean, I was going to anyway because you asked me to, but this conversation - isn't done."

Leaving the room with that parting shot, Heather braced the length of her spine against the wood of the door, picking at her cuticles while she waited.

She'd have fallen had Oliver not caught her after jerking the door open. Tipping her chin up so she looked at him upside down, she poked his firm jaw.

"Spill it."

"I don't know, Heath. There's no big, secret reveal or revelation," Oliver muttered tiredly, pushing her ahead of him and then following through the stables to the arena. "I just—things feel different for me now. Somehow."

"Now—as in after Isla?"

Shrugging, Oliver's jaw tightened further and Heather couldn't prevent herself from asking, "What is happening between the two of you, Ollie? I've never seen you this twisted up about a woman, not even—"

Glancing at her when she cut herself off, Oliver's lips twisted wryly. "Not even for Connie. You can say it, Heath. It's the truth."

"Wow," Heather whistled, opening the large double barn doors into the back stable. "That's…"

"Yeah," Oliver scrubbed his face once more. "What's the chore for this morning?"

"Ahh, well. I was just gonna clean equipment. Oil up bridles and saddles. Put on a load of blankets."

"Why not give those chores to the Juniors?"

"Occasionally I like to do it myself. That way at least I'm assured once a week everything is getting done properly."

"Anal much?"

"I prefer the term *perfectionist*."

"Yeah, I'm sure that's exactly what they call you behind your back," Oliver laughed, tugging the first load of horse blankets from her arms. He moved out back towards the large washing machines, used only for washing rags and horses gear.

The familiarity of time had them settling into an easy banter, as they performed the menial tasks of cleaning. At some point, Oliver turned the radio on and they laughed at the host's antics on the local station.

It was here that Constance—with six-month-old Leo strapped to her chest in a sling and her arm linked with Isla's—found them, the two women coming to a halt at the threshold of the stable doors.

"Good morning, you two," Constance greeted cheerily. "You're both up early."

"Lots to do," Heather said by way of explanation.

Glancing at Isla, she smiled, though the woman's gaze didn't seem able to lift from the toes of her boots. "Morning, Isla."

"Morning, Heather." Finally dragging her gaze up, Isla glanced at Oliver and swallowed. "Morning, Oliver."

He smiled, the expression infinitely different to the usual smile his face held. This smile seemed more intimate and softer somehow.

Or perhaps Heather was just romanticising things. She didn't think so though—especially when she noticed Isla's cheeks heat as her gaze dropped once more to her toes.

"We were gonna head into town," Constance said, clearly oblivious. "Did you guys wanna come? Or want me to pick anything up?"

"I do need a lift back to my truck," Oliver said, wiping the palms of his hands on the seat of his jeans. He'd changed into a pair of Wranglers and a simple T-shirt with work boots—all of which he stashed in Heather's office for backup.

"Wait a minute," Heather raised her hand. "Connie, Happi and Annabelle are coming in this morning, remember?"

"Oh my gosh!" Slapping a hand to her forehead, there was a false note to her voice which had Heather studying her carefully. "I flat out forgot! Isla, would you do me a solid and drive Ollie into town? Please?"

Looking a little shell-shocked, Isla spluttered as Constance produced the keys from a pocket in the baby carrier. Taking them finally between her thumb and forefinger, she held them gingerly.

"That okay with you?" Constance asked, turning wide, innocent eyes on Oliver—whose expression resembled that of a young boy waking up on Christmas morning.

When neither replied, Constance clapped her hands together loud enough to make a sleeping Leo, Isla, and Oliver jump in surprise. Her tone was gleeful. "That settles it then. Thanks a bunch, Isla. I'll call the store later, Oliver, to place an order for some more feed."

Practically shoving the couple from the stable, Constance firmly closed the stable doors in Isla's face as she finally roused enough to argue, then leaned against the door and pressed her finger to her lips.

Curious, Heather crossed her arms and waited until, deciding the coast was clear, Constance released a breath.

"And what was that?"

Grinning, Constance patted Leo's back in the sling and bounced slightly from side to side. "They needed to talk."

"Evil genius or matchmaker—you decide," Heather joked rhetorically. "Heard from Faith?"

"A text last night," Constance rubbed her son's head. "They'll be off to the Whitsundays this morning. Maria and Samuel drove the kids to the airport to meet them there."

"Two weeks on the beach," Heather contemplated the idea for a moment. "It does sound like a nice change of scenery."

"Kids are gonna love it," Constance agreed, carefully taking a seat on an upturned bucket. She pulled Leo out of the carrier and plopped him down on the blanket Heather laid out.

Immediately Leo squealed happily, reaching for anything within range. Luckily, Constance produced a couple of toys which she scattered close by.

Accepting one of the bridles handed to her, Constance immediately set cloth to leather. "I'm excited to see Annabelle and Happi again. Their parents have posted pictures from every single event they've participated in. But it'll be good to see them in person. It's been months since they visited last, and I still can't believe how grown-up they are."

Heather nodded silently in agreement, tipping some more leather oil onto her own rag. Bending over the saddle in her lap, there was companionable silence for long moments.

Broken only by the sweet babbles of Leo and Constance's soft coos in response.

**

The silence in the RAM was a lot less comfortable, Isla's grip on the steering wheel so tight her fingers were white, the expression on her face unapproachable.

"If I didn't know better, I'd say Connie set this up," Oliver joked finally, refusing to be cowed by the look she slid him. "Sleep okay?"

"You know I didn't," Isla said between tight teeth. "I could have slept well. I could have slept real well."

Annoyed now too, Oliver turned slightly in his seat to face her. "We can't keep having drunk hookups, Isla. It's not the way a healthy relationship works."

"Relationship?" Isla snapped, instantly regretting it as she watched Oliver's expression close down.

Feeling hurt, Oliver angled his body back to the front, the silence now deafening.

Reaching the pub's car park, Oliver unclipped his belt, about to leave, when he turned to Isla—who, mimicking him, had been turned towards him with her mouth opened, poised to speak.

"I'm a good boyfriend," Oliver said softly, stalling whatever Isla may have been about to say. "I'm not the kinda guy who'll break your heart or play games. I like to think I'm pretty straight up about my wants and needs. I'm a good person to rely on."

Feeling lower than dirt, Isla swallowed. "I know. I'm sorry—I shouldn't have said what I did. It was... unnecessarily cruel."

"A lot of women have been with me because they wanted the idea of me rather than the reality of me." Oliver cleared his throat, a little uncomfortable. "Girls chased me when I was in high school and playing footy. That continued at university. Even after I was injured and couldn't play anymore, I didn't struggle for dates."

Ashamed, Isla let her hands rest in her lap, her face turned down—though the large man in the seat beside her had her full attention.

"But they were all chasing something I'm not. And I'm not in the market for the late-night booty calls, Isla. I want something more than that—I think I deserve something more than that."

Then, before she could reply, he'd exited the car and was halfway across the car park, heading in the direction of his truck.

Sitting still in the driver's seat, Isla released a deep breath.

She didn't want any ties here.

Didn't want to be charmed by the community, or find the locals enchanting, and she definitely didn't want to fall in love with the local hero.

Isla would have to have been deaf not to hear the rumours about Oliver—the town's golden boy who had represented New South Wales in rugby. Before a career-ending tackle that left him with nerve damage along his spine – benched him permanently.

Oliver had returned and been folded into the family business, and he'd thrived there. Isla hadn't met a person here who didn't have wonderful things to say about him.

If she was honest, his shiny reputation was almost too wholesome for her—the mask she wore when placed next to him uncomfortable.

Oliver was entirely too good for her.

Remembering what her therapist had said, Isla slipped her sandals off and pressed her feet into the firm floor, grounding herself in the here and now.

Breathing through the clawing fingers of anxiety wrapping around her throat, she then followed the three-by-three-by-three rule she'd learnt.

In her mind, her therapist's voice—calm and unhurried —reminded her of each step.

3 objects.

"Car. Wheel. Floor mat."

3 sounds.

"Birds. Trucks backing up. People talking in the bistro."

Move 3 body parts.

Carefully Isla rolled her shoulders back into the chair, wriggled her fingers to relax their grip on the wheel, and scrunched her toes hard for three seconds.

How do you feel now, Isla? Are the fingers loosening?

"Yes," Isla answered, shifting to rest her hands palms down on her thighs. "Yes, I can breathe."

Good. Keep breathing.

Opening the eyes she'd closed, Isla dropped her gaze to the cuffs of her long-sleeved silk blouse, pads of her fingertips rubbing along the raised scars she could feel beneath the satin.

Oliver deserved someone whole, who was as uncomplicated as he was. And Isla came with too much drama. She'd only ruin him.

Pushing her feet back into her sandals, Isla adjusted her seat and took a moment to check her mirrors, before turning the engine over and making her way back to Emerson Station.

Parking the car exactly where Constance had left it, Isla took a moment to draw in a deep breath, glancing up at the stone building with a wistful sigh.

Just then her phone rang, startling her from thoughts that were quickly becoming depressing. "You've got Isla."

"Isla, it's Nate. You haven't left for the airport yet, have you?"

"I haven't, no. My flight isn't until tonight."

"Rebook it for tomorrow."

"Nate," sighing, Isla slumped and covered her eyes. "I've said I need to think—"

"Heather found me before the wedding. You could have told me your underlying doubts about leaving Perth."

"Would you have listened?" Isla asked, her tone amused. Nathaniel had the good grace to grunt in response, and feeling she'd won this round, Isla smiled.

"I'm listening now," Nathaniel said finally. "So my counterproposal to that is this. We bring in Matteo."

Sucking in a surprised breath, Isla loosed it on an awkward laugh. "God, really Nate?"

"He is my brother, has the necessary qualifications and intelligence to do the job. Seems like the next logical step to me."

"I think it's a wonderful idea," Isla muttered finally. "Do

you think he'll go for it?"

"I've reached out to organise a face-to-face call. He's currently in Spain, I believe—developing a security system for one of the big tourist hotels over there."

Whistling, Isla glanced down at the screen of her wrist as it vibrated—alerted to an incoming text message from Constance.

Connie: *Girl, where are you?*

Isla: *Just got back then Nate pulled me into a quick meeting over the phone, wrapping it up now.*

Connie: *You'd better be. I have you until 7. Tell him to stop being so greedy!*

Isla: *You tell him.*

"Well, let me know how it goes once Matt gets in touch," Isla said, plucking the keys from the ignition and opening her door. "I'll see what I can do about rescheduling my flights."

"I don't know why you insist on using commercial planes. I could have mine filled and ready to go whenever you wanted."

"I like the normalcy," Isla quipped. Then before Nathaniel could continue, added, "Laters, boss."

Ducking in the backdoor, Isla cast her gaze around, looking for Mary. Seeing no one, she quickly returned Constance's keys to the pegs next to the door.

Figuring she'd find Heather and Constance where she left them, Isla made her way through the stables with a swift smile at the long, curious faces who appeared over the doors.

In the arena, there was a class in progress—pre-teens, Isla would guess, by the awkward braces and poorly applied makeup. The coach, a young woman Isla had met once before, nodded briefly her way as she passed.

As she'd thought—still seated on bales of hay, sans Leo now—Constance and Heather paused in their cleaning to glance up.

"How'd it go?" Constance asked, returning her attention to the large pile of blankets she was folding.

With determined guiltlessness, Isla asked, "How'd what go?"

"Don't be annoying," Heather piped up, her gaze focused on Isla as she squirmed. "You know he slept on my office sofa last night."

"Don't see how that's my fault," Isla replied mulishly, reaching out to snatch a blanket from the pile. She folded it badly. "Plenty of beds inside the house."

Sharing a look with Constance—who was trying and failing to hide her smile—Heather capped the oil bottle at her side.

Standing, she hung the last of the bridles back up and stuffed the rag she'd been using into a bucket that had maybe a dozen more in there. Taking the bucket over to the washing machines, she threw them in and started the machine.

"Alright, ladies. Enough gossiping. Our guests will be arriving any minute—let's go open the paddock gate so they can drive straight through."

"Thank God," Constance said, promptly dropping her blanket into the basket half-full of neatly folded material. "I'm handing this off to one of the juniors."

Standing, Constance moved away and pulled the walkie-talkie out of its clip on her belt. While she did this, Heather reached down and tugged the badly folded blanket from Isla's hands.

Letting the material drop back onto the unfolded pile,

Heather studied Isla's pinched expression, searching for words of comfort—only she didn't know the other woman well enough to know how to ease the tightness in her shoulders.

"Oliver is the very definition of a 'good ol' country boy,' Isla. Caring, hardworking, dedicated to his family—he's the most uncomplicated person you'll ever meet."

"Maybe that's the problem," Isla muttered softly, as she fell into step beside Heather, who followed Constance's trek towards the front of the barn. "Maybe he's too uncomplicated. Maybe once he gets to know me a little better. Is exposed to the quirky, city-girl hang-ups that I have, I won't be so mysterious or exotic anymore."

Stopping, Heather mulled that over quietly, then added, "Or maybe you're his brand of spice—and you'll both find something more rewarding there than previously expected."

Thankfully, that was the end of the conversation, as a familiar four-wheel-drive with horse trailer pulled through the gates Constance had opened, parking in the middle of the open paddock.

From the driver's seat slid a familiar face, and smiling wide, Heather accepted Ian's hand and shook it firmly. "Hey Ian, how was the drive?"

"Uneventful," Ian said with a smile. At his side, Annabelle slid beneath his arm and smiled—her small face matured and sharper with age.

"Hello, Heather."

"Hey Anna." Opening her arms was instinctual—the squeeze of Annabelle's arms around her waist reciprocated before Heather held her back. "Look at you! You've had another growth spurt."

Lisette joined the group then with an indulgent smile.

"Has her daddy's height."

The greetings repeated once Constance had joined their small group, Isla hanging back slightly but smiling with a short wave once she'd been introduced.

Following Annabelle around to the back of the float, Heather and Constance stood chatting companionably while the pre-teen unloaded Happi.

Whistling in appreciation, Heather ran her hands over Happi's flank. "My, my—aren't we looking handsome?"

Preening under the attention, Happi made soft, contented sounds as both Heather and Constance lavished him with attention, Annabelle giggling as his long face took on an expression of bliss.

"Spoilt," Lisette commented, but Heather noticed the small chunk of liquorice the other woman slipped from her back pocket. Glancing away with a smile as Happi quickly snuffed the sweet up.

"We've popped you guys in the first stall," Heather said finally as Annabelle walked Happi slowly to help stretch any stiff muscles. "You can leave the gate open to the round yard there, or close it off depending. Weather for the next few days is relatively mild, so it's up to you if you rug him."

"I brought it," Annabelle piped up as Happi paused to nibble at grass. "I'll get it out once Happi is settled."

Expression approving, Constance unlocked the side door that led to the inside of the first stall, running her hand down the length of Happi's side as he passed inside.

"You'll recognize this room, buddy. It was yours while you stayed here."

His long horsey sigh made them all grin as he padded straight over to the clean water trough to drink, lifting his head long enough for Annabelle to remove his lead rope and bridle.

"He's looking really good, guys," Constance said, leaning her forearms on the open doorway. "Real good."

"Anna's strict with his feed routine and hygiene. He's been a massive learning curve for our girl." Lisette said with a quiet smile of pride. "Mucks his stalls twice daily, has a calendar to keep track of the farrier coming, worming schedule, and even pins receipts and other Happi-related paraphernalia up there. Honestly, Ian and I refer to that thing daily to keep track of what's happening."

Smiling because it reminded her of when she was Annabelle's age, Heather stood at Constance's side while Annabelle unpacked all of Happi's gear.

Suddenly, Ian asked, "Did you guys ever hear anything about what happened with Manuel Perez?"

Lips twisting angrily, Heather released a very horsey snort. "I may or may not have reported the entire operation to the RSPCA and authorities. About a month after Happi went home, they raided the farm."

"Perez was charged with animal cruelty. He's not allowed to train or own horses for the next few years," Constance muttered.

"Longer, if I have anything to say in the matter." Heather pulled her hat off and slapped it angrily against her thigh. "I've made it known throughout the whole horse community exactly how bad news this guy is. Thankfully, his reputation was already taking a nosedive. I don't think he'll be finding any work with horses once his ban is lifted."

Sighing, Ian and Lisette shared a long, grateful look before Ian whispered, "Thank God. To think how things could have turned out if we hadn't had you both... it would have broken Anna—which would have broken us."

'CHAPTER THREE'

Having left Constance with the little family to settle Happi in, she unlocked her office door closing it behind her, quickly running through her emails and answering the important ones.

Leaving her office a few minutes later, she turned in the direction of the equipment room, smiling at Ryan as he loitered with Sascha at Happi's inner stall door. "What are you two up to?"

"Saying hello to Happi," Ryan replied with a boyish smile, the gelding standing with his head hanging out the top half.

"He's looking good, isn't he?" Heather asked with a sigh.

"Better than two years ago, anyway," Sascha replied, her pretty face flushed sweetly.

If those two didn't announce they were dating in the next several days, Heather would eat her hat. Turning away, she left the two lovebirds to coo over the pleased gelding.

She quickly grabbed a horse blanket and Charlie's saddle and bridle from his peg, swinging out of the room a moment later. She slid the teens a fleeting smile of amusement as they sprang apart.

Heather headed towards the stall closest to the arena, her smile almost splitting her face when Charlie's long black face appeared, ears pricked forward as he snorted excitedly in welcome.

Ditching the equipment on the open half of the door, Heather spared long moments to rub his face, paying special attention to his eyes and inner ears.

Gently, Heather manoeuvred him back enough to slide into his stall. With the bristled brush she'd tucked into her back pocket, Heather groomed Charlie, speaking softly to him as she worked, admiring the deep black undercoat and asymmetrical white splashes of his coat. Once she'd brushed him down and spent a little time lavishing him with attention, she moved to drape the blanket over his back along his spine, finishing with securing his polo saddle and bridle in place.

Feeding him a bite of liquorice, Heather led him from his stall and towards the front of the barn. Happi's guests had disappeared, the gelding now standing sleepily in the shadows.

Outside in the sunshine, Heather drew in a deep breath and released it, noticing Constance with Lisette and Ian on the back veranda. Raising her hand in response to their waves, Heather swung herself up into the saddle.

Leading Charlie head-first towards the latch end of the gate, Heather made sure his whole side was lightly touching the gate's rails. Then, leaning down, she lifted the latch free.

Tapping her toes lightly behind Charlie's opposite armpit, the well-trained gelding smoothly side-stepped, his body pushing the gate open.

When the space was wide enough, Heather gently nudged him through, spinning him easily on the other side. Nudging him once more—this time to sidestep back—he returned to the gate and closed it.

Latching the gate, Heather glanced up and saluted

Constance, who had come to lean against the veranda fence. Reaching down to pat Charlie's neck, she murmured softly, "Good boy."

"See you in half an hour?" Constance asked, familiar with Heather's training routine.

"Yep."

A final smile shared between the two friends, Heather urged Charlie into an easy walk to start, waiting until they cleared the two posts signifying the car park.

Along the gravel, Heather urged Charlie into a trot, relaxing her body into his easy gait, the breeze kissing her face as she turned it up slightly to the sun's rays.

She loved this.

Loved being on the back of Charlie as they both indulged in the fresh air, sun, and thrill of riding.

Reaching the end of the driveway, Heather and Charlie turned to the left, heading towards Hart territory along the nature strip running parallel to the road.

Occasionally a local would pass, tooting, to which Heather would raise her hand or tip her head in acknowledgement, Charlie steady beneath her, unfazed by the noise or sudden zip of passing cars.

Running between Hart and Emerson was a well-disguised trail used by the two properties, winding and criss-crossing between the combined thousand-plus-acre spread—the perfect endurance trail for exercising horses.

Reaching the start of the trail, Charlie suddenly balked, his large body shuddering as he snorted. Surprised, Heather flowed with the sudden movement, tightening her thighs to prevent tumbling from her seat.

Frowning now, Heather gazed up the sunlight-dappled trail as something uneasy slid down her spine. Charlie's snorts, and deep shuddering breaths as he stood—ears pricked and alert—were so unlike the easy-natured gelding.

"What is it?" Heather asked, her tone low. "It's just our normal trail, Charlie-boy. Nothing new or unusual about it."

Unconvinced, the gelding loosed another huff, his nostrils flaring as he tested the air. Suddenly, Heather noticed the silence around them.

No birds.

No rustle of small animals in the undergrowth.

Something wasn't quite right, and it made the hairs on the back of her neck stand up. Carefully, Heather backed Charlie up, turning him towards home.

But whatever had sent the animals to ground was enough of a threat that Charlie refused to give it his back, swinging around to keep his gaze focused on the trailhead as he backed slowly up.

Finally, five hundred meters from the trail's entrance, Heather was able to convince him to turn. Riding back towards Emerson, she couldn't help the urge that encouraged her to glance occasionally over her shoulder.

At the start of the driveway, she paused, looking back the way they'd come. The sound of birds chattering filled the air as butterflies swarmed around her.

Unaccountably troubled, Heather urged Charlie back up the long driveway, unsurprised to find Constance still seated on the veranda as she returned—the other woman now standing with a frown.

Watching as Heather and Charlie manoeuvred through the gate back into the back paddock, Constance asked, "What happened? It's not been ten minutes since you left."

"Not sure." Heather sat relaxed on Charlie's back, rubbing his ears comfortingly—though he seemed to have recovered. "Charlie didn't want to go anywhere near the trail."

"Really?" Surprised, Constance left the veranda to stand by the gelding's head, rubbing his nose. "That's unlike him."

"Tell me about it." Shimmying her shoulders as she shivered, Heather admitted, "There was something off today—about the trail. No birds. No animals of any sort."

Nodding slowly, Constance said thoughtfully, "Oliver mentioned some of the locals in town have been losing livestock. A sheep here. A goat there. Some chickens. Could be dingoes. Perhaps a pack of wild dogs?"

"Might explain it," Heather nodded.

"I'll send Josh with one of the hands out to have a look," Constance said, running her hand down Charlie's neck.

"Maybe send them on the ATVs—horses might balk like Charlie did."

"Good idea. What's your plan for Charlie's training today then?"

"We'll go to the arena. He and I can get some work in, then set up the drills for this afternoon's class."

Nodding, Constance patted Charlie's rump as he passed. "I'll come find you later, let you know what Josh says."

"Thanks, Connie." At the stables, Heather dismounted, walking Charlie through the laneway and out the back to the indoor arena.

Starting at a walk, Heather led Charlie through a series of figure eights at the centre, making sure he changed his leading leg, slowly increasing from a slow walk to a trot to a canter.

After a good twenty minutes, Heather slowed Charlie to a walk, catching sight of movement at the corner of her eye—Ryan, who lifted his hand in greeting. She called out,

"Ryan, can I ask a favour?"

The teen paused, propping the saddle he carried on his hip, his young face open as he nodded.

"Can you grab my racquet from the office?"

"Do you want me to saddle up and do some shadow exercises with you?"

"Thanks for the offer." Heather patted Charlie's neck as the gelding released a deep sigh. "But I've only got another twenty minutes or so before I'll start cooling him down."

Smiling in that wide, easy way of his, Ryan ambled off, and Heather refocused her attention on Charlie, urging him into a trot, directing him into a relatively wide circle. After a few passes, she encouraged him into a faster trot.

Beneath her, Heather could feel Charlie's big body move with each inhale, his muscles bunching and shifting. With a leading nudge, he picked up the pace, and Heather tightened the circle.

By the time Heather noticed Ryan standing at the side fence, her racquet held casually in one hand, Charlie's circle had decreased to ten metres and was being done at a smooth canter.

In a practised movement, Heather brought Charlie around in a sharp one-eighty turn, the powerful feel of his back haunches releasing like a spring towards where Ryan stood.

At the last moment, Heather pulled lightly on the reins.

Locking his muscles tight, Charlie came to a screaming halt, his long, drawn-out huff of breath blowing moist air across Ryan's laughing face.

"You're rollbacks are so smooth," Ryan complained half-heartedly, handing over the racquet. "What's your secret?"

Eyes alight with mischief, Heather replied, "Well, I'm not too busy showing off to all the girls pulling tricky manoeuvres that I spend hours practising at home—I spend my hours at home working on... rollbacks."

Pulling a face, Ryan deliberately rolled his eyes. Then, from his back pocket, he produced one of the soft, rubbery balls used in Polocrosse. Cocking his arm back, he loosed the ball with a short grunt.

Quick as a whip, Heather and Charlie spun on the spot, taking off after the ball in a canter—the arena so large that the ball had made it as far as the centre line.

Without slowing, Heather leaned her body to the right and scooped the ball up as Charlie thundered past. Pressing her heels down in the stirrups, she brought Charlie to a stop.

Panting slightly, Charlie's ears flicked back once, and to acknowledge his good behaviour, Heather used her left hand to rub up and down his neck, crooning. "Good lad."

Settling back into her circles, Heather now added in a bit of ball work, tossing the ball from side to side and practising scooping it up.

Noting a small body seated on the top rail where Ryan had stood, Heather smiled at Annabelle. Giving Charlie a moment to catch his breath, she walked him closer.

"You guys are so fast," Annabelle breathed, her small, thin face animated. "What's it called?"

"It's called Polocrosse. And this is nothing." Heather

rubbed Charlie's neck again, boasting a little. "When Charlie and I are playing, everything—including the other players—is moving three times as fast."

"Polocrosse," a tiny frown creasing lovely features. "I've never heard of that. Is it like Polo?"

"Yes and no. It's a combination of lacrosse and polo, invented right here in Australia."

Expression alight with curiosity, Annabelle offered her hand for Charlie to sniff as the big gelding sidled in closer. "Wow. Can anyone play?"

Thoughtful, Heather nodded. "Yeah. All ages and genders. Happi is tall enough too, at fifteen hands. Maybe a smidge on the smaller side, but he'd hold his own on the field."

Giggling softly as Charlie playfully lipped the flat of her palm, Annabelle lifted her gaze after a moment. "While we're here, could you maybe show me and Happi a little bit about it?"

"Tell you what," charmed, Heather compromised, "let's talk to Mum and Dad about it first. I'll bring you a couple of books I have on it tomorrow—after your competition in Armidale."

Patient, Heather waited as Annabelle thought about it, rewarded shortly afterward by another large grin, Annabelle extending her hand towards Heather.

"Alright," the pre-teen's tone was perky. "I think Happi and I will be good at this, though."

"Kid," forgoing the hand to move close enough to tug at the end of Annabelle's ponytail, Heather smiled, "I think you and Happi could take on the world, if that was what you both choose."

Giggling in response, Annabelle fluttered her fingers along Charlie's nostrils, causing the big softy to huff and sneeze. Then she was swinging her lithe body down off the rails and turning towards the front stable.

Watching the young girl disappear, Heather hummed appreciatively. Already thinking through how she was going to phrase inviting Annabelle to join her afternoon class, the group small and full of local kids who played Polocrosse.

**

Half an hour later, and Heather was done, leading Charlie towards the wash bays, his body covered in dark patches of sweat.

Backing him into the bay, Heather grabbed one of the rope halters and two lead ropes hanging on the wall, murmuring to Charlie as she slipped the new halter up his long face and over his ears.

Once it was secure, she unbuckled and removed the bridle, hanging it out of the way. Clipping the lead ropes to both sides of the halter—the ends of which she then clipped to hooks on each side of the bay—she stepped back.

Rubbing his nose, she ran her gaze over the ropes, noting how Charlie comfortably disengaged his hind quarters.

Running her hand down the long line of Charlie's side towards the back of the bay, she checked the hose had the correct nozzle and then turned the water on.

Turning back towards Charlie, she started at his feet before moving slowly up his body, making sure each section was soaked.

Reaching his neck, Heather chuckled as Charlie dropped his head low, the water running like a waterfall over his closed eyes, his sides contracting as he blew great horsey sighs.

From a foal, Charlie had adored bath time, and with a smile Heather joked. "You should have been a water buffalo."

Turning the water off once she'd soaked his whole body, Heather approached the open shelf along the back wall where the water taps and hoses hung. Then she picked one of the full bottles of shampoo, designed specifically for horses.

Making sure the nozzle was twisted to spray, she covered him in shampoo, rubbing it into his coat before rinsing him completely down.

More shampoo went into his tail and mane. Heather scrubbed the cleaner into his tail, picking occasional blades of hay out—which she then brandished at him when he turned to check on her.

Rinsing thoroughly, she shut off the water and then dumped a big helping of conditioner into the palm of her hand, working it into his tail first and then following the same process with his mane.

Back to the shelf, she picked one of the scrapers from the jar where a dozen stood upright, starting at his neck to work her way down his body.

Clean and slightly damp, Charlie's eyes drooped lazily, his back leg disengaged as he appeared all but asleep. Chuckling, Heather unclipped the two leads from their wall points.

Leaving one attached to the halter, she hung the other back on its peg and took down the bridle to lead a slow-moving Charlie back to his stall.

Once inside, Heather checked he had fresh water. Noticing the tidy stall and figuring one of the juniors would have been through by this stage, she nodded.

By the back door which led to the outside, hung a hay

net that also looked to have been replaced with fresh feed. So running her hand along his neck, Heather pressed a kiss against his nose.

"Good boy, Charlie. I'll see you later."

Pace brisk, Heather headed back into the arena. Ryan and one of the newer juniors, Mark, were carrying an armful of equipment each to drop at the very centre.

"Thanks, fellas." Jogging over, Heather checked through what they'd brought. "New box of paints? Nice."

"I was gonna bring out the rebound nets," Ryan said, "but I figured I'd check first."

"The nets are a good idea. I spotted the Darcy twins practising against a piece of corrugated tin yesterday."

Smiling, Ryan wiped at the sweat along his brow. "Yeah, been there, done that."

"Same. So they'll know exactly what to do with a net."

Chuckling, Ryan nudged Mark's shoulder and nodded back the way they'd come. Heather watched the two lanky teens disappear into the back stables before returning her attention to the pile.

Grabbing a canister of water-based spray paint in white from the opened box, Heather made her way towards the far left-hand side of the arena.

There, she began by spraying a straight line on which she printed the word 'START' in large letters on one side. Following that, in 30-foot increments, she sprayed a circle until she had five all in a line, concluding that setup with another straight line labelled 'END.'

Thirty feet back in towards the centre, she repeated the process until, by the end, she had three drills set up, the parameters laid down on the soil in white, water-soluble paint.

Heading back into the centre, Heather then laid the

foundation for a traditional barrel-racing cloverleaf pattern, using the paint to spray circles to represent the barrels.

For the next drill, Heather grabbed a heap of the traffic cones and headed towards the right-hand side of the arena. Mapping out a large 20-metre circle, she left the rest of the right side completely free and open for exercises.

Spotting Ryan and Mark carrying a rebound net each, she pointed towards the fences along the right. "Just prop them there if you can, please, fellas. We'll set them up when we're ready for them."

"Do you want all four?" Mark asked.

"Yes, please. The group has eight booked in, so they can work in pairs."

Nodding, the teens leaned the nets against the fence as instructed and jogged back to get the next two. Turning to consider the arena, Heather ran through the lesson plan in her head.

This particular group's skill level was intermediate, and all eight played for the local club and had been riding their whole lives. Aged eight to twelve, they were familiar with each other and all the mounts.

'CHAPTER FOUR'

"Now this looks like a fun course. Are those the rebound nets?" Constance called out, and turning, Heather smiled in welcome and nodded.

Short legs striding across the arena at a quick clip, Constance brandished some paperwork in one hand while the other held Leo's hand as he cooed from the carrier on her chest.

"What you got for me?" Heather asked, accepting the paperwork after smiling down at Leo, who chuckled, his little legs kicking enthusiastically.

Bouncing on her heels and rocking, Constance ran her gaze over the drills. "Latest invoice from Ollie—just wanted you to quickly check everything ordered on it is what we need. Then I'll process the payment and organise a couple of the boys to go in and pick it up from the store."

Nodding abstractedly, Heather ran her gaze down the list, tugging her hat from her head and slapping it on her thigh. "Yeah, that all looks right to me."

"Sweet," grabbing Leo's feet in her hands after one particularly exuberant kick hit her pelvis, Constance blew a breath out. "How many for today's class?"

"Eight."

"I noticed on the booking sheet the Darcy twins are down to come today?"

"Yeah, I spoke to Johnny yesterday. He booked them in over the phone."

Amused, Constance said, "They about ran me over on Monday. I was coming out of the fruit and veg store, and they came screaming up the pathway on their bikes, literally lobbing a tennis ball between them with their racquets."

"Probably exhausted their ponies," Heather remarked, her tone dry. She reached out and cradled Leo's face between her palms, grinning as he drooled all over her and squealed loudly.

Grunting as another kick connected with her pelvis, Constance muttered, "I already know Leo is gonna grow up to be the Darcy twins—a total menace to society."

"But so damn cute he gets away with it," Heather said, her tone pitched high as she made nonsensical sounds to Leo, who delightedly copied her chirps with his own.

"How's Johnny going?" Constance asked, referring to the twins' father, recently single after his wife left him with full custody of the boys and moved to the city.

"Adjusting," Heather shrugged slightly. "From what I can gather, his role hasn't changed all that much. Jessica wasn't an active presence in their lives."

Making a face at that, Constance checked her watch and then sighed. Taking the papers back, she motioned with her chin towards the house.

"Better get this sorted. Have you seen Graham?" Constance asked, referring to one of the stable hands who had worked at Emersons for the last thirty years.

"Pretty sure work detail puts him out in paddock six, mending fences. Should be in range of the walkie-talkie."

Nodding, Constance was already moving to pull hers

from its clip on her belt, a preoccupied wave over her shoulder for Heather as she left the arena.

"That's the final two nets," Ryan said once it was clear Heather and Constance had finished their conversation, the two boys having rested the final nets against the others at the fence a few moments earlier.

"Thanks, fellas. You're good to return to your other tasks. Ryan I've left Charlie in his stall eating, would you mind in around forty minutes or so saddling him up, and bringing him out for me?"

Rubbing his hands over his thighs Ryan nodded quickly, his expression bright, "Sure thing Heath."

At his side Mark pulled his ball cap off, dragging his fingers through his hair, Ryan nudging him and nodding to indicate further in to the stables.

"We're off then. See you in a bit with Charlie," Ryan called. "We'll be transferring feed into the feed bins out back, if you need us before then."

"Good idea. I'd hazard a guess this afternoon you'll be helping Graham unpack the next lot of produce from the ute."

Ignoring their groans, Heather turned back towards her pile of equipment, checking the sketch and lesson plan she'd worked on the night before in preparation for today's class.

Spotting one unread text, Heather opened the message and felt the muscles in her stomach tighten—the fuzzy picture undoubtedly of her.

She was wearing white jodhpurs and a polo shirt dark enough to make its colour indistinguishable. Seated comfortably on Charlie's back, her racquet was resting on her shoulder as she smiled.

The angle suggested whoever had taken the photo

had needed to zoom in, possibly meaning they'd been sitting in the crowd.

Glancing at the background, Heather recognised it— remembering one of the local events during which they'd essentially held a 'family fun-day' for people to come and try.

That had been two months ago.

"Sorry! Sorry, we're here!"

Startled by Johnny's loud, booming voice, she took a moment to gather her thoughts while the other parents laughed good-naturedly, slapping Johnny on the back as he led one of his sons' mounts into the arena.

Followed closely behind by his twins, Hudson and Cooper Darcy, who were both leading the last horse, and by the time the boys had settled into their saddles and Johnny had left the arena, Heather had shoved her unease aside.

"Alright, alright guys, let's settle down." Waiting as the kids' amicable chatter quietened, Heather smiled from her spot on the ground. "First things first, let's start with some stopping."

Chuckling at her own joke, Heather paused when she caught the kids eyeing each other. Tutting, she rolled her shoulders and then lifted her whistle to her lips.

One single long blow and the kids immediately formed one line, Hudson leading the charge as he set his heels into his horse's ribs and squeezed. After a short distance, Hudson sat back in his seat, squeezing the reins to tuck his horse's nose and encourage him to a quick stop. No doubt reacting to Hudson's own energy, his horse listened. However, not completing the stop fully, the horse popped in place and Hudson's body rocked forward as he set his heels once more, urging the horse off.

After a few stops like this, Heather blew her whistle in a quick sharp toot, encouraging Hudson to round the witches' hat Heather had set up marking the boundaries of their warm-up space.

"Alright, Huds, you gotta make sure you're pulling to a stop. Get Rayne's backend under him so he's using his haunches, and you aren't getting thrown around in your saddle."

Nodding, Hudson's little face creased with concentration as he adjusted his seat and worked at collecting Rayne at the end of each stop, Heather calling encouragement.

"That's it, mate—get his butt low, that's how he stops."

Hudson joined the end of the line, patting Rayne's neck before refocusing on the next student.

After a successful ten minutes during which all students, including Hudson, managed successful stops with their mounts, Heather was ready to move on to the next exercise.

Using her whistle to release one long and then one short toot, Heather raised her voice and called out, "Ok guys, divide yourselves into two groups of four and put yourselves into line-up."

Like tiny soldiers, they split down the middle into groups of four and settled into the familiar 'T' line-up positioning. Once done, the two teams faced off, their horses angled and staggered slightly side-by-side.

Front and centre, Heather raised her voice slightly to be better heard. "So we're just gonna run through a reverse line-up stack drill to help practise the initial umpire throw. One at a time—either in a slow trot, trot, or slow canter—I'll throw the ball. I want you to peel off, pick the ball up, and then remember to settle racquet and ball on your dominant side. Then you'll bring the ball back to me. Starting right—number off one to eight."

Dutifully, Hudson—who happened to be leading the right-side grouping—called out, "One."

After all eight had called out their number, Heather nodded. Turning, she grabbed her racquet from its spot leaning against the fence. On the ground at her feet, she opened a bag filled with practice balls.

Emptying half the bag onto the ground, Heather used her racquet to scoop the first ball into her racquet's net, then, bringing the head back over her shoulder, called out "One" before launching the ball into the air.

Quick as a rabbit, Hudson and his horse Rayne turned out to the right, heading towards the ball at a slow canter.

Slowing slightly to a fast trot two feet from the ball, Hudson bent his body to the right, dragging the netted end of his racquet through the dirt. With a quick scoop, he had the ball and was sitting straight back up in his saddle.

From the sidelines, Heather heard Johnny's loud clap but kept her gaze fixed on Hudson as he returned to his spot. Close enough to hear her, she motioned with a tip of her head for him to drop the ball at her feet.

"Nice job, Hudson. Did everyone notice how he was only bending from the waist? That way his legs stayed under his body, supporting him. This way, he could have leaned either side without overbalancing and falling off."

His sharp little face swallowed by the size of his grin, Hudson puffed his chest out and slid his brother a sly look. Obviously refusing to rise to the bait, Cooper rolled his eyes.

Grinning, Heather scooped up her next ball and glanced at the girl seated on her mare slightly behind and next to Hudson. Finding her attention locked on the ball, Heather called "Two" before tossing it out into the centre of the arena.

Half an hour later Heather called a halt, directing everyone to take their horses for a drink, and to dismount and have drinks themselves.

Quickly checking the time and her lesson plan, Heather waited for five minutes and then lifted her whistle to her lips, releasing three short and sharp toots. She waited in the centre for the kids to mount and form a wide half circle around her.

"Alright, now that we've been watered—" Heather was cut off as one of the mounts loosed a loud fart, all the kids peeling off into laughter as the culprit—a pretty roan mare—snorted loudly and shook her body. Her rider, an equally pretty brunette called Eve, blushed bright red beneath her hot pink riding helmet. "Sorry."

"Better out than in, my dad always says," called out Hudson, Cooper agreeing easily as they lifted their racquets to bash them together in solidarity.

Rolling her eyes as this brought on a fresh round of laughter, Heather noticed Eve was no longer beet red. Clearing her throat once the noise calmed down, she tried again.

"As I was saying—next up today we are gonna work on our racquet side and backwards pick-up technique. Now I know some of us are more comfortable than others, so you will decide on how slow or fast you'll complete the exercise. But first, Charlie and I will run through a quick demo."

As the kids all nodded, Heather quickly pulled herself up into Charlie's saddle. Then, producing one of the red, rubber training balls from a net tied to Charlie's saddle horn, she pulled her arm back and threw the ball as far as she could across the arena. Noting its placement, she then turned back towards the kids, taking a breath to explain what she was about to do.

"Now I'm gonna do it at an easy trot, and keeping my eyes on the ball I'm going to use my thighs to stand up in the stirrups. When I'm closer to the ball I'm going to shift my weight forward and over Charlie's shoulder, pressing my racquet down so it bends over the top of the ball. Then I'll drag the racquet back, cradling the ball as it lifts, and then I'll swing the racquet forwards into the normal holding position."

Meeting the interested faces around her, Heather nodded once, then accepting her racquet from Siobhan, one of the older students in her class, Heather proceeded to execute the pick-up technique she'd just detailed.

Quickly heading back to her class afterwards, Heather remained seated on Charlie. Moving from one student to the other and handing them out a ball, she instructed, "Ok, one each to practise with. I want you to find your own space—your own spaces, Hudson, Cooper —to practise. You don't need to throw the ball as far as I did, and keep an eye out on your fellow classmates. I'll come around to each of you and give you a hand if you need."

Making her way to each of the kids, she spent time correcting form and answering questions, pleased by the end of the allotted twenty minutes that everyone was working and improving their technique.

"Miss Heather?"

Turning to face the youngest member of their class, just six years old and with the longest name—Zachariah William FitzPatrick the Second—Heather couldn't help but smile wide as he navigated his huge horse closer.

The horse, a whopping eighteen hands tall and impressively named Warhorse, was possibly the most docile creature Heather had ever met. He utterly adored his little passenger, who had been plopped onto his wide back before Zack was even walking.

"Are we gonna use the nets over there today?"

Grinning, Heather capped the lid of her water bottle. "We are indeed, Zack."

"You knowed that I played with these kinda nets at school," Zack said excitedly as he bounced in his saddle. "Miss Teacher had us throwing—uh—throwing these —bean bags and they—they bounced so hard back! We laughed and laughed and laughed," Zack recalled, chuckling now as he shook his little head. "Such a funny day."

God, some days she just wanted to squeeze his little cheeks. Smothering the urge, Heather instead licked her lips and blew once more on the mouth of her whistle.

As everyone gathered, Heather set up the rebound nets. "Alright guys, we are actually gonna give the horsies a bit of a break." Ignoring the groans around her, Heather made a shushing sound, continuing loudly, "Throwing, catching, bouncing and everything in between. You can use the nets, you can have partners—NOT you two," Heather pre-emptively pointed at Hudson and Cooper, her eyebrows raised. "Either of you want partners, you can have me and your father," she'd already cleared it with Johnny, in fact. "I heard all about the two of you ripping through the streets of Glen Innes. Bicycles, guys? Really?"

Refusing to be placated by their matching smiles, Heather returned her attention to her remaining students. "Alright guys, off you get."

Prepared, the parents had already moved within the arena, Zack's father reaching up to pluck his son from Warhorse's back, accepting his son's exuberant hug with a soft smile.

By the end of the class the horses had cooled down enough to be ready to get floated home, and the kids had done a heap of running, jumping, throwing and catching to be pretty well exhausted.

The last to leave, Johnny moved closer while his boys removed their horses' saddles and unwrapped their legs. "Appreciate today, Heath. I know you normally like to cap the class at six."

Waving away his thanks, Heather asked, "How you doing, Johnny?"

Shrugging, Johnny checked on his boys. "I watched her walk out that door, Heath, and as relieved as I was that it was all finally over, it was still a punch to the gut. She wasn't just leaving me; she was leaving us—leaving the two little boys we'd raised together. How'd she do that, Heath? How'd she turn off her feelings, how'd she walk out that door? I look at them now, at the confusion in their tiny faces, their sadness when they ask me where she is and why she isn't coming home."

"Oh, Johnny." Reaching out and clasping his hand in hers, Heather sighed. "Jessica's always been a law unto herself."

"That's not the way things work once you have babies," Johnny argued. "We built a life together. She made promises not just to me, but to them. And now she's just gone, and I'm here, trying to hold everything together, trying to be both mother and father, and I know I can't be everything they need."

Unable to offer any real insight, Heather simply laid her hand on one of his broad shoulders, knowing he appreciated her silence by the way he slowly softened, until finally he expelled a deep breath.

"See you next week?" he asked finally, and smiling, Heather opened her arms, saying jokingly,

"Where else am I possibly gonna be, Johnny?"

Chuckling, he nudged her arm with his own, then moved off towards his boys, helping them collect the reins and urging them out of the stable towards the car park and their trailer.

Finished gathering all the equipment to leave it piled in the centre to deal with later, Heather turned her attention to the grandstands.

Having noticed Isla's arrival a half hour into the lesson, Heather had watched the small woman sit close by the other parents, who nodded in welcome her way.

Dwarfed by a large, stylish coat, her long hair curled fashionably and her make-up subtle, Isla looked every inch the city girl she was.

Until you noticed the muddy, steel-capped work boots Constance had insisted she buy two days into her very first visit to Emersons—her insistence that Isla wear them everywhere when visiting an unbroken rule.

"Whatever you and the kids were doing then," Isla called out, "was freaking amazing."

Smiling at the compliment, Heather dismounted Charlie, leading him over on foot to the rails closest to lean there. "Thanks. It's Polocrosse. Been doing it my whole life pretty much. Took up coaching at sixteen for extra pocket money."

Sniffing, Isla rubbed her cold fingers against her thighs. "Well—it's impressive. And fast! I'd love to watch a game —if that's what they're called—one day."

Nodding, Heather rubbed Charlie's neck. "Well, when you move here, that'll be inevitable. They're a weekly recreational sport here for a lot of the kids."

"If I move here," Isla muttered, standing. Her smile looked forced. "Just coming to say bye. I'm heading back to Perth tonight."

"I thought you were staying until Matteo visits next week?" Heather asked with a frown. In her back pocket, her phone vibrated. Absently, she pulled the device out and checked the screen.

"Hang on," Heather interrupted Isla with an apologetic smile. "This might be a client. Hello, this is Heather."

Pressing her phone to her ear, Heather waited in silence, the dead air on the other end of the call she attributed to poor reception moments later.

Hanging up, she shrugged apologetically. "Sorry, Isla."

"No, no, totally understand." Waving Heather's apology off, Isla stood and made her way down the seats. "Yeah. I was supposed to stay. But with the merger happening in the next few days, I can't risk leaving Perth to manage itself. Nate is just gonna have to have his little family reunion as just the two of them."

Expression sliding into something sly, Isla reached the bottom of the stands and moved closer to the rails. "Or, you could be his backup."

"Backup?" Snorting, Heather busied herself moving Charlie towards the gates. Isla opened them for her a moment later. "It's his brother. Does he need the backup?"

"Not necessarily," Isla latched the gate securely once Charlie had followed Heather through. "They could do with the buffer, though."

Inside Charlie's stall, Heather paused and glanced over her shoulder. "Nate said they were okay. Why would they need a buffer?"

Snorting, Isla watched Heather start brushing Charlie in long, sweeping strokes. "Because they're men. Because they're Sicilian men. Nathaniel is the eldest and does his best, but Matteo always knew his precarious position as his father's illegitimate love child. There's a tension there that neither one acknowledges verbally— and which Nathaniel's mother encourages."

Surprised, Heather paused. "Nate said—"

"Nate lied," Isla interrupted. Then, smiling apologetically to blunt her sharp tone, said, "Nathaniel is a fixer. Who takes on way too much responsibility —especially for the people around him. He's charming and competent, and people forget that his shoulders are only so wide. He shouldn't have to be everyone's rock when his own support network is scarily precarious."

Feeling unaccountably guilty, Heather nodded slowly at what settled unspoken between the two women. After a moment, Isla nodded and then cleared her throat.

"Anyway, it's been good seeing you again. I'll catch up with you the next time I'm here."

Face hot and feeling uncomfortable, Heather nonetheless smiled warmly. "Thanks, Isla. It's been great catching up."

'CHAPTER FIVE'

The silence that settled once Isla had left afforded Heather a moment to collect her thoughts, her sigh deep and causing Charlie to swing his long face back towards her in question.

"I've never been accused of being selfish before," Heather muttered. "But Isla has a point, Charlie-boy. I mean, two years and I didn't know he had a brother. He knows everything about me—what do I know about him?"

"What do you want to know, *Tesoro*? Ask me. I have no secrets from you."

Heather looked at the open stall door and, surprised, asked, "Nate, when did you arrive?"

Having listened to Isla and Heather conversing inside the stall some time ago, he chose not to answer and simply shrugged instead.

However, the memory of Isla's parting words as she caught him eavesdropping lingered in his mind like poison. Isla had a way of cutting to the heart of things, of forcing him to confront what he didn't want to face.

Nathaniel had always believed that by keeping Heather in the dark about his family, he was protecting her from the unpleasant aspects surrounding his family name.

But now, after Isla's blunt honesty, Nathaniel wasn't so sure.

What if he was setting her up to fail?

"She deserves to know everything." Isla's voice echoed in his ears again. The words struck him harder than he'd expected—because they rang with a truth he couldn't deny.

His family was toxic in ways Heather couldn't even begin to understand. His mother's affection, the family dinners, were all part of a larger game he'd navigated his whole life. And his father? A man who knew how to make people bend without even raising his voice.

Nathaniel wasn't naïve. He knew the kind of wounds his family left, how easily they broke a person down. They were manipulative, controlling, and they never let you go.

He'd been raised to maintain the family's image, keep their secrets, and never let anyone see how warped those bonds really were.

But in doing so with Heather, he'd made a choice for her —one that now seemed unfair.

"You're either naive or deliberately obtuse," Isla had said, her words heavy with accusation.

She was right. He had been both. He couldn't continue to shield Heather from something she would inevitably have to face. Because when that day came—and it would come—what hope would she have if she wasn't prepared?

Nathaniel clenched his jaw, a knot tightening in his stomach. He had always thought he could handle it all on his own. But if he wanted Heather to survive in his world, he needed to give her the tools to navigate it. And that meant pulling her into the storm—showing her the parts of him and his family he'd tried so hard to bury.

"You led me to believe all was happy families between

your brother and your family," Heather said in that direct way of hers. "So what are you leaving out?"

"The time it would take to explain a loaded question like that," Nathaniel said on a sigh, "would see Charlie's patience for dinnertime well and truly worn out."

Making a face at the gelding, who unhelpfully chose that moment to snort softly and lip at her pockets, Heather gently redirected the horse's face away.

"Nate—"

"Have dinner with me tonight," Nathaniel suggested. "I'll answer all the questions you want."

Rubbing Charlie's face, Heather hovered a moment, her expression undecided. "Alright. Fine. Only because I'm hungry and I'd prefer something homemade to the frozen meals I have."

Smiling, Nathaniel leaned one wide shoulder against the doorframe. Having come from an online meeting, he'd rolled the cuffs of his crisp white dress shirt and left his jacket in the car.

His gaze dark and unreadable, he watched in silence as Heather finished grooming Charlie, her attention fixed on a list in her head that he couldn't see.

Turning to him with an empty bucket, she startled to find him still hovering there. "Jesus, Nate. You're still here?"

"Is it a crime," Nathaniel asked lazily, "to watch a beautiful woman and her horse?"

Colour flagged her cheekbones, and tutting, Heather paused right in front of him, raising her eyebrows when he remained blocking her way.

"Whatever you do, *Tesoro*. Walking from house to stables before the sun's even up. Lugging feed bags off the back of that old work ute. Covered in sweat and horse manure and God only knows what else. You are poetry in motion."

"That silver tongue of yours will get you into trouble one day," Heather chuckled awkwardly, squeezing between his hard body and the doorframe to pass.

"And you've never been able to take a compliment," Nathaniel sighed dramatically, turning to press his back against the wall. He bent one leg casually and crossed his arms over his chest.

Ignoring him took effort—and some days she managed it better than others. Today was one of those 'other' days.

Having mixed up Charlie's evening meal, Heather walked purposefully back toward the stall. Leaning in to hook the bucket in its usual spot, she paused long enough to see Charlie take a mouthful.

Locking the stall securely, Heather subtly glanced around the shadowy interior. Then she pressed the length of her body against Nathaniel's, resting her forearms on his shoulders and her hands on the wall by his head.

Nathaniel shifted his stance wider so now their hips pressed firmly together, his hands swooping down beneath the waistband of both jeans and undies to sit on the bare curve of her arse.

"What are you gonna cook me for dinner?" Heather asked, her tone soft with desire, her gaze tracing the length of his jawline.

She wanted to take a bite out of it—and gave into the urge moments later, rewarded by his low groan and the hard nudge of his arousal.

"Something spectacular," Nathaniel muttered, arching his neck to allow Heather better access to the column of his throat. "*Tesoro*, you make me wild."

"Good," Heather murmured, her hands tangled in his inky black hair. "It's only fair. You have no idea how crazy you drive me."

"Oh, I think I do," Nathaniel's tone was rough as he hauled Heather to her toes, shifting to press one leg between hers, opening her to his touch.

Dipping his fingers down and around, he followed the curve of her bottom until finding the molten heat of her entrance. Lips against the shell of her ear, Nathaniel purred.

"So wet, *Tesoro*. You are dripping."

Mindless, Heather all but hung in his arms as his fingers slipped and slid in and out of her body, her soft gasps the only sound outside the thunder of her heartbeat.

A split-second later, Nathaniel froze. Heather's gasp of denial was muted by his sudden shift. Before her mind could catch up, he had her pressed against the wall inside Charlie's stall.

His dark eyes serious but sparkling with humour, he covered her mouth with one hand. Hearing the voices and footsteps now, Heather acquiesced and stood pliant.

As the group passed by outside the stall, Heather and Nathaniel frozen, the atmosphere charged—made worse as Nathaniel lifted the fingers of his other hand to his lips.

Shuddering, Heather watched as he sucked those fingers into his mouth—fingers that only moments ago had been buried inside her—her legs liquid with longing as his tongue dragged across his own skin, tasting her.

Once the jovial sounds of voices raised in spirited

conversation had finally dissipated, Heather wrapped her hands in the silky material of his shirt.

"Come to my office," Heather demanded, her lips against his.

Instead, Nathaniel took her lips in a hard, fast kiss, the sound of his palm cracking against her rump startling Charlie into a surprised snort.

Then he was setting her back from him. "My rooms. Seven. You will be wearing a dress, *Tesoro*. With nothing underneath it."

She wanted to scoff in denial, wanted to knock him down a peg or two, but her tongue wasn't cooperating— and then he was gone.

Standing there for long moments, her body thrumming with unfulfilled desire and frustration, Heather started as Constance's head popped around the corner of the door.

"Heath? What are you doing, girl?"

Blinking slowly, Heather cleared her throat. "What?"

"This door is wide open. I thought one of the juniors must have forgotten to latch it."

"Nope. Just me." Still struggling for composure, Heather finally moved her feet, leaving the stall and closing the door behind her.

Staring at her strangely, Constance shrugged finally. "Okay. Well, I've just got back from dropping Isla off. Nathaniel had her use his private plane, so I only had to go down to the local airfield."

Stomach fluttering at the sound of his name, Heather cleared her throat and tapped her thighs with her palms. "Private plane. That man has entirely too much money."

Laughing, Constance looped her arm through

Heather's. "That wouldn't be the first time someone's said that to him. How the other side lives."

"You can't talk," Heather managed with a grunt. "Do you even know how much money you stand to inherit as the only living Emerson?"

Face twisting, Constance shrugged. "Bleh. Not a topic I want to discuss."

Heather's phone vibrating diverted her attention momentarily. Opening the text message, she frowned —the picture blurred and of what she could only guess was rusty knives.

"Problem?" Constance asked, catching the frown on Heather's face as she dropped into the chair opposite her desk. The tall woman was quiet for a moment before shaking her head.

"No. Just weird texts lately. Probably a wrong number."

When it seemed Constance was going to ask more, her gaze was deflected by the arrival of Leo and Josh. Her pretty face transformed into one of love and adoration as she stood.

"Ladies," Josh smiled widely. Leo, spotting his mother, started kicking his legs enthusiastically, his little hands reaching out as he babbled.

Cooing, Constance accepted Leo's warm little body, Josh's arms moving to circle her as she cradled their son. Deep and buried beneath layers of self-preservation, something resembling want gripped Heather fiercely.

Ripping her gaze from the little family with concentrated effort, Heather glanced down at her phone just as a new message flashed on the screen.

Unknown: Time to break in a new set of knives. Tell me, Heather—your place, or mine?

Ice slid down her spine. Instinct took over, and she hit block, then delete.

Glancing up, she found both Constance and Josh staring at her.

"What?"

"You've gone awfully pale," Constance muttered. Handing Leo back to Josh, she moved closer and pressed the back of her hand to Heather's forehead. "You feeling okay?"

Swatting Constance's hand away, Heather forced a laugh. "Healthy as a horse, thank you very much. You guys scram—I've got a mountain of paperwork and I'm not gonna be late leaving this office."

Expression uncertain, Constance nonetheless shrugged. "Yes, you've got a hot date."

Spluttering, Heather dropped her pen. "Wait—what?"

"C'mon," Constance said, backing out and using her body to usher Josh ahead of her. "The juniors aren't completely blind. Fast as Nate was in hustling you two into Charlie's stall—"

Hooting with laughter, Josh resisted just long enough to make a parting shot. "The hallway, Heath? You and Nate, with your little private tête-à-tête!"

"Maybe ask him for some lessons in how to seduce a woman, then!" Heather shouted as Constance shoved Josh hard and quickly shut the door behind her.

Face warm, Heather groaned just once in mixed embarrassment and annoyance, then glanced back at the neat stack of paperwork by her elbow and sighed.

**

At exactly five to seven, Heather entered the downstairs landing of the old pub, briefly ducking her head into both sides to wave at the staff and a few locals she recognised.

Taking the stairs to the top landing, she turned right toward Nathaniel's private rooms. Outside, she paused and smoothed her hands down the length of her body.

As requested, she wore a short silk dress in deep blue, simple low-heeled black sandals on her feet, and her chocolate-coloured hair loose for a change.

Lifting her hand to knock—a needless gesture—Nathaniel already had the door open. One hand tucked into the pocket of his trendy jeans, the other reached out to settle on her waist.

Rocking closer, Heather took a few steps until she settled against his chest with a sigh. "How do you always look perfectly put together, even when you're not wearing a suit?"

Shrugging carelessly, Nathaniel leaned closer to inhale her perfume. "I'm Italian."

Shaking her head, Heather smiled, flowing into the room with very little urging. She glanced briefly around the dark outer office, noticing the light from his laptop. "Working in the dark? That's not good for your eyes," she chastised half-heartedly.

"One or two emails," Nathaniel waved her concern away. "Come. Dinner is ready."

"Ready?" Heather asked, surprised, preceding him through the double French doors that opened into one large room—Nathaniel's inner sanctum.

Completely open-plan, the space was light and airy, with large windows and soft lighting. Against the left wall was a modern kitchen with open shelves displaying Venetian glassware, and an island flanked by four stools.

On the opposite wall sat a round mahogany dining table

polished to a shine, with four matching chairs tucked neatly in place. Nathaniel had already set the table with placemats, cutlery, and wine glasses. Two candles stood proudly in the centre.

In the middle of the room was a large, cream-coloured three-seater lounge with matching end tables. Heather knew from experience that a large screen descended from the ceiling, a projector cleverly tucked into the kitchen shelving—Nathaniel's preferred setup for watching classic Westerns.

Behind the lounge, an extra-large king-sized bed stood against a partially partitioned wall. Beyond that was a modern ensuite with a jacuzzi bath and rain-head shower.

Smooth jazz played through the surround sound system, and Heather smiled as Nathaniel wrapped his arms around her waist and pulled her close to his chest.

"How was the rest of your day?" he asked, his lips brushing her temple.

Shrugging, Heather sighed as she melted into his embrace. "Uneventful. Finished my paperwork—always an accomplishment."

Open-mouthed kisses trailed from her ear to her collarbone, drawing a low groan of appreciation from her.

"You promised me a meal."

"Consider this an appetiser," Nathaniel said, his hands moving down her sides to bunch the fabric of her dress. When he found the smooth skin of her thighs, he grinned.

"You finally going to finish what you started this morning?" Heather asked breathlessly, rewarded as Nathaniel cupped her heat in a firm, possessive move.

"Did you drive over here without anything on underneath?" he asked. "Or did you take it off in the car?"

Smiling, Heather shrugged. "Does it matter? I'm here without anything on underneath, as instructed."

One hand collared her throat while the other fluttered between the lips of her sex, with unerring accuracy his fingers found the hard nub hidden there.

"I suppose you're right. But I liked the idea of your bare pussy kissing the silk of your dress."

"Nate," she gasped grinding back against the hard press of his arousal, as he dipped a single finger inside the wet heat of her body. "Please."

"Please what, *Tesoro*?"

Her hand gripped the wrist of his hand around her throat, eyes rolling as his fingers tightened slightly in response. "You know what."

"I want to hear you say it," he said darkly sliding another finger alongside the first, thrusting both and making Heather gasp. "Say it, Heather."

"I want you inside me. Now."

Nathaniel's tone turned rough. "Don't move, *Tesoro*. Keep your hands right there." He guided her to the kitchen bench, pressed her palms to the marble.

Heather obeyed, panting, as she heard the zip and the rustle of fabric. The heat of his body returned a moment later, his hands on her bare backside.

He knelt behind her and Heather mewled when his tongue replaced his fingers, alternating between long, slow swipes from bottom to top. He gripped her thighs with bruising force as he stabbed his tongue deep into her wet channel, Heathers legs trembling as she shouted.

Only after he'd drawn climax after climax from her did he relent. Standing, he turned her to face him, lifting her to sit on the cool marble.

Panting, Heather fumbled with the buttons on his shirt as Nathaniel slid his hand back between their bodies, unapologetically burying two fingers deep inside her pulsing pussy.

"You want me right here?" He whispered, lining the blunt head of his hard cock up with her entrance, he froze waiting for her response.

"Yes."

"You want me buried deep?"

"Yes."

"You love me?"

"Yes."

Wait. What?

She ripped his shirt open the same moment he thrust inside her. Gasping, her head fell back as pleasure overtook her.

"You love me?" he asked again, his weight heavy and comforting against her.

Vulnerable, Heather didn't deny it. "Yes."

His gaze flared. "I love you. I love you to distraction. To madness. You're mine, *Tesoro*. Until our last breath—you're mine."

And just like that, she shattered, pulling him over the edge with her.

Breathing ragged, limbs tangled, Heather finally whispered, "You love me that much?"

Nathaniel gathered her close and carried her to bed, curling around her. "From the minute I met you. I'd have laughed if someone told me you could be instantly so devoted to a person."

"I was horrible to you," she muttered, lips pressed to his chest.

He chuckled, pinning her hand over his heart. "I wanted to needle you. Everyone said how level-headed and calm you were. I liked being the one to get under your skin."

"Vain creature," Heather teased, kissing him softly.

Serious now, Nathaniel palmed her backside. "I've seen you with Charlie. You love me *because* I'm vain."

Hunger tamed, Heather finally caught the scent in the air. "Mmm, what is that smell?"

"My Nonna's recipe," Nathaniel replied smugly. He slapped her rump and dodged her swing as he headed for the kitchen, leaving his shirt open and jeans hanging low.

She followed, her hand resting on the small of his back as he pulled the lasagne from the oven.

When she reached to steal a bit of cheese, he swatted her hand away with a grin.

"Nona's recipe, you say?" Heather asked, sucking her fingertips. "I didn't know you could cook."

"I enjoy cooking," he said, plating two hearty servings. "Probably because it's one of the better memories I have of childhood."

"I would've thought money made things easier," she murmured.

He let out a dry chuckle. "Money doesn't solve everything."

With a plate in each hand, he nodded at the fridge. "Grab the wine, please."

Heather pulled out a chilled bottle of Sangiovese and followed. "Fancy."

"Sangiovese has a tart, savoury flavour that complements the creamy intensity of the lasagne,"

Nathaniel said, pulling her chair out.

"To dinner," Heather said, clinking her glass. "You've outdone yourself, Mr Feria."

His gaze warm, he took her fingers. "Many don't find me nice, *Tesoro*. But for you—I can be."

Dinner passed in a haze of laughter and warmth. Dessert was homemade cannoli dipped in chocolate and crushed pistachios, served with coffee.

Later, they packed the dishwasher together, falling easily into routine. When they made it to bed again, it was quiet and tender, the world narrowing to just the two of them.

Heather didn't dream that night—she didn't need to. She was already exactly where she wanted to be.

'CHAPTER SIX'

Entering the stables the next morning, Heather frowned in surprise. "Isla! You're still here?"

Pretty face twisting in annoyance, Isla held still at Constance's glare, leaning as far away as she could from the long horsey face whose bridle she held.

"Unfortunately, yes. Nate had me fly back in early hours this morning."

"It's a good thing Isla loves flying," Constance muttered from somewhere behind the horse, "otherwise that would have been extremely annoying."

"It was extremely annoying either way," Isla huffed, twin spots of heat making an appearance high on her cheekbones. "I was home less than six hours. Six hours!"

"Well—why did he bring you back then?" Constance asked, shuffling into view with the end of a hose in one hand, her pretty face curious.

Sighing, Isla shrugged, then eyed the mare, who—picking up on her annoyance—tossed her head in agitation. "Apparently he heard back from Matteo sometime in the night. He's on his way here today to have a chat."

Feeling her own stirrings of annoyance, Heather crossed her arms. "He didn't mention it this morning."

"Why would he have called to tell you his brother was coming today?" Constance asked, her tone sly, clearly already knowing the answer. The smaller woman gasped theatrically. "Did you spend the night with Nate, Heath?"

Lips twisting with mock mirth, Heather swatted Constance on the butt as she tugged the mare's reins free. "I don't know what you're laughing about. I got a full eight hours last night.

"I'll bet," Isla said, her expression light with amusement. She made small movements with her hips, her tone breathless as she announced, "I would have slept eight hours after all that exercise too."

At the sound of a throat being cleared, all three women swung their gaze to the open door—and Isla could have died of embarrassment at seeing Oliver standing in the doorway.

Tall and broad and more handsome than he had any right to look, he stood with his short apron slung low on his lean hips and a toolbox in his hand.

"Morning, ladies." Smiling, Oliver tipped his chin as he studied Isla's expression, her gaze studiously focused on her boots.

Smooth as a cucumber, Constance smiled in response. "Morning, Ollie. Thanks for coming last minute. Meet Sandi. She's one of our new tenants, and her feet need a little help."

Out of the corner of her eye, Heather noticed Isla slipping out of the stable, a phone appearing from her back pocket.

"Apparently Sandi is a fan of standing knee-deep in water," Constance said, her tone affectionate as she rubbed the mare's ear. "Her owners have moved her here for a bit. They're low-lying and have a bit of a problem with water laying in the low spots on their property.

They didn't think it'd be an issue since the other horses head to higher ground, but Sandi is new to the group and they're still learning all her quirks."

Chuckling, Oliver ran his hands slowly down her front leg, urging Sandi to lift her hoof for him to inspect it. "Yeah. These are a little soft."

"Shoes?" Constance asked, to which Oliver nodded solemnly, and she sighed. "They figured that might be the case. Happy to pay whatever needs to be done."

Nodding, Oliver placed the hoof he held down on the ground and straightened. "I'll be back—need to go out to my truck to grab a few extra things."

"No dramas," Constance said, lavishing attention on the mare, who looked sleepy.

On his way past, Oliver pinched Heather's side, causing her to flinch in response. "You're such a brat."

"No, you are." She poked her tongue out and crossed her eyes, watching as he disappeared from sight a moment later.

"So," Constance drew the word out, her gaze bright, "you stay over at Nate's often?"

Sighing, Heather rubbed Sandi's side. "Sometimes."

"Is it serious?"

"Sometimes."

"What does that mean—sometimes?"

"I don't know, Connie. He drives me mad. Sometimes."

Chuckling, Constance made a 'no duh' expression. "Isn't that why men were put on this planet? To drive women mad?"

Laughing, Heather shrugged. "I suppose that would make sense."

"Do you want it to be serious?" Constance asked, her expression solemn.

"I told him I loved him last night," Heather admitted shakily, her tone barely a whisper. "Most terrifying moment of my life."

"What did he say?"

"He said he loves me too."

Face going soft, Constance carefully moved closer and bumped Heather's hip with her own. "That sounds pretty serious to me."

"Yeah," Heather muttered. "I guess it does."

Oliver's arrival forestalled whatever Constance may have been about to say, and handing the reins to the smaller woman, Heather nudged Oliver and smiled.

"I better get to work. Got paperwork to do."

Saluting her, Oliver's attention had already dropped to the mare's hooves, his 'Later, Heath' distracted. Constance's expression silently told Heather they weren't finished with their conversation.

More than ready to make her escape, Heather opened the door to her office and set her hat on the hat peg by the door. Heading towards her desk, she noticed a pile of letters and a small box wrapped in brown paper and twine.

Frowning at the package, she set it aside to go through the letters, systematically sorting invoices from local businesses, bills, and the occasional pamphlet for upcoming events and competitions.

Opening her computer a moment later, she pulled up her ledger and was looking through the current adjustment lists when she was distracted by the feel of her mobile vibrating in her front pocket.

With a small wriggle, she pulled the device free and opened her screen to read a new message from an unknown number.

Unknown: You haven't opened my package...

Heather: Who is this? What package?

Unknown: Don't play games, Heather. Open the package.

A shiver of unease and the cold touch of instinctual, primal fear had Heather reaching out to tentatively touch the brown package.

"What is going on?" Heather whispered to herself. Wrapping her hand around the box, she pulled it closer —before the shrill ring of her mobile made her gasp in fright.

Heart pounding, Heather glanced at the screen and sighed at the familiar name flashing up. Pressing one hand against her heart, she hit answer.

"Hey, Vicki."

A beat of silence. "Hey, Heath. Sorry, did I interrupt you?"

Suspicious, Heather swallowed. "No—why?"

"You just sounded weird when you answered. Figured you must be in the middle of something."

Sighing deeply, Heather covered her eyes with her hand. "Yeah, no—sorry. What's up?"

Vicki Darcy—Johnny's little sister—was also the event coordinator and marketing representative for the local Polocrosse team, a friend of Heather's from when they were both young and playing on the same team.

"Are you free this weekend?"

"I am, yeah."

"We need another umpire for the club event this weekend."

Nodding, Heather recalled having seen a post on social media asking if any umpires were available to help out.

She had in fact been about to offer her services, but then…

Glancing at the package, Heather flicked the tail end of the twine. "Happy to do it. Might even enter one of the games."

"Of course," Vicki laughed—the sound high and tinkling, inviting Heather to join her. "It's mixed groups, so we have some kids on the books."

"Ah," Heather waved her hand. "They're more fun to play with anyway."

A soft knock at the door—Isla entering a moment later with a sheepish smile. Waving her in, Heather wrapped up the call with Vicki.

"Hey Isla, what's up?"

"Waiting for Nate," Isla said, tossing her body carelessly into the seat opposite Heather. She stretched her legs out and linked her fingers over her flat stomach. "He was supposed to pick me up ten minutes ago. Something about Stan and the renovations."

"So you're hiding in here?" Heather asked, noticing the unread messages in her email account. She opened them up. "Ollie's not gonna bite—you'd have to ask very nicely."

"Har-har." Expression sour, Isla glanced around curiously. "So what was the call about? You're an umpire? Soccer?"

Shuddering, Heather quickly typed a reply to one of the emails. "God, no. Most boring sport in the world—apart from golf, in my humble opinion. I play Polocrosse."

"Ahh yes, Polocrosse." Isla smiled. "Tell me about it."

"Basically it's a group of people, on horseback, using a racquet to throw the ball from one end of a field to the other."

"So... hockey on horseback?"

Laughing, Heather shrugged. "I guess, kinda."

"Have you always played?"

"Long as I can remember." Seeing the interest there, Heather set back a little and gave the tiny woman her whole attention. "My grandparents were originally from the Netherlands and emigrated here as young adults. They had my mum—who, as you know, married my dad. They settled here, with Dad working with cattle and Mum having a hair salon in town. Long story short —I was on horseback before I could walk, tagging along with Dad while he cut and mustered cattle. Polocrosse was his sport. I grew to love it as much as he did."

Expression soft, Isla smiled. "I like that."

"What about you?" Heather asked. "You have a family sport or hobby?"

"Neurotic tendencies don't count?" Isla asked wryly, brushing at non-existent dust on her suit pants.

Studying the woman closely, Heather said softly, "You don't seem neurotic to me."

"I'm an accomplished liar," Isla's tone was flippant, but beneath all that Heather could see she truly believed it.

"Isla—"

Without warning, Constance pushed her way into the office, her hair slightly wild and her skin flushed with health. "Here you guys are! Hey—they're in here!"

Stomach tightening as warmth and arousal flooded her system, Heather loosed a sigh as Nathaniel stalked confidently into her office, making a beeline for her.

At her side, he ran his hand over the tight braids of her hair, recalling that morning as he'd watched her plait them, standing in a simple pair of undies before the mirror in his bathroom.

"Why don't you leave your hair loose?" Nathaniel had asked, leaning against the doorway, his gaze hungrily fixed on the heavy sway of her unfettered breasts.

"Do you know how hot it can get with my hair out? Lifting bags of feed, mucking out stalls, working with horses—blech. No thanks."

"You always braid your hair," Nathaniel observed slowly. "When you have work, you wear them in two braids either side. But even for special events, you braid them—it's just more elaborate then."

"My mum always braided my hair," Heather had said softly, tying off the end of her second braid. She tugged them gently—something else her mum used to do once finishing the hairstyle off for the day.

Warmth at her back, his hands had wrapped around her body in a tight embrace.

Whispering against her temple, "My mother would have loved a daughter. She got me instead, and I was always closer to my father."

Turning in the circle of his arms, she had wrapped her arms around his neck and pressed her breasts against the silk of his shirt.

"Mmm. Well—I'm glad you are you and not a daughter... frankly, I'd miss your—"

Covering her laughing mouth with his, he'd growled and backed her up to the sink, lifting her until she sat balanced on the edge.

Recognizing the way his eyes darkened and the pulse in his neck started thumping, Heather cleared her throat and wrapped her hand around his tie. "I have a bone to pick with you."

Tugging at his tie, Nathaniel made a face. "Words every

man wants to hear from his woman."

Ignoring the thrill that sent down her spine, Heather sent him a look. "You didn't mention your brother called last night."

"Forgive me, *Tesoro*. My attentions were otherwise— occupied—this morning."

Sending Constance a quelling look at her snort, Heather crossed her arms. "I still think you could have mentioned something, considering you had time to organise Isla to come back."

"Oh no," said Isla, standing and smoothing the bottom of her suit jacket. "Don't pull me into this."

"Indeed—let's go have a cuppa, Is. I have it on good authority Mary made cookies."

"Oh," Isla's eyes lit with greed as she linked her arm through Constance's. "Chocolate chip?"

"Of course. By popular demand she makes a batch every few days."

"My godson around?" Isla asked as they left the room. "I'm in the mood for snuggles."

Waiting until the two women had left, Nathaniel then pushed Heather's chair back slightly to move in closer. "*Tesoro*, he messaged me at some ungodly hour telling me he had today, and today only, to speak to me. I fired off a message to Isla and my pilot to be ready for a five a.m. take-off, so that Isla could get here and the plane would have time to get to Sydney and back again before nine-thirty."

Hating his reasonable tone, Heather sighed. "Okay. Fine. We wouldn't have had time with the rush we were in this morning—your fault, I'll add."

Smiling at her beleaguered tone, Nathaniel tipped her chin up and leaned in close, his lips coaxing her open so that he could dip his tongue in for a slow, languid kiss.

Her phone ringing interrupted the tender moment, and smiling at his growl, she reached out and answered without first checking the caller ID.

"Hello, this is Heather."

Silence.

Deep and eerie, it made all the hairs on her body stand upright. Swallowing, her gaze tracked Nathaniel as he stood and moved away, his own attention diverted to his phone.

Hanging up, she managed a brittle smile when Nathaniel glanced at her. "All good?"

"Wrong number."

Gaze sharpening at the false note in her tone, Nathaniel went to press—but it was his phone ringing this time. Noticing it was his brother, Nathaniel smiled apologetically before answering.

"Matteo."

"I've landed and can see your driver waving me over. Tell your pilot to keep the plane going. This won't take long."

Sighing at Matteo's gruff, belligerent tone, Nathaniel asked, "Can we not have a nice lunch, without any fighting? I made us reservations at the Italian restaurant in town—"

"*Porco cane*, Nate. I've just come from Italy. Can we not have something else?"

"There is a popular sushi place in town," Nathaniel said after a long moment. "If you'd prefer."

"Hallelujah. *Si*, that sounds good."

"I'm glad you're here, Matt," Nathaniel said finally, his gaze locking on Heather.

A long, loaded silence before a gusty sigh. "As am I, Nate.

See you soon."

Hanging up, Nathaniel sighed and took the seat Isla had sprawled in. Concerned, Heather studied him closely.

"Penny for your thoughts?"

"Isla thinks my hope is misplaced," Nathaniel said. "Matteo and I—we clash."

"That's what siblings do, isn't it?" Heather asked. "Can't tell you the arguments I witnessed between Josh and Jackson. Oliver and his three younger siblings. Hell, even Faith on occasion with her sisters."

"You'll remember Matteo's illegitimate," Nathaniel shrugged. "Before, when I told you my mother welcomed him into the fold, I was maybe stretching the truth a little."

Face twisting sympathetically, Heather guessed, "She wasn't as 'let bygones be bygones' as first suggested then?"

"She is Italian," Nathaniel said, as if that were answer enough—and thinking about it, Heather decided it probably was.

"So you and Matteo. Strained sibling relationship?"

"At its very best, 'relationship' would be a stretch. I attribute it more alike to rivalry."

Standing, Nathaniel tucked his hands into his pockets and slid Heather a warm look. "Will I see you tonight?"

"Do you want to see me tonight?" Heather asked.

Prowling around the table, he hauled her up and against his chest. The kiss he laid on her lips—hot and wet.

"That you even ask that makes me wish I had more time, *Tesoro*. My place at seven."

"Actually," Heather rested her hands on his chest and gave a little, embarrassed laugh, "mine at seven would be better. I need to check on my plants."

Charmed, Nathaniel took her lips in another deep kiss. Breaking away finally, he nodded. "Yours then. We will finish our conversation later..."

Leaving Heather behind her desk, Nathaniel's long legs ate up the distance to the house. Familiar with his welcome, he stuck his head through the back door, looking for Isla

Finding her finally on the floor, killer curves displayed by a pristine Armani suit, her heels kicked off to the side. Leo had a chubby fistful of Isla's incredibly long, raven black hair, seemingly dazzled by the way her ringlets wrapped around him.

Sitting at the dining table, Constance sent Nathaniel a warm smile. "You got time for a coffee?"

"Unfortunately not." Stepping into the room, he slid Leo an amused look when the toddler caught sight of him, releasing an authoritative grunt.

"Sorry, *bambino*. I must steal your godmother away."

Gaze sharp, Isla asked, "Matteo landed?"

"And on his way to the pub as we speak."

Helping Isla disengage Leo's grip on her hair, Constance stood with the little boy balanced on her hip. "Well, thanks for coming by, Is. You gonna stay here?"

"Yes," Isla stood with a groan. "I'm not flying home tonight. In fact, I think I might just stick around for a few days—and catch up on some sleep."

Chuckling, Nathaniel waited as Isla moved his way and used him to carefully slip her heels back on. Once she'd done that, he gestured her ahead of him.

"I'll see you later, Connie."

"But you'll be seeing Heath first, right?" she asked cheekily, her gaze knowing and her smile sly.

When Nathaniel said nothing, she chased them as far as

the top step of the veranda. "Just wanna let you know you have my firm seal of approval. You and Heather are adorable together!"

Gaze deadpan, Nathaniel held the gate open for Isla. "Goodbye, Connie."

Giggling, Isla slid her legs into the car and closed the door firmly behind her. Watching as Nathaniel joined her a moment later, she wiped the smile clean at his expression.

"I think it's nice," Isla said carefully. "Heather is an amazing woman."

Eyebrow lifting, Nathaniel replied simply, "I know."

"So what is your game plan?" Isla asked, turning her upper body slightly to face him. "Have you thought about what you're going to say to Matt?"

Blowing a breath out, Nathaniel rolled his shoulders. "I was going to go with the truth."

"The truth?" Frowning, Isla asked, "What would that be?"

"That I am moving here to Glen Innes, because this is where the woman I love is. That you are moving here to take over the pub—"

"Allegedly," Isla muttered, Nathaniel ignoring her to continue.

"I'll still be able to travel between here and Perth, but I need someone whose full attention will be firmly fixed on business deals and operations there."

"Matteo makes a lot of money as an independent security specialist," Isla murmured, her fingers plucking at the necklace she'd worn around her neck the whole time Nathaniel had known her.

"I have thought of that. I won't object to him taking on independent contracts. I know how long and hard he has worked on his career. But I'll offer him three times his current going rate, and it'll be a steady income."

"Ah," Isla clucked her tongue. "Because Matteo is going to care about the money."

"Well then what would you suggest?" Nathaniel asked, his tone silky.

"Shares in the business," Isla answered immediately, pushing through the silence that filled the car. "He is your brother, Nate. It's gonna take more than just a good pay check, considering the money he makes through his private contracts is nothing to sneeze at. Give him a vested interest in the company—that's what will make it worth his while."

Finally releasing his breath in a deep sigh, Nathaniel rolled his shoulders again. "Alright. Alright, you're right. Call Hutch, have him draw up a contract giving Matteo—"

"Half your majority shares."

Chuckling, Nathaniel nodded. "Half."

Smiling, Isla pulled her phone out, hitting speed dial on the company's lawyer. A quick conversation later and she was checking her emails.

"Got it," Isla muttered.

"Print it off once we get inside," Nathaniel instructed, pulling into the car park behind the pub reserved for the employees.

Already parked; the car Nathaniel had sent to pick Matteo up. He took a moment to draw in a deep breath, Isla glancing at him sympathetically.

"C'mon. Not gonna get an answer sitting here."

Laughing dryly, Nathaniel agreed and then exited the car.

'CHAPTER SEVEN'

Feeling smug, Nathaniel put the keys in the ignition and carefully backed out of his spot in the car park. As always, he merged smoothly into traffic, heading up the main road toward the sushi spot Matteo had requested.

"I will need several days to put some changes in place for my own company," Matteo announced from the back seat, his dark eyes stormy.

A clear indication of his anxiety, which made Nathaniel sigh slightly, knowing Matteo's nerves had nothing to do with the job and everything to do with sharing the car's interior with him. Matteo did all he could normally to avoid situations that put them in close range of the other.

Having been folded into the Feria household at thirteen after his mother's sudden passing, Matteo had often felt the disapproving gaze of the family matriarch—and suffered for it.

Sofia Feria had never recovered from her husband's transgression, and while well known for her benevolence, she hadn't quite managed to be so charitable with the angry teenager dropped in her lap.

As soon as Matteo had turned eighteen, he'd left—and to this day, had yet to return.

"There," Isla said, pointing at a car park right outside the store.

Following her direction, Nathaniel pulled into the spot, meeting Matteo's gaze in the rear-view mirror. "You asked. This place has good reviews."

Nodding, Matteo's gaze slid aside, his face—an almost exact replica of Nathaniel's—tight and uncomfortable. "Thank you."

Inside they found seats around the conveyer belt, and started helping themselves to the various dishes that passed. Isla had seated herself between them and was easily holding the conversation together.

She was well-versed in doing so, having known the brothers since she was a teenager—their families close. "Nate, Isla? Hey."

Turning, Nathaniel smiled to find Faith and one of her younger sisters standing there. Rising, he gathered Faith close in a quick hug.

Leaning back, he took in her lightly tanned complexion and felt his expression soften. "When did you get back from your honeymoon? I can't believe it's been two weeks already."

Grinning, Faith chuckled and gestured to her sister. "This morning. Wanted to show Hope where I work before she leaves the state."

The younger woman beside her smiled—a distant expression that didn't quite reach her eyes. A carbon copy of Faith, Nathaniel blinked slowly at the resemblance.

"Hope, I've heard a lot about you. We met very briefly at the wedding."

Silent, Hope shook his hand firmly, her skin smooth beneath his. Her tone, when she spoke, was low and pleasant—and as remote as her expression.

"Pleasure to meet you. Faith's told me a lot about you."

Stepping aside as Isla muscled her way in to hug Faith and greet Hope, Nathaniel turned to his brother, opening his mouth to make introductions.

Matteo's expression—normally so closed—was open in a rare unguarded moment, his gaze fixed on Hope with a look Nathaniel could only describe as curious admiration.

Turning back to study Hope with fresh eyes, Nathaniel admitted he could understand the appeal. Where Faith kept her hair short in a blunt bob, Hope's was long and caught elegantly in a French twist.

Faith was casually dressed in a pair of old jeans and a faded shirt, her feet stuffed into boots Nathaniel knew were steel-capped and courtesy of Jackson.

Her sister was the complete opposite, dressed in a smart two-piece suit of charcoal grey, her powder-blue blouse tucked in neatly.

"So, where are you headed?" Isla asked, her smile open and inviting as she looked expectantly at Hope.

"Queensland," Hope answered politely, and when she offered nothing more, Faith hastened to add:

"She's been offered a job with Hackett's and Noble."

"Oh," Isla nodded, then confirmed, "Law office?"

"One of the best," Faith said, her tone warm with pride. Slinging one arm over Hope's shoulder, she smiled wide. "My little sister is a hard nut. Soon the whole world will see it—and bow down before her."

A tiny crack, a minuscule thawing. The eyes Hope turned on her sister were alight with something soft.

"This is my brother, Matteo," Nathaniel said then, pulling Faith and Hope's attention more effectively than a spotlight.

Arm still draped over Hope's shoulder, Faith smiled warmly. "Hello. I must confess I haven't heard a great deal about you, but what I have heard has all been wonderful."

Expression shadowed, Matteo nodded slowly, his gaze fixed on Hope—who returned his stare boldly. "I've heard many wonderful things about you too. Congratulations on your recent nuptials."

"Thanks." Finally seeming to catch the undercurrent between her sister and Matteo, Faith cleared her throat. "Well, we'd best be off. Nice to meet you, Matteo. I'll see you, Isla and Nate, when I'm back at work tomorrow."

Waving, Isla turned her gaze to Matteo and raised her eyebrows, waiting until the younger man had returned to his seat before reclaiming her own.

Wetting her lips, Isla shared a glance with Nathaniel. "Well, that was—"

"Interesting," Nathaniel interrupted, picking up his chopsticks and the salmon sushi roll he'd been eating. "Hope is lovely. Looks very like her sister."

"Not really," Matteo argued, returning to his meal in a way that could almost fool someone into believing he was unaffected.

Except Nathaniel had seen the admiration in Matteo's face as he and Hope sized each other up. He thought it interesting that Matteo now endeavoured to downplay the instant chemistry.

"Not that I don't adore you, Isla," Matteo said suddenly, his gaze turning to encompass Nathaniel and Isla both, "but I am surprised not to be meeting this remarkable Heather character. The family cannot stop talking about how smitten you are, Nate."

If not for the underlying defensiveness in his brother's tone, Nathaniel might not have recognized the subject change for what it was—but he knew Matteo, and knew he was inclined to 'attack' first when feeling threatened. "Heather I left very diligently bent over paperwork at Emerson's. You are more than welcome to accompany Isla and me there this evening."

"Oh?" Perking up, Isla glanced at Nathaniel. "You're going to Connie's for dinner?"

"Yes. Josh messaged me when we arrived here. Apparently, his team is playing tonight. He wanted to know if I'd like to go around for dinner, watch the game. Mary is making homemade pizza."

Moaning, Isla dropped her chopsticks into her half-eaten bowl. "Why would you do that? Now my tastebuds want homemade pizza. Is Josh gonna use his new pizza oven?"

Scoffing, Nathaniel sent her a 'what do you think' look, raising his eyebrows. Leaving her to salivate in peace, he looked back at his brother's closed expression.

"What do you say, Matt? Ready to fall in love with Mary's cooking?"

Extended silence before Matteo slowly shook his head, using his napkin to delicately wipe his mouth. "Thanks. But I'll have to pass. Rain check?"

It was a subtle dig—a reminder of memories past.

Amerigo Feria, an absent and often inattentive patriarch, had made a career of promising father-son activities that never eventuated.

Matteo had stopped expecting his father to show up to movie nights, soccer games—even his high school and university graduations.

"Next time," Isla said softly, her hand beneath the table

patting Nathaniel's knee, her expression bland. "In that case, though, why don't we get this show on the road?"

"Indeed." Nathaniel cleared his throat and stood, adjusting his tie. "I'll go pay. You two wait here."

Automatically, Matteo moved closer, silently helping Isla shrug into her suit jacket, which she'd removed to avoid getting sauce on it during the meal.

"He's trying, you know," Isla muttered, her gaze tracking Nathaniel even as she kept her tone low, speaking to the big man behind her. "You could cut him a little slack."

"You, better than anyone, know how hard this is." Matteo's tone was low and even, almost completely masking the hint of strain beneath.

But Isla knew Matteo as well as she knew Nathaniel.

"You're both adults now. There's no reason the same games played in childhood should still apply."

Big hands turned her slowly under the guise of fixing the collar of her blouse, Matteo's gaze dark and turbulent. "You, better than anyone, know why they must."

"Amerigo passed away, Matt. Years ago—"

"He wasn't the one in charge of the games."

It was a dark reminder. Sighing, Isla nodded slightly. "I still think you and Nathaniel should stand up to her. She shouldn't still be controlling your relationship."

"Lectures, Is? Or is it someone else's mother— a woman perhaps, also by the name of Isla. Whose mother has purportedly entered into a business merger for her daughters hand in marriage. You really need to be back home, in Perth, sorting that out. Otherwise you'll find yourself married by proxy, by the end of the year."

Lips tightening in annoyance, Isla nonetheless bowed

her head. Silently, they both waited until Nathaniel returned.

"Alright, Matteo. Let's drive you to the airport."

**

"Heather?"

"Hmm?" Glancing up from her computer screen, Heather rubbed her eyes tiredly, her gaze refocusing on Ryan's tall, lanky form in the doorway.

"Sorry. Connie wanted me to pass these along."

Frowning at the handful of letters, Heather sighed. "More? I've only just cleared away the last lot."

Smile apologetic, Ryan dropped the tidy bundle onto her desk and handed over a small package. "Sorry."

"All good, kid—off for the afternoon?"

"Yeah. I'll see you tomorrow?"

Gaze dropping to the first letter, Heather waved distractedly. "Yep. See you tomorrow, Ryan."

Thumbing through the letters, her attention was drawn to the package. It was exactly the same as the first one she'd received. She shook the box slightly.

Unlike the first, which had been empty when she'd finally opened it, this one rattled. Plucking at the twine, she slowly unwrapped the brown paper.

As before, beneath the wrapping was a plain brown cardboard box. Lifting the lid, she made a short noise of disgust, immediately closing it and pushing her chair back.

Poised to rise, she paused, then hardened her resolve. Sliding her chair closer, she glanced at her closed door before tentatively lifting the lid again.

Inside: a small plastic toy horse, its coat a perfect match to Charlie's. An otherwise cute gift—perhaps from one of her students.

Except the legs and head had been cut off. Red smears—paint or nail polish, she hoped—splattered the body and the wounds.

No note.

The address had been handwritten, with no return.

Closing the lid, Heather used the twine to tie the package tightly again, then turned to the bin beside her desk and dropped it in.

Swallowing against nausea, a sixth sense drew her gaze to her phone screen. A new notification flashed. She reached out slowly.

Unknown: Did you like my gift?

Heather: The butchered toy horse? No—I didn't, you sicko. Who is this?

Radio silence.

Frustrated, wondering if this was just a sick joke, Heather tried for the next thirty minutes to focus on the paperwork she needed to finish.

Eventually giving up with a sigh, she closed her computer and stood with a stretch. Tucking her phone into her back pocket after frowning at it, she left her office.

She headed toward Charlie's stall, taking a few moments to stand with him, rubbing his long face comfortingly.

The package had thrown her more than she wanted to admit. Every small shift of air made her flinch, her gaze wide and alert as she studied the darkened stable interior.

A noise behind her preceded a shift of warmth at her back. All the hairs on her neck lifted as instinct told her someone was there.

Whirling, she would have screamed—had her body not been strung so tight. Instead, all she could do was gasp loudly and flinch back.

Green eyes narrowed, Josh studied her posture for a long, silent moment, gaze taking in her pallor and the way her pulse throbbed in her neck.

"Heath? What the hell is going on?"

"I don't—what are you—" But she couldn't finish. She'd been frightened so badly that Heather's legs slowly crumpled.

Josh was already there. He caught her by the arms and lowered her to the floor, his expression a terrifying mix of fury and concern.

"Seriously. What was that? What's going on?"

Shaking her head, Heather flapped a hand, needing a minute to catch her breath. But her lungs refused to cooperate. It felt like a hand gripped her throat.

With every heartbeat, those phantom fingers squeezed tighter. She didn't resist as Josh shoved her head down between her knees.

"Breathe, Heath. Jesus—don't make me call Connie. Hell —don't make me call Nate."

Ripping free, Heather straightened and gripped the lapels of Josh's flannel shirt. "Don't—you—dare."

Gaze hard, Josh gripped her wrists tightly. "Then breathe."

The warmth of his rough hands anchoring her to the here and now helped. Ten agonizing minutes later, Heather could finally breathe.

As her lungs evened out, she and Josh sat with their backs pressed against the wood of Charlie's stall. The silence in the stables was no longer ominous.

"Care to explain what just happened?"

"You scared me," Heather replied, exhausted. The look she sent him was arched.

Josh shook his head. "Nah, Heath. I've seen you scared. I've seen you pissed off, black with rage, even deliriously happy. But I've never seen *that* expression on your face before."

She wanted so badly to tell him.

Wanted to talk about the weird phone calls where no one answered. The jumbled texts from unknown numbers.

More than that, she wanted to show someone the damn parcel—the miniature of Charlie, hacked to pieces and covered in fake blood.

But she'd been silent too long, and Josh took it upon himself to fill the gap. "Is this because it's almost that time of the year?"

For a moment, Heather had no idea what he meant— then reality slammed into her, crushing her heart.

How could she have forgotten?

The anniversary of her parents' death. The first in a long line of "people Heather loves" to die suddenly, without warning.

Josh didn't wait for a reply. He pulled her into his side for a tight hug, his chin resting on her head as he sighed. "I'm sorry, Heath. So damn sorry they're gone."

A wet drop on her hand. Reaching up to touch her face, Heather released a shaky breath. Tears. "Damnit, Hart."

"I know," Josh's voice rumbled against her ear. "Feelings —yuck."

As always, he lightened her sadness with a touch of humour. But so close to the anniversary, it only muted the grief—it didn't erase it.

"Rugby's on tonight," Josh muttered. "Came out here to

ask if you wanted to stay for pizza and beer."

"If it was any other night," Heather murmured, "I probably would've said yes. Damnit." Remembering her dinner with Nathaniel, she sagged a little further. "I forgot... I've already got plans this evening."

"With Nate?"

Sitting up, Heather leaned away and glared at Josh. "How would you know that?"

"I'm not as blind as everyone around here seems to think I am," Josh said, exasperated. "I've seen the way you two are together. If you're not doing the horizontal tango, I'll eat my hat."

Disgusted on his behalf—and eyeing the filthy hat with concern—Heather sighed. "Fine. You're not blind."

Josh waited a beat. "That's it? That's all I get?"

"Well, I'm not giving you a play-by-play," Heather said dryly.

When colour flagged Josh's cheekbones, Heather spluttered with laughter—only to be sent sprawling a moment later when Josh shoved her.

"No, you perv. That I can do without. But I did expect more validation than 'you're not blind.'"

Smiling, Heather righted herself and brushed off her jeans. "Fine. We are—dating."

"You don't sound awful sure there, Ross."

"It's relatively new, Hart."

"Please. You two have been dancing this waltz since you met two years ago." Standing, Josh pulled Heather to her feet. "For what it's worth—I like the guy."

Smile turning soft, Heather patted the seat of her jeans. "Yeah. I like the guy too."

"Does he know?" Josh asked as they walked toward the front doors of the stable.

Somehow Heather knew they'd swapped topics again, and shaking her head Heather murmured, "No. Not the specifics. Not the dates."

"He needs to know, Heath. He'll want to be there."

"When have I ever wanted anyone there?"

"Never. But he'll push his way in, as is his right."

Sliding him a look, Heather didn't argue. At the door now, she glanced back into the stables.

Peace. Quiet. Tranquillity. Every shadow and grain of wood as familiar as her own face.

But the earlier disquiet refused to be banished, and Heather's voice was a whisper. "Josh?"

Turning to look over his shoulder at her frozen figure in the doorway, he raised an eyebrow. "Yeah?"

"What did you find on the trail?"

Distaste shifted his expression. His sigh was deep, troubled. "Canine bodies."

A brush of icy fingers down her spine. "What?"

"Let's just say the wild dog pack that's been hunting these parts? They're not gonna be a problem anymore. Someone trapped them, skinned them, and hung them along the trail."

Lips bloodless, Heather croaked, "You're kidding? Why?"

"A warning?" Josh shrugged. "You know some of the old boys around here. Probably figured they'd deter other wild dogs and dingoes."

"But why *my* trail?"

Alerted by her tone, Josh turned fully, arms crossed over his broad chest, gaze suspicious. "I don't know, Heath. Is there something you want to tell me?"

A charged silence. Then Heather shook her head—just once—and before Josh could argue, she was already walking towards the house.

Suddenly, heading home to curl up and grieve didn't feel like a safe option. Something instinctual and ingrained sent Heather into the bright lights and warmth of the crowded Bed and Breakfast.

Her foot hit the first step of the veranda, and suddenly Nathaniel was standing in the open back door, his expression centred on her.

"*Tesoro*, I was just about to come and find you."

Striving to match his tone, Heather tried to smile. "Well, look no further. Here I am."

His gaze sharpened. He took in the lines of stress on her face, then shifted to the tight, angry set of Josh's shoulders. Nathaniel stepped smoothly onto the back veranda, closing the door behind him.

"Something wrong?"

"Ask your girlfriend," Josh griped.

Just as fast, Nathaniel warned, "Watch your tone."

For a minute, the two large men considered each other. Then Josh took a step back. "This isn't about me. Has very little to do with me, in fact. So—I'm gonna go inside and make up some kind of excuse that'll give you two fifteen to twenty minutes, tops."

Then he was gone, the back door opening and shutting quickly, leaving Heather and Nathaniel alone. Moving to follow Josh's path, she huffed in annoyance as Nathaniel stepped in her way.

"You two were arguing about something?"

"It's nothing," Heather shrugged. "Seriously. Let's go inside."

"You two never argue, so whatever it is, it must be big."

"Nate, you're not listening to me. It's nothing. Please, let's go inside."

"The only thing I've ever seen you two argue about is Connie. Is—"

"Nate! We need to get inside!" she snapped, unable to help herself.

Freezing, Nathaniel studied her carefully. "*Tesoro*. Why do we need to go inside? What's out here that's frightening you?"

Hovering on the edge, Heather realized this was another big moment—another choice. She could finally tell someone what had been happening. But a very small voice cautioned her.

Maybe she was imagining it. Maybe she was just stressed about the anniversary of her parents' deaths.

Without conscious thought, Heather reached into her pocket and pulled out her phone. Unlocking the screen, she brought up the texts from the unknown number and handed it over to Nathaniel.

She watched as his eyes scanned the messages, his full lips tightening with fury, his expression darkening into something unreadable.

With effort, he set the beer bottle he'd been holding down on the veranda railing. Then he ran one hand through his hair while the other scrolled back to the top of the thread.

"Who, Heather?"

"I don't know. I don't know who the messages are from —I—" She hesitated, but his gaze met hers, steadying her. Warning her not to stop. "I don't know who's been calling me or sending me packages. I don't know."

"How long?"

Rubbing her palms against her thighs, Heather blew out a breath. "Ahh. Well. The calls with dead air have been happening the last few months. The texts and packages started around Faith's wedding, I think."

"And you didn't think to mention it before now?"

"I—I mean—I just—" Thrown by the cold anger in his tone, Heather swallowed thickly.

Nathaniel's gaze was direct. "What's changed? Obviously something big—otherwise I doubt you'd have shown me these."

Accepting the phone he handed back, Heather haltingly explained what had happened that morning with Charlie, and Josh's gruesome discovery on the riding trail.

"Who else knows you ride that trail?"

Pulling in a shocked breath, Heather made a helpless gesture. "Everyone, Nate. Everyone knows. We even mentioned it in that magazine article Connie did a couple months ago."

Closing his eyes, Nathaniel let out a deep breath. His mind raced, considering every possible angle.

His Heather was a creature of habit—just like the horses she trained. She lived each day to a schedule. A schedule anyone could memorize after just a few days of watching her.

Heather resisted change to a fault. She was possibly the least spontaneous person he'd ever met.

Regimented.

Consistent.

Steady.

Three of her greatest qualities. The same three someone could have used against her—to figure her out. To threaten her.

The tighter his chest became, the more Nathaniel saw one blinding truth.

He needed Matteo.

He needed him—now.

'CHAPTER EIGHT'

"This is silly," Heather muttered, fiddling with the string of the tea bag in her mug. "Nate. Are you listening?"

"No," Nathaniel's fingers didn't pause as he communicated with his brother through a secure link Matteo had set up. "Frankly, I'm still annoyed with you for waiting until now to tell me."

"Because this is probably all nothing, just a prank from the local hoodlums—albeit in poor taste."

Breaking from his furious typing, Nathaniel reached down and hooked his fingers underneath the seat of her chair, physically jerking her closer so they sat outer thighs pressed together.

Pinching her chin gently between thumb and pointer finger, his gaze was serious. "*Tesoro*. Your safety is the only thing I'm concerned with right now. If it turns out to be a bad prank, fine. But I'm not going to assume it's nothing without first exhausting all other possible angles."

"My brother has a point," Matteo's young face—so like Nathaniel's—stared sternly back at her from the computer screen.

Not the way she'd have preferred to meet Nathaniel's younger brother, but Heather was a practical kind of girl and realised some things she really had very little control over.

"I still think it's a waste of resources," Heather argued, but even she could hear the give in her tone and wasn't surprised by the flash of triumph in Nathaniel's deep brown eyes.

A sigh from the computer drew her attention once more. Matteo's features, no less stern, softened by an almost imperceptible light in eyes several shades lighter than his brother's.

"You shouldn't give in to him so easily; you must push back, just to make him work for the victory."

Tone laced heavily with affront, Nathaniel replied, "Oh, she made me work for it. Two years she made me work for it."

Smiling, Heather returned to plucking at her tea bag, her body fairly aching with exhaustion.

"*Tesoro.*" Noticing the way she drooped, Nathaniel dropped his hand on her thigh—the action hidden by the table. "Go to bed."

"Not unless you're coming with me." Heather shook her head stubbornly, rubbing her eyes briskly. But ten minutes later, when Nathaniel turned to ask her something, he smiled.

Determined as always, she'd fallen asleep with her head pillowed on her arms. Murmuring something to Matteo, he stood and carefully slid his arms beneath her knees.

Gently tipping her upper body back, she sighed as she relaxed into his arms. Coiling his muscles, Nathaniel stood, Heather tucked firmly against his chest.

Walking to his bed, he deposited her on what he'd begun to call "her side," unlacing her boots to tug them off. He tucked her in a moment later.

Quietly, he studied her—features softened by sleep and

vulnerable in a way Nathaniel knew she never was when awake.

Pressing his lips to her forehead, he shushed her when she rolled, whispering his name in her sleep as she reached for him.

Returning to the kitchen, he picked his laptop up and headed into his office, turning off the kitchen light as he went and closing the double French doors behind him.

Switching on his desk lamp, he settled with a groan and met Matteo's considering gaze.

"What?"

"She's really important to you," Matteo said finally, his tone surprised.

Insulted, Nathaniel raised both eyebrows. "You knew I was seeing her."

Shaking his head, Matteo interrupted. "No. The way you look at her is not how I've seen you look at the other women in the past. You want to marry this woman."

Quiet, Nathaniel finally nodded, admitting faintly, "Yes. I want to marry her."

"You want her as the mother of your children."

"Yes. There is no other woman I could see fulfilling that role - I will allow no other woman in this role."

Uncharacteristically, Matteo's expression gentled. "I did not realise this was who your heart had settled on. I think I will need to return soon to meet her."

Heart hurting for all the very best reasons, Nathaniel's tone was gruff. "I would like that. Heather and I—we'd like that. Perhaps... perhaps you could stay a while."

A smile—open and honest in a way Matteo hadn't shown since he was a young boy—took over features made light by the expression.

"You cannot keep bringing people over to your Glen

Innes, Nate. Soon you will have no one left to maintain your interests over here in Perth."

Shrugging in that careless fashion of his, Nathaniel leaned back in his chair and steepled his fingers over his abdomen. "It is easy to fall in love with the town, yes?"

When Matteo chuckled but nodded, his attention returning to whatever he was working on, Nathaniel felt his expression slide into something sly.

"The people," he said, struggling to keep his tone even, "are also easy to fall for. Many beautiful women here, many single. You met Hope—Faith's little sister. She told me Hope hasn't been on a date in four years. Imagine a woman as beautiful as that, spending her weekends alone. What a crime."

Expression souring somewhat, Matteo grunted. "I know what you are up to. I do not need your help with women."

Nonetheless, Nathaniel could read the consideration on his younger brother's face. Deciding to leave that topic for now, he asked instead, "What have you found?"

"I'm going through Heather's contacts, trying to see if I can pick up anything unusual."

"The one she's been getting those texts from—that's not listed in her contacts book."

"I know. There are a lot of different ways people can hide their calling ID, but the tone or the way they construct their texts would come across in their emails and other communication threads. That's how we'll figure out the who, and then we can start working on the why."

"The why?"

"People don't just stalk another person for no reason, Nate. Maybe this person feels Heather slighted them somehow. Maybe they think they're in a relationship with her. Could've started as simply as Heather smiling at them at a game or in the shops."

"That's..." Searching for a word but not coming up with anything, Nathaniel said, "Unhinged."

"Depravity has many different faces," Matteo muttered, hitting enter as the software he'd just loaded started downloading. "Alright. I'm running a program in the background of Heather's systems. It'll start analysing everything coming through and look for those patterns."

"But for the time being, we just have to let things progress?"

"Yes." Pinning his older brother with a look, Matteo warned, "Heather needs to try and go about her life as per normal. Any major changes and her stalker might get wind that he is now the hunted party. He'll go to ground and we'll lose him."

Nathaniel didn't like doing nothing. What he wanted to do was surround Heather with the biggest men he could find.

Better yet, he wanted to lock her in this home where he could track every single person coming in or out. But he also knew Heather better than she probably knew herself.

She'd buck at that kind of authority, and while he enjoyed pushing all her buttons, he knew she'd just as soon cut him out of her life than let him run it.

"I know that goes against what your instincts are telling you," Matteo said softly, his expression apologetic. "But it's what we need to do for right now, so my software can do what it needs to and find the bastard."

"Thanks, Matt. For doing this for me."

Shrugging, Matteo cleared his throat. "I'd better go. I

have a meeting with the board in the morning."

Nodding, Nathaniel asked, "So you're all settled in?"

Another smile peeked out quickly before Matteo's face settled back into its customary stern lines. "I didn't have time to call the cleaners, so my place is dusty and smells a little stale. I'll fix that in the morning on my way into the office."

"Call me when you get something," Nathaniel said, ringing off after Matteo had agreed quietly. Then, closing the lid on his laptop, he stood with a groan.

Heading back into his main living quarters, he didn't turn on any lights, moving through the shadows with the ease of familiarity.

At the end of the bed, he watched Heather sleeping for a long moment as he loosened his tie, pulling it over his head to drop at his feet.

Tugging the ends of his shirt free from the waist of his pants, he shed it and his pants in smooth succession.

Completely nude now he crawled up the length of the bed, sliding the sheets down Heather's form and gently pressing his lips against the long column of her throat.

Fingers unbuttoning her jeans, he slowly slid them off.

Rolling slightly to help, Heather sighed and made a small murmur of sound.

Kissing the smooth skin of her thighs, Nathaniel watched her wake slowly, his hands slipping up the hem of her shirt to close over her breasts.

Moaning now, Heather arched, blinking slowly awake. "Nate?"

"Mmhmm." Dipping his fingertips into the cups of her bra, he yanked the material down slightly, his hands palming the soft flesh as he moved to settle his body firmly between her legs.

"What time is it?" Heather asked, her hands tangling in his thick hair as his mouth closed over her shirt-covered nipple.

"Late," Nathaniel whispered a long, lazy heartbeat later. When he pushed her shirt up, she didn't hesitate to finish the job, pulling the material up over her head. "Or early, depending on how you look at it."

Gasping as his fingers dipped between her legs, Heather lost her train of thought. "Nate—"

Lips pressed against hers Nathaniel parted the lips of her sex, moving her hand down until it wrapped around hard cock. "Shhh, *Tesoro*. Let me take care of you."

**

Sunlight streaming through a crack in the blinds the next morning woke Heather from the deep, dreamless sleep she'd fallen into after Nathaniel had driven her to blissful madness.

Lying on her stomach, the sheets pooled carelessly over her nude body. Heather lifted her chest slightly and glanced around. Noticing the bathroom door closed, she could hear the sound of the shower, the waterproof radio Nathaniel kept in there playing low, set to an Italian news channel.

Lowering again to stretch her body, her limbs felt heavy and lazy, her mind helpfully replaying small moments from the night before. God, that man knew his way around her body.

Smiling, she rolled over onto her back, the covers twisting around her legs, brushing sensitized skin still singing with awareness. Nathaniel chose that moment to leave the bathroom, one towel hung low on his hips while he used another to dry his hair.

Catching sight of her straining nipples, Nathaniel

paused on the threshold and smiled, the expression heated. "Good morning, *Tesoro*. Did you sleep well?"

Deliberately moaning softly, Heather sent him a look from beneath lowered eyelashes. "I believe I did."

Prowling towards her side of the bed, he leaned down, caging her body between his arms, and took her mouth in a wet kiss. He tasted like mint and smelled good enough to eat. Reaching for him, she settled her hand on his knee and dragged her hand up beneath the towel. Unsurprised to find him hard and ready, her grip around him firm, he ripped the towel aside and climbed into the bed. Nudging her legs apart, he had just settled the tip of his cock at the heated entrance to her body when both their phones went off. Freezing, Nathaniel growled something in Italian while Heather cursed.

Rolling away, Nathaniel answered his phone while Heather checked her caller ID. Seeing Constance's name, she slid Nathaniel a longing glance and hit accept.

"Morning, Connie."

"Morning, Connie. Morning Connie! Don't you 'Morning, Connie' me! What the hell is going on? Josh said you have a stalker?"

Sighing, Heather sat up slightly, pulling the sheet with her. She watched as Nathaniel turned away and headed to his closet, his round, firm backside making everything feminine in her ache with want.

"Connie, it's not a big deal—"

"I disagree! It's a big deal, Heath. A big, fucking deal!"

In the background, Heather could hear a deep voice—Josh—attempting to calm the shrill in Constance's tone. But clearly the small woman was on a roll.

"Don't downplay this, Heather. One in six women experience stalking, and one in three women experience some form of physical violence. At the hands, of their stalkers. This is something that you should have told me was happening!"

"Someone's been on the internet this morning," Heather tried for flippant, a little shocked by the animalistic growl she received in response to her attempt at a joke.

"Hurry up and get to work. We're doing a safety demonstration and implementing some new 'stranger danger' processes for the farm."

Feeling a little meek in the face of Constance's ire, Heather slid Nathaniel a glance as he reappeared, his attention fixed on her even as he buttoned his cufflinks. Her gaze trailed down the tanned expanse of his chest, bared by his unbuttoned shirt. Whatever Heather replied with clearly enraged Constance further.

"Heather Ross! Put on some clothes, get in your car and be at the farm in an hour. Otherwise, I will get into my car, drive to the pub, and drag you off Nate's dick myself!"

Mouth dropping open in surprise, Heather didn't get the chance to answer—Constance hung up on her. Setting the phone back on the bedside table, she stared at Nathaniel.

"Connie's mad."

"I heard," Nathaniel replied wryly, moving to the bed and physically plucking her from it. Pressing the naked length of her up against his body, he took her mouth in a long, lazy kiss that left her boneless, her body demanding more. Then he stepped back and turned her toward the bathroom.

With a hard swat to her rump, which did nothing to ease the arousal tightening every nerve, he nodded toward the empty room with a grin. "Better hop to it. I, for one, make it a rule not to get on Connie's bad side. I'll get you a coffee and a cream cheese bagel to go."

Pouting, Heather offered him her side profile and trailed her hand down her body, delving her fingers to the wet heat between her legs. "Join me?"

Heat flared in the depths of his eyes, but Nathaniel pointed sternly toward the bathroom again. "You think Connie won't barge in here and do just what she threatened? You and I will finish what we started—tonight."

"Argh!" Sexually frustrated but also kind of enjoying the idea of hovering on the brink all day—because that would make tonight's release that much more spectacular—Heather complied.

A short fifteen minutes later, Heather had showered, braided her hair into a single heavy tail that lay against her spine, and spent longer than necessary making out with Nathaniel. On her way out, with her coffee in a to-go cup and a bagel wrapped in baking paper, she was coming down the stairs as Faith entered through the front doors.

Glancing up from her phone, Faith paused and smiled. "Hey, Heather."

"Morning, Faith. How are you going today?"

"Good! I'm running a little later this morning. Harmony spit up half of what she ate on my shirt."

Chuckling, Heather paused once she'd reached the ground floor. "It's still amazing to me that they can smell so adorable, considering how much they vomit."

"Baby powder," Faith revealed with a slow chin tip. "It's all about the baby powder."

Laughing, Heather brandished her bagel and travel mug. "Alright, I better be off. I'm also running late."

Having turned toward the kitchens, Faith sent Heather a wicked smile over her shoulder. "Hazards of going to bed with a handsome man. They also have a tendency of making you late."

Chuckling into her mug, Heather waved as Faith disappeared around the corner. Out the back door, she was unlocking her car when she noticed something sitting beneath one of her wipers.

Slowly, Heather glanced around the empty parking lot and then at the closed gate—the only access to this car park a back-alley road that ran between the pub and neighbouring shops.

Straightening her spine, Heather plucked the envelope from her windscreen and hustled into her car, locking it immediately once she'd settled.

Setting her coffee and breakfast down in the centre console, she slowly opened the envelope. Inside—another Polaroid.

The angle was from the road, looking in through the double doors of the pub. Heather was dressed in a slinky black dress and standing on the second stair. Nathaniel, dressed as ever in one of his suits, had his back to the cameraman, his hands settled on her hips, and Heather's arms rested on his shoulders.

Chilled despite the warmth in the sun, Heather slipped the photo back into the envelope. Opening the glove box, she stuffed the envelope and its contents in with the rest of the junk she stored there.

Sitting for a moment, she drew in a deep breath and then turned the car on, following the familiar route to Emersons with the music playing a little louder than necessary.

On the main highway headed out of town, Heather

glanced in her rear-view mirror and noticed a truck sitting a little too close. She motioned for him to overtake her.

Whoever the driver was didn't seem inclined to pass, and feeling anxious, Heather pulled off at one of the service stations.

For a moment she wondered if the truckie was going to follow her—his indicator blinking a heartbeat after she'd turned hers on.

But when she took the turning lane to exit, he continued by, the noise of his truck screaming in her ears and making her hunch her shoulders.

Feeling stupid now, Heather stopped illegally on the white stripes rather than continue toward the service station, drawing in a slow, shaky breath. She held it for the count of five before exhaling slowly.

Indicating, she came back out onto the highway, her nerves settling slowly. Then, just before the exit she'd usually take to pull into the road that led to Emersons and Harts, her instincts screamed at her.

Sitting in one of the truck stops was the same truck from before—its lights on and engine running. Once she passed, it slowly started pulling back out onto the road behind her.

Pressing her foot down on the accelerator, Heather didn't care if she was speeding. Spotting her exit just up the road, she whipped into the turning lane without slowing.

Taking the corner faster than she should have, the truck went flying past, the driver sitting on the horn and making Heather's heart jump into her throat.

"What the hell is his problem?" Heather demanded aloud, her hands shaky as she gripped her steering wheel tightly.

She'd never been more grateful to hit the end of Emerson's driveway than she was then, and still driving a little faster than necessary, she fairly flew up the loose gravel road.

Reaching the car park, Heather reversed into her usual spot and then turned the car off. Sitting there for a long, silent moment, she reached for her phone and opened Nathaniel's number.

The urge to call him and tell him about what had just happened drove her hard, and with her thumb hovering over the 'call' function, she paused—undecided.

Slowly, with great reluctance, she closed her phone app down and opened her door. Sliding out, she shoved her phone into her back pocket and took a few deep breaths. Scary as that had been, equally alarming was this weakness—this softening—that demanded she call Nathaniel. Because he could fix this.

He could make her feel better.

When had Heather started needing Nathaniel to handle things for her?

Her. Heather Ross.

Who hadn't needed or leaned on another person since watching her last family member being lowered into the ground.

She didn't like feeling this vulnerable, this out of control.

The only constant in life was that you had only yourself to rely on—and no amount of promising could hold out against things like car accidents, kidney disease, or a broken heart.

Annoyed now, for reasons she didn't really want to look too much into, Heather grabbed her to-go mug and bagel, slammed her door behind her, and stomped toward the paddock gates.

As if having waited for her, Constance stood from one of the chairs to meet her at the bottom of the stairs, her expression marred by a frown.

Sighing, her own anger flaring, Heather raised her hand when Constance went to speak. "C'mon, Connie. Don't start."

Expecting a heated reply, Heather froze when instead Constance launched her small body in Heather's direction—arms surprisingly strong as they wrapped around her waist and Constance huffed, burying her face into Heather's chest.

For a moment, Heather didn't know what to do—her anger suddenly deflating like a balloon. Then, dropping her shoulders from their tight position, she wrapped her arms around Constance's neck.

Tipping her head slightly so she could rest her cheek against the top of Constance's head, she slid Josh a glare as he stood with Leo balanced on his hip, watching from the back door.

"You scared me," Constance whispered, the admission low and full of emotion. "You scared me, Heather. What would I do if something happened to you?"

Suddenly, Heather was reminded that she wasn't the only person at Emersons who had lost a loved one—that Constance had loved and lost her mother to cancer at a much younger age than Heather.

Had grown up in a system because her remaining family hadn't wanted her.

Had scars and cracks of her own.

"I'm sorry," Heather whispered. "I just... didn't think about telling anyone else. Figured I'd handle it on my own."

"We're family. You don't need to handle it alone."

Nodding—though Constance's face was still hidden—Heather sighed. "You're right. I won't do that again. If I'm ever unlucky enough to have another stalker, I'll tell you as soon as I know."

Snorting a laugh, Constance finally stood back, dashing at the tears clinging to her eyelashes, and for a moment Heather pulled a face.

Even crying, Constance looked beautiful and elegant. Some women got all the luck.

Hooking her arm through Heather's, Constance started pulling them toward the stables, saying, "C'mon. I told everyone to gather in the arena. We're gonna go through some new safety procedures."

"I really don't think that's necessary—"

"It is, Heath. We have juniors we need to think about. I want everyone to be vigilant. Any unknown visitors are gonna need to sign in, and we're gonna close ranks on new clients for a little while."

"Okay, I agree with letting the juniors and employees know—their safety is my priority. But no new clients? Are you sure, Connie?"

"Positive."

Thinking about it, Heather said gently, "You know, my stalker could be anyone. Including one of the regular clients. They aren't necessarily gonna be new."

Steps faltering, Constance gazed up at Heather—horrified. "I hadn't even thought of that."

Patting Constance's hand, Heather started them walking again. "It's fine. Neither had I until I said it. I don't think turning away new clients is gonna fix the issue, is all I'm saying."

Groaning, Constance glanced at Josh, who had taken up position on Heather's other side. "You couldn't have thought of that angle and said something before?"

A hand raised in the air his tone a slow drawl Josh replied, "Woman, any thoughts I've had on the matter. You've steamrolled over, since I told you about the stalker this morning."

Sniffing, Constance turned her face forward again. "I don't appreciate your tone."

Sighing and running one large hand through his hair —the action tousling already dishevelled blond locks— Josh glanced down at his small son and said, "Women. Eternal headaches."

Gasping in outrage, Constance pulled Heather to a stop again, leaning around the taller woman to pluck Leo from his father's arms.

"Don't listen, bubba. Your father doesn't know the first thing about women." Then, without another word to either of them, Constance stormed off—Leo gurgling happily from his mother's hip.

"You had to tell her," Heather muttered wryly, poking Josh in the side with her elbow.

"Oh, shut up."

Chuckling, Heather entered the stables and followed in Constance's path, Josh ambling along behind her, his face dropping comically as he sulked.

'CHAPTER NINE'

The weekend couldn't have come soon enough. With the sun still an hour off, Heather had arrived at Emersons to tightly braid and wrap Charlie's tail.

Accustomed to the usual event-day preparations, Charlie stood there half-asleep, compliant as Heather finally deemed her handiwork acceptable.

She'd then prepared his typical feed of grain and chaff before packing her ute with all of Charlie's gear—and her own. Dressed in white jodhpurs with her club shirt beneath a black, skin-tight, dry-wicking jacket, Heather stuffed her feet into high tan leather riding boots.

After double-checking she had everything—Charlie's tack, hay, and a small portion of his final feed—she loaded him into the float.

Constance chose that moment to exit the house, a to-go cup in each hand as she yawned widely. Climbing into the passenger seat, she clipped in her belt and set the cups down.

When Heather opened her mouth to speak, Constance shook her head. "No. It's too early."

Smiling, Heather watched as Constance rolled toward the window, burrowing into her oversized jacket and promptly falling asleep.

Opening her maps, Heather typed in the destination. Her sense of direction was poor enough that even though she'd been to this location before, she didn't trust herself not to get lost.

For the next hour, Heather staved off sleepiness by drinking the coffee Constance had prepared, occasionally checking her rear-view mirror—half-expecting to see the same truck from the day before.

Beside her, Constance slept, murmuring now and again or snorting loud enough to wake herself, then glancing blearily around.

It was amusing, but when they were eight minutes out from the venue, Heather reached over to shake her shoulder gently.

"Connie. We're almost there, time to wake up."

Groaning, Constance wrapped her arms around herself. "No. This has been the best sleep I've had since Leo was born."

Chuckling—Heather had a front-row seat to how easily that little boy ran his parents ragged—she indicated and pulled into a nearby service station.

"C'mon. Let's get you another coffee."

Blinking dazedly, Constance looked at her empty to-go mug. "Why? What happened to mine?"

"I drank it," Heather said cheerily. "You left it sitting there, unclaimed."

For a moment, Constance looked like she might argue —then she yawned. "Alright. Whatever. Make mine a triple shot of caffeine, would you?"

Having already anticipated that, Heather slid from the car without replying. Walking along the ute and float, she peeked in at Charlie.

He looked much like Constance—sleepy. Leaving him to it, Heather headed through the sliding doors and waved to the gentleman behind the counter.

At the self-help station, she placed paper cups under the machines, listening to them splutter and whine until the rich smell of coffee filled the air.

Soon after, she had the two cups fitted with travel lids and headed for the counter, grabbing a packet of lollies on the way.

Back in the car, she tossed the lollies into Constance's lap and slotted the coffee cups into the holders.

"Oh yes, sugar."

"Figured you'd appreciate it." Heather started the engine and merged back onto the main road. A quick glance at the time showed she was running right on schedule.

They pulled up outside the school hosting the event. The carpark was already packed—cars, floats, people, and horses everywhere.

"Wow," Constance whistled as she met Heather at the back. "This place is huge."

"Yeah, we come every year for the Polocrosse event here."

Helping lower the ramp and open the gates, Constance rubbed her palms against her jeans. "Don't the Lockharts—"

"Yeah," Heather laughed. "The family lives on a few hundred acres on the outskirts of town."

"Mmm." Her expression hardening, Constance shoved her hands into her back pockets. "Would it be asking too much to not see them today?"

"I doubt they'll be here. Both Nicole and Lily ride show jumping and equestrian, not Polocrosse. But this is their school—and an opportunity to flex their hypothetical muscles."

"Ugh." Constance's face twisted before she drew in

a deep breath and smoothed her expression. "Never mind. We are here with a purpose today."

Smiling, Heather raised a brow as she backed Charlie out. "We are?"

"Yes. I'm here to drum up some business. Your classes are extremely popular, Heath. Kids love you."

"No idea why," Heather muttered, rubbing Charlie's long face. "I try to have as little to do with them as I can."

"Maybe that's why they love you. Like cats—they flock towards people they get 'stay back' vibes from. Besides, what are you talking about? You're amazing with Leo."

"Leo is different."

Expression turning dreamy in that motherly way, Constance sighed. "Yeah. He's pretty amazing."

Nudging her shoulder as she passed, Heather led Charlie to his open stall—already pre-assigned from the paperwork she'd reviewed earlier.

Once he was settled, she joined Constance, who had started unpacking the trailer, hanging Charlie's saddle and blanket over the fence.

Leaving Constance with Charlie, Heather headed toward the sign-in tent, spotting Vicki behind the pop-up table with a clipboard in hand.

**

Umpiring a mixed group, one side had just scored. The two teams worked their way back across the field toward the sideline.

Ryan was there on his mount Samson—a sixteen-hand blue roan gelding with just enough sass and showmanship to complement Ryan perfectly.

Grinning, Ryan bumped racquets with Mark, who was also playing. The two galloped showily side by side, and Mark, with more force than necessary, sent Ryan's racquet flying.

Heather smiled as Mark galloped off, laughing boisterously while Ryan—the exhibitionist—turned Samson on a dime. Hooking his soft spurs into the his stirrups for leverage, he leaned down low along the gelding's side.

Hanging off Samson as he cantered full-tilt toward the dropped racquet, Ryan scooped it up one-handed and hauled himself upright in the saddle.

Slowing to a jaunty trot, Ryan turned toward Heather's sideline. Sitting on the top rail beside her, Constance chuckled.

"Show-off."

Unrepentant, Ryan rested the racquet on his shoulder. "C'mon, Heath. Like you can't do that too."

Annoyingly, she couldn't anymore. Every year her hips and knees got a little stiffer. Not about to admit that, she sniffed and shared a knowing look with Constance.

"Line it up," Heather called, directing Charlie to stand opposite the scoring team, facing those on the defensive side. The players froze, their attention locked on her.

Setting the ball behind her right shoulder, she let it fly between them at racquet height—and all at once, they peeled off, racing to scoop it up.

Six minutes later, the chukka ended, and the teams swapped out. On the adjacent field, Heather spotted Johnny lying along his horse's side, scooping the ball before flipping upright and launching it to Cooper.

Cooper caught it midair and bolted toward the goal.

It didn't surprise Heather to see the Darcys here—the family well known in Polocrosse circles, especially in Glen Innes.

She turned her head toward the gazebo canteen.

Constance stood talking to the volunteer serving—but Heather's attention was caught by the tall figure next to her.

Nathaniel.

Even from a distance, she felt the weight of his gaze, her stomach fluttering happily. His head was tilted toward Constance, listening intently as she gestured animatedly.

Dressed in black jeans and a plain T-shirt, he looked too good for her sanity. The cap—probably Josh's—suited him.

Then Heather saw *her*.

Nicole.

Painted-on white jodhpurs, a blood-red blouse, and her signature smile. Heather tensed as she laid a hand on Nathaniel's arm.

Constance's expression froze. Nicole tipped her head back in a rehearsed move, exposing the long line of her throat.

Heather gritted her teeth, ready to ride Charlie right through the crowd—possibly run Nicole over—but paused as Nathaniel brushed Nicole's hand aside.

His smile was polite, but firm. In one smooth move, he placed Constance between himself and Nicole.

Heather nearly laughed at Nicole's pout.

"Heather, are you okay?" asked Eden, one of the players, her elfin features curious.

"Yes, sorry. Yes. Got... distracted. We ready to go?"

"Yeah."

"Yes."

"Yep, let's do this!"

Nodding, Heather drew in a deep breath. She spared Nathaniel one final glance. He smiled—a slow, heated caress that sent arousal arrowing straight to her core.

Turning back to the lineup, Heather drew in a deep breath, then resolved let the ball fly.

Heather lost track of time, the rhythm of the games pulling her into its familiar flow. At the end of the day, with the sun low and golden, she finally floated Charlie, her smile wide and genuine. Constance stood nearby chatting with Vicki, who had her doubled over in laughter.

A throat cleared.

Turning, Heather spotted Nathaniel standing at the bottom of the ramp. She smiled.

"You two looked good out there today," he murmured, his voice low and warm.

"Pretty cruisy day really," Heather replied, matching his tone. Charlie stood dozing beside her, his weight shifted onto one hind leg, utterly relaxed.

With a final rub against the gelding's soft nose she exited, accepting Nathaniel's offer to help lift the ramp. They latched the gate securely before she turned and stepped into the circle of his arms.

With a deep sigh Heather relaxed, resting her forehead against his collarbone.

She wasn't going to say anything.

Didn't need to.

She trusted Nathaniel.

"I saw you had a visitor today," the words dropped like bombs into the quiet that had settled between them.

Shit.

Annoyed with herself for bringing it up—Heather cleared her throat and tipped her chin up to meet his amused gaze.

"She claimed she was a friend of yours." Nathaniel

raised an eyebrow at Heather's snort. "But she seemed far more interested in ruffling your feathers —and Constance's, for that matter—than having any meaningful conversation with me."

Rolling her eyes, Heather smoothed her hands over his shoulders in a familiar caress. "Nicole Lockhart and I... well, we don't get along."

"I got that impression. If looks could kill, *Tesoro*, that woman would've dropped dead right where she stood."

Shrugging uncomfortably, Heather studied his face. "She's very beautiful. One of those girls who could—and did—have any guy she wanted. They dance to her tune. Have been falling all over themselves since she was thirteen."

Nathaniel's hands slid lower to palm her backside. He made a low, appreciative sound in his throat.

Against her stomach, she felt him harden. Surprised, she looked up and found warmth in his eyes.

"*Tesoro*," he said softly, "women may come and go, but all my attention—all my affection—is fixed firmly on you."

Heather melted against him, her chin tilting up as he bent to kiss her.

His possession was a leisurely slide of tongue, teeth, and lips - soft, wet heat - arousing her in all the ways he knew she loved best.

Charlie shifted nearby, letting out a heavy sigh that snapped them gently back to the present.

Laughing quietly, Nathaniel leaned his forehead against hers. "You're coming home with me tonight."

"Fine. But we need to stop at Emerson's first, get Charlie unpacked—and I promised Connie I'd stay for dinner."

Having already invited himself around earlier that

afternoon, Nathaniel grunted in acknowledgement. He hauled her up onto her toes for a shorter, but no less heated kiss before releasing her.

"Show me how to pack your equipment, then let's get on the road. It's a long hike home, and I'll be following close behind."

Trailing after him, Heather allowed a slow smile to form, hidden by the shadows. "Fine. No need to be so bossy."

"You haven't seen bossy yet," Nathaniel murmured, voice dropping. "Bossy will be later tonight when I'm shoving my cock down your throat and telling you to swallow every last drop—"

"Jesus!" Constance squealed, clapping her hands over her ears. "I did not want to hear that!"

Blushing, Heather shoved Charlie's saddle toward Nathaniel. "Girl, please. I heard about you and Josh in the equipment room last Friday."

Mouth dropping open, Constance's hands fell away. "What? Who!"

"The 'who' is irrelevant. But seriously—you two need to stop hooking up in the stables. You're an old married couple now. And parents to boot. Behave already."

Sniffing, Constance snatched up Heather's equipment bag. She brushed past with a terse, "I don't think you have much of a leg to stand on, to be perfectly frank."

Closing the tray of the ute, Heather smiled at Constance's retreating back as she stomped toward the driver's seat. Nathaniel's hands settled low on Heather's hips, pulling her attention back to him.

"I'll meet you both at the entrance. Then we'll stop at the servo—grab some fuel and something to eat before heading home."

"Sounds good," Constance called, already climbing into the ute. Poking her head out the window, she added, "Since you're both coming back to the house for dinner, we don't need more than some snacks. Mary's made a roast."

Nathaniel kissed Heather quickly, and a moment later she slid tiredly into the passenger seat.

Buckling herself in, she caught Constance watching her with a soft expression. "What?"

"I just like how happy he makes you," Constance said with a shrug. "And how happy you make him."

Smiling, Heather reached over and squeezed her friend's hand. "Thanks, Connie. I'm so happy most days, it's almost scary."

"Yeah," Constance nodded slowly, returning the squeeze before starting the engine. "I feel the same way some days too."

Heather settled into the seat and smothered a yawn. Constance humming along with the radio as she drove, content to let Heather rest in silence after a long day.

Two hours later, they pulled into Emersons. Heather stretched and sighed, accepting the ute keys from Constance and tucking them into the console along with her phone.

She met Constance by the tray who, hands propped on her hips, gestured towards the vehicle. "Need a hand with anything?"

Shaking her head, Heather raised her voice slightly to include Nathaniel. "Nah. You two go on inside. It won't take long to unpack and get Charlie settled."

"Okay." Constance squeezed her arm and turned away. She paused halfway along the row of cars, waiting as Nathaniel prowled closer to Heather, his arm reaching out to haul her in for a short, heated kiss.

Heather remained still, listening as Nathaniel and Constance's voices slowly drifted away. When it was finally just her and the soft nighttime noises of the bush, Heather released a long breath.

The float was quiet—Charlie clearly snoozing—so she focused on unloading the ute first, ferrying his equipment into her office to clean tomorrow.

Only her own personal gear remained when she turned back towards the float.

Lowering the ramp, Heather smiled as Charlie fixed one sleepy eye on her.

"Sorry, bud. I know you're tired. Let's get you settled —Graham would've left your dinner mixed up and waiting."

The magic word—dinner—perked him up. Without fuss, he followed Heather across the paddock to the stables.

Inside, soft breaths and shifting hooves echoed around her. A few curious heads peeked out before ducking back in, recognizing her.

Sure enough, Charlie's feed bin held a fresh helping of cool feed. Graham had left everything prepped, just as she'd expected.

Unclipping the lead and slipping off the rope bridle, Heather leaned against Charlie's warm body, her hands smoothing his coat.

"Good boy, Charlie. I'll see you in the morning."

She checked his water and lingered a moment longer before stepping out.

Retrieving her hat from its peg in her office, she slapped it lightly against her thigh as she walked one last time across the grass towards her ute.

From the back of the house, she could hear Nathaniel and Constance's laughter drifting on the breeze, warm and familiar.

Heather reached for the driver's door, intending on grabbing her phone.

Then she saw it.

A medium-sized package on the passenger seat.

Blood chilled in her veins, a shiver of awareness crawling down her spine.

Stepping back, she scanned the paddocks—dark and still. No muffled scratching, or chirps from nocturnal animals and insects; the night quiet. Too quiet.

Her stomach turned.

Slamming the door, she circled the ute, threw open the passenger side, and ripped the lid off the box.

Inside was a plastic horse mask—torn, stained.

Heather stared at it, bile rising.

"Sick, twisted—" She couldn't finish the sentence. Swallowing hard, she glared out into the darkness.

Whoever this was—they wanted her afraid.

But Heather was done playing their game.

With more bravado than she felt, she stuffed the mask into her back pocket. Turning her back on the night, she walked toward the stables.

Every step was harder than the last.

She could swear she felt her stalkers moist breath on her neck. Could feel unknown eyes watching her, hands reaching towards her intent on harm.

She passed the warmth and safety of the house, not wanting to bring that ugliness into her home. Close to her family.

Inside the stables, she closed the wooden door behind her. It clicked shut like a vault, offering little comfort.

She still didn't feel safe.

She switched on the office light and stepped inside.

Another door. Another layer.

Reaching into her back pocket, she pulled out the mask.

Her stomach churned. Her hands shook.

It was patterned like Charlie.

Deliberate.

Heather stuffed it into the top drawer and slammed it shut.

For a frozen moment, she just stood there.

Then something inside her cracked.

And for the first time since she was eighteen—Heather cried.

Tears came hot and fast, her chest tight and heaving.

"Damnit," she whispered, reaching blindly for the tissue box in the bottom drawer.

But the tears didn't stop.

The sick feeling only grew stronger.

'CHAPTER TEN'

Glancing at the door and then his watch for the tenth time in the last five minutes, Nathaniel frowned—he had expected Heather well before now.

"What did you make of your first Polocrosse event?" Josh asked, appearing at his elbow with a fresh beer.

Accepting, Nathaniel offered a distracted smile. "Fast. Impressive. Intimidating. I've never seen such big horses all collected in one place before."

Chuckling under his breath, Josh nodded and tipped his head back to draw on his own beer. "Regulations state horses need to be at least eleven hands, but the average size of most is fifteen hands at least."

"The taller the horse, the better," Constance said from her seat on the floor, Leo bouncing on his nappy-covered butt on the rug.

"I was speaking to one of the coordinators—Vicki, I think she said her name was. She mentioned the event was smaller this year than last, that fewer and fewer people join up or participate in events each year."

"Once upon a time, it was a popular sport," Josh said, sprawling his long frame in the dining room chair closest to his wife and child. "Rugby on horseback, I think they likened it to. But interest's petered off over time, which is a shame. It's a real family event."

"I noticed that," Nathaniel murmured, recalling the

fathers, mothers, and children who had played as teams throughout the day—often found picnicking between events. One group even had grandparents. The whole atmosphere had the flavour of inclusiveness and community.

"Did Heath play?" Josh asked.

"No," Constance answered, shaking her head with a smile as Leo made an unsuccessful attempt at standing, his little face determined as he gripped his father's jean-clad leg. "She decided just to umpire wherever Vicki needed her."

Whatever Nathaniel had been about to say was forgotten as awareness lifted the hairs on his neck. Turning to the door, he smiled as Heather stepped inside, bracing one hand on the door while using the other to pull off her boots.

Her face was downturned, her braids falling over her shoulders, but he could tell from the set of her frame that she was exhausted. He frowned, noting the tension in her forehead, curious when she turned to glance back out into the darkness.

Without conscious thought, Nathaniel was moving— away from Josh and Constance, whose attention was diverted to Leo. In a few large strides, he was at Heather's side, checking to see if Mary was busy in the kitchen.

"What's wrong?"

Her eyes, when they lifted to his, held shadows that made Nathaniel's stomach clench. "I had another package."

"With the mail on your desk?" Nathaniel asked, his tone low and sharp as he glanced out toward the stables, where light from her office spilled across the night-drenched grass.

"In my passenger seat."

A long beat passed as the implications of her words sank in like stones. "What?"

"The package was on the passenger seat, Nate. My car was locked the whole day, and I was in that seat the entire drive home. Whoever delivered it did so after we got here—would've had to while I was still unloading the ute."

"That means they were here," Josh growled, startling Heather badly enough that she jumped. Wrapping his arms around her, Nathaniel pulled her into his chest.

Sharing a look with Josh—whose gaze was dark and dangerous—Nathaniel lowered his lips to Heather's ear, instinctively keeping his voice low.

"What was in the package, *Tesoro*?"

"A mask," Heather whispered. "It's in the top drawer of my office desk."

Another glance at Josh, who nodded grimly, and Nathaniel gently pushed Heather farther into the house. "Stay here. Josh and I will be back in a minute."

"Wait—" Subconsciously, Heather reached out and fisted the fabric of his shirt over his abdomen, her wide, searching eyes begging him not to go.

She couldn't find the words—but somehow, he knew. Pulling her close, he kissed her hard.

"I promise, *Tesoro*. I'll be right back. Close the door behind us."

Unclenching her hand was the hardest thing she'd ever done. It was the fear coursing through her veins that finally convinced her to release him.

This was her farm.

These were her people.

Shakily, Heather stepped back and closed the door, refusing to watch as Josh and Nathaniel disappeared into the shadows, swallowed by the dark.

Sitting on the floor, Constance watched her with piercing eyes. "Everything alright?"

Shaking her head, Heather sank onto the rug and cuddled Leo's soft little body close. "Got another package. The fellas are checking it out."

Reaching out, Constance rubbed Heather's shoulder and glanced toward the door, worry on her face. In the kitchen, Mary moved silently to the sink, staring out into the inky night beyond the stables.

"Top drawer," Josh rumbled, standing in the office doorway with arms crossed and legs braced. Knowing the fury leaking off him would only distress the horses, he stepped inside and closed the door behind him.

Crossing to the desk opposite Nathaniel, he swore when he saw what lay between them.

"What the hell is that?"

"A horse mask," Nathaniel replied icily, tossing the rubber mask onto the desktop.

"Looks like Charlie," Josh muttered, his jaw tight. "Sick bastard had to know that would hurt Heath more than a regular horse mask."

"That's almost a guarantee."

"What the fuck does this bastard want?" Josh snapped. "What's the fucking end goal here, Nate?"

Sliding into Heather's seat, Nathaniel steepled his fingers low over his abdomen, leaning back as he considered the question.

"Fear. Control. That's the M.O. for most stalkers—making their victims feel powerless. That's the end goal."

Josh growled. "How are you so fucking calm about this, Feria? This sicko is terrorising your woman. They let themselves onto my land! I'm gonna knock his fucking block off—"

"We don't even know if it is a *he*," Nathaniel interrupted, waving a hand. "We don't know who it is. Like it or not, they've got the advantage."

"And you're okay with that?"

"Of course I'm not. You've not met my brother yet—Matteo is a security specialist. He's got something in motion right now. A trap the stalker won't see coming." Josh exhaled and eased into the seat beside him. "Security specialist, huh?"

"Yes. I think it's time to install some cameras, motion detectors, maybe even floodlights."

"Yeah. Constance has already told the staff to be on alert, but it's hard when we have new clients coming and going for both the stables and the B&B."

"Hence the cameras," Nathaniel sighed, rubbing his eyes. "Not foolproof, but a good start. Maybe even dogs —for added security."

Josh nodded. "Connie sent Patton to live with Jack in town. In hindsight, maybe we should've kept him around. He's smart. Knows the place. Grew up here."

"Talk to Jack," Nathaniel said. "Maybe Patton can come back for a while."

"Jack'll do it," Josh agreed. "But that dog'll pine—and so will Jack. We've been talking about getting working dogs anyway. Might just bump that up."

"Not a bad idea," Nathaniel murmured, his tone heavy. Josh studied him. "What about Heath?"

"Don't worry about Heather," Nathaniel said, his smile razor sharp. "I'll handle her."

Chuckling, Josh scrubbed a hand through his hair. "You might be the only man on the planet who can."

Heading back to the house, Nathaniel searched the room for Heather, spotting her seated at the dining table, her expression tense.

Seeing him at the same time, Heather stood and hurried to his side, her gaze skimming over his face, his chest, his hands.

"You okay?" she asked, her voice low.

Shaking his head slightly, Nathaniel wrapped an arm around her waist and pulled her against his chest. "Am I okay? *Tesoro*, you look half-dead on your feet and pale with worry. I'm fine. Are you?"

Was she okay?

Heather wasn't sure she had the answer, so instead she shrugged with a short, self-deprecating laugh.

"Food's ready," Mary declared, placing the final tray down in the centre of the table. She smiled at them both. "C'mon, you two."

In a move so unlike Heather, she linked her fingers with Nathaniel's, tugging him toward the table with a small smile.

Lazily sprawling at her side, Nathaniel draped one arm across the back of her chair, reminded of a similar night two years ago. Only this time, Heather turned to smile at him, placing a hand on his thigh beneath the table.

Across from them, Josh and Constance sat with Leo in the middle, chatting away as Josh carved the roast. At the head of the table, Mary was making faces at Leo, who giggled each time. The atmosphere was warm, familiar, uncoiling the last of Nathaniel's tension.

**

Saying goodbye to Mary as she waved from the driver's

seat of her car, Nathaniel and Heather watched as the older woman's brake lights disappeared up the long driveway.

"That was a nice ending to what was shaping up to be a shit evening," Heather murmured with a sigh, tucking herself against Nathaniel as they leaned against his car. Snickering softly, Nathaniel let his hands drift down the length of her spine, resting them low on her back to slip beneath the waistband of her jeans.

"What do you say we get you back to my place, run a nice warm bath, and I wash your back for you?" Nathaniel asked, placing nibbling kisses along the column of her throat.

Usually, Heather made it a point never to stay two nights in a row, but in a move that was becoming achingly familiar, she nodded. "Alright. I'll leave the truck here for the night."

Moving them just enough to open the passenger-side door, Nathaniel helped her into the car, then detoured to her ute. Grabbing her equipment bag, he tossed it into the back seat and handed her the keys.

Once he was belted in, Heather hit the lock button, leaving her keys in his centre console after her car flashed its confirmation. Leaning back into the seat, she reached over to link her fingers with his, resting their joined hands on her thigh.

The drive to the pub was quiet and comfortable. Once parked out the back, Heather didn't fight the urge to lean over and kiss him.

Liquid fire ran in her veins, and somehow—between the car and the front door—Nathaniel had her pressed down into the soft mattress of his bed. Caging her beneath him, he kissed her long and deep, waiting until she was pliant and melting.

Sliding his way down her body, he tugged on her clothes and whispered, "Take these off. I'll go start the bath."

As he disappeared into the bathroom, the sound of water hitting porcelain filtered through. Heather wiggled on the bed, pulling off her jodhpurs and shirt and tossing them aside.

Appearing in the doorway a moment later, Nathaniel prowled toward her. Caging her back against the mattress, his gaze devoured her nearly nude form.

"Do you have any idea what you do to me?" he asked huskily, grinding the evidence of his arousal against the apex of her thighs.

Wrapping her legs around his hips, Heather moaned softly as he kissed her jaw. "I can guess."

"I told you to get naked," Nathaniel murmured, sweeping his tongue into her inviting mouth. He broke the kiss and moved lower, kissing her navel before hooking his fingers through the waistband of her underwear and dragging the cotton down her legs.

Her thighs fell open in shameless invitation, and she arched as he pressed kisses up the inside of her leg, retracing the path her underwear had just taken.

His hands urged her knees wider, splaying her to his gaze, and Heather gasped as he latched his mouth to her centre.

"Oh God, Nate!" Reaching down, she fisted his thick hair, hips bucking with every skilful lash of his tongue.

Sliding his hands up to her breasts, he tugged the cups of her bra down and groaned in appreciation. Heather's legs alternated between tightening and trembling around his head.

"Nate. Nate, I'm—oh God, Nate!" The tension that had

built steadily snapped like a rubber band, her body jolting as she came hard.

Afterward, he soothed her with gentle kisses and licks, gazing up at her through lidded eyes.

She lay there, utterly wrecked—loose-limbed, her stomach twitching with aftershocks, her breath ragged, her nipples taut.

Getting up, Nathaniel disappeared into the bathroom to turn off the tap, checking the temperature with a satisfied smile.

Back in the room, he stripped off his shirt and pants, then sat beside her and ghosted his fingers along her sensitive skin, chuckling as she flinched.

"C'mon. The bath's ready."

Heather groaned and rolled halfway onto her side. "Can't you bring the bath to me? I'm exhausted."

Laughing, Nathaniel tipped her over his shoulder and delivered a firm slap to her upturned bottom.

"Hey," she protested weakly—but they were already at the bathroom door.

As he lowered her into the steaming water, she sighed in delight. "Mmmm."

Sliding in behind her, he tugged her so she lay back against his chest. Grabbing the loofah and body wash, he lathered her slowly, washing one arm, then the other, fingers lingering.

"I have something to ask you."

Bones liquid, Heather snuggled closer. "Yeah?"

"I love you."

Smiling, she tipped her head back, heart aching. "I know. I love you too."

Dropping the loofah into the water with a plop, Nathaniel tipped her chin farther and leaned down, sealing her mouth beneath his for a long, thorough kiss. Then he drew back just enough to meet her eyes. "Marry me?"

As relaxed as she was, it took a long moment for the surprise to register.

"What?" Heather asked, blinking.

"Marry me," Nathaniel repeated calmly. "I love you more than words can express. You challenge me. You delight me. You surprise me. You make me a better version of myself. Marry me, Heather."

Mouth open, she sat upright, twisting to face him fully. Panic fluttered in her chest as she stared at him.

"You—I mean, we—Nate, this is a knee-jerk reaction—"

"No, it's not." He reached for her calves, dragging her back toward him, water sloshing around them. "I'm not asking you because some psycho is stalking you. I'm asking because I want to point to you and say: that woman there, she's mine—*my* wife. I want rights to you, Heather. Call me a Neanderthal, but my feelings for you are primeval and, yeah, a little possessive."

She couldn't deny the thrill his words stirred. God knew she'd had to smother the urge to shoo other women away from him more than once.

But deep down, Heather was scared—terrified by the depth of her love for him. Because everyone she'd ever loved tended to die or leave, taking pieces of her heart with them.

Nathaniel read her too well. Gently, he drew her back into his arms until she lay against his chest again.

"Don't think too hard," he murmured near her ear. "Don't dwell on the past or worry about the what-ifs. Do you love me?"

"You know I do," she whispered instantly.

"Then say yes." He caught her left hand in his and reached over to the ledge where a ring sat waiting. Sliding it onto her finger, he held her gaze.

"Wow," Heather breathed, studying the elegant design.

Set in rose gold, the pavé band wrapped around a cluster of small diamonds, raised slightly in a delicate basket setting that twinkled in the soft light.

"I designed it especially for you," Nathaniel said, arms closing around her. "It matches the jewellery you inherited from your Oma."

Heather's tight chest eased a little, a sigh escaping her lips. He remembered. The rose gold earrings and tiny diamond necklace she rarely wore but treasured. He remembered.

Sniffling as emotion threatened, she glanced up at him.

"You really want this? I mean—how long have you had this ring?"

"Twelve months," he said. "I was in the city, lost thanks to a fill-in driver. We stumbled down this side alley and I spotted a little jeweller's shop. It wasn't flashy—tiny place, tucked away. Inside, this old guy with the thickest glasses was sketching a design. When I asked about it, he told me he'd known I'd walk in. Said the ring was for the woman I loved—elegant, but tough."

Heather exhaled shakily, then turned to face him completely.

"I'll marry you," she whispered. "I accept. Yes, Nate."

His hands smoothed up her back as she straddled his thighs, knees on either side of his hips. His eyes held nothing but warmth.

"I love you," Nathaniel said, voice husky.

Heather rested her forehead to his, heart pounding. "I love you too."

A wicked glint lit his gaze. His hands slid down to her hips, then lower, lifting her just enough before guiding her down onto him.

Their sighs mingled.

And as water splashed over the edge of the tub and doused the candles, they sealed their engagement with shared passion.

'CHAPTER ELEVEN'

The following morning dawned bright and warm, Heather having woken up before the sun had even risen, and now she sat at the breakfast bar with a mug of coffee, wrapped in a blanket.

Next to her mug, her phone lit up with a notification from her calendar, all the happiness from the night before giving way to heavy sadness.

Sighing, Heather covered her eyes with one hand, leaning on that elbow, the urge to crawl back into bed strong.

Hands, warm and familiar, settled on her shoulders, and she was unresisting as they tipped her backwards against a hard chest.

"How long have you been up?" Nathaniel asked, his voice gravelly with sleep.

"Long," Heather whispered.

Moving around to her side, Nathaniel stared down into her pale features, felt his stomach clench at the aged grief he found there.

"What is today, *Tesoro*?"

"The anniversary of my parents' death," Heather closed her eyes and leaned into his arms, "one of the worst days of the year in my opinion."

Kissing her hair, Nathaniel sat silently with her for long moments, asking finally, "What do you need from me today?"

Warmth fought with the grief and won; her gaze appreciative as she looked at him. "Just you."

Nodding slowly, Nathaniel urged her to stand, then led her into the bathroom. Turning the shower on, he slowly undressed her, pressing a warm kiss to her shoulder.

Urging her underneath the warm spray, he then discarded his own clothes quickly, closing the glass door behind him.

With gentle hands, Nathaniel washed the long, lean lines of her body while Heather stood quiet beneath the spray.

Afterwards, he wrapped her in a fluffy towel and sat her on the edge of the bed. Unable to create the intricate braids she usually did, he used her brush to make sure her hair was smooth and tangle-free.

Pressing a soft kiss against the corner of her lips, he smoothed the shadows beneath her eyes. Handing her the brush, he turned back to the wardrobe and quickly dressed.

Still seated on the edge of the bed, Heather started her braid from one ear, braiding across to the other and then continuing along until the braid had followed the circle of her head. Tucking the remaining section behind the rest, she clipped it all into place and pulled the hair in the braid until it was loose.

The end result: a pretty crown with wisps framing her face. Standing, she then entered the wardrobe to the shelves Nathaniel had cleared for her stuff.

He had pulled on a pair of black dress pants and was tightening his belt. Glancing up, he smiled softly, his eyes tracking over the braid with interest.

Smiling, Heather turned her attention to the shelves, pulling out a new pair of black jeans and a soft cotton blouse in navy blue.

Leaving Nathaniel in the wardrobe, she tossed the clothes onto the bed and shrugged into a matching set of bra and undies, then pulled her clothes on over the top of that.

Coming out of the wardrobe, Nathaniel tossed a pair of socks Heather's way with a "Here."

Catching the garments instinctively, Heather glanced up to thank him—and froze, her heart flopping in her chest as she noticed he'd found a matching navy-blue dress shirt in silk and wore it now.

Stalking the final steps between them, Nathaniel cupped her face between his palms. "We'll stop for some flowers, and I'd like to hear some stories about your parents. I hate that I'll never get to meet them, to tell them how thankful I am for raising such an amazing woman. But I'll honour their memory by loving them alongside you."

Startled laughter ending on a broken sob, Heather folded into his arms, soaking the front of his chest with tears she'd sworn she wouldn't shed.

"Damnit," Heather groused a long time later, checking her reflection in the mirror and sighing over her red nose and swollen eyes, "I wasn't gonna cry today, Nate."

Fixing silver studs into the cuffs at his wrists, Nathaniel sent her a lazy look and shrugged maddeningly, "Tears are good for the soul, *Tesoro*."

Swiping at the drop sliding slowly down her cheek, Heather huffed. "I won't be able to stop now—it's better if I just keep it together."

Hands on her hips, Nathaniel kissed her cheek. "No one

expects you to keep it together, Heather. I think your expectations on yourself are too harsh. Lean on me and the others who love you. We won't let you fall today."

Face twisting as fresh tears hit, Heather turned and slapped his chest in complaint. Wiping the wet off her face and then shaking her hands, she stepped away. "Alright. Better get going."

Following along behind her, Nathaniel pulled his phone from his pocket and fired off a text. Waiting for the three thumbs-up he received before sliding the device back, he managed it without Heather noticing.

The car trip to the local grocery store was quiet but comfortable, Nathaniel staying in the car as Heather went inside and picked out a bouquet of mixed flowers.

Sliding back into the car, Heather cleared her throat, touching the pads of her fingers to the vibrant yellows and pinks. "Can we stop by my place?"

Studying her downturned face, Nathaniel said softly, "Sure."

A few minutes later they were pulling into her driveway, and lifting her gaze, Heather sighed. By her front door, underneath the roof of the veranda, sat half a dozen flower deliveries.

Silent for a moment, Heather whispered, "Friends and family who live too far away send flowers. I take them to my parents' graves."

Already undoing his seatbelt, Nathaniel was silent as he followed Heather's slow walk up the stairs, taking the flowers she handed to him and setting them carefully in the backseat.

Once they'd all been loaded, Nathaniel tucked his hands into his back pockets, staring up the pathway at Heather, who sat hunched on the top step of her house.

Moving slowly, she hauled herself upright—solemn and distant—as she slid back into the passenger seat of his car. Closing the door behind her, Nathaniel hurried around to his side.

During the drive to the cemetery, he slid her careful looks—having no experience with this version of Heather, so still and so quiet, her face unreadable, unreachable.

Following the signs, Nathaniel pulled and drove over the cattle grate leading into the cemetery, noticing the open walker's gate just to the side.

Hugging the lawn, Nathaniel followed the direction that Heather gestured. Noticing the cars parked up ahead, he pulled in next to Jackson's Ram.

For a moment, Heather could only gaze out the window at the cars and the headstones, feeling raw and uncertain, so lost in thought her door opening a second later startled her.

"C'mon." Nathaniel reached in, undoing her belt, hands gathering her body up to help her from the interior.

Tucking her arms into her body, she leaned into his warmth, closing her eyes to seal out her surroundings.

"Connie, come take Heather. I need to help unload the flowers," Nathaniel commanded, his tone low and soothing. He passed Heather to Constance, who wrapped one arm around her waist.

Nathaniel stood watching their halting progress towards the graves, then turned to Josh, who stood framed in by the backdoor, his face strained as he handed flowers to Jackson.

Waiting in the line, Oliver clapped Nathaniel's shoulder, saying softly, "Thanks for keeping us up to date this morning. Heather's stubborn and usually tries to do this all alone."

Lips twisting, Nathaniel nodded, unsurprised by this information. Stepping in behind Oliver, he waited for Josh to load his arms with the flowers.

As a small group, the men all headed in the same direction as Constance, finding the women five hundred metres up the road.

Heather had sunk to the grass and sat with her arms wrapped around her legs, her expression eerily blank as she gazed at the headstone.

Constance stood with one arm wrapped around Faith's shoulders, Isla slightly off to the side, watching as Nathaniel and the other men approached.

Reaching out, Isla accepted one of the bouquets Oliver handed her, nodding at Nathaniel when he smiled slightly in appreciation for her having come today.

She hadn't had much time, as Nathaniel hadn't realised what today was until the night before. Having messaged Isla after Heather had fallen asleep, he was grateful.

Isla hadn't offered anything more than, "I'll be there."

Her car, one of the first he'd recognised when pulling up—no doubt she'd driven up that morning to support them.

"Where do you want these?" Jackson asked, kneeling at Heather's side, his gaze very green. "Heath. Tell us where you want these."

Rousing from what seemed a deep slumber, Heather blinked and glanced around. Unable to take in all the faces, she instead refocused on the headstones.

"Pass them to me, I'll do it." Repositioning herself to the side on the double, raised concrete slab, Heather leaned towards the headstone, one hand extended behind her.

Silently, they handed the flowers to Heather one at a time, and she, in turn, arranged them to sit in a cluster around the headstone.

Once done, Heather scooted back till she was once more huddled at the feet of the graves, her hands wrapped around the stems of the flowers she'd picked up from the store.

Slowly, she felt the air behind her shift—felt the hands that caressed her shoulders or the kisses they pressed against her hair.

But in this moment, she was lost.

Lost to the memories of her parents.

To the night that took them from her.

The sun was hot, beating down on her from a sky mockingly clear, and when a shadow moved to cover her body, she roused enough to look up and to the side.

Standing in stark relief: Nathaniel, his lips tight and his gaze watchful as he studied her. "Tell me about that night?"

Her tongue felt glued to the top of her mouth, but somehow she unstuck it to answer. "It was raining. It was late. They'd gone out to dinner and were on their way home. I was supposed to have already gone to bed but... I was still up playing a game on the computer. Oma and Opa were looking after me—they'd both passed out watching some talk show on the TV. I heard a knock on the door..." Breaking off, in her mind's eye Heather could hear the hard rap of fist on wood, remembered the spike of alarm and then the curiosity as she'd paused her game.

"You answered the door," Nathaniel breathed, feeling horrified at the thought of Heather—young and fresh-faced—answering the door to the police.

"I could see their lights flashing through the glass," Heather recalled, her tone distorted. "I recognised the police officers—small town being what it is—I'd known them my whole life."

"I'm sorry, *Tesoro*. I'm sorry you lost them so young."

Swallowing, Heather accepted the hand he held down to her, let him lift her to her feet and fit her against his chest.

Sniffing, Heather pulled back a moment later and, leaning down, placed her flowers between the two graves. "Love you both, so much. This is Nate. Nathaniel Feria. He's asked me to marry him, and—I've said yes."

Expression grave, Nathaniel bowed his head slightly. "Pleasure to meet you both. I promise you, I'll take good care of your girl."

Smiling sadly, Heather placed her hand on his chest, leaning into his side. "Mum would have adored you. Dad would have come around, eventually."

Nodding, Nathaniel said, "Can't say I'll be too quick to welcome any of our daughters' partners—but that will be my right as their father."

A jolt right to the core of her, and leaning back slightly, Heather stared up at him in surprise. "Daughters?"

"Of course. Personally, I'd like a son and a daughter to balance it out—" trailing off, Nathaniel studied her expression. "You don't want kids?"

More than anything, Heather thought, her lips sealed. I want kids. I want your kids.

But fear, insidious and crippling, slid through her system—the irrational fear of dying in an accident and leaving her own children orphaned overwhelming.

"I—I—" Unable to push words through her tight throat, Heather said nothing, folding into his embrace when

Nathaniel pulled her against his chest.

"I'm sorry, *Tesoro*. That is indeed too much to ask of you today." Squashing his own fears about her lack of response, Nathaniel tipped her back from him slightly, changing the topic. "Come with me?"

"Always," Heather responded immediately—her answering going far to soothe his own anxieties—and tucking her under his arm, Nathaniel led the way back to his car.

"The only one remaining," Heather asked, "Where did everyone go?"

"After about an hour they started heading off. Josh said they'd said their goodbyes."

"An hour?" Heather asked, shocked. "It only feels like we've been here a few minutes."

Unsurprised by her answer, Nathaniel tucked her into her seat and belted her seatbelt. Taking his own spot in the driver's side a moment later, he turned the car on.

One hand braced on her headrest, he checked the coast was clear while backing out, saying, "Oliver said usually someone stays behind to—help you get back home end of the day."

"So what— I normally just sit there all day?"

Pausing in the driveway, Nathaniel glanced over at Heather, absorbing her shock with a frown. "*Tesoro*, what did you think happened every year?"

Frowning, Heather sat back into her seat, thinking about it, but drawing a blank. She shrugged. "I don't know. I remember waking up and being sad and then it's the next day and I'm just—" breaking off, Heather shrugged again, this time a little frustrated. "I don't know."

Lips tight, Nathaniel reached out and settled his hand

on her knee, realising he needed to be more thankful to her friends than he'd first realised.

She hid it well, but Heather had a softness that left her vulnerable—and too open for Nathaniel's liking.

Lucky for her, Nathaniel was good at protecting those he'd decided were his—and Heather had taken top spot mere minutes after he'd met her, and stayed there since.

"Where are we going?" Heather asked finally, her gaze wide as she blinked slowly. "Are we heading to the airport?"

Smiling, Nathaniel squeezed her knee. "Maybe."

"What are you up to?" Heather asked, sliding him a suspicious look.

"I'm taking you to dinner," Nathaniel responded idly, his tone ringing with honesty.

But ten minutes later, when they were standing next to a small aircraft, Heather glared at him. "I thought you said we were going to dinner?"

"We are," Nathaniel herded her up the steps, smiling at the flight attendant he kept on retainer. "Just a nice, quiet, celebratory dinner."

"That requires a trip in an airplane to get to?" Heather pursed her lips to hide her smile, stepping inside the aircraft. Opposite her, the flight attendant stood in front of a closed cupboard.

Pretty face holding a polite smile, the attendant gestured to the interior seats. Glancing at them, Heather whistled appreciatively at the fawn leather seats and deep mahogany finishes.

Along the back, Heather noticed a closed door which she presumed led to a bathroom. Slipping sideways into a set of seats with a tabletop suspended between them, Nathaniel picked the one opposite her and sat with a lazy sprawl.

The flight attendant, who until then had been silent, stepped to Heather's elbow asking, "Could I interest either of you in a drink?"

Adjusting his tie, Nathaniel hooked one ankle negligently over his knee, bumping Heather deliberately. "Red, Laura. Thank you."

Laura dipped her chin before moving back to the small cupboard, opening the shutter to reveal a fridge, bench, and top cupboards.

"Laura?" Heather asked, raising a questioning eyebrow in Nathaniel's way. "Pretty."

"Married," Nathaniel said with a wide smile, "to the pilot."

Said pilot appeared then, and Nathaniel stood to quickly shake hands with the tall, attractive man in his mid-thirties.

Turning, Nathaniel gestured to Heather, introducing them. "Wyatt, this is Heather, my fiancée."

"Pleasure to meet you," Wyatt replied, showing all of his teeth in a large smile. His accent decidedly American, he took her hand in a firm shake.

Turning his attention back to Nathaniel, Wyatt checked his wristwatch, saying, "Flight time is an hour and a half, so we should be getting in by four. I've already spoken to Ian, who'll meet you both on the tarmac at the other end."

"Excellent." Sitting once more, Nathaniel accepted the glasses a returned Laura handed to him, setting one in front of Heather, who smiled sheepishly in thanks.

A moment later, Laura had returned, her manner polite and professional as she poured into first Heather's and then Nathaniel's glasses. Waiting while Nathaniel tasted the beverage, she left once he'd nodded.

Feeling slightly displaced, Heather sampled a sip of the wine herself, just barely managing to hold back a moan of appreciation.

A girl could get used to this kind of pampering, Heather thought, realising with a somewhat belated start that she better start considering—she was now engaged to him.

"So are you going to tell me where we are going now?" Heather asked, clearing her throat awkwardly, feeling like an imposter sitting in the comfortable seats.

Gaze dark and lidded, Nathaniel stared at her from his seat opposite hers, a small smile flirting at the corner of his lips.

"It's a surprise."

Choked laughter, Heather took a larger mouthful of her wine. "How very secretive, Nate."

Uncrossing his legs, Nathaniel deliberately stretched out so that his long legs pressed against the outsides of Heather's knees. "Persuade me to spill my secrets, *Tesoro*."

Warmth settling low in her abdomen alongside arousal, Heather asked, "How do you propose I do that?"

"That door," Nathaniel said, tipping his head in the direction of the rear of the plane, "leads to a bathroom, through which one reaches a bedroom. What do you think, would you like to join me back there for a—rest?"

Heat flooding her cheeks, Heather glanced over her shoulder, noticing Laura standing in the doorway of the cockpit. "Shh! Anyone could have overheard you."

Sighing, Nathaniel took a small sip of his drink. "Then you will just have to console yourself to waiting for the surprise, hmm?"

Shaking her head, Heather took another swallow from her glass—surprised to find it empty. About to say something, she leaned towards Nathaniel but startled when seconds later Laura was at her elbow.

"Would you like a refill, ma'am?" Laura asked, her tone smooth and professional.

"Oh—ahh. Yes, please. Thank you, Laura."

The smile Heather received this time was warmer, as Laura refilled her glass, then disappeared back to the entrance to the cockpit.

"You don't think she heard anything, do you?" Heather asked, gnawing on her lip.

Chuckling, Nathaniel reached out and set his thumb against the corner of her mouth, gently tugging the flesh of her lip free.

"*Tesoro*, Laura and Wyatt are professional and discreet. Whatever they see or hear will remain private, trust me."

With an effort, Heather relaxed, casting her gaze around the interior. "It is lovely and comfortable."

"With my company, I spend many hours travelling from place to place. I wanted to make sure to do so as comfortably as possible. This particular design—the chairs are arranged in a four-club seating configuration—which allows for meetings while also reclining all the way back for sleeping."

"And the bedroom down the back," Heather reminded, lifting her glass in the rear with a head tip.

"Yes. Although, to be perfectly frank, I've never used it. Never had any reason to."

Surprised, Heather glanced at him. "I'm the first woman you've had on the plane, other than Laura?"

"My mother often uses the plane. Other female

relatives, and even a few close friends with their wives. Not to mention Isla often accompanies me, being my right-hand man."

"Isla you consider a sister," Heather said with a wave of her hand. "You know what I meant—I'm talking about the other type of woman men take home."

Delighted, Nathaniel smiled. "In which case, no. You're the first woman I've brought onto the plane."

Something tight uncoiled then, her stomach relaxing, and able to read her easily, Nathaniel watched the way her shoulders softened.

Just then, Wyatt's voice came over the speakers built into the seats. "Welcome aboard Mr Feria and Miss Ross. Flight time today is an hour and a half, and clear skies. Please sit back and get comfortable, we will be taking off in the next five minutes."

Smiling, Heather released a soft chuckle, explaining when Nathaniel nudged her, "I just—no one would believe that I'd be sitting here, in a private plane. About to get whisked off to places unknown by my rich boyfriend."

Sharing her amusement, Nathaniel advised, "Enjoy it. This is just the beginning."

The flight itself uneventful, Heather was introduced to Ian, Nathaniel's driver, once they'd touched down in Sydney.

Bemused, Heather ran her palms along the black leather of the limousine seats, glancing up at Nathaniel a moment later to say, "You really grew up different to me, didn't you."

It was a rhetorical question, but Heather couldn't help but worry as she asked, "Does your family know you proposed to me?"

"Matteo does."

Glancing down at her lap, Heather murmured, "Yes. But —your mother?"

"I don't want you to worry about my mamma, *Tesoro*."

That's a no, her subconscious supplied.

Somehow, Heather doubted the woman would be overjoyed to hear of her son proposing to a foreman in the middle-of-nowhere Blue Mountains.

Pride pricked, Heather withdrew her hand from Nathaniel's, her tone cool. "I think you should probably let your family know, Nate. They might not approve—"

"*Tesoro*, I am an adult. My mamma doesn't dictate my life."

Before Heather could argue, the car slid to a smooth stop, and glancing out her window, Heather felt her breath catch.

Exiting the car after Nathaniel, she barely heard him speak to Ian, her attention fixed on the view of the Sydney Harbour Bridge.

A hand pressed low against her spine urged her forward, and unresisting, Heather preceded Nathaniel into the restaurant.

Dark walls and floors, huge, picturesque windows taking in the view—the whole establishment screamed money and class.

Feeling underdressed and out of place, Heather would have stopped, would have turned around and walked straight back out again—

Except Nathaniel stood an immovable presence at her back. The host, having already spotted them, was now weaving his way through the people and tables to their side.

"Mr Feria, pleasure as always to have you here." The

small man smiled widely in welcome, his attention firmly fixed on Nathaniel. "Please follow me—we have reserved you the table you requested."

Nodding, Nathaniel urged Heather along by anchoring her to his side, perfectly able to read the flight instincts in her gaze.

Having asked for a table near the windows overlooking the Opera House, Nathaniel wasn't disappointed when a moment later they were shown to their seats.

Sighing, Heather sank down, her shoulders deflating in awe as she rested her chin in her palm, drinking in the sight of the Opera House and the crowds of people milling around.

"Wow."

Watching the way the sunlight streamed through the large windows, picking up those subtle hues of red in her deep chestnut hair, Nathaniel couldn't agree more.

Addicted to the soft smile that touched her lips as she watched a small family right outside the window—how she intuitively turned to include him, tethering him to her more effectively than anyone could have guessed.

"Have I surprised you, Tesoro?" Nathaniel asked, his tone low and intimate. Reaching out, he tangled their fingers and set them down on the tabletop between them.

"Oh yes," Heather sighed, squeezing his fingers in silent thanks. "That you certainly have."

'CHAPTER TWELVE'

It had been a busy month between wedding plans, taking on a more permanent coaching class for Polocrosse, and weekends spent as an umpire or playing herself.

So it was that Heather found herself bent over her computer, having to put in a late night to finish off some of the office work she'd avoided for the month.

Earlier that day, Constance had advised her she'd be starting the annual BAS, and that Heather needed to get all her reports and expenses in for that quarter so Constance could enter it on her end.

Phone vibrating, Heather didn't bother checking the caller ID, answering with a distracted, "Hello?"

"*Tesoro*, you sound harried."

"I have a heap of paperwork to get done—no idea why I've left it to the last Friday of the month, but here we are."

"I'll go out on a limb then and assume you forgot we had dinner plans?"

Freezing, Heather sat back in her seat. "No. We did?" Opening her diary, Heather ran her finger down the page, and there in red 'dinner with Matteo' had been circled a few times.

Sighing, Heather slapped the diary shut. "Damnit. I'm sorry, Nate, I forgot."

A warm chuckle wrapped her up in a tight embrace she

could feel through the phone. "It's alright—Matteo is going to be here over the weekend."

"Oh." Frowning, though she knew Nathaniel couldn't see her expression, she chewed thoughtfully on the end of her pen. "I thought he was only passing through."

"Change of plans," Nathaniel drawled lazily.

Attuned to the nuances in his voice, Heather guessed, "There's more to it, isn't there?"

"Perhaps."

Rolling her eyes, Heather snorted in laughter. "Fine. Stay mysterious. You and Matteo should still go out to dinner, regardless of me needing to stay here late."

"But who will protect me?" Nathaniel asked, his tone baiting.

"I'll see you later tonight. Don't be such a baby—take your little bro out for a meal." Hanging up before he could respond, Heather chortled beneath her breath, returning her attention back to the computer screen in front of her with a groan.

Half an hour later, Constance poked her head in. "Hungry?"

"No," Heather said with a sigh. Pushing her chair back, she stood and stretched, her spine popping. Dropping her arms, she moved in Constance's direction. "I do need to step away from this computer for a minute."

Smiling, Constance moved back so that Heather could exit. Turning towards the house, she said, "Let's grab a cuppa. I'm craving something sweet too."

Eying the small woman, Heather said, "You don't really eat sweets, Connie. Unless it's chocolate cake."

"Well," shifting, a small smile blooming, Constance spread her arms wide and said, "might have something to do with the fact that I'm pregnant again."

Freezing, Heather covered her mouth with a short laugh. "You're kidding?"

"Nope."

Wrapping Constance up in a tight hug, Heather pulled back a moment later. "Oh wow! Congratulations!"

"Thanks. Confirmed eight weeks—little early to be telling people, but Josh wants me to take it easy, so we're breaking the rules a little."

"Duh," Heather laughed. "Oh wow, Leo is gonna have a playmate really close to his age."

"I know—two under two, what the hell are we thinking?"

"Hey, get it over with early," Heather said as they started walking again, "that way they're all grown and moving out around the same time, and you and Josh can go start on old people things sooner."

"Old people things?" Constance asked, opening the door and stepping back for Heather to enter ahead of her. "What does that even mean?"

"You know. Like… couples' cruises where there's no kids allowed. Travelling overseas without having to worry about long flights, and crying toddlers – stinky babies."

Raising her eyebrows, Constance hit the button for the kettle to boil, leaning on the kitchen benchtop to face Heather, who slid onto one of the stools.

"I've thought about this. I think the people who choose to have kids young come out on top the other end. Kids are all grown up, but they're still young enough to go on adventures."

Laughing, Constance nodded. "I suppose you do have a bit of a point there."

Exiting the hallway leading to the laundry, Mary smiled widely, propping the washing basket on her hip. "Get me a mug out, would you, Connie? I'm about ready for a cuppa myself."

Moving to the cupboards above the kettle, Constance took out three mugs, deftly tossing teabags and sugar into each mug.

Filling the mugs with water, Constance moved them to Heather. Grabbing the milk from the fridge, she served milk in hers and Mary's before handing the carton over to Heather.

Tipping milk into her own mug then putting it away, Heather was stirring her drink with the spoon Constance used as Mary slid into the seat at her side with a groan.

"That last group that came through," Mary muttered, shaking her head, "how many towels can four people go through?"

"A lot, I'm guessing by the look of that basket," Constance said with a grin, leaning her arms on the benchtop as she glanced at the overflowing hamper.

"Each girl needed two towels for their hair. One of them had a pixie cut—what exactly was she drying?"

Snorting, Heather spared a glance at Constance, who wiggled her eyebrows suggestively. Burying her own smile in a mouthful of hot liquid—

"You here for much longer?" Mary asked, the whole interaction between Heather and Constance going unnoticed. "Don't you have dinner with the Feria brothers?"

Straightening, Constance's mouth opened in surprise. "That's right! I forgot you had dinner with them tonight. You'd better get a move on if you wanna get home and showered."

"I've already called Nate—I'm not going. I've gotta get

the reports done."

"Heath," gaze serious, Constance propped her hands on her hips, "take the computer home and work on it over the weekend. Seriously, I'm not starting the BAS until next week."

Raising her eyebrows, Heather asked idly, "Did you, or did you not say to me earlier these reports were ASAP, done yesterday, in your inbox by midnight—or not?"

"Okay, so maybe I was trying to light a fire beneath your arse 'coz you've put them off all month. But seriously—do them over the weekend. Go put on one of the three dresses I know you have in your cupboard. Go out to dinner. You work hard enough as it is."

Chuckling, Mary chose that moment to interject, "I suggest you wear the velvet red one I bought you three Christmases ago."

Faking confusion, Heather hummed, "I don't think I still have that—"

"Yes, you do," Constance interrupted. "I remember seeing it a month ago, shoved way in the back of your wardrobe, but definitely there."

Frowning, Heather poked her tongue out at Constance, who mimicked the expression. "Traitor."

"You have Nate call us later to thank us," Constance said, winking at Mary, who was snickering into her mug.

"You two are incorrigible, you know that."

Ignoring her, Constance slid her half-drunk tea away and then nodded at the door. "Go, Heath. I'll see you on Monday."

"Bossy," Heather said with a nod. Standing nonetheless, she sniffed and tipped her nose into the air. "Both of you —meddlesome."

"Love you too," Mary said, adding another spoonful of

sugar to her drink, while
Constance raised her eyebrows.

Slipping out to the sound of Constance inquiring sassily, "Would you like any tea with that sugar, Mary?" Heather was smiling as she entered her office, startled to find Mark there, the teenager's face going bright red.

"Hey, Heath. Sorry—was looking for you."

"Sure." Waiting as Mark came around from behind her desk, she took a seat and glanced up at him. "What can I help you with?"

"I was just wondering if I could get you to print my roster off?" Mark asked, rubbing the back of his neck sheepishly. "Mum's printer is outta ink, and I've run out of data, so I can't download it to check it on my phone."

Rolling her eyes, Heather quickly pulled up his roster and hit print. "You know you should talk to your mum about putting you on a plan. You chew through more data than any other teenager I know—which is impressive, considering the amount of videos I catch the girls watching when they're supposed to be mucking out stalls."

Laughing easily, Mark accepted the sheet of paper Heather handed him. Studying the paper in his hands, he gave a distracted thanks and left, closing the door behind him.

Spotting her phone on her desk, Heather pulled open her messages and started typing one to Nathaniel.

Heather: Hey, so plans have changed and I'm in for dinner tonight.

Nathaniel: Excellent. I was really hoping you'd change your mind.

Heather: Constance bullied me into it.

Nathaniel: Then I will thank Constance ☐ Be at my place

by half six.
Heather: I'll be wearing red.
Nathaniel: Red? Hmmm. In that case, be here at five...
Heather: Down boy! See you soon.
Nathaniel: Love you. Drive safe.

Sending him a quick heart emoji, Heather packed up the work computer and a handful of files, stuffing them all into a material tote which she then slung over her shoulder.

Locking her office door, Heather noticed Mark bent over picking up a handful of blankets. Pausing for a moment to frown, Heather recalled his chore list should have placed him in the arena.

Mentally shrugging, Heather headed off, and a short drive later, she was unlocking her front door. Setting the tote on the hallway table, Heather started stripping off her clothes on her way to the bathroom.

A fast five-minute shower later, Heather used her hand to clear the condensation off the mirror. Quickly running her brush through her hair, she deftly braided the length of it into a single tail.

Leaving the bathroom door open so the rest of the heated air from her shower could dissipate, Heather threw open her cupboard and dug around until finding the velvet red dress.

Turning to the full-length mirror, Heather held the dress up against her body and sighed. Long and with an A-line bodice that sat just underneath her bust, it was elegant.

Too elegant almost.

Returning to the hallway table, Heather found her phone and reopened her messages:

Heather: How fancy is tonight?

Nathaniel: As fancy as you like.

Heather: No. Are you wearing a suit?... What am I saying—of course you're wearing a suit.

Nathaniel: Wear the red velvet dress.

Heather: Wait a minute... I never mentioned the dress was velvet.

Nathaniel: Busted. Constance messaged me.

Rolling her eyes and making a 'tsk' sound, Heather returned to the bedroom. Tossing her towel across her bed, she pulled on a more raunchy set of matching underwear in red lace.

Stepping into the dress, Heather wiggled to get the material over her hips, then, with a lot more twisting than she liked, she wrestled the zipper up the back.

Turning this way and that, Heather acknowledged that the dress did wondrous things for her figure. Hugging the long, slender line of her body, it dipped at her waist. Built-in shapewear created more of an hourglass figure than Heather was used to seeing in her own reflection. Searching through the cupboards for a pair of shoes, the only ones that would work had a slight heel.

Shrugging, Heather strapped the low-heeled black heels on, appreciating the way they gave her just enough added height that her dress sat just above the floor.

Back in the bathroom, she applied makeup and a spritz of perfume, then, throwing some more clothes into an overnight bag, she grabbed the tote with her computer and locked the door firmly behind her.

Walking tentatively through the soft grass to her car, Heather waved at her elderly neighbour who sat in a rocking chair on his front veranda.

Close as she was to the pub, it still took Heather ten minutes to get across the busy traffic, pausing at the intersection where she needed to turn onto the main road.

Movement at the corner of her eye caught her attention. Glancing over, Heather smiled to see Johnny and both twins mounted on their horses.

Casually walking down the main road, Johnny spotted her first. Tipping his hat her way, he loosed an appreciative whistle as he caught sight of the bodice of her dress.

"Yeah, yeah, yeah," Heather muttered beneath her breath, smiling as she waved him along.

Pulling out into traffic once it was clear, Heather turned towards the pub. Taking the back alleyway to reach the staff car park, she pulled in next to Nathaniel's Rolls Royce.

Shaking her head at the ostentatious vehicle, Heather locked her own, heading through the back doors. She paused as another familiar face came strolling out of the bar side.

"Well lookit here," Oliver drawled. "Never seen you in that dress before, Heath."

"I love how people assume intimate knowledge of my wardrobe," Heather said with a weary sigh. "Honestly, don't you people have better things to do than harass me all day about what I choose to wear?"

"Not really," Oliver commended idly. Taking a large mouthful, he leant against the stair's wooden banister. "Date night?"

"In a manner of speaking." Heather smoothed her hand down her side. "Nate's brother is in town."

Oliver's smile vanished, his gaze darkening slightly.

"Yeah. I know."

"Woah," Heather said after a charged moment of silence. "You have a problem with Matteo?"

"Nope," Oliver argued, popping the 'p' at the end of the word with a frown.

Moving closer, Heather nudged his shoulder with hers. "C'mon, Ollie. I can read your face like an open book. What's—"

Laughter from inside the pub made Oliver's shoulder tighten, and understanding hit Heather like a bolt of lightning. Moving around the big man, she dodged the hand he automatically threw out.

"Don't, Heath."

Too late—Heather was peering around the large archway, easily spotting Isla as she sat next to Matteo, the low table before them showing evidence of a few drinks already.

"Ahh," Heather whispered, watching the way Isla's face lit up and she punched Matteo's shoulder. "I think I get it now."

"You don't get shit," Oliver barked, but his tone lacked any real anger. Feeling for him, Heather moved away from the archway.

Groaning, Oliver leaned against the wall opposite the stairs and next to the entrance into the bistro. "I don't know how to explain it, Heath. She turns me about— muddles it all up inside my head."

Thoughtful, Heather moved to stand beside him. "This is only what I've picked up in bits and drabs over the last twelve months, but Isla's family is close to Nathaniel and Matteo's. The boys view her more as a younger sister than—with any sort of romantic inclinations."

"I get that," Oliver said, and from his tone, Heather

realised he did in fact see that familiar vein.

Confused, Heather glanced back at the archway. "Then why are you—"

"She laughs with him," Oliver muttered. "Really laughs. Tells him things. He knows her. She doesn't let me get close enough to scratch anything more than the surface."

Sighing, Heather rubbed his arm. "Have you tried talking to her?"

"We just end up in bed."

Startled into laughter, Heather asked, "And that's a bad thing?"

"I want more than that," Oliver said, his voice so soft Heather almost missed it.

Heart clenching, Heather instinctively tucked her head beneath his chin and wrapped her arms around his body, angry on behalf of him now because damnit— Oliver deserved the sun and the moon combined.

"Want me to beat them up?" Heather asked finally.

Chuckling, Oliver relaxed and wrapped one arm around her shoulders. "Nah. As one of my best friends, I shouldn't have to ask you to do that—you should just do it."

Moving back now that the dark edge had smoothed out of his tone, Heather patted his chest. "My advice—talk to her, tonight. Matteo is coming to dinner with Nate and me. I know Isla is staying here in one of the upstairs rooms tonight, because all three have a meeting in the morning. Subtly cut off the alcohol and start plying her with water. Then get her upstairs into her rooms and push for the hard topics. You matter too, Oliver— so maybe it's time to lay it all out there, ask for exactly what you want."

"Just like that?" Oliver asked, his tone light.

"Just like that." Heather patted his shoulder briskly, then headed towards the stairs. Over her shoulder, she called back, "I'll be calling you tomorrow to find out how it went. So don't bitch out."

At the top of the stairs, Heather turned towards Nathaniel's end. Finding his outer door open and Nathaniel seated behind his desk, she leaned slightly in the doorway.

His face creased in concentration as he read something off the computer screen, Heather cleared her throat and watched in amusement as he glanced up and away before his gaze yo-yoed back.

"Wow."

Silently pleased by the heat that immediately flushed his olive skin a soft red, Heather sauntered in. Closing the door behind her with a satisfying snick, she turned the lock for good measure.

"Good afternoon, Mr Feria."

Leaning back into his office chair, Nathaniel followed her slow trek towards his chair with hungry eyes. Reaching his desk, Heather trailed her fingertip along the smooth top.

"I'm sorry for taking such a long time to respond to your message, but that file you asked for was a little difficult to find."

Catching onto the game quickly, Nathaniel tsked. "Not good enough, Miss Ross. When I ask for a file, I expect the file on my desk ASAP."

Nodding, Heather reached him and stood framed between his legs. Smoothing her hand through his hair and down the side of his face, she shivered when he caught it and pressed a kiss against her wrist.

"You understand what needs to happen now?" Nathaniel asked, his tone rough. "You need to be punished."

"Yes," Heather breathed, carefully bunching her dress up to her hips as Nathaniel lifted slightly to unbuckle his pants. She was sitting down on his hard length a moment later with a gasp.

Hands squeezing her hips, Nathaniel punched out a curse, his gaze intense as he demanded, "Ride, *Tesoro*."

Afterwards, Heather giggled as Nathaniel pressed kisses against her mouth, his hands more of a hindrance as she tried to fix her skirts.

"I'm going to buy you a thousand dresses," Nathaniel declared as she slapped his hands away playfully. "Then I'm going to throw out all of your underwear."

Rolling her eyes, Heather pulled the undies she'd slipped off in the car out of her overnight bag, slipping them up underneath the dress as Nathaniel's gaze heated.

"I vote we send Matteo out to dinner with Isla, and you and I go back to the bed and—"

"No way," Heather interrupted, pressing her pointer finger against his lips as she flowed into his lap. "Two reasons. One, a simple dinner with your brother isn't that big of a chore and gives me more of an opportunity to get to know him."

Beneath his breath, Nathaniel muttered, "Maybe it is a chore. For me."

"Secondly, Oliver needs to get Isla on her own—which he'll never manage with your brother monopolising all her time down there."

Frowning, his attention piqued, Nathaniel sent her a curious look. "Oliver and Isla are dating?"

"I'm not sure that's the word for it. Acquaintances with benefits, perhaps, fits a little better."

Immediately self-righteous, Nathaniel glanced at the closed door. "I'm not sure I approve of Oliver breaking Isla's heart—"

"Oh, baby." Laughing, Heather cupped his chin between her palms. "Pretty sure it's Isla doing the heart-breaking here."

Mollified somewhat, Nathaniel sighed before a sly look made its way into his expression. "Hmm. This would kind of be perfect. If Oliver and Isla start a relationship, she'd one hundred percent move to Glen Innes."

Annoyed, Heather groaned and stood. "You're like a dog with a bone sometimes."

Imitating a dog, Nathaniel growled and took a bite out of Heather's butt. Swatting at him, she was nonetheless laughing as she helped him out of the seat.

Catching her laughing mouth in a deep kiss, Nathaniel rested his hands on her hips while she settled the palms of her hands on his chest.

Breaking away slowly, Nathaniel smiled. "I love you."

Melting a little like she always did when he said those three words to her, Heather mirrored his expression. "I love you, too."

Downstairs, they found Matteo at the base, his attention fixed firmly on his phone, a small smile lightening normally grave features.

Curious, Nathaniel asked, "Who are you texting to put that smile on your face, brother?"

Quick as a flash, Matteo's expression smoothed, and his phone disappeared into his back pocket. "Took you two long enough. I won't ask what you were up to in your office just now—I think I can guess."

Embarrassed, Heather flushed but accepted the kiss Matteo pressed to each of her cheeks. "Sorry. I hope you aren't too hungry—you've probably been waiting a while."

Before Nathaniel could utter a word of reproof, Matteo was catching Heather's hand, his expression genuinely contrite as he said earnestly,

"No. Forgive my manners—I was teasing Nate, and you got caught in the crossfire. You two are newly engaged and in love. I'm sorry for my bad-tempered words."

Nodding at the sincerity in his eyes, Heather sent a smile Nathaniel's way as he pressed her towards the car park, Matteo falling into step just behind them.

"I remembered what you said last time about being sick of Italian," Nathaniel said over his shoulder, "so I booked a table at another one of the restaurants in town."

"They do a really nice Angus rib fillet," Heather said, nodding in thanks as Nathaniel opened the door and stepped aside for her to exit first.

"Is the meat local?" Matteo asked.

Nodding again, Heather went to open her car door, but once more Nathaniel was there in a smooth sidestep that left no room for disagreement.

Taking her seat, she was quiet for a moment as both men took their own seats and belted in, then continued, "Yes. The meat is likely from Harts."

"That name sounds familiar," Matteo muttered, then snapped his fingers moments later. "Friends of you both."

"Yes," Nathaniel agreed, navigating the car out into the alley. "You've not yet had the opportunity to meet them—however, if you are staying for the weekend, you'll accompany Heather and me this Saturday to Emersons."

"Will I?" Matteo asked.

"Connie and Josh host a weekly Saturday night dinner —it has become a bit of a tradition. Everyone who is important to us, important to me here, will be there. I'd like for you to come."

If Matteo was surprised by Nathaniel's candour, his tone didn't reflect it. "Alright. Then I accept your invitation— thank you."

Pulling up to the restaurant a moment later, Matteo was out of the car before Heather had unbuckled. About to open her door, Nathaniel reached over and prevented her by pulling the door shut.

Amused, Heather raised her eyebrow, her tone low and challenging. "I can open my own doors, Nate."

"I know. But if you do in my presence, I'll turn you over my knee and spank you."

Just that quickly, Heather was wet—and slightly annoyed. Now she sniffed but released her hold on the door. "You say that like it's a punishment, but you and I both know that isn't the case."

Smiling, Nathaniel exited the car and rounded the bonnet, sparing Matteo a quick glance to notice that same smile from earlier once more fixed on his brother's face.

Reaching Heather's side, he opened the door and extended his hand. Helping her from the car, he manoeuvred her slightly so that he could close the door. Her body blocking the way, his hand strayed down to shape the flesh of her backside as he pressed a seemingly chaste kiss against the bare skin of her shoulder.

Sending him a look, Heather cleared her throat slightly. "Behave."

Grinning, Nathaniel pressed his lips against the shell of her ear. "I will if you will."

'CHAPTER THIRTEEN'

Exhausted from the night before, Heather nonetheless rolled over and silenced the alarm on her phone. Glancing towards Nathaniel, who remained asleep, she sighed.

With effort, she slowly sat up and slid her legs over the side of the bed. Just as she was about to stand and head for the shower, she squealed as a strong arm wrapped around her waist.

With a firm tug, she was plastered against Nathaniel's chest as he rolled them slightly so she was pinned half beneath him. One of his hands pushed between the bed and her body to squeeze her backside; the other smoothed up the length of her torso to shape her breast as he buried his face into the crook where her shoulder and neck met.

"Nate?" Poking at his big body, Heather sighed when he remained motionless. "Nate, I have to get up."

A low noise of complaint was her only answer. Heather tried sliding out from beneath him, thwarted when his grip on her tightened warningly.

"Nate, I've got work to do, and I need to get to the farm and exercise Charlie."

Another grunt—this time accompanied by him

nudging his way between her legs. Both of them having slept naked, Heather felt the hardness of his arousal instantly.

"Nate, I don't have time. Charlie—"

"Exercise me first," Nathaniel muttered, his tongue darting out to drag along the pulse in her neck. The action was rounded off as he sucked deeply on the spot just beneath her ear.

Moaning, Heather couldn't help the way her legs lifted to cradle him more firmly against her body. "Don't you dare leave a hickey, Nathaniel."

Growling again, Nathaniel leaned back just enough to pin her in place with his hands on her wrists. "Say my name like that again, while I'm buried deep inside you."

An hour later, Heather was pulling into her spot at Emersons. Checking her rear-view mirror, she spotted the dark bruises on her neck and cursed.

"Damnit, Nate. I said no hickeys."

Getting out of the car, Heather headed through the gate and towards the stables at a quick clip. As usual, this early in the morning, no one else was around except for her.

The house lights were on—at least one person was up and most likely brewing the first pot of coffee. Knowing she'd catch one of the later ones, Heather quickly greeted Charlie.

Waiting with his head half-hanging out of his stall, he nickered softly in welcome. Stepping back as Heather entered, his lead lowered as she patted him firmly.

"Ready to go for a run?" Heather asked, moving too quickly to saddle him up. As she led Charlie from his stall, the sun sent pale shards of yellow and orange across the dew-tipped land.

Taking the side gate from the arena, Heather swung herself up into Charlie's saddle. Pursing her lips, she made a kissing noise to urge him into a walk.

Obediently, Charlie started off at a fast walk—or slow jog—blowing deep breaths out occasionally through his nose. The crisp air was revitalising as he shook off the remnants of sleep.

Passing through the first paddock, Heather closed the gate behind her. This time, clicking her tongue, she prompted him again. Proving he was listening, Charlie picked up the pace to a slow trot.

Increasing his stride, Heather and Charlie completed the six kilometres they'd worked up to at a steady canter. Finally, Heather turned him towards home, following the same steps down: from canter to trot, to jog, then walk

Breathing elevated, Heather took Charlie through to the wash bays. His clipped body cooled quickly beneath the spray

Back in his stall, Heather mixed him an oats-free muesli mix with added electrolytes. Making sure to replace his water, she patted his haunches and left him to his breakfast.

Heading for the house, Heather poked her head inside and smiled to find Constance, Josh, and Mary all standing in the kitchen. "Good morning, all."

Surprised by their matching looks of trepidation, Heather stepped inside, hooking her hat next to all the others as she kicked off her boots.

"What? Has something happened? Is Leo okay?"

"Leo's fine," Constance said strangely, her gaze shifting to the stairs that led to the next level. "It's just..."

"We have a guest," Mary offered when Constance

seemed unable to continue.

Making a face, Heather shrugged and pinched one of the apples from the fruit bowl. "It's a Bed and Breakfast, guys. Guests usually come with the territory."

Snorting, Josh hid his expression in his coffee. Pleased to have lightened the mood somewhat, Heather walked around the breakfast bar towards the coffee machine.

"I'm exhausted. Dinner ran so late last night. Think I'll need to make one of Nate's espressos," Heather was saying as she reached for the cupboard above the machine where all the mugs were stored.

An unfamiliar voice piped up from behind her. "*Si*, an espresso sounds wonderful. *Grazie, cara.*"

Turning, Heather felt her smile freeze as she came face-to-face with the 3D version of Nathaniel's mum. Before she could think to censor it, her mouth popped open, and she said, "Oh, shit."

Expression bland, nevertheless, Heather got the distinct feeling Sofia Feria didn't approve. Swallowing, she let Mary nudge her aside and slowly crossed over to Sofia.

Extending her hand, Heather cleared her throat. "I'm sorry—that was rude. I'm—"

"Heather, yes, *cara*. Of course I know who you are." Very deliberately, Sofia reached out and pulled Heather into a hug, the action still managing to be stiff and impersonal.

"Now," Sofia announced, setting Heather back and dragging her dark brown eyes over every inch of Heather's face, "let me get a look at you. My son tells me he has proposed, and you have accepted. *Si*?"

"Yes—yes. Yes, Mrs Feria—"

"No, you must call me *mamma*," Sofia chided, gently

tapping her fingers against Heather's cheek. "We are family now, after all."

Uncomfortable, Heather merely smiled, using the opportunity to study the older woman right back. Obviously, the two boys must have got their height from their father.

A whole head and shoulders shorter than Heather but taller than Constance, the woman held herself rigidly poised, her slender, well-maintained figure displayed in a tasteful linen dress.

Hair as dark and thick as her sons' was artfully collected into a French twist, and her subtle makeup highlighted long lashes, full lips, and high cheekbones.

She was a beautiful woman who had aged extremely well, and it didn't take a magnifying glass to see that beneath the polite veneer of welcome lay a deeper vein of disapproval and dislike

Heather couldn't have explained how she knew this, but the longer she stood held in place by fingers tight enough to hurt, the more certain she became: Sofia *really* didn't like her.

"Does—does Nate know you're here?" Heather asked, her tone higher than she'd like.

"No, *cara.*" Sofia released her suddenly, and Heather stepped back out of reach, unconsciously rubbing her arms. "I thought it would be a wonderful surprise, you see. To visit my son and his *la signorina.*"

Nodding slowly, Heather glanced around for backup. Finding Constance and Mary in the kitchen watching closely, she said, "Of course. Nathaniel always speaks so highly of you—"

"*Scusati*, but I find that hard to believe. I've heard practically nothing about you, other than you are *la futura padrona di casa, pare.* Hmm?"

Unsure if the disdain in her tone was all in Heather's head or very real and aimed directly at her, she cleared her throat and shifted uneasily on her feet.

"What do you say you and I spend the day together?" Sofia asked, the smile on her face not quite reaching her eyes. "A wonderful way for us to get to know each other better, don't you think?"

Wanting so very badly to say no, Heather knew that alone wouldn't be enough. As if sensing her silent plea for help, Constance chose this moment to appear at her elbow.

Carrying two steaming mugs of coffee, Constance handed one to Sofia and the other to Heather, her voice firm and polite as she said, "Oh, I'm sorry, Mrs Feria. But Heather has obligations she needs to attend to here today. I can't really spare her."

"Obligations, *pah*." Sofia waved her hand through the air as if shooing away flies. "I think you can make an exception, hmm?"

"No, I'm afraid I cannot. Heather is my foreman; she handles everything outside these doors. We are coming to the end of a very busy breeding session. I don't have the time to spare her right now. Perhaps you can spend the time with Nathaniel, and next time you visit—given enough warning—Heather can request some days off."

Impressed by Constance's moxie, Heather stared down at the tiny redhead beside her, meeting Constance's expectant look with a somewhat dazed expression of her own.

"Heather. Those reports, by midday please."

Hearing the dismissal, Heather barely repressed the urge to salute the little general. Instead, turning back to

Sofia, she spread her hands wide.

"That's alright, *cara*. Next time."

If the somewhat threatening undertones didn't spell it out clearly enough, the expression on Sofia's face as she watched Heather back away certainly did.

Oh yeah. Mama Feria didn't like Heather—not one little bit.

Escaping—because there was really no other way to look at it—back to her office, Heather drew in a deep breath after closing the door.

At her desk, she grabbed her phone, typing out a quick message which she fired off to Nathaniel.

Heather: So... your mum's in town?!

Nathaniel: I've just got off the phone to Josh. I'm on my way.

Heather: You didn't know?

Nathaniel: I would have told you had I known she was coming. It's past time you both met. I'd have preferred introducing you properly. But it was a necessary next step, don't you agree?

What could Heather possibly say to that?

Gnawing on her lip, Heather glanced idly down at her engagement ring—some inner sense making her slip it off and tuck it into the top drawer of her desk.

With a sigh, she pulled her computer from the tote bag and plugged everything back in the way she liked. As it booted up, she couldn't help the way her gaze strayed to the bay window.

Hoping to catch a glimpse of Nathaniel when he showed up, although rationally she knew she was tucked around a corner in her office and couldn't see the front entrance or the whole carpark.

As time slowly ticked on, Heather became resigned to the fact that Nathaniel wasn't coming to find her. Feeling glum, she slouched in her chair, swivelling from side to side.

"Here you are."

Startling hard enough to drop the pen she'd been using to poke random keys on her computer, Heather glanced up to find Nathaniel framed in the doorway.

"You're here?"

Frowning at her tone, Nathaniel stepped into the office, closing the door behind him. Having stood in the doorway for five minutes unnoticed, he studied her expression

There was a careful vacancy in her eyes that made Nathaniel sigh internally. He'd hoped Josh, Constance, and even Mary had exaggerated the tense first meeting between Heather and Sofia.

"I'm sorry, *Tesoro*," Nathaniel said gently. About to round the desk to pull her from her seat, he paused —something in her face told him he might not be welcome.

"So am I," Heather said, her heart aching. "I did kind of expect it, though. I'm well below your social standing, after all."

Feeling confused, Nathaniel shook his head. "I don't understand how social standing is relevant—"

"Your mum wasn't too impressed with me." Heather glanced away now—mostly to hide the bitterness in her expression, but also to escape the dawning realisation in his.

"Heather, I've discussed this with you already. My mother doesn't control my— You're not wearing your engagement ring."

Idly glancing down at her hand, Heather drew in an unsteady breath. "No."

Covering the space between them quickly, Nathaniel drew her up, ignoring the way her hands pushed ineffectively at his chest.

Dropping into her chair, he then pulled her back down into his lap, rearranging her limbs the way he wanted so she was draped flush against him.

"Don't," Heather said, futilely trying to wriggle away. "I don't think we should—"

He silenced her by pulling her head down to his and taking her lips, refusing to let her breathe until she was limp and still against him.

Then—and only then—he let her lift away, his hands still gripping her face as he glared at her. "You do not get to run. You do not get to leave. You and I are too far past that point."

Swallowing, Heather shook her head. "You didn't see her, Nate—"

"Give her time to adjust. Mamma is used to everyone falling into line. She grew up with older brothers and, as the youngest, is perhaps used to getting her way. Lord only knows Papà never pulled her up for it."

Heather felt Nathaniel was being naïve, but weakness when it came to him made her swallow the retort. She wasn't able—or willing—to argue with him.

"Where is it?"

Eyes flicking to the top drawer, Heather was silent as Nathaniel opened it and pulled out her ring. Pliant, she let him take her hand and slip it back onto her finger.

The familiar weight settled like a puzzle piece, and Heather automatically moved her thumb to rub the cool metal—something she'd caught herself doing multiple times throughout the month when lost in thought.

"I love you," Nathaniel said, his hands once more capturing her face in his palms. He drew her closer for another soul-searching kiss, resting his forehead against hers after he'd released her mouth.

Slowly nodding, Heather wound her arms around his neck, leaning into him slightly. "Yeah. I love you too."

"You left too early this morning; I'd wanted to talk to you about something," Nathaniel said. Rubbing her thigh, he paused a moment before continuing, "I think you should move in with me."

Smiling a little with bemusement, Heather parroted, "Move in with you?"

"Yeah, just hear me out. You spend pretty much every night with me anyway. You could put your place up for rent or sale—whatever you wanted. We're engaged; we knew we'd get to this bridge eventually. I don't see the point in putting it off anymore."

If he'd asked her this morning, Heather wondered if she'd have been more inclined to jump in with a yes, wondered if she wouldn't have hesitated as she did now. But the fact was, she'd met his mother now and sensed the woman's immediate and deep dislike. She wanted to believe Nathaniel when he said his mother didn't control his life.

Yet a small, careful voice deep within her told her to wait—just wait—because when the other shoe dropped, Heather was going to need her home.

"Just think on it," Nathaniel said into the charged silence, reading the expressions on her face all too easily. He pressed a tender kiss to her temple, frustrated with the ground he'd lost today.

Quiet for a few minutes, Heather sighed and shifted

slightly. "I better get back to work. And you probably should go find your mum and take her out. Maybe you, Matteo, and your mum can go sightseeing—"

"Matteo has left," Nathaniel interrupted, his tone gruff. "He's borrowed the jet and returned to Perth."

"But-he was here for the weekend."

Observing Heather for a long moment, he admitted, "As soon as Matteo heard mamma was in town, he was resolved to leave. And nothing I could say or do would have convinced him to stay."

Having met Sofia now and felt the sharp blade of her disapproval, Heather suddenly felt a kinship with the younger Feria. Growing up under such blatant dislike would have been demoralising, and it was little wonder Matteo and Nathaniel's relationship was strained.

Because even now, Heather knew Nathaniel was hoping the first meeting with his mother would be forgotten —that by some miracle, the damage done in that one meeting would be undone.

Naïve, her inner voice whispered as she shifted off him —terribly naïve.

**

By late afternoon, Heather had somehow managed to finish all her paperwork. Glancing around her tidy office, she sighed, silently acknowledging how easy it had been in the end.

Throwing herself into anything that distracted her from this morning, her brain had latched onto the office work like a drowning swimmer to a life raft.

She'd gone so far as to go through her filing cabinet and burn documents older than seven years, reorganising the rest into alphabetical order.

Then she'd cleaned her office until every inch sparkled,

and now sat on her freshly steamed sofa thinking about tackling the equipment room next.

A soft tap on the door had Heather reflexively calling out, "Come on in."

Entering, Constance cautiously glanced around and released a low whistle. "When Ryan told me you were on a cleaning bender, I couldn't have imagined he meant this. Heath, are you okay?"

"Sure." Standing, Heather slapped her hat against her thighs, then jammed it onto her head. "But the equipment room is a pigsty. I'm gonna start reorganising it—it's been on my to-do list since New Year's."

"Wait." Catching Heather's arm as she would have passed, Constance smiled slightly. "You haven't eaten anything, haven't taken a minute to just catch your breath. Come back up to the house. Mary'll fix you some lunch, and you can just take a break."

"I can't, Connie. There's just so much to do—"

"Sure. But half an hour isn't gonna make a difference at this point. And it's almost five."

Surprised, Heather checked her phone. Her stomach dropped to find no new notifications, no missed calls—and that it was, in fact, quarter to five.

"You okay?" Constance asked, studying Heather's profile.

No. Heather glanced up with a forced smile. *He hasn't called or messaged all day; I can't remember a day that's gone by without him touching base at some point.*

"It's just been a long day," Heather said finally, her tone unsteady. "And you're right—I'm starving."

Linking her arm through Heather's, Constance pointed them in the direction of the house. "Are you and

Nathaniel staying for dinner tonight?"

Closing her eyes as they exited the stables, Heather swallowed. "You know, I forgot it was Saturday. I don't know—"

"Look at it this way: better to have dinner with the new mother-in-law with backup than be out in public playing to her tune."

Backup, Heather thought glumly. "That doesn't sound like a bad idea, Connie."

Taking the stairs up to the back door, Heather toed off her boots and stored her hat. Glancing up, she found Mary in the kitchen, checking on the roast she had in the oven.

"Heather," Mary said with a smile, gesturing to the fridge. "I put aside some lunch for you—it's in the fridge."

Ravenous, Heather pulled the fridge door open, spotting the plate immediately. Checking beneath the tin foil, she smiled at the large sandwich.

"Thanks, Mary. You're the best."

"And don't forget it," Mary said, brandishing the basting tool she was using in Heather's direction as the younger woman took a seat next to Constance at the breakfast bar. "How's Nathaniel going with his mother?"

Stomach souring, Heather set down the sandwich she'd been about to bite into. "I'm—ah. Not sure. Haven't heard from him."

Frowning, Mary turned slightly to face her. "Is that normal?"

No, Heather wanted to admit. Instead, she just shrugged and picked at the crusts.

"You two were okay after this morning though, right?" Constance asked, her attention diverted to her phone. "I mean, he didn't blame his mum being rude on you, did he?"

"Connie." Mary tipped her chin in Heather's direction once Constance looked up.

Following the gesture, Constance hurriedly set her phone down, turning in her seat to fully face Heather.

"Sorry. I didn't—that came out wrong."

"It's alright. I know what you meant." Heather smoothed the tin foil back over the sandwich, no longer hungry.

"He's probably just busy," Mary soothed. Leaving her spot in front of the oven, she patted Heather's hand. "His mother seems the high-maintenance sort."

Obviously grasping for a topic change, Constance smiled and asked, "Will we finally get to meet the elusive Matteo?"

"No." Sighing, Heather smiled somewhat tiredly. "He jumped ship as soon as he heard Sofia was here."

"Wow." Failing to hide her surprise, Constance tried, "Well, thank goodness Isla's coming? I've heard she's known Sofia her whole life. She might come in handy as a sort of... buffer."

"I shouldn't need a buffer," Heather griped. Then, "She's my mother-in-law. It should just be easy. Maria Hart— perfect example of the kind of mother-in-law I want."

Snorting, Mary turned on the tap at the sink. "C'mon, Heather. Maria is a one-in-a-million exception to the rule. Most mothers-in-law are monster-in-laws and you know it."

"God, I love that movie," Constance said reflectively— then blushed under Heather's glare a moment later and shrugged apologetically.

'CHAPTER FOURTEEN'

"Well, I'll admit the place has a certain... rustic charm to it," Sofia said, her elegant face creased by a slight smile. Reaching across the centre console, she patted Nathaniel's knee. "But *figghiu miu*, do you have to live here? Where are the shops? The theatre? The... excitement and life? Hmm. You cannot expect me to believe you are truly happy—"

"I am, mamma," Nathaniel interrupted smoothly. Ignoring her arched brow, he glanced at her briefly. "I'm really happy here."

"But you have no family here to make sure you are taking care of yourself. Who will bring you dinner when you forget and work through lunch? Heather? She is so busy she cannot even take a day off to get to know her new mamma. Not right for you at all. Now Isla—"

Interrupting again with a sigh, Nathaniel shook his head. "Never gonna happen, mamma. And you know it."

"Then there are plenty of women back in Perth better suited to caring for your needs, *figghiu miu*. You needn't settle—"

"I'm not settling, mamma. Enough! I am in love with Heather, and only Heather. You need to get on board with this."

Changing tactics, Sofia's voice turned low and soothing. "I only push because I love you, because I worry for you. You are so serious, Nathaniel. With so much responsibility. You need someone who will lighten that load, not add to it."

Suspicious, Nathaniel hit the indicator and turned into the driveway headed to Emersons. "What are you talking about, mamma? Who have you been speaking to?"

Shrugging, Sofia spread her hands. "I don't know what you're insinuating, Nathaniel. I merely question how well you know Heather—"

Slamming on the brakes in the middle of the long trek towards the house and stables, Nathaniel turned his upper body to pin Sofia beneath a stern look.

"You've had Heather investigated?"

Smiling softly, Sofia reached out and cupped his jaw. "As your mamma, it's my responsibility to check these things. I need to know about the women you are involved with! I asked Mathew to place a few discreet inquiries, that's all."

She'd dragged the family lawyer into this?

"Unbelievable, mamma! Unbelievable! You had no right to invade Heather's personal boundaries that way."

Mouth tight with anger, Sofia folded her hands in her lap. "On this, you and I disagree. *Figghiu testardu*, it falls to me when these things fall apart—and they do, Nathaniel. They fall apart! I am the one working behind the scenes to make sure any—and I mean any— blowback is in your favour. I am protecting our family and our family name so that we can hold our heads high."

Speechless, Nathaniel could only glare out the

windscreen, his grip tight on the steering wheel.

"She's important to me, mamma," Nathaniel said as the silence stretched uncomfortably between them. "She is... the air in my lungs, the blood pumping through my veins."

Gaze dark and troubled, Sofia rested her fingers against his shoulder, and once he turned to face her, she cupped his face.

"*Figghiu miu.* I felt the same about your father, and you and I both know how that turned out."

Sighing, Nathaniel trapped her hands against his face. "I need you to back off. You've made your opinion clear— she's not your choice. But she is mine."

After a charged moment, Sofia released a soft pulse of air. Tugging her hands free, she raised them, palms facing him, either side of her head.

"Okay, *figghiu miu.* I trust you. If this is who you want—"

"It is." Shifting the car out of park, Nathaniel eased his foot onto the accelerator. "Get to know her. Heather is loyal and smart and kind. You have a lot in common with her."

Rolling to a smooth stop in one of the free parks beside the office entrance, Nathaniel was out of his seat and rounding the car to his mother's side in an instant.

Holding her door open, he accepted the kiss she pressed against his jaw with a slight smile, tucking his hand into his pocket as Sofia linked her arm through his.

Bypassing the main entrance, Nathaniel headed towards the gate, as familiar with Emersons as he was with his own house in Perth.

Leading his mother through the back door, he was oblivious to the sudden silence their entrance caused. His gaze roved the room to hone in, and focus on

Heather.

Wearing the same jeans and shirt from earlier, she'd lost her hat and boots, Leo and Harmony propped on each hip.

Their small faces still chuckling, Leo swooped in to place an open-mouthed kiss against Heather's cheek, breaking the tension in the room as all the adults chuckled at Heather's reaction.

"Eww, Leo. At least take a girl to dinner first."

"Watch out, Feria," Jackson piped up from his lazy sprawl at the dining room table, his gaze dark with challenge as he said, "Competition for your girl."

"Of all the men in this room," Nathaniel loosened his tie, prowling slowly across the room towards Heather, "he is the only one who stands a chance of stealing my girl away. Lucky for us both then, that he's merely keeping her entertained until my arrival."

Having watched his approach silently, Heather was unsurprised when Nathaniel plucked each babe from her hips, handing them off to their respective mothers.

"I feel like it's been hours since I saw you last," Nathaniel said, his tone deep as he settled his hands low on her hips.

Not feeling very charitable, Heather resisted the urge to wind her arms around his neck, instead keeping them limp at her sides.

Reading the intent in his gaze, she turned her head to the side at the last minute. Nathaniel's kiss fell short and landed high on her cheekbone.

Shifting back, Nathaniel frowned down at her closed expression. "*Tesoro*?"

"Dinner," Constance announced cheerily as she stood at her regular chair. Handing Leo over to Josh, who strapped him into his high chair, she gestured to Nathaniel and Heather to come join.

Without waiting for him, Heather headed to the table —something akin to annoyance flashing through her system as she noticed Sofia sitting in the chair she normally claimed.

Changing direction, Heather slid into another seat. "Is Ollie still on his way?"

"He was picking up Isla," Faith murmured, serving up a plate for Bastien, who sat between her and Jackson.

"I'll save them a seat beside me—" Breaking off, Heather smothered a sigh as Nathaniel smoothly took the chair at her side.

"They'll fit next to mamma," Nathaniel replied idly, ignoring the pointed look she sent him. Accepting the salad bowl Josh handed him, he asked, "Salad, *Tesoro*?"

Moving to take it, she frowned when he lifted it out of reach. "I can serve my own plate, Nate."

Making a low noise of assent, he then proceeded to heap a spoonful of the crisp cabbage salad onto both her plate and his.

The direction the plates moved around the table meant that each time Josh handed one to Nathaniel, he served both her plate and then his own.

Heather's annoyance by the end was at an all-time high, but all attention was diverted as Isla and Oliver entered from the library landing.

"You're like a wet mop sometimes, Oliver. It's exceedingly annoying," Isla said as she unwrapped a scarf from around her neck. Behind her, Oliver loomed like an angry giant.

Expression tight, Oliver shrugged out of his Driza-Bone. "I'm the wet mop?"

"Evening, you two. Running a little late?" Josh piped up, reminding them that whatever they were arguing about now had an audience.

The two shared a look that Heather was pretty sure was scorching enough to set either of them on fire. Then Isla tossed her scarf over Oliver's head and turned away.

Ripping the soft material off his face, Oliver stalked toward the coat rack by the back door. As he passed Heather, she caught him mumbling something dark beneath his breath.

"Isla," said Sofia, standing with open arms to accept Isla into a tight embrace. "Dearest. It has been far too long since I saw you last. Look at you—skin and bones. Do I need to tell Nathaniel not to work you so hard, hmm?"

Chuckling, Isla moved back slightly once Sofia had all but crushed her. "It's okay, Sofia. I enjoy the challenge of keeping up with him."

"Keeping up, *pah!* You and I both know you run rings around him. His company does so well only because of all *you* do in the background."

Sinking slightly in her seat, Heather watched as Sofia folded Isla into the seat beside her, lavishing attention on the tiny woman shamelessly.

Sending Heather a questioning glance, Oliver muscled his way behind Constance to slide into the seat beside Isla, meeting Sofia's look head-on.

"And who are you?" Sofia asked, her tone imperious.

"Oliver."

Her eyebrows lifted. Sofia watched the blond behemoth load his plate and then Isla's with food. "Oliver?"

One platinum blond eyebrow disappearing into his hairline, Oliver glanced down at Sofia for a long moment. "That's right."

When it looked like Sofia was about to step the inquisition up a gear, Constance leaned her head slightly around Oliver, her tone pleasant. "So, how was your day? Did Nathaniel take you sightseeing?"

"Sightseeing?" Sofia parroted, her tone suggesting she found the idea amusing. "Yes, we walked up and down your main street. It did not take us long."

From the other side of Jackson and Harmony, Mary sat forward excitedly. "There's a rather beautiful gem store along there. Did you go inside? All the gems are from around Glen Innes, and some have been crafted into the loveliest pieces of jewellery."

Heather could tell that what Sofia termed jewellery and what Mary termed jewellery were probably vastly different. She half-expected a thinly disguised mocking rejoinder from the poised woman.

Only Nathaniel chose that moment to place his hand on her knee beneath the table. Glancing at him sharply, Heather reached down to shove it off.

But he tightened his hold on her leg, saying from the corner of his lips, "Careful, *Tesoro*. I am almost done with your temper tantrum."

Laying her hand over his, she dug her nails into his skin, gratified by his subtle wince of pain.

"Move it, or lose it," she warned beneath her breath, smiling when Constance slid her a bemused look from across the table.

Ignoring her, he moved his hand up her inner thigh until, in a move all sorts of bold, he cupped her possessively. Any movement on Heather's part did nothing to dislodge it from its resting place.

"Don't," Heather warned, ineffectively squeezing her thighs together to prevent any further movement.

"Don't, Nate."

"Look at me," he ordered.

Desperate, Heather complied. Her gaze was heated with anger and bright with unwilling arousal.

"I missed you today."

Trying to hold on to that anger, Heather argued, "You didn't message me once. Not once, Nate. What was I supposed to think?"

Hearing what she didn't say, Nathaniel leaned closer—and like a moth to the flame, Heather copied him.

"My phone died, *Tesoro*. And do you think I could find my charging cable? No. I bought a new one from the servo—the damn thing doesn't work. Either that or the stereo won't acknowledge the cable. I knew I'd see you here tonight. I didn't think about how my silence might seem. I'm sorry."

Just like that, all the wind left her sails. It wasn't the first time he'd been out of communication, prone as he was to running his phone battery dead.

Usually, he had it back up and running in a matter of hours, but Heather believed that was mostly down to the fact he had cables stashed all over the place.

It was a quirk Heather never would have expected in the otherwise organised businessman, and she'd teased him mercilessly the first time his phone died mid-conversation.

Watching the way her shoulders relaxed, Nathaniel rubbed his thumb over her jean-clad leg, happy to leave his hand exactly where it was, eating with his free one.

Picking up her own fork, instinct forced Heather's gaze up—meeting the ice-cool fury in Sofia's expression.

Heather froze.

Then the older woman blinked and turned her face

toward Isla, engaging her in conversation—and the moment passed.

Glancing around, Heather realised no one else had caught the expression on Sofia's face. Shivering slightly, she swallowed.

Noticing, Nathaniel leaned in. "Cold?"

"No. Just—someone walking over my grave, I guess."

Smiling at what he assumed was a silly turn of phrase, Nathaniel squeezed her leg and returned to his conversation with Josh, who sat at the head of the table.

Appetite nowhere in sight, Heather moved the food around her plate, draining the beers as they appeared in front of her—courtesy of Jackson, who handed them via Faith down the line.

Once the dinner plates had been cleared—with all the women except Sofia helping tidy up in the kitchen— Heather was feeling decidedly dizzy.

Tipping back the rest of her beer, she stumbled slightly, Nathaniel already having placed himself at her back, chuckling.

Arms wrapping around her waist, he nuzzled her neck. "We should get you home."

Drying one of the pans, Mary smiled. "I think that's a smart idea, Nate."

Resisting when he would have led her away, Heather frowned at him. "I'll just sleep on my sofa bed in my office. It's super comfy and kinda why I bought it."

"You will not sleep on the sofa bed in your office," Nathaniel said, his tone brooking no argument, "when you have a perfectly comfortable bed to sleep in already."

Smiling, Heather nodded. "Good point. I saved up for ages to afford my mattress, and I about drove the mattress man mad. Laid down on every single one in the shop."

"I meant our bed, in our rooms, *Tesoro*," Nathaniel said, amused. He caught Josh's gaze from across the room. "Hang here for a minute—just gonna say goodnight to mamma."

Waiting until he was out of earshot, Heather made a face. "Mama? He's a grown-ass man. Why is he still calling her Mama?"

Snorting, Isla took a long pull from her own beer. "Everyone calls Sofia 'Mamma.' She demands it, as is her right as *la capu di la famigghia*."

"*La capu di la famigghia*?" Heather asked.

"The Matriarch of the family," Isla muttered sliding a glance at Oliver as he reached across her body to take a sip from her glass.

"You don't," Heather realised. Turning, she ran her gaze up and down Isla's body. "You don't call her mamma. She loves you."

"Because I call my own mother 'Mama,'" Isla responded, poking out her tongue.

Taking a page out of Leo's book, Heather blew a raspberry in Isla's direction, receiving a good-natured swat with the tea towel from Mary.

"All right," Mary announced to someone over Heather's shoulder, "take her home and tuck her in, for the love of God. She's tipped over into sass-pot mode."

"Sass-pot, hmm?" Having collected her jacket, Nathaniel wrapped it around Heather's body. Trapping her arms against her sides, he used her momentum to tuck her against his chest, then grinned down at her frowning face.

"I still maintain I could sleep here tonight,"

Heather said, following along nonetheless as Nathaniel manhandled her toward the door.

Going to his knee, Nathaniel tapped her foot. Feeling her hands settle on his shoulders to brace herself, she lifted the foot he'd indicated so he could slip her boot on.

Repeating the process with the other foot, Nathaniel stood and wrapped one arm around her waist. Anchoring her against his chest, he waved to everyone in the room.

"Night, all. Thanks for dinner. Mamma, I'll see you in the morning."

To the chorus of "good night" and "drive safe," Nathaniel shifted Heather outside. Sliding her into the passenger seat, he buckled her in when, for all intents and purposes, Heather had fallen asleep.

In his own seat, Nathaniel paused a moment to tuck a strand of hair behind one of her ears, studying the smooth panes of her face, now relaxed in sleep.

The drive home was punctuated by the soft, occasional snore from the passenger seat but was otherwise silent and comfortable. Nathaniel sighed a little once they reached their destination.

Leaning over slightly, he ghosted the pads of his fingers along her cheek. "*Tesoro*, time to wake up."

A long moment later, she sighed, eyelashes fluttering. "Nate?"

Kissing her lips softly, Nathaniel released her seatbelt. "We're home. Let's get you upstairs and into bed."

Making a low noise of complaint, Heather was otherwise compliant, falling into bed minutes later after completely stripping off.

Nathaniel merely pulled the cool top sheet up over her

naked body. Loosening his tie and pulling it off, he watched her sleep in comfortable silence.

**

"When is she going home?" Heather hissed, corralling Constance into a corner of the office. "Seriously, Connie. When is she booked in to leave?"

"I don't know." Constance shrugged helplessly, glancing around the empty office. "Her stay is a little... open-ended at the moment. She came by this morning to extend it by another day."

Overcoming the irrational urge to stomp her foot, Heather sighed and slapped her hat against her thigh. "It's Monday. I thought she said she was only staying the weekend."

"Well, she obviously changed her mind! I don't know what else to tell you, Heath. You need to find a better hiding spot, though, because she asked for a tour of the stables."

Moaning, Heather brought her Akubra to her mouth and bit into the material. Releasing it a moment later on inspiration, she asked, "Aren't there fences to be mended today?"

Frowning, Constance's gaze turned contemplative. "Yeah, actually. I think I did see it on the chores list—"

"I don't care who it's been assigned to. I'm pulling rank." Heather turned on her heel and headed toward the front door, shoving her hat back onto her head.

"Heath."

Stopping with her hand on the door handle, she raised a quizzical eyebrow in Constance's direction. The small woman's face was serious.

"You can't let her speak to you like that."

Blood freezing, Heather tried to smile and failed. "I don't

know what you—"
"I heard her. The morning after dinner, when you were making coffee. I heard what she said to you."

"You think I don't know what you're doing?" Sofia hissed, her hair still up in the overnight curlers she wore. "You are not the first woman to pursue Nathaniel for money and social standing. But mark my words—Nathaniel will see through you, and you will be tossed back out onto the streets, you grasping slut! Buttana maledetta!"

Sighing, Heather let her hand fall from the handle back to her side, staring out through the glass across the paddocks beside the bed and breakfast car park.
"I don't even know what to say to her," Heather murmured. "I tried—every topic under the sun—but Sofia is just... unbending in her dislike for me."
"She blames you for why Nathaniel moved here," Constance guessed, shrugging when Heather glanced at her in surprise. "C'mon, it's not that hard to pick. Tell me you have an overbearing mother-in-law without telling me you have an overbearing mother-in-law."
"What should I do?" Heather asked, though she could already tell by the expression on Constance's face that she didn't have a real answer.
"Personally, I think you need to tell Nate."
"No." Shaking her head, Heather gnawed on her bottom lip, her thumb rubbing against her engagement ring. "That's his mother. I just—I can't."
"Then you need to stand up for yourself," Constance said. "Don't let her walk all over you. Tell her to shove it up her butt."
"Shove it up her butt?" Heather raised her eyebrows. "Did university teach you all that fancy language?"

"No. But for the amount of money I ended up repaying the government for that degree, they should have."

Laughing, Heather rolled her shoulders and sighed. "I just need to get to the end of her visit. That's all."

Wanting to be supportive, Constance nodded and slid back into her desk chair. She nodded toward the door. "Sofia's tour is at nine. Make yourself scarce if you don't want to be around for it."

In record time, Heather had found Graham and swapped him out for fencing duty. Taking the work ute, which he'd already packed with the necessary equipment, she was gone.

Turning the radio to her favourite local channel, Heather wound the window down, leaning her elbow on the sill and luxuriating in the feel of the crisp air.

She didn't care what anyone else thought—Glen Innes was the most beautiful place in the world.

And if Sofia couldn't see that?

Well... then that wasn't Heather's problem at all.

'CHAPTER FIFTEEN'

"Can we talk about this later?" Heather asked two weeks later, pausing in the bathroom doorway. She gazed back at Nathaniel's naked form, admiring the way the early morning sun played shadows across smooth muscle.

"That's what you said yesterday," Nathaniel argued, clasping his hands behind his head. He smiled at the way her gaze traced the muscles in his arms and chest. Not above using his body to seduce the answer he wanted from her, he continued, "And the day before, and the day before that. Give me one good reason, *Tesoro*. Just one."

"Because I like having my own space," Heather tried.

"You're kidding, right? I can't even remember the last time you stayed at your place instead of here with me. Not a valid answer. Try again."

Crossing her arms, Heather leaned her shoulder against the doorframe. "Because all my stuff is there."

"Already said to bring the important stuff here. The rest we can put into storage or leave for the renters."

"I pay rates on the place—I should spend some time there!"

Rolling his eyes, Nathaniel directed his gaze to the ceiling. "Again, that's what the renters are for. You'll make enough in this market that they'll be paying your rates for you."

"God, you're persistent."

"I've been called a lot worse." When she laughed, Nathaniel glanced back over to her and held out his hand, waiting as she crossed to his side and took a seat. "Is it so terrible that I want my fiancée here, every night, by my side?"

Sighing, Heather rested her hands either side of his head, leaning over him slightly to study his face.

"It's hard to let go of that last piece of my independence," she revealed softly.

Gripping her waist, Nathaniel smoothed his hands up and down her sides comfortingly. "Because you're still expecting this to go pear-shaped."

Unwilling to admit it aloud, Heather shrugged, her expression pensive. She'd have to be a fool to forget Sofia's disastrous visit last month.

Reaching up, Nathaniel tucked her hair behind her ear. "If it takes until we're both old, and grey, and grumpy, I'll prove to you just how devoted I am. You're stuck with me, Heather. I'm not going anywhere."

He said it with such conviction that Heather almost believed him, but all the hard knocks in her life crowded her throat and prevented the 'yes' she desperately wanted to give him.

"Just—give me a little more time?" Heather asked, her expression pleading.

Sighing deeply, Nathaniel cupped the back of her neck and tugged her down until her lips met his, pushing his tongue past her defences until she was limp and thoroughly kissed.

"Because I love you, I will wait," Nathaniel growled once he'd released her. "But when we're married, I don't care what you say—we will share a home."

Laughing lightly, Heather dropped another quick kiss against his lips. Standing, she moved into the bathroom, closing the door behind her.

Moments later, the sound of the shower turning on prompted Nathaniel to reach for his phone. Opening his emails, he checked to see if the one he'd been waiting for had arrived yet.

When a quick refresh revealed that no, it hadn't, he checked the time and then groaned. Forcing himself upright, he scrubbed his hands over his face, grimacing at the rough stubble.

Pulling on the discarded dress pants from the day before, Nathaniel padded on bare feet toward the kitchen, starting up the coffee machine as he grabbed a mug and a travel cup.

Falling into the easy familiarity of his morning routine, he brewed two cups of coffee, preparing Heather's in the travel mug.

He then toasted a couple of bagels he'd frozen from the local bakery, adding avocado, cream cheese, and salmon to both and taking the plates to the dining table.

Knowing Heather preferred orange juice with her breakfast, he poured some into a glass and placed it beside her plate, his own mug set beside his.

By this time, Heather had finished her shower and exited, dressed in jeans and an opened checked shirt with a singlet beneath. Her typical outfit for her days spent at Emersons'.

Taking the seat at his side, she kissed his mouth in thanks, working her way through her bagel as they shared easy conversation.

"Mmm, before I forget," Heather said, using a napkin to

wipe the corner of her mouth, "got an email from the florist. She has some ideas for the table centrepieces?"

Nodding slowly, Nathaniel tapped his phone, which sat off to the side. "Forward the email to me—I'd like to have a look at what she's designed."

Knowing he'd say that, Heather smiled and leaned over to peck his lips quickly. Standing, she took her plate and his to the sink, rinsed them quickly, then added them to the dishwasher.

Brushing her teeth, she pulled the towel from her hair and quickly fixed it into its usual two braids.

Nathaniel had moved from the dining table to the sofa, his coffee sitting on the table at his knees, one ankle draped over the other as he balanced the laptop in his lap.

He'd found his reading glasses—stylish black frames that complemented the sharp angles of his face—and made Heather's lady parts squeeze in a wholly feminine way.

Ignoring the urge to tip the computer off his lap and slide into that spot herself, Heather instead slanted his chin up for a quick kiss.

Nathaniel deepened the kiss until it teetered on the edge of the carnal. When he pulled away, her breath came fast—matching the wild beat of her pulse.

"See you tonight," he remarked with a lazy smile, knowing he'd just smashed her equilibrium to shreds.

Later that morning, Heather was still sighing in frustration. Ignoring the look Constance sent her, she glared at Oliver's wide back.

Sensing her stare, Oliver slid her a careful look over one broad shoulder. "What?"

Frowning, Heather straightened slightly. "You what?"

Turning, Oliver propped his hands on his hips. "You started it."

"Started what?"

"All right, you two," Constance made the letter 'T' with her hands. "Heath, babe. You're scaring the horses."

"I'm scaring the horses?"

"Yeah. What've you got—a rock stuck in your hoof?"

Lips twitching as she unsuccessfully tried to hide a smile, Heather asked, "Hoof? Really, Connie?"

Bumping Heather's shoulder with her own, Constance grinned. "What's up?"

"Nathaniel's pestering me about moving in with him again."

Surprised, Oliver paused—bent almost in half with one hoof clenched between his thighs—to glance up. "Wait. I thought you two were already living together."

"No! I still have my place, Ollie."

"Yeah, but aren't you basically at Nathaniel's every night anyway?"

"So?"

"So, that's you two living together."

"He kinda has a point, Heath," Constance chimed in, pulling a chocolate bar from her pocket and munching happily. "Everyone in town knows you're pretty much living out of Nate's place now. Word's gone 'round the pub."

"Shit," Heather said, resting her hand on her hip. "Sneaky. I didn't even notice—he's moved me in."

Rolling his eyes, Oliver returned his attention to the hoof between his legs. "You're hopeless."

"I'm hopeless?" Heather arched her eyebrow, sharing a look with Constance. "What is going on with you and Isla lately?"

Releasing the mare's hoof gently back to the ground, Oliver stood upright and brandished the file in Heather's direction. "Don't deflect. We're talking about you, not me."

To the sound of Constance snorting, Heather wiggled her finger. "Talking about you is more interesting to me. Spill it, big guy. Did you have the big feelings talk?"

"If I say yes, will you leave it alone?"

"Unlikely," Constance said, licking chocolate off her fingers. "Better just spill the details—save us all the hassle of hounding you for the next hour."

"God, you two are so much work," Oliver groused, but Heather could tell he meant it playfully.

"What did she say when you told her you wanted to be more than just bed-buddies?"

"She wasn't expecting it," Oliver said slowly, patting the rump of the mare he'd just finished. He waited until Heather had returned her to her stall, then returned with Charlie, whose feet were due next. "To be honest, I haven't heard much from her since."

Feeling bad for him, Heather glanced at Constance, who in turn shrugged her shoulders.

"Maybe she's just been busy? Even with Matteo taking over in Perth, Nathaniel's still been as busy as ever."

"Considered that," Oliver said, raising his voice above the sound of him clipping Charlie's hoof, "so I went to Perth."

"Wait." Shocked, Heather shifted so she could see his face. "You flew? To Perth?"

"Yes, I flew to Perth."

When he seemed disinclined to elaborate, Heather prompted, "And?"

Placing Charlie's hoof back on the ground, Oliver stood

and turned. "She's a different person in Perth. She has a Glen Innes version of herself, and a city Perth version." Sighing, Constance tucked her hands into her pockets. "I'm sorry, Ollie. I should have said something—maybe." When Oliver shrugged, Heather glanced between them. Hating being left out of the loop, she waved her arms. "Hello? What are you guys talking about?"

"Isla is an heiress," Constance said slowly. "The eldest daughter of a business mogul who's made an absolute fortune manufacturing and distributing vaccines."

Mouth dropping open, Heather asked, "Our Isla?"

"Not ours," Oliver muttered. Then he shrugged when Heather glanced at him. "You'd have to meet city Isla to understand, Heath. She fits more comfortably there than she does here in the country."

Frowning, Constance shook her head slowly. "I'd have to disagree, Oliver. Isla wears a very successful mask in Perth, but it's not the real her. The real Isla is the woman who lays on the floor playing with Leo—the same woman you can't help but argue with every time she's nearby."

"Maybe." Oliver returned his attention to Charlie, and they continued in silence for a few moments.

Before the silence grew too long, Heather muttered, "Well, I guess I should probably speak to a real estate agent about getting my place up for rent, rather than continue beating around the bush when I'm pretty much living at Nate's."

Snickering, Constance produced another chocolate bar from her pocket. "I can't believe you're the last one to figure out that you're living with Nate. How did you miss that?"

"Great sex," Heather shrugged, ignoring Oliver's

spluttering groan about that being 'too much information.'

Ducking out of Emersons early that afternoon, Heather slid her sunnies onto her face and turned up the stereo, singing along to the country tune blaring from her speakers.

A quick half-hour later, she was pulling up out the front of her house. Noticing the car already parked on the sidewalk, she smiled at the older man who met her at the front gate.

"Heather, good to see you."

Accepting his handshake, Heather nodded. "Hey, Peter. Good to see you too. How's Samantha and the kids?"

Smoothing the front of his crisp white shirt, Peter shrugged. "You know how it goes. Feels like every other week Sam or I are being called up to the school. Jimmy can't seem to keep his nose clean."

"Teenagers," Heather replied with a sympathetic twist of her lips.

"It's these friends of his," Peter grumbled as Heather unlocked her front door. "None of them are in any sort of extracurriculars. They just loiter around town."

Not an uncommon issue in small towns. Stepping aside to let him enter, Heather closed the screen door behind them.

"I could get him work in the stables," she offered. "We have a number of juniors working for us already. Might encourage him to make new friends. He was an enthusiastic rider, if I remember correctly—I doubt he's forgotten all those lessons."

Expression thoughtful, Peter smiled. "Thanks, Heather. I'm not sure I'd be able to get him there, but I'll have a chat with Sam and figure out a way to talk to him about it."

Changing gears, Peter glanced around, his expression softening. "This house always did have good bones. She's looking real good, Heather. Your grandparents would be proud of how well you've taken care of her."

Warming with the approval, Heather tucked her hands into her back pockets and trailed after Peter as he worked his way through the rooms.

"So what are you looking to do, Heather? Your message mentioned you wanted to put it up as a rental?"

"Yeah, I'm not really living here at the moment. As a decent-sized three-bedroom, she'd be perfect for a family. Opa built her for a family."

"Congratulations on the engagement," Peter added with a nod. "Heard about it through the grapevine."

Stomach warm, Heather grinned. "Thanks."

"Well, like I said, the house is in immaculate condition, and as a three-bedroom it won't sit empty long once it's on the market. There are a couple of things I'd encourage you to look at before we get the photographers in."

"Sure," Heather said, gesturing to all her furniture. "As you can see, I still need to empty the place."

Nodding, Peter gestured out the back window. "You'll probably want to get the back veranda fixed, and the backyard fences too. If we're marketing toward a family, they'll want a safe, secure area for kids—or to keep pets contained. Speaking of—pets: pro or con?"

"I wouldn't mind if they had pets," Heather replied with a shrug.

"All right, then. Next, you'll need to update these smoke alarms—I'd suggest getting them hardwired."

Glancing up at the nearest smoke detector, Heather

tried and failed to remember if it even had a battery. She vaguely recalled a night, more than a year ago, when she'd been naked and used a broom to knock it down.

"Okay. New smoke alarm system—check."

"I can give you the number of the guys my business uses," Peter offered. Then, moving toward the windows in the dining room, he added, "Pedantic as this might sound, I'd also get all the locks, screens, and blinds checked."

"Blinds are less than twelve months old," Heather said with a nod. "End of last year I finished installing the last lot in the bathroom. I'd still been using the curtains Oma put up—it was time for a change."

Nodding, Peter tested the closest blinds, making a low sound of approval when they slid open and closed easily. "Good, good. Still check the locks and screens. Wouldn't hurt to do the same with the front and back doors."

"All right. That's simple enough."

"The kitchen—you updated that recently?"

"Yeah. I got one of those flat-pack ones delivered, and then Stan pulled the old kitchen out and put the new one in. Appliances are all new too."

Admiring the off-white cupboards and deep mahogany-polished benchtops, Peter nodded. "Perfect."

"Should I get a fresh lick of paint run through the place?" Heather asked, eyeing the walls in the lounge room. She'd repainted the whole house herself for her twentieth birthday—but that was several years ago now.

"Up to you. It's tidy as is, but if you want to unify the rooms to the same cream colour, that's not a bad idea."

Fifteen minutes later, Heather had a list on her phone

of everything Peter had recommended. Waving as he pulled away from the curb, she decided to swing by the pub on her way back to work.

Parking out back, she quickly ducked into the bistro side and poked her head through the double swinging doors, scanning for Faith.

In the far back corner, Faith was smiling as she mixed something up. Seated on the benchtop next to her: Hope.

Surprised, Heather made a beeline for the two women, waving to Corinne, who was efficiently manning the stove.

"I don't understand how he even managed to get my number," Hope was saying, her tone low with annoyance. About to respond, Faith caught sight of Heather and her smile warmed with welcome.

"Heather, hey! I didn't know you were coming to lunch today."

Swatting Hope's knee playfully as she passed, Heather wrapped Faith up in a one-armed hug. "Just dropping past after stopping in at my place. Thought I'd go upstairs and bug Nate for a bit."

"Matteo's upstairs with him," Faith said, a sly note in her voice as she flicked a glance in Hope's direction.

Curious, Heather looked at the middle Bianchi sister. "Oh? Do we not like... Matteo? I'm kind of obligated to— being as he's my brother-in-law."

Nothing like the young girl Heather remembered, Hope had grown into a very solemn young woman. Understandable, given what Heather now knew about her upbringing.

Still, in rare moments, the mask lifted—and Heather could see the quiet girl with the wicked, dry sense of humour peek through.

Today, Hope was coiled tightly. Her elegant skirt suit and reserved expression hid almost all emotion—except her hands kept smoothing her skirt and her lips were too tight.

"Matteo has been sexting Hope."

That being the last thing Heather expected, she choked out a sharp laugh while Hope gritted through her teeth, "Faith!"

"What?" Unashamed, Faith continued stirring the batter. "Is it or is it not the truth?"

"Actually sexting you? Are you sure? Matteo's so..." Heather trailed off, tipping her head to the side, considering. "Huh. You know... maybe I can see him doing that."

High cheekbones stained an attractive red, Hope slipped off the bench, pulling the hem of her buttoned blazer down firmly with a sniff. "It's not that funny, Faith."

Unable to respond—because it was that funny—Faith braced her hands on the benchtop as she laughed.

Looking miffed, Hope crossed her arms. "Seriously. I didn't come here for you to laugh at me, okay?"

More curious now, Heather asked, "Why are you here? Last I heard, you were in Brisbane."

"I'm back in New South Wales visiting Mum," Hope replied. "Thought I'd also drop in on my older sister."

"After she heard Matteo was going to be here," Faith whispered conspiratorially to Heather.

Throwing her hands up, Hope gave in. "Fine! Yes, okay—I heard Matteo was going to be here. I need to speak to him privately and ask him to stop messaging me."

"You want him to stop?" Heather asked, reaching for the batter Faith had just finished. She grinned when the other woman slapped her hand away. "Whatever for? That man looks like he knows his way around the bedroom—if you know what I mean."

Blushing again, Hope shifted slightly on her feet. "Regardless. I don't have time for it, and I never gave him my number in the first place."

Accepting the finished cupcake Faith handed her, Heather took a too-large bite and moaned slightly.

"Oh my God, Faith. How do you stay so thin when you bake stuff like this?"

Chuckling, Faith began pouring the batter into tins lined with cupcake wrappers. "I have two children and an active husband—my body burns the calories as fast as I put them in."

Laughing, Heather turned her attention back to Hope, noticing the way the younger woman now plucked at the gold cross hanging on a thin chain around her neck.

"These messages are really bothering you?" Heather asked, reading the poorly hidden anxiety on Hope's face.

"Yes," Hope replied, but her tone lacked any real conviction.

Finishing the cupcake, Heather tossed the liner into the bin beside Faith and dusted her hands off. She waved for Hope to follow her as she exited the kitchen.

Suspicious, Hope asked, "Where are we going?"

"To interrupt their meeting," Heather replied.

A hand fisting in the back of her shirt paused her forward momentum. Glancing over her shoulder, she raised an eyebrow in question.

"We don't have to interrupt—it's not that important—"

"Hope, honey. I came here to interrupt Nathaniel's day anyway. I'm just going to position you so you can grab Matteo on his way out."

Unwilling to cause more of a scene than she already had, Hope released Heather's shirt and trailed her up the stairs to the top landing.

Having no experience with the pub's layout, Hope was slightly relieved to follow Heather, who turned confidently and headed toward an open door.

Leaning against the doorframe, Heather smiled as Nathaniel paused mid-sentence, his gaze warming with welcome as he spotted her.

"*Tesoro*. I wasn't expecting to see you till tonight."

Moving confidently into the room, Heather slid Matteo a small smile and wiggled her fingers in greeting. Circling the desk, she leaned down to press her lips to Nathaniel's.

Reaching up, Nathaniel anchored her with a firm hand at the nape of her neck, and as the kiss deepened, Matteo stood, muttering, "I'll catch up with you both later. If I wanted a peep show, I'd have stayed in Perth."

Turning, Matteo caught sight of Hope in the doorway —his annoyance quickly morphing into something else entirely.

"On second thought, you two take as long as you like. I'll be down in the bar."

Waiting in the hallway, Hope straightened her shoulders in response to the challenge in his gaze. Deliberately relaxing her arms at her sides, she hoped she projected disinterest though her stomach churned.

"Well, well, well. You didn't mention anything about being in Glen Innes at the same time as me. Convenient."

"Lose my number," Hope demanded, her tone flat and unfriendly. She startled slightly at the hand he settled low on her back.

"Join me for a drink."

"I don't drink. I want you to delete my number from your phone. In fact I want you to explain how you got it in the first place."

Smiling instead, Matteo gently guided Hope ahead of him into the liquor side of the pub, tipping his head toward the bartender.

"Two glasses of the red Zinfandel, please. Thanks, Jerry."

Annoyed, Hope stared up at him. "I told you I don't—"

"Humour me," Matteo advised. Accepting the two glasses, he gestured toward a set of comfortable-looking black sofas near a large floor-to-ceiling window overlooking the sidewalk.

Acquiescent—but only because she had a goal to achieve—Hope accepted the glass and took a small sip.

Savoury and rich, the flavours of plum, berries, and hints of red currant exploded on her tongue. Unable to stop herself, she moaned slightly before quickly cutting the sound off.

Lifting her lashes, she met Matteo's hungry gaze and felt her stomach flutter in response. Reminded of her purpose, she set the wineglass down.

"If you please, Matteo—my number."

"It truly bothers you, my having it?" he asked, echoing Heather's earlier question with a curiosity Hope didn't appreciate.

"It does when I wasn't the one who gave it to you."

Sighing, Matteo sprawled his long legs out, loosely caging Hope between them. "How else was I going to contact you?"

"Why would you need to contact me?" Hope asked, bewildered. "We met for five seconds months ago. We're not even acquaintances."

"Hmmm," was his only response.

Uneasy, Hope reclaimed her wineglass and nursed it in her lap—more for something to do with her hands than anything else.

"If you can look me in the eye and tell me you haven't thought—*not even once*—about me in return, I'll delete your number right here and now. Never bother you again."

Tension thrummed between them. Hope took a deliberate sip, stalling for time—but her answer came too slowly.

Smiling, and looking entirely too smug for her liking, Matteo nudged her knee with his.

"That's what I thought."

'CHAPTER SIXTEEN'

Early Saturday morning, Heather chuckled as Johnny recounted something silly the twins had done, his face serious though his eyes sparkled.

"When I asked what they were thinking, Cooper looks me dead in the eye and goes, 'We thought the dye would wash out with the rain!'"

Chuckling, Heather patted Charlie's neck as he shifted beneath her thighs. "God, those two are a handful."

"Tell me about it. I call my mums almost every day to apologise for what a shit I must have been growing up."

Amused, imagining Johnny's mothers with their dreadlocks, green thumbs and penchant for silk scarves, Heather murmured, "You know they relished every minute of it. I still remember the rally they led when I was a teenager. What were they protesting again?"

"Which time?" Johnny asked, his tone dry. Well aware of his alternate mothers' lifestyles and ideologies, he and his sister Vicki considered themselves lucky to be as normal as they were, considering some of the radical beliefs their mothers held.

Vicki liked to credit their relatively well-adjusted minds to their grandparents—the Darcys were part of the founding families for Glen Innes.

Johnny credited Polocrosse, which in a roundabout way also thanked his grandfather. The sport had been part of his life since he was first sat on horseback at three.

Johnny was umpiring this weekend's event at the local showgrounds. Heather took her place as the third of her team for this chukka. As soon as the ball was set loose, the next six minutes passed in a blur.

Caught up in the game, Heather laughed, exhilarated, as Charlie pressed the length of his side into Samson. Taller by a good hand, Heather jostled Ryan expertly, the teen swearing beneath his breath as she popped the ball free of his racquet.

Thundering after the ball, Heather barely caught the incoming racquet from the corner of her eye. Too slow to dodge, pain exploded from her mouth as it contacted her unguarded face.

"Hey!" shouted Johnny, appearing at her side a moment later, his face black with anger. "Watch where you're swinging that thing!"

"Yeah!" Cooper piped up, slotting in behind his father. "You did that on purpose."

"No, I didn't!" Mark's angry voice announced.

Blinking through stars, Heather lifted a hand to her mouth and drew it back covered in blood. Shocked, she glanced at Mark, who glowered at those around him.

"I saw that. Coop's right—you did it on purpose," Hudson chimed in, pointing. "What are you even doing swinging your racquet around like that? The ball's all the way over there."

"There was a bee," Mark defended heatedly. "I'm allergic! I'll admit I shouldn't have been swinging the racquet around, but I didn't deliberately clock Heath across the face."

"Take a walk," Johnny advised. As the official umpire, his expression was cautious. Watching as Mark sulked away, he manoeuvred his horse closer. "You okay, Heath?"

Baring her teeth, she asked awkwardly, "Do I still have all my teeth?"

Staring into her mouth as she opened it wide, Johnny nodded. "Yeah. No chips either. You're bleeding all over the place though. Better go get cleaned up."

As the chukka paused, Heather nudged Charlie over toward where Constance and Josh stood, Leo hoisted high on Josh's shoulders.

Accepting her reins, Josh held Charlie still while Heather dismounted. Feet planted firmly, Constance met her, gaze bright with worry.

"That looks bad, Heath. At the very least, you've split your lip."

"That's what it feels like," Heather muttered, pressing the towel Constance handed her to her mouth. She hissed slightly at the pain.

Glancing over, she caught Josh watching something across the field. Turning, Heather felt her blood freeze as she found Mark's gaze fixed on her.

Confused, a headache brewing, Heather pulled the towel back to find it soaked with blood.

"Maybe we should go to the hospital," Constance suggested, hovering. "You might need stitches. Can they even stitch a lip?"

"Give it ten minutes," Josh advised, jiggling slightly to entertain Leo. "If the bleeding doesn't stop, then we'll take her to the ER."

"It's fine," Heather said, waving a hand but accepting the seat Constance guided her to. "It'll stop in a minute, then I'll get back in the game."

"You're kidding, right?" Constance asked. "With that

much blood? No way."

Chuckling, Heather shrugged. "C'mon, this is nothing. Trust me."

"I dunno, Heath," Josh piped up, attention on the deep, red-stained towel. "Connie's got a point. You're bleeding like a stuck pig."

Rolling her eyes, Heather sighed. "Thanks for that charming visual."

"That's why I'm paid the big bucks," Josh said with a smile. Leaning down so Constance could lift Leo, he gestured to Charlie. "I'll let him into the field there so he can grab a drink and pick at some grass."

Nodding, Heather rubbed her forehead, feeling very tired and slightly woozy. A shadow fell over her, and she looked up to meet Johnny's concerned gaze.

"How you going?"

Carefully removing the towel, Heather reapplied pressure when it continued to bleed. "It sucks, but they might need to sub me out."

Nodding, Johnny gestured with one hand. A moment later, a young girl on a tall grey mare trotted onto the field.

Leaning on his thigh, Johnny studied her pale features. "You're not looking too flash, Heath. Go home. Vicki will call you later tonight to check on you."

Lifting her hand in recognition, Heather sighed, limbs heavy. "Nate's gonna have kittens when he sees my face."

"Understatement of the year," Constance snorted, Leo chortling alongside her, happily kicking his legs. Her eyes narrowed, lips tightening. "Incoming."

Confused, Heather lowered her hands and stared up at Mark on horseback. His face was embarrassed as he swallowed. "Sorry, Heath. It really was an accident."

Unable to smile—the action tugged painfully at her lip —Heather shooed him off with a rough, "Don't worry about it. Hazard of the game."

Mark hovered a moment longer before trotting back toward his team. Heather couldn't explain why the unease in her stomach continued to swirl. Something about it didn't sit right.

"Connie, babe. Why don't you and Leo take Heath home? I'll handle Charlie, get him washed and fed."

Hating leaving Charlie's care to others, Heather at least knew Josh would treat him with as much care as she would.

Nodding, Constance tucked her phone back into her pocket. Her focus returned to Heather. "Wait here. I'll bring the car around."

"Sure," Heather muttered. She slowly lowered the towel, grateful the bleeding had finally stopped, and began collecting what she could reach.

Once Constance returned, she finished packing the rest, quickly hauling everything into Josh's truck.

The last item to pack was the seat Heather sat on. With Constance's arm wrapped around her waist, Heather eased into the passenger seat.

A short trip later, they were parked behind the pub. Nathaniel stood waiting, arms crossed, mouth tight.

Before Constance had even put the car into park, he opened the door. Releasing her seatbelt, he hissed when he saw her lip.

The front of her shirt and thighs were covered in dried blood. The skin on her chin was stained red, her bottom lip swollen and split open by a nasty gash.

"Jesus, who?" Nathaniel demanded.

"Mark," Constance replied with a sigh.

"Mark. Seventeen-year-old, Junior at Emersons, Mark?"

"Yeah."

"What the hell?"

"He said he was trying to fend off a bee. Didn't notice Heather until after his racquet hit her."

Jaw clenching, Nathaniel helped Heather from the car, directing his words at Constance. "I hope he got raked over the coals for this?"

"It's Polocrosse," Heather forced out, wincing. "Not the first time I've taken a racquet to the face."

Because he didn't want her arguing further, Nathaniel nodded his thanks. Constance lifted a hand in parting, knowing from his expression she'd be hearing from him later.

Arm wrapped around her waist, Nathaniel guided Heather inside. Just as they reached the stairs, Faith, Jackson, their small family, and Grace exited the bistro.

"What the fuck?" Jackson demanded, handing Harmony to Faith, who froze. "What happened?"

"Polocrosse," Heather muttered before Nathaniel could answer.

Expression relaxing somewhat, Jackson's mouth twisted. "That's a hell of a split lip, Heath."

Shrugging and just wanting to lie down, Heather said, "It happens."

But her stomach wobbled at Faith's expression—the other woman frozen in place, eyes wide with fear.

Noticing, Jackson moved to shield her, torn between removing Faith from the obviously triggering situation and finding out more about what had happened to Heather.

It was Grace who broke the tension, her tone no-

nonsense. "Jacko, take Faith and the kids home. Nate, take Heather upstairs. I'll come give you both a hand."

Nathaniel frowned but complied, overhearing Jackson ask Grace if she was sure. He was out of earshot before he could catch her response.

Groaning as she finally got to sink into the soft comfort of the lounge, Heather didn't even smile in thanks as Nathaniel sat on the coffee table, lifting one leg at a time to strip her of boots and socks.

"Have you guys got a first aid kit?" Grace asked as she entered the room with a determined air. Following Nathaniel's pointing finger toward the bathroom, she veered instead to the kitchen sink.

Checking the cupboards, she spotted the tell-tale bright red box and manoeuvred it free with a satisfied smirk.

Returning to the lounge, she paused. Nathaniel had finished removing Heather's boots and now sat gently massaging her feet, tenderness in every line of his expression. Grace felt like an interloper.

Clearing her throat, she lifted the first aid kit in victory. "Found it."

"What do you need from me?" Nathaniel asked.

"Ice wrapped in a flannel. Probably a glass of water too."

Taking his spot again on the coffee table after delivering what she asked for, Nathaniel watched as Grace knelt beside Heather and smiled kindly. "That's gotta hurt like nobody's business."

Heather nodded, staying quiet as Grace pulled a heap of items from the kit—gloves included, which she snapped onto her hands.

"This is a good kit," Grace said, accepting the glass and ice from Nathaniel. She held up a packet of Steristrips. "These are invaluable."

Heather swallowed, recognising the skin-coloured wound closures. She'd had them before—alongside stitches—after a nasty fall.

"This is gonna hurt like a mother..." Grace warned, uncapping a lime green antiseptic bottle. She gave Heather a look, and at her nod, moved closer.

Holding Heather's jaw in a gentle but firm grip, Grace pressed the soaked cotton ball to the jagged wound at the corner of her mouth.

Heather moaned and jerked, her whole body tensing. She smothered the urge to pull away, keeping her face still.

Nathaniel, now seated beside her, hissed and reached for her hand. She gripped his tightly.

"Easy," Grace murmured, blowing gently on the skin as she swapped out cotton balls, cleaning the wound until she was satisfied.

Opening the box of Steristrips, she sat beside Heather, placing the strips in her lap as she studied the split.

"I don't think it'll take many. It's in an awkward spot. I'll cut one of the strips in half and use just the one to pull the edges together. Sound okay?"

Heather gave her a thumbs-up. She tensed again as Grace picked up the scissors and sliced a Steristrip into shorter pieces.

"You really know what you're doing," Nathaniel observed quietly. "I thought Faith said you studied Marketing and Economics?"

Grace faltered for a split second—so slight it might have gone unnoticed. But Nathaniel was watching her hands like a hawk.

After a loaded silence, she met his gaze and said simply, "Let's just say I've had a lot of practice."

"In stitching people up?" he pressed.

"For a start, yes."

Nathaniel hadn't known Rory. And normally, he didn't judge someone without meeting them. But he made an exception in Rory's case—and thought it lucky the man was already dead. Had he not been, half the town might've wanted his blood.

"As bad as the antiseptic rub was," Grace said, her tone gentler now, "this is going to hurt more. I need to press the skin together while applying the strips. It'll be quick —just two."

Before Heather could nod, a sharp knock sounded at the outer door. A familiar voice called out, "Heather? Nathaniel? It's Johnny Darcy. Are you guys in there?"

Kissing Heather's forehead, Nathaniel stood and crossed to the office door, opening it. "Hey, Johnny. We're in."

With his twins roughhousing behind him, Johnny's hazel eyes were more green than brown. Tucking his hands in his pockets, he said, "Sorry to drop in. I was umpiring Heather's game. Everything wrapped up quickly. I wanted to check in."

Stepping aside, Nathaniel let them in. Before doing so, Johnny knelt down to speak to his sons, his tone firm. "Behave. We're going in to see Heather. She's hurt, remember?"

Sober nods followed, the boys trailing in behind their father with exaggerated innocence. Nathaniel smirked, remembering seeing them two days earlier, hanging upside down from trees, trying to knock each other down with racquets.

Back in the main area, Nathaniel resumed his seat beside Heather, retaking her hand.

"Wow," Cooper muttered, leaning in. "That looks gnarly."

"Look at your shirt and pants," Hudson added, impressed. "You look like a zombie attacked you."

Johnny sighed and sent them both a stern, if loving, look. His gaze flicked to Grace, who had gone still upon hearing his voice.

"Hey, Gracie. Long time no see."

Heather glanced between them, confused by the expression on Grace's face. How did they know each other? Grace was six years younger than Johnny—Heather wouldn't have expected her to register on his radar.

Then Grace smiled. It was perfectly polite. Too polite. Heather's eyebrows shot up.

"Johnny. You've got old."

Something quick and calculating flashed across Johnny's handsome face. Then he smiled wide, showing even white teeth.

Heather couldn't remember the last time she'd seen Johnny smile like that. She studied Grace anew.

Interesting.

"Shall we get this lip sorted now?" Grace asked, turning her back to Johnny.

"What are you gonna do with those?" Cooper asked, pointing to the Steristrips.

"Use them to patch Heather's lip up."

"Won't that hurt?" Hudson asked.

"Probably."

"Why are you wearing gloves?" they both asked in sync. Smiling slightly, Grace replied, "I just made sure the wound is clean. I don't want to introduce new germs from my hands. The gloves are to protect Heather."

They shared a look and drew out the word "cool," examining their own hands with interest.

To distract them, Grace tipped her head toward the kit. "If your dad and Nate say it's okay, you could each grab a glove to take home. Fill it with sand or rice—it makes a good stress ball."

Eyes lighting up, they turned to the men. Both nodded. Johnny crouched in front of the kit, pulling two gloves from the box.

As he handed them over, he studied Grace's profile, intrigued in a way he hadn't been in a long time.

"Squeeze Nate's hand, Heather. This is gonna hurt."

With sure, firm movements, Grace peeled a Steristrip free, stuck one end down, and pulled the skin together as she laid it across the wound.

Heather hissed, squeezing Nathaniel's hand tightly. Tears leaked from the corners of her eyes despite her efforts.

"There. That's one," Grace said. "One more should do it. I was worried I wouldn't be able to seal the worst of it, given the placement. But luck's on our side—it should seal up nicely. Probably won't even scar."

Heather wasn't one to worry about scars, but she glanced at Nathaniel anxiously.

Reading her easily, he rubbed his thumb over her hand and smiled.

Releasing a jagged breath, Heather turned her attention back to Grace, who gave her a silent, reassuring nod.

As Grace applied the second strip, she dabbed away fresh blood, reapplied antiseptic, then pressed the ice pack gently against Heather's mouth.

Snapping off the gloves, she said, "All done."

Heather moaned something unintelligible, sinking

deeper into the chair. She nudged Nathaniel's knee. He stood, frowning slightly.

"I'll drop you home, Grace—"

"It's okay. I'll figure something out—"

"We can drop you," Johnny interrupted easily. "Right, boys?"

"We can!" Cooper and Hudson chorused with enthusiasm.

"You still live here in town?" Grace asked, already knowing the answer. "I'm staying out at Hart Station with Faith and Jacko."

Shrugging, Johnny rubbed Hudson's head. "We don't mind."

"It's a half-hour drive out of your way."

"The boys have a gift for Bastien's birthday from earlier this year. We've been meaning to drop it off. Keep forgetting."

About to argue, Grace was interrupted by Heather. "Thanks, Johnny. We appreciate it."

Sealing her lips, Grace could do little but nod and follow Johnny and the boys out.

In the passenger seat of Johnny's Hilux, Grace folded her hands in her lap and stared straight ahead. The boys were buckled in the back, chattering quietly and fiddling with their new glove-shaped "stress balls."

"Hope you don't mind, but we need to make a brief pit stop," Johnny said.

Curious, Grace glanced at him. "What for?"

"Bastien's present is at home."

Her brow lifted. "You said you had it in the car."

"I implied," Johnny corrected smoothly. "How've you been?"

Flabbergasted, Grace scoffed. "Implied? And—'How've I

been?' Fine, Johnny. I've been just fine."

"I heard some rumours a few months back," Johnny said, lifting a hand in casual greeting as a ute passed by and honked. "Is it true what people are saying about your dad?"

Grace's body went cold. She slid him a look from the corner of her eye. "Why does it matter to you?"

His jaw tightened. He checked the rearview mirror—the boys were preoccupied.

"You should have come to me, Gracie. I could have done something."

Genuinely confused, Grace asked, "Why could you have possibly done, Johnny? I was six years younger than you. Barely on your radar. You'd just had the twins. Newly married. What did it matter what my father did behind closed doors?"

He went silent, just as she'd expected.

"I always noticed you," Johnny said quietly after a moment. "You might've been younger. I might've been married. But I noticed you, Grace."

They pulled up to a gate, where the boys quickly decided who had to open it via rock-paper-scissors. Cooper groaned and unbuckled.

Grace glanced around. The small cottage sat on five, maybe ten acres on the edge of town. White-washed wooden posts, four taut strings of wire, well-maintained.

"This looks nice," she admitted, flicking her fingers toward the fence.

"Yeah. Traded in the townhouse about six months ago. The boys and I prefer it here. We can breathe. We've got the horses."

Six months. Grace did the math. That would've been

right after Jessica left for good this time—gone in a blaze of fury, leaving the boys in Johnny's care.

"I'm sorry," Grace said quietly once Hudson jumped out to help his brother. "About Jessica."

"It was inevitable," Johnny said, voice flat. "We were never going to last. We're both better off now."

Grace didn't understand that. Not really. Her memories of them as a couple were fractured, but they always seemed like a team. Still, she stayed quiet.

The boys finally got the gate open, and Johnny eased the ute through. The driveway was short and well-kept, curving toward the house. Pulling up underneath an open carport, Johnny put the car into neutral and turned the ignition off. Glancing across to find Grace staring resolutely out the windscreen he cleared his throat.

"You can come in, if you want."

Surprised, Grace studied his face. "Really? Uh, yeah. Okay."

The boys swept past her and into the house, the door thunking shut behind them. She frowned.

"You don't lock up when you leave?"

"Nah. My neighbours are lovely—and nosy. Plus, it's Glen Innes."

Chuckling, Grace followed him inside, mimicking him as she took a seat on one of the breakfast bar stools. "It's Glen Innes. I check my windows, screens, and doors twice before leaving my apartment."

Johnny grinned and started rummaging in the fridge, pulling out ingredients to make sandwiches. "Faith mentioned you live in the city now?"

"Sydney. Dover Heights. Just down the road from Mum's place."

Without glancing up from buttering the slices of bread he'd laid out he asked, "How's your mum?"

Uncomfortable, Grace cleared her throat. "She's—yeah. Good." She changed the subject. "So where's this present?"

Johnny didn't miss the dodge. He raised an eyebrow but said nothing. "The boys are probably getting it from their room."

Thumps and bursts of laughter echoed from down the hall. Grace couldn't help but smile. "They're kind of adorable."

Johnny glanced at her for a long moment, his voice quiet when he asked. "Any boyfriends? Plans for kids?"

Laughing, Grace shook her head. "Boyfriends? Not by a long shot. Kids? Sure, eventually. When I meet the right person."

His gaze lingered on her, intense and slow. When he smiled again, it curled something warm and tight low in her stomach.

Johnny set a plate on the counter in front of her—a simple ham and cheese sandwich, cut in halves.

"I'm out of mustard. Hope mayo's okay," he said, also sliding her a napkin.

"Perfect, thanks." Grace accepted it, tucking her hair behind her ear as she leaned on her elbow. "You always this hospitable with the people you ambush then practically kidnap?"

Johnny gave a low laugh. "Only when they look like they could use it."

"I'm not sure if that's a compliment or an insult."

"Take it however you like."

Their eyes locked for a long, tense moment.

From the hallway came the sound of bickering. Then a

shout—"We found it!"—followed by hurried footsteps.

Hudson entered first, proudly holding a badly wrapped box. Cooper trailed behind, his expression just as triumphant.

"Here it is!" Hudson declared, placing the gift on the bench beside Grace.

She eyed the gift unable to help her smile.

"Good job, boys," Johnny said, ruffling their hair as they beamed. "Now—grab your shoes and socks again. I've made some sandwiches you can eat in the car. We've gotta head to Hart Station."

Groaning, the twins trudged back towards their bedroom.

Johnny poured two glasses of water and leaned back against the counter opposite Grace. "Plan on staying long?"

Grace shrugged. "I suppose. It's just for a couple weeks. Needed some air."

Johnny tilted his head, watching as she licked a smear of butter from the corner of her lips, arousal coiling low in his stomach.

"Never was much of a fan of the big, city smog myself," he commented easily.

Chewing slowly Grace watched as Johnny turned away, easily packing everything back up into containers, which he then returned to the fridge.

She'd managed to finish her lunch by the time the twins had returned, sliding off her stool to take the dish to the sink. Smiling as she dodged Hudson who accepted his sandwich from Johnny, her attention focused on rinsing her plate.

Rubbing her damp hands on her jeans Grace froze, as turning she found Johnny's gaze locked on her. Lost for words she muttered softly, "Thanks again, for lunch."

"Your welcome," trying not to analyse the warmth flooding his system at the moment, Johnny gestured towards the door leading to the carport. "Ready?"

Nodding Grace quickly moved towards the exit, "Sure. Yes. Thanks."

Seated once more in the car Johnny turned the music on low managing to keep his gaze on the road, when really all he wanted to do was study the quiet woman in the seat beside him.

A woman who he'd honestly never expected to see again.

A woman who had looked too damn good, sitting there in his house, eating a sandwich off his plates.

'CHAPTER SEVENTEEN'

In the end, it took three weeks for her lip to heal and her face to return to normal. Studying her reflection in the bathroom mirror, Heather smoothed the pads of her fingers over the slight, pale scar.

"Everything okay?" Nathanel asked from the doorway.

Turning, Heather leaned against the bench and crossed her arms. "Fine. Just... thinking."

Moving into the room, Nathaniel placed his hands on her hips, pulling her to settle against his chest. He made a low noise of approval as her arms wrapped around his neck.

"Penny for your thoughts?"

Shrugging, Heather honestly didn't know how to make sense—much less voice—her thoughts. A part of her was still unwilling to believe what many people said about that weekend. About the way Mark had watched her and then calculatingly placed himself in position on the field, how he'd been waving his racquet around chaotically but intentionally.

She'd spent the last two weeks observing Mark, trying to pick up on any unsettling vibes—but frustratingly, she got nothing.

He was exactly as he'd always been: slightly awkward,

with his floppy, too-long hair and tendency to get flustered in big groups. If anything, he seemed a little lonely, with a big chunk of the junior employees giving him the cold shoulder. Ryan, apparently, was still unimpressed.

"Polocrosse is a sometimes-hazardous sport, which you know."
Heather had pulled Ryan aside when the teen point-blank refused to partner with Mark.
"He didn't do it on purpose."
"Sorry, Heath, but respectfully, bull. Mark's been riding and playing Polocrosse his whole life. When he got you with his racquet, it all looked way too practiced."
From behind him in the arena, Annabelle piped up from Happi.
"Is that the guy that's always skulking around corners?"
Glancing up at the tween, Heather asked, "What?"
"Now that I finally convinced Mum and Dad to bring me every fortnight for classes, I notice him around a lot." Annabelle shrugged. "I mean, I didn't think too much of it, considering how busy this place is. People everywhere. But I dunno... he kinda feels—different."

From that point on, Heather had started paying attention to where Mark was. The feeling of being watched sometimes became overwhelming. She hated walking on eggshells but wasn't sure what else to do.
Glancing at Nathaniel's reflection, she sighed.
Telling him any of her suspicions would be a mistake—especially if it all ended up being unfounded and Mark was just a regular, albeit unusual, seventeen-year-old.
"Just busy with work and the wedding plans," Heather said, tucking her head beneath Nathaniel's chin.

Not so easily appeased, Nathaniel tightened his arms around her, tempted to call her out on how poorly she'd been sleeping, how she'd seemed to have lost weight.

Wanting to shift the conversation to happier things, he said, "Real estate called. He thinks he's found somewhere that might suit us perfectly."

Craning her neck, Heather slapped her palm against his chest and leaned away. "I don't understand why we're house shopping. You tell me to rent my place out, then immediately turn around and start house hunting? We have a house!"

"I want to find something that's both of ours," Nathaniel soothed, swaying them gently. "Somewhere on the edge of town, maybe, where you can have Charlie. So I don't have to wake up before the sun just to make love to you before you leave."

Winding her arms back around his neck, Heather sighed. "That does sound nice."

Smiling, he settled his lips over hers. "It does, doesn't it?"

When his phone vibrated several long moments later, he gave her one final lingering kiss, then left the bathroom with the phone pressed to his ear.

Glancing once more at her reflection, Heather smoothed her finger over the faint scar at the corner of her mouth. Leaving the bathroom, she grabbed some clothes from the wardrobe.

Moments later, dressed, she pressed a kiss to Nathaniel's temple where he sat at the dining room table, speaking rapid-fire Italian into his phone.

In the kitchen, she reached for her favourite travel mug. She'd completed the final move of her belongings several days ago. Whatever hadn't fit into this space had gone into storage. She had to admit, a bigger place would be nice.

Nathaniel had shifted and gotten rid of furniture to make space for her, and she appreciated it. But she understood his reasoning. A place that was theirs would make life easier.

Pouring coffee into her mug, she wandered back to the table, topping up Nathaniel's cup and smiling at his appreciative grunt.

After adding sugar and milk to taste, she screwed on the lid and did a quick no-leak test over the sink. Checking her tote bag for everything she needed, she paused by the table once more.

Nathaniel covered the mouthpiece and tipped his head back so her kiss landed on his lips. "Have a wonderful day. Am I still seeing you at lunch?"

"Yes, I'll see you then."

Forty minutes later, she pulled up at Emersons and headed toward her office. Unlocking the door, she dumped her things on the sofa—then froze. A box sat on her desk.

With everything going on, she'd almost forgotten about the strange messages and packages. The box was nearly identical to the earlier ones.

Feeling slightly sick, Heather sank into her seat, her fingers hovering over the twine. With a quiet lecture to herself, she plucked it open and removed the lid.

Letting out a breath, she lifted out a jewellery box and opened it with a soft gasp.

Nestled in dark blue velvet was a necklace of finespun white gold, a large blue sapphire at the centre surrounded by sparkling diamonds.

A note was tucked beneath it. Pulling it free, Heather

relaxed when she saw the single name written in cursive: Sofia.

Dialling Nathaniel, she waited until he answered.

"Your mother sent me a necklace. Know anything about that?"

"Forgive me, Tesoro. I should have mentioned it sooner. She asked if you had anything blue or borrowed. When I said no, she told me she had it covered. That necklace has been in our family for generations. It's an heirloom."

"Why would she send it to me then?"

"Tesoro, she's sorry for her behaviour when she visited. These jewels—among others—will pass to you after our marriage. She wants you to feel welcomed."

Heather highly doubted that, but unable to voice it, she made a low sound of acknowledgment. "Well, thank her for me. That's very kind."

"I will see you at lunch," Nathaniel murmured before hanging up.

Closing the box, Heather locked it in the bottom drawer of her desk and headed out to saddle Charlie for their usual morning exercises.

Later, she was washing Charlie down in one of the bays, singing the lyrics to a newly released country song under her breath.

"My turn next," Nathaniel teased, his tone warm and suggestive.

Smiling, Heather straightened and slanted him a narrow-eyed glare. "Vain creature."

"That's one of the reasons you love me," he said, stepping closer. "How'd he go?"

"Normal eight kilometres," Heather said, rubbing Charlie's neck. "Ryan's mixed his breakfast, and I was just finishing scraping him dry."

"I called mamma. Let her know you received the package."

"That reminds me." Heather clipped Charlie's rope lead and led him back to his stable. "I'll get you to take the necklace home with you."

"Oh?"

"All morning, I've worried about it being stolen."

Indulgent, Nathaniel held the stable door open. Once inside, Heather removed Charlie's halter and rope lead. Closing the door behind her, Nathaniel took her hand as they headed toward the office. "How likely is it to be stolen? You know the ins and outs of this place better than anyone."

"I was still terrified it would get taken. You should have had it sent to the pub."

"Mamma wanted to send it to you. Not me."

Easier to blame me when it gets stolen, Heather thought —then immediately felt guilty for it.

"She's glad you like it," Nathaniel said, pressing a kiss to her head.

In the office, Heather let him back her against the door, which he pressed closed, sighing as his lips trailed down her throat.

Her phone vibrated in her back pocket, and Nathaniel groaned. Wiggling slightly to retrieve it, Heather smiled and answered.

"Hello?"

"Heather, hi. It's Peter."

Bracing her hand against Nathaniel's chest, she nudged him back. "Hi, Peter. How are you?"

A long pause. "You need to come to the house."

Heather blinked. "My house?"

"Yes. I'll see you in half an hour."

He hung up.

Staring at the phone, Heather turned to Nathaniel. "Peter wants me at my place. Now."

"I'll drive," Nathaniel said, already moving.

No arguments. Heather slid into the passenger seat and linked her fingers with his once he joined her. As he drove, she described a funny moment from yesterday's Polocrosse class to distract herself.

But as they approached her house and saw the police wagon behind Peter's car, dread sank into her bones.

Sensing her reticence to exit the car, Nathaniel pulled her attention to him by kissing her knuckles. "Let's get this done fast, then we can have an early lunch. It's probably nothing."

"Cops coming to this house's door rarely means nothing," Heather said sickly. Nonetheless, she exited the car, heading up the walkway to the open door.

Catching sight of the smashed living room window, her pace quickened until she took the stairs in one leap, stepping over the threshold with a loud gasp of dismay.

Glass littered the carpet of the front living room, the walls bearing crude renditions of male and female genitalia, as well as the words 'Die bitch, die' in red.

As she stepped further inside, the smell assaulted her nostrils—acrid and overpowering—making her gag and cover her nose quickly.

"Dios mío," Nathaniel muttered beneath his breath. Taking her elbow firmly in his hand, he tugged her back outside to the front veranda.

"Oh my god," Heather felt her throat start to close over as her lungs struggled to draw in enough air. "Oh my god, Nate. Did you see my—my house—my grandparents' house? Who would do such a— That's my house!"

"Shhh." Rarely was he speechless, but in this moment, he had nothing more to offer. Pulling her unresisting body against his chest, he locked his arms tightly around her.

Shivering, Heather couldn't prevent her gaze from swinging back to the open door, the urge to take another look, to confirm, overwhelming.

Unknown minutes later, Peter and local Sergeant Michael stepped out onto the veranda, their expressions grave and uncomfortable.

"Thanks for getting here so quickly." Peter cleared his throat, loosening the tie at his neck. "Terrible business, this, Heather."

Unsure if she felt like crying or laughing aloud, Heather decided the best thing to do was remain silent. Tucked firmly against Nathaniel's chest, she felt his body rumble as he questioned,

"What happened?"

"That's actually what I was going to ask both of you," Michael interrupted, his shrewd brown eyes piercing. "Heather?"

Flabbergasted, Heather glanced between the police officer and her open doorway. "What are you talking about? Are you implying I'd do this to my own house?"

A charged silence, before slowly, Michael shook his head. "No, of course not. Can you think of anybody who'd do something like this though? Do this to you, specifically, Heather?"

"I grew up in this house," Heather murmured, her eyes dry as her stomach started burning. Swallowing back nausea, she felt lost and cold and uncertain.

Violated.

"I spent almost as much time here as my own before my parents died. Then afterwards, I lived here permanently. My—my Opa built this house for Oma when they—when they emigrated. My mother was born in the back bedroom—"

In the end, it was all too much, and Heather felt herself give in to the dam, unable to suck back the agonizing wail that ripped its way from her throat.

"This is my house!" Heather sobbed, clinging to Nathaniel's wide chest. "How could someone do this to my house?"

When her knees gave way, Nathaniel tightened his arms, anchoring her to him—not that she was present, her despair a living entity in the air.

Uncomfortable now, Michael cleared his throat and shifted on his heels, his gaze studying Heather's limp and sobbing form for a long moment.

"How bad is it?" Nathaniel asked, his jaw clenched so tightly it physically hurt.

Peter and Michael shared a look before the officer flipped open a notebook, the pen tip moving down the page as he listed it off.

"Every room has shattered windows, damage in the form of holes to the walls, stained carpet and flooring. Blinds have been ripped down and there's graffiti all over the place—"

Moaning a low, tortured sound, Heather shoved out of Nathaniel's arms and threw herself down the stairs, moving as far away from the small group as she could—towards some bushes.

Bracing her hands on her knees, Heather was then violently sick. When the cramping in her stomach finally eased, she became aware of Nathaniel's large hands bracing her.

"Email me a copy of the report," Nathaniel commanded. Bristling, Michael tucked the notepad back into his pocket. "I'll need Heather to come down to the station, do up a report."

"Not today," Nathaniel said, his tone leaving no room for argument.

"I'll come back to the station with you now," Peter piped up helpfully, stepping in when it appeared the two men were about to argue further. The older man gestured to Heather, who stood listless. "Take her home."

Without waiting for a response, Nathaniel bundled Heather back up into his arms. Whisking her back into his car, he was pulling away from the sidewalk seconds later.

Checking the rear-view mirror, Nathaniel held his phone against his ear. "Josh? Hey, look, Heather is taking the rest of the day. Yeah. No, she's not. Someone broke into her house, it's—it's not good. Yeah. I'll talk to you later. Thanks."

Any minute now, Heather reasoned, someone was going to say 'just joking.'

She was going to wake up, because this was a nightmare.

But every second that ticked over, she felt herself sink further and further into helpless misery. The idea that this was actually happening so utterly abhorrent, Heather wrapped her arms around herself.

It didn't matter though, and it didn't stop her whole body from breaking, her heart a bruised mess that sat heavy and aching in her chest.

"C'mon, *Tesoro*." Nathaniel's voice pulled her from her

agony. Blinking to clear the darkness from her gaze, Heather found him in the space made by her opened door.

Muscles stiff, Heather slowly eased her legs out until she heard her boots crunch on the gravel, but that was as far as she got.

Voice shaking, Heather managed to squeeze the words out. "I—I don't think I can stand."

Easing his arms beneath her knees, Nathaniel wrapped one arm around her back. "Hold onto me, *Tesoro*. I have you."

Doing as she was told, Heather buried her face in the crook of his neck, closing her eyes because keeping them open took too much effort.

A blink of lost time, and Heather roused enough to find herself tucked into the bed, her hair wet from a recent shower. She was comfortably draped over Nathaniel's chest as he lay above the covers.

If she'd had the energy, she might have questioned how they got here—might even have asked who undressed her and slipped the large, soft sleep shirt in place of her work clothes.

Instead, Heather sighed as the weight of the day settled like heavy rocks on her chest. The easiest escape at this point was to close her eyes.

A blink of lost time, and on opening her gaze this time, the shadows stretched from one side of the room to the other, indicating late afternoon.

Over in the kitchen, she could hear Nathaniel speaking rapidly in Italian. Laying on her side, curled into a small ball beneath the blankets, Heather didn't move to confirm his whereabouts. Instead, she let the comforting press of oblivion pull her back under and, with a sigh, Heather pulled the blankets up and over her head.

A blink of lost time—only now Nathaniel was sat towering over her, his expression pinched with determination as he forced a smile for her benefit.

"Are you hungry, *Tesoro*? Mary dropped around her famous chicken soup, and fresh-made garlic bread."

Now that he'd mentioned it, Heather could smell it, her gaze finding the food on her bedside table—but almost immediately, her stomach rebelled.

Turning away with a groan, Heather once more buried beneath the blankets, making herself small beneath the heavy quilt and closing her eyes tight.

Nathaniel had never felt so helpless in his life. It wasn't an emotion he felt comfortable with, but he had no other way of describing those following twenty-four hours.

Had hovering been an Olympic sport, Nathaniel would have been a gold medallist, able to do little else as Heather slept.

When she cried—great gulping sobs that seemed to come straight from her soul—Nathaniel could do nothing more than wrap his body around hers.

Despite the many blankets he piled onto the bed, she was cool to the touch, often shivering loud enough that he could hear the clack of her teeth.

The rare times she woke, she stared straight through him, her skin pale and her expression listless—so out of place on Heather's face that his stomach turned.

People dropped in—Heather's people.

Nathaniel was surprised that it wasn't only her they dropped in for, Mary pulling him into a bone-cracking hug and asking him how he was doing.

Jackson rested one large hand on his shoulder and squeezed, before he told Nathaniel to take a moment and just go outside to breathe.

It had been such a gradual process that Nathaniel had missed the moment Heather's people had become his. And if he hadn't been so concerned about Heather, he might have been annoyed by that.

Famously observant Nathaniel Feria—missing that pivotal moment he'd stopped being Nathaniel Feria, Constance's ex-boss, and become Nathaniel Feria, family.

Right now, all he wanted was for Heather to open her eyes—wanted to hear her drawl something sexy and smart and sharp his way, just because she had that kind of dry humour.

Instead, she slept.

Evening gave way to night, which eventually lightened to early morning, the sun reaching its trajectory at the height of the sky before Heather released a deep sigh.

Having been laid on his back above the covers at her side, Nathaniel glanced over. Meeting her gaze, his heart hiccupped at the sorrow there.

"Did I imagine it?" Heather asked, her voice rough with tears. "Tell me I imagined it."

"I've never wanted to lie to you more in my life than at this very second."

Tears—this time cathartic and healing—as she burrowed into his side. Silent, Nathaniel lent his support in the strength of his arms and the warmth of his body.

Long moments later, Heather pulled away, sniffing but no longer breaking apart at the seams. Mustering her strength, Heather slowly pulled herself upright.

"Shhh." Nathaniel tried to press her back down into the bed. "There's no need to get up, *Tesoro*. Rest."

Shaking her head, Heather swung her legs over the side of the bed. "That police officer—he said he wanted a statement?"

Wary, Nathaniel hurried around to her side. "Yes. I told him he could wait—"

"If you have his number, give him a ring," Heather encouraged, taking his hand and standing on wobbly feet. "I'll take a shower, and we can head down to the station, get it over with."

"Heather—"

"It's OK, Nate. I need to do this."

Proud of her, Nathaniel wrapped his arms around her shoulders, pressing his lips against her hair and breathing in her subtle scent.

Relaxed in his hold, Heather couldn't manage a smile once he'd released her, but she did lift slightly to her toes in order to kiss his cheek.

Watching her walk carefully towards the bathroom, Nathaniel waited until she was out of hearing, before dialling the number on the card Michael had provided.

"Sergeant Reeves." Michael answered, his voice brisk and making Nathaniel's hackles rise instinctively.

Squashing his annoyance, he said slowly, "We'll see you in half an hour."

'CHAPTER EIGHTEEN'

"I can't believe there's absolutely nothing here to use," Heather sighed in frustration, hitting the play button for the millionth time on the keyboard.

On the computer screen, the grey image pixelated slightly as dark shadows danced here and there, passing car lights occasionally piercing the deep night in the recorded image her neighbour had given the cops.

Michael had provided Heather with a copy, but the poor quality and darkness prevented her from noticing anything unusual.

All Heather could see was the appearance of a dark truck pulling into her driveway at midnight, the plates hidden and the occupants indistinguishable by the angle and cover of night.

They departed before dawn, their faces concealed by ski masks and hoodies, with their plates obscured and impossible to make out.

Having returned to the house after giving her statement to the police, Heather had walked, tight-jawed and silent, through the remains of her house.

The ache still as piercing as the day before, dulled somewhat by the anger that coursed through her body.

How dare they, had been all she could think, *how dare*

someone break in and do this to my grandparents house.

News had spread quickly through the town, and Heather hated to say it, but every genuine caller and nosy well-wisher, she'd answered with a deep vein of suspicion.

Michael had said he had no leads, no evidence outside of the video captured by her elderly neighbour's door camera.

"Heather." Glancing up from the screen of his phone, Oliver frowned from his seat on the sofa. "Johnny messaged. Said Coop and Hudson noticed a truck sitting in your street the morning before your place got trashed."

Straightening, Heather screenshotted the paused frame showing the front section of the vehicle. Sending it through to Oliver, she urged, "Send that to Johnny, get the boys to look at it, see if they recognize it."

From the kitchen, Nathaniel brought over the mugs of coffee he'd been preparing. Setting Heather's down, he sat on her armrest to be closer.

"Coop said he thinks yes, but that they didn't pay too much attention to it. Apparently, they were running from Mrs Johnston's dog and thought it unusual to see a truck in the neighbourhood—but were too busy to investigate further."

"Did they happen to catch sight of the person driving it?" Nathaniel asked.

Opening the latest message that came through, Oliver read it quickly and then sighed, shaking his head. "Unfortunately not. Boys said so far as they could tell it was two of them. Passenger was smaller—maybe a woman? They were both wearing caps and the hoodies, looked like they were sleeping. Even then, it was too high either way to tell much more than that."

Deflating, Heather closed the lid of her laptop with a snap. Standing to pace away, she planted her hands on her hips.

"Damnit!"

It was too little to go with, and logically Heather knew it wasn't the twins' fault—but in this moment, she'd have preferred they said nothing so her hopes hadn't been dashed.

Contemplating her, Oliver asked finally, "What are you gonna do, Heath?"

Confused, Heather glanced at him. "What?"

"I know you were just about to put the place up for rent—makes sense, considering you and Nathaniel are living together now and here at the pub. But the house is gonna need some major renovations before it'll be market ready."

"That's already been sorted," Nathaniel said then, settling into Heather's seat comfortably. He continued, "I hired Stan, wrote him a cheque. Anything and everything at his disposal to get the house squared away."

"When did you speak to Stan?" Heather asked slowly, her tone cold. "Why did *you* write him a cheque?"

Surprised, Nathaniel studied Heather carefully. "While you gave Michael your statement. I thought it a good use of time and locked Stan down. Lucky, considering he was working through a few quotes for others needing some work done."

"You didn't think to mention this sooner? It's my house, Nate. You can't just steamroll over me—I should have been the one to hire Stan. To write that cheque. Make those decisions."

"You are my fiancé. I was trying to help."

"No, you were stepping in and taking over. *Watch out! Crisis!* But don't worry, because Nathaniel Feria is here to save the day."

Without either of them noticing, Oliver stood and left on silent feet, feeling too much like a trespasser on a moment he knew neither would appreciate him witnessing.

"I wanted to make this situation easier for you, Heather. I'd just spent the last twenty-four hours watching you lay there in bed like a zombie. *Forgive me!* For trying to be supportive."

Hating that he threw her weakness back in her face, and shoving aside the voice that told her she was being unreasonable, Heather sneered at him. "You come across like the benevolent entrepreneur, Nate. But I'm not an idiot—I know you are five steps ahead of everyone else around you. In the background turning this and manipulating that so things always go your way."

"Why are we fighting?" Nathaniel asked seriously, his expression deliberately blank. "I'd really like to understand how we got to this point, right here, and right now Heather."

Hating the reasonable tone he used on her, the way he sprawled so casually in his chair, the figurative 'kid gloves' he was using to handle her—the final straw breaking the camels back.

Furious for reasons she didn't understand, Heather headed for the door, catching her keys up on her way past—the reason for Oliver's visit as he'd returned her car; also something else Nathaniel had organized.

"Where are you going?" Nathaniel asked, his tone no

longer cautious but deep and commanding as he came to his feet to follow her.

"I just need a god damn minute, Nate. Is that ok with you? Do I need a written note of permission?"

"Heather—"

"I'm going to Emersons, to ride Charlie. *Back off*."

He wanted to argue. God only knows he wanted to chase her out the door, tip her over his shoulder and bar her exit from the rooms.

But Nathaniel had never been accused of being a stupid man, something telling him that if he were to push any harder in this moment, he wouldn't be coming out on top.

So instead, against his instincts and against the ringing warning alarm going off inside his head, Nathaniel said nothing as Heather shoved her boots on and swept from the rooms without a word.

Five minutes ago, Heather had wanted the silence of her empty cab so badly it was a physical taste in her mouth. Now that she was leaving Glen Innes and heading towards Emersons, the silence was oppressive.

In the quiet, she replayed the argument, picturing Nathaniel's face turning pale with hurt before shutting down as she walked away.

"I can take care of my own disasters," Heather growled aloud, the resounding hush that followed her statement mocking her. "I can take care of my own disasters! I can pay my own bills and hire my own builder; I don't need Nate or anyone else running my life. I've been doing it alone since I was eighteen—I'm not helpless!"

But there was something comforting in having someone firmly in your corner, a sly inner voice observed—*so completely in your corner he'd let you say all those hurtful things to him and never once defended himself.*

Feeling like scum, Heather reached for her phone, half her attention trained on the road as she deftly plugged the device into her stereo system.

As her address book loaded, a prickling sensation at the back of her neck warned her of danger.

Reflex drew her gaze to the rear-view mirror, and shock combined with cold resignation sank into her bones—approaching fast, the truck from all those months ago.

The same one from the recording.

She'd just been too shell-shocked and too furious to recognize it.

Pressing her foot down on her accelerator, Heather cursed her stereo as it hummed and hawed, taking its time connecting with her phone.

Less than a car length from hers, Heather frowned, trying to make out the driver—but the truckie had his lights on, and a second later, even the shine of those disappeared.

Pressure on the steering wheel told Heather the truck was now touching her, and naively she hung onto the wheel hopeful that he'd come to his senses and back off. Maybe he'd fallen asleep.

Or had zoned out.

Any minute he was gonna realize he was pushing her along the road, and slow down.

Reaching for the radio, Heather broadcasted, "South along the NEHWY exiting Glen Innes—you're sitting right up my clacker, mate."

Nothing but static replied, and about to repeat herself, she paused as the truckie backed off slightly—her unsteady inhale turning into a choked squeak as he deliberately shunted her.

Heather kept herself in her lane despite the 'danger' warnings echoing through her system. The knowledge that things were about to get worse—instinctual, and with it a sense of helplessness that made her breathless. The truck advanced, the larger vehicle hitting hers and making Heather jolt painfully as the wheel she gripped attempted to wrench free.

Looking for the radio with the intention of telling the driver to *fuck off*, Heather swallowed in dismay as she spotted it on the floor of the passenger side.

Returning her attention to the stereo screen, Heather almost sobbed in relief, hitting the top number in her last dialled list with shaking fingers.

Ring.

"Pick up, Nate," Heather muttered, watching the truck move closer.

Ring.

Although braced for the impact, Heather still felt the jolt through her whole body, hissing at the pain in her shoulders and hands from hanging onto the wheel so tightly.

Ring.

This time, the truckie didn't slow—instead speeding up, and in a split second, Heather knew she wasn't going to be able to hold onto it much longer.

"Heather?"

Opening her mouth, she managed a breathless, "Nate—" before all of a sudden her world was a disorienting blur as she felt her body whiplashed from side to side.

With a loud *thwack*, her head connected with her window—the sound of shattering glass lost amid the noise of metal crunching and the screech of tyres.

Her airbags exploded, hitting her face with such force

that her neck snapped back, momentary darkness a blessed relief.

Coming around to a weird feeling of weightlessness, Heather cracked her eyes open as much as swelling would allow, confused to find her arms above her head.

Unable to feel them, Heather grunted, otherwise unable to move—a hand appeared in her peripherals, and if she could have, she'd have flinched away.

But whoever's hand it was wrapped comfortingly around one of hers, a voice distorted by distance too much for her to understand.

Staring through her windscreen, she tried to make sense of the black skies—only moments ago the day a sunny, clear blue.

Shoes entered her line of sight then, before a body was spreading flat, the face ashen with terror even as he smiled soothingly.

"It's ok. You're ok. I called and paramedics are on their way."

Shaking her head, Heather wanted to ask why there was an ambulance coming—wanted to know how it was that he was hovering over her car like that.

The hand gripping hers squeezed as lips pressed against her ear. "Don't move, Heath. We don't know if there's been any damage done to your spine or neck."

She knew that voice—recognized Jack's gruff tone—but still unable to find the muscles for her mouth, she simply squeezed back in acknowledgement.

Slowly, rational thought returned, as Heather slowly realised she was hanging upside down—her seatbelt tight across her chest and hips, painfully biting into her skin.

The annoying drip was coming from her as blood ran

freely along her skin, getting into her eyes, nose, and mouth.

Eyes fluttering shut, she did her best to listen to Jack as he ordered her awake, as he promised that help would be there soon.

But every second felt like a lifetime—the pain in her body slowly becoming inescapable. She whimpered, feeling weak in this moment, and squeezed Jack's hand a few times to get his attention.

He shifted closer. "Yeah, Heath. I'm here, girl."

With phenomenal effort, Heather located the muscles in her jaw, and ignoring the way unlocking them sent agonizing pain screaming through her system, she whispered, "Tell—tell Nate I'm—I'm sorry and I love—"

"No," Jack interrupted. "No, I ain't carrying that message. No, Heather. You're gonna stay awake. The paramedics and fire department are gonna get here. And you're gonna be fine, do you hear me? I ain't losing you, girl. No ma'am, not on my watch."

Wanting to smile at the pure steel in Jack's voice, Heather squeezed his hand weakly, her lashes fluttering as—regardless of Jack's stern tone—darkness sucked her under.

**

Slowly, Heather became aware of her surroundings. Spreading her fingers wide, she tested the firm but soft sheets beneath her.

Something close by beeped at regular intervals, and hazily, Heather realized that had been what woke her.

After a long search, she located her eyes and forced them open, managing to get one halfway while its partner stayed stubbornly sealed shut.

The air shifted at her side as a large hand encompassed

her own. "Oh my God, *Tesoro*."

Prevented from turning her head, Heather was forced to wait until a familiar face leaned over her prone body. Releasing a sigh, she felt her chest burn.

Tutting softly, Nathaniel smoothed the single tear that managed to force its way out of her swollen eye. Leaning over, he pressed a kiss against her forehead gingerly.

Covered head to toe in open cuts caused by the windows shattering as her car flipped, her face and head had taken the brunt of the trauma.

She'd cracked her skull open against something hard, and the airbags deploying had broken her nose, giving her spectacular matching black eyes.

While she'd been out, doctors had sent her for CAT scans, MRIs, and a myriad of other tests before determining that, thankfully, she would have no lasting spinal issues.

She'd gotten away with a bad case of whiplash despite the fact that her car had cartwheeled down the highway at one hundred kilometres an hour.

Her body would be tender courtesy of the belt marks left across her chest and pelvis—but again, the doctors said it was a miracle the restraints hadn't done more damage to her internal organs than bad bruising.

"Do you remember what happened?" Nathaniel asked gently, holding her hand and being careful to avoid the IV line placed to feed antibiotics and pain relief into her body.

Frowning, Heather tried—her mind unhelpfully blank. Wetting her lips, she swallowed painfully. "No—I. I can't remember anything after leaving the police office."

Trying to hide his surprise, Nathaniel lifted her hand

gently to kiss her knuckles. "Doctor said to expect a bit of confusion. Your head took a big hit."

Confused, Heather used her peripherals to look around. "Where are we?"

Casting his own gaze around the white, sterile room, Nathaniel returned his attention quickly back to Heather. "Sydney."

"Wow," she mumbled.

"Helicopter airlifted you here," Nathaniel revealed, his voice turning unsteady. "Scared the hell out of me, Heather. I never wanna get another phone call like that again—are we clear?"

Squeezing his hand, Heather smiled apologetically. "Promise. Can you tell me what I did to get here, so I can make sure to avoid it in the future?"

He knew she'd said it tongue in cheek, but struggling to find any humour in the situation, Nathaniel sighed. Leaning forward completely, he pressed his forehead against her hand.

"Someone ran you off the road."

In the ensuing silence, you could have heard a pin hitting the floor—Heather's shock palpable in the air. "What?"

"Jack was behind you, but he said a Kenworth wore you like a hood ornament before shoving hard enough to make your car spin out of control. Jack cannot say how far or how long you rolled, but there's very little left of your car—and that speaks for itself."

"The truck?"

"Kept going. Jack had taken down half the license plate before everything happened—was going to report them for tailgating."

"Tailgating?" Laughing, Heather winced in pain and

groaned. "Ahh, don't make me laugh, that hurts."

Frustratingly, the hospital decided to keep Heather for several days, and by the end of the week she was so ready to leave she was dressed and in a wheelchair by eight a.m. and before the doctors' rounds.

Amused, Nathaniel glanced over the top of his computer screen. "*Tesoro*, do not scowl—you'll scare the baby doctors away."

Rolling her eyes, Heather tried to rearrange her expression into something more approachable, reminded of a day earlier that week when she'd accidentally made one of the residents cry.

Heather never had been a good patient—too many days left sitting idly around always put her on the back end of a foul mood.

"I'm not sure that expression is much better," Nathaniel remarked idly, chuckling when Heather poked her tongue out. He half closed his laptop lid as their doctor finally arrived.

Followed in by three residents, Doctor Paensuk was a tiny Asian man in his mid-seventies with sharp features and keen, intelligent brown eyes.

Smiling wide at finding Heather seated expectantly, her bag packed and sitting in her lap, Doctor Paensuk tucked his hands into his white coat.

"Good morning, Miss Ross. How did you sleep last night?"

"Like a log."

"How is your pain today?"

"What pain? Turn on the tunes, Doc. I'll dance a jig."

Under his appraising eye, Heather fidgeted—her face warming as she finally admitted, "It's a steady eight."

"Even after painkillers?"

"Yes."

"Headache?"

"The mother of all headaches, Doc."

Making a low noise at the base of his throat, he accepted her patient folder from one of his residents. With a nod towards another, he opened the charts with an absent sigh.

While he looked through the observations recorded by the night nurse, the resident he'd picked—a tall, cool-eyed beauty who watched Nathaniel from beneath her lashes—booted up the freestanding computer beside Heather's bed.

"Read them out," Doctor Paensuk encouraged, glancing at the Amazonian resident with a parental smile. Needing little prompting, the resident rattled off the nurses' notes for that night.

Trying and failing to smother her blush as the woman also recounted her toileting habits for the last twelve hours, Heather shifted uncomfortably in her chair—but froze as that drew Doctor Paensuk's attention.

Deciding on some honesty, Heather hid her fingers in her lap beneath her bag. "I gotta go home, Doc. I promise I'll take it easy, keep my dressings dry—I won't even leave the bed... but I cannot stay another day in this hospital."

Smiling kindly, Doctor Paensuk moved closer until he could sit on the edge of her bed. Then, leaning over, he patted her knee. "I get the same way after a long day. I'm inclined to release you. But I expect you to comply without question to my instructions for home—you were incredibly lucky to have survived that accident. I'd hate to see all the hard work of your guardian angel undone because you have itchy feet and a phenomenal work ethic."

Before Heather could speak, Nathaniel was there, his voice cool with a hint of authority. "Trust me, Doc — Heather will follow your instructions to the letter. I will ensure it."

Eyes twinkling, the doctor stood and glanced at the blonde resident. "Doctor Tara, I'll leave organizing Miss Ross's discharge in your hands?"

Nodding quickly, the young woman smiled widely at Nathaniel, her voice low as she answered, "It would be my pleasure, Doctor Paensuk."

Lips pouting, Heather held her silence until the resident had left. "God, could she be any more obvious?"

Having returned his attention to his computer, Nathaniel's fingers froze over the keys as he lifted his gaze. "Excuse me?"

"What a wonderful boyfriend you have," Heather simpered in a poor imitation of the blonde doctor. "So handsome. So attentive. My, what strong muscles you have—bleh."

Charmed into silence by the stain of red on his high cheekbones, Heather sighed. "I guess I cannot really blame a girl. Any woman with a heartbeat cannot help but look at you and imagine you between her legs."

Jolting, Nathaniel glanced at the open room door and loosed a chuckle. "*Porca puttana, Tesoro*. Lower your voice, woman."

"You're my fiancé," Heather argued stubbornly. "I can objectify you if I want."

Laughing, Nathaniel closed his laptop with a snap and set it on the table at his side. Then, reaching out across the space, he caught her wheelchair and pulled her close until she sat caged between his knees.

Feeling her muscles loosen at that all-too-familiar glint in his eye, Heather automatically tipped her chin back, ignoring the slight twinge in her neck as the feeling of his lips on hers settled her emotions completely.

"Better?" Nathaniel asked against her lips.

"Yes, thank you."

"So demanding, *Tesoro*." Nathaniel sighed in mock exhaustion. "Lucky for you, I have the stamina to keep up."

"You're so vain," Heather said, smiling as she wound her arms around his neck, tugging him closer to press another deep, searching kiss against his mouth.

His expression careful, Nathaniel rubbed the pads of his thumbs along her jaw. "Marry me."

"I've already said yes," Heather rolled her eyes, moving to sit back.

Nathaniel tightened his grip. "Next month."

Shocked, she hovered on the knife edge of indecision. "Nate—there's no reason to rush into something that—"

"You think I will change my mind? That somehow I will decide I no longer wish to marry you?" Nathaniel gripped the arms of her wheelchair, dragging her closer still. "You are mine—have been mine since the very first moment I laid eyes on you. I would marry you here and now if I thought you'd let me. But you deserve the wedding of your dreams. Do not keep me waiting, *Tesoro*."

"Planning a wedding takes months..." Heather hedged, her resolve crumbling.

"Leave it to me," Nathaniel coaxed. Dipping his chin, he sipped gently from her mouth. "Just say yes."

Sighing, Heather capitulated. "Yes."

'CHAPTER NINETEEN'

That morning had been a whirlwind, full of excitement and a touch of nervousness. Heather had woken up early, the sun barely peeking over the horizon, to get ready for the most important day of her life.

In front of the mirror, a makeup artist worked her magic, Heather's reflection a blur of happy anticipation. Her heart had been racing, but not from nerves—rather from anticipation.

As she'd slipped into the dress, the one she had picked out barely two weeks ago, Heather couldn't help but marvel at how everything was falling into place. The fabric hugged her in all the right places, the lace delicate and intricate, and for a moment, she felt like she was in a dream. The soft bustle of the bridal suite around her, the quiet excitement, the low hum of conversation—it all felt surreal.

She glanced at her phone one last time, waiting for Nathaniel's message, unable to prevent the slow smile that spread across her face at the texts they'd exchanged that morning. His words were a perfect mix of excitement and reassurance. It made her feel like everything would be okay, that they were embarking on this new chapter together, no matter what.

And now, here they were, standing together as husband and wife, a quiet happiness between them as they shared this moment. Nathaniel's hand was warm and solid in hers, anchoring her in the present even as Josh's voice filled the air.

"...and then Nathaniel, in his infinite wisdom, decided that he could 'definitely' build the bookshelf himself, what with his last name being Feria after all."

Heather chuckled, remembering the story Josh was sharing, the way Josh was really leaning into the story causing Nathaniel's cheekbones to darken to an attractive pink.

The crowd laughed along as Josh finished off his toast with a flourish, and for a moment, Heather lost herself in the joy of the evening—the love surrounding her, the promise of all the tomorrows they would face together.

In the end, moving the wedding date up had been the right decision.

Heather raised her glass to her lips, letting the fresh, sparkling taste of the expensive champagne flood her taste buds.

With a happy sigh, Heather turned her gaze to Nathaniel. When he squeezed her fingers gently, meeting the warmth in his gaze, she softened and leaned slightly closer.

"Are you happy, *Tesoro*?" Nathaniel asked softly.

"More than words can possibly describe," Heather murmured. "Are you happy?"

"Si, *Tesoro*." Bridging the distance between them, Nathaniel released a gusty sigh, his lips resting softly against her temple. "I will be happier still once I have you alone..."

Shivering at the promise in his tone, Heather subtly nodded. "I don't think we would be missed if we were to make our way towards the exit."

Needing no further encouragement than that, Nathaniel had her on her feet, hand clasped warmly in his, moving them towards the exit.

"Can I get a final picture of the new Mr and Mrs Feria?" Johnny called out, interrupting Heather's train of thought. She blinked until her surroundings once more filled her gaze.

Already, Nathaniel had tucked her close to his side, and glancing around, Heather realised they were slowly making their way towards the exit.

"Quickly, Johnny. I want Mrs Feria all to myself now—no more sharing."

Chuckling, Johnny snapped a few candid shots before raising his hands and moving away. Standing in front of the large double doors, Heather smiled as Nathaniel gave her space.

Around her, the single women who had attended the wedding gathered, their faces bright with teasing mischief as they jostled each other.

"Here, Heath!" Isla yelled, shoving her elbow towards Grace, who, having had her attention diverted off to the side, stumbled.

"Oi!" Recovering quickly, Grace mock growled as she threatened to kick, her gaze bright with amusement even as something slid slowly off her expressive face.

Waiting a few more moments until everyone was in place, Heather turned, finding Nathaniel's gaze hot and demanding on her body.

Smirking at his bold perusal, Heather raised her eyebrow, then with a casual toss sent her bouquet flying over her shoulder.

The clatter of heels on wood and the sound of rustling silk and chiffon—until a sudden silence. Surprised, Heather turned and couldn't contain her bark of laughter.

Heather's wedding bouquet held stretched away from her body, Hope was staring at the pretty floral arrangement with a look that was a cross between dismay and horror etched onto her pretty face.

Behind her, Heather noticed Matteo stood, one hand casually tucked into the pocket of his slacks, the other holding a sleek mobile phone to his ear.

But it was his attention—dark and focused on Hope as she tried unsuccessfully to give the flowers away—that made a small sliver of concern slide down Heather's spine.

Matteo was Nathaniel's brother, and therefore he was now a part of Heather's family—and Heather had no boundaries when it came to her family.

Hope had been Heather's family longer, the older woman able to remember Hope's first period—hell, her first training bra.

"I know, *Tesoro*." Nathaniel's voice, smooth as silk, as his arms wrapped warm around her waist, his lips at her ear as he joined her in watching the scene before them. "I have noticed it too."

Relaxing somewhat, Heather nibbled on her lower lip. "Hope has demons, Nate. Same as Faith—same as Grace…"

"Matteo knows of demons, Heather. He has his fair share of them himself."

Nodding slowly, Heather resisted somewhat when Nathaniel would have moved them away. "Still…"

"Not today, *Tesoro*. Today is for us."

Sighing, Heather took a long moment to deliberately relax her shoulders, turning her attention away from Matteo and Hope.

When Nathaniel wrapped his arm around her waist, she let him continue leading them towards the exit, accepting the well-wishes and congratulations.

By the door they connected with the wedding planner, an attractive woman in her mid-thirties so scarily competent the day had run without a hitch.

"Thank you," Heather said on a gusty sigh. Reaching out, she accepted the hand extended her way. "I'm so grateful for everything you've done to make this day the success that it's been."

"My pleasure, Mrs Feria. Now, I've already had your bags packed into the boot of the car—it's waiting for you both now. Pilot has been notified, so he and the flight crew will be ready for take-off once you both have arrived. It's been my pleasure, and thank you both for including me in your special day."

Nathaniel gently placed his hand on Heather's back. With one last look at the room and the ongoing celebration, they left.

As promised, the car destined to take them to the airport idled silently at the curb, Nathaniel and Heather sharing a slow, intimate glass of champagne as the black town car slid effortlessly through traffic.

Delivered on the tarmac to the bottom of the stairs of Nathaniel's jet, Heather felt overwhelmed and happily exhausted, tucked close to her new husband as he ushered her onboard and into her seat.

Buckling her in, Nathaniel tipped her chin up and took her lips in a scorching kiss, his words low and for her alone as he promised, "As soon as we are in the air, *Tesoro*, I will show you the rest of the cabin—including the large, comfortable bed I have at the back of the plane."

Shivering, it was all Heather could do to contain her arousal, forced to sit there for the next twenty minutes as the cabin crew ran through their checks, and the pilot came and spoke in deferential tones to them both.

Once they'd reached cruising altitude, Nathaniel stood and held his hand out for her, his expression both compelling and demanding in this moment.

"They'll hear—" Heather whispered, her hand already reaching for his, her body pliant as he pulled her from her seat and flush against his hardening body.

"They wear headphones," Nathaniel slid his hands down the length of her spine to settle them on the curve of her hips, "will do so until breakfast. Scream as loud as you please, Tesoro. I want to hear my name on your lips."

Gasping as he took her mouth in a demanding kiss, Heather felt her body moving, knew he manoeuvred her past the line of seats towards a door she'd spotted at the back.

Hands greedy, Nathaniel filled them with the soft globes of her bottom, shaping and plumping the flesh. He closed the door with his heel, the cabin's light muted. A hand in the centre of her chest sent Heather sprawling across white silk sheets, her giggle punctuating the soft atmosphere.

Unbuttoning his white dress shirt, Nathaniel dragged his gaze over her supine form, his jacket and tie having already been discarded in the backseat of the limo.

"Shall I undress?" Heather asked, lifting to her

elbows. She watched hungrily as Nathaniel exposed the smooth, tanned skin of his chest.

"No." Voice rough, Nathaniel prowled towards her until she lay beneath him, caged by his body. "All day I have fantasized about what I would do, once we were alone. I want to ruin you, *Tesoro*."

Heather shivered as he bent his head to nibble the plumped-up flesh displayed above her corset, and he released a deep groan as he ground the hardened length of his cock between her thighs.

Sighing, Heather lifted her arms to wrap them around his shoulders. "Show me…"

So he did.

**

Forty-eight hours later, Heather sighed as the gondola glided through the serene canals of Venice, its slow, steady motion barely causing a ripple in the water. The golden light of dusk was falling over the city, casting soft shadows over the centuries-old buildings that lined the waterways.

Heather leaned back against the plush cushions, her fingers intertwined with Nathaniel's as they both relaxed into the evening's quiet rhythm. The air was warm, a gentle breeze carrying the scent of saltwater and freshly baked bread from nearby cafes.

"Venice," Heather whispered, her voice filled with wonder as she looked around at the majestic city. "It's everything I imagined—and so much more."

Nathaniel's smile was lazy, his gaze soft as he watched her face light up in the glow of the fading sun.

"I'm glad you like it," Nathaniel murmured, squeezing her hand gently.

Heather turned her head to meet his gaze, her smile

tender and full of love. "I love you."

They passed under a low archway, the water darkening as they moved into a quieter section of the city. The gondola's oars dipped silently into the water with every stroke, the soft splash blending with the distant sounds of the city—laughing children, the clink of glasses, the occasional call of a gondolier guiding his passengers.

The gondola's wooden sides creaked gently as the boat moved through the calm water, but it was the silence between Nathaniel and Heather that felt most comforting—a shared space where no words were necessary.

Tucked into his side, Heather leaned her head on his shoulder, her eyes closing as tranquillity settled into her bones.

Nathaniel's fingers brushed the skin of her thigh above her knee, revealed by the short hem of the pretty sundress she wore. The light was fading quickly now, the sky deepening into shades of lavender and pink, and the city's lights began to twinkle to life, reflecting off the water like thousands of tiny stars.

Heather sighed, "I'd return if Venice was ever an option as a holiday destination."

"Even with how long the flight was?" Nathaniel asked, his tone amused—between them hovered Heather's annoyance and edgy energy from the almost twenty-four-hour long flight.

Gaze lit, she lifted her eyebrows as she slid him a look heavy with intent. "You managed me quite well. I'm confident you're up to the task of getting me through another flight."

Gaze darkening, Nathaniel recalled the hours he'd spent buried in her willing body. "You can count on it," he said, his words quiet, carrying the weight of burgeoning arousal.

Heather's fingers tightened slightly around his. "I wish I could freeze time—stop it right here, right now."

Nathaniel shifted slightly, his thumb tracing small circles on her hand as the gondola passed under another bridge, its reflection rippling in the water.

Slowly, the vessel bumped into the stone of the canal walls, drawing Nathaniel and Heather from their small bubble. They met the kind smile of their gondolier guide.

Having returned them to where they started, Heather waved her thanks, accepting Nathaniel's hand as he helped her onto firm ground.

"Are you hungry, *Tesoro*?" Nathaniel pressed his lips against the shell of her ear, his hand possessively low on her abdomen.

"Yes." Reaching back for him, Heather led the way back to their room, blind to the splendour around her as the hunger of her need for him drove her to the privacy of their hotel.

Hours later, Nathaniel sighed, his hand tracing lazy patterns against Heather's back, her moan of complaint a soft puff of air against his chest as she sprawled naked across his body.

"Time for dinner," he said as he rolled her unceremoniously off onto the cool sheets of their bed, smiling when she grumbled and continued rolling away until she lay on her stomach.

The sheets now bunched beneath her exposed the long, slender lines of her naked body, and unable to help himself, Nathaniel moved down until he was able to bite the pale flesh of her bottom.

Squealing slightly, Heather swatted ineffectively in his direction. Nathaniel, dodging easily enough, sent a stinging slap across the globe closest to his hand.

Enthralled as the flesh bounced, he shifted until he sat above her, his legs caging her own so that any kicks she aimed his way were now impossible.

In quick succession, he rained short, stinging slaps down on Heather's upturned bottom, loving the way they jiggled after each touch and Heather's ineffectual struggles.

"Nate!" Panting in a confusing mix of anger, embarrassment, and need, Heather tried twisting her upper body to dislodge him—and failed.

Unable to move, she had to submit, her gasps coming louder until a final sharp swat. She felt his legs loosen, thinking to scramble to her knees and escape. Heather made it as far as lifting to her hands and knees.

Then Nathaniel planted one firm hand between her shoulder blades, shoving her face down into the mattress.

About to call him every name under the sun, Heather instead loosed a wail, Nathaniel using the new position to drive his hard cock balls-deep in a single thrust.

"Oh God," Heather moaned, gripping the sheets beneath her now, her body tight as need sang through her veins. The anger, the confusion she felt at being so worked up by what she considered an embarrassing spanking, completely forgotten by the bite of pain and pleasure his possession created.

"Good girl," Nathaniel grunted, his hands on her hips bands of steel as he moved her body however he wished. "That's my good, beautiful, sexy *Tesoro*. So wet. So ready. So mine."

"Nate!" Shouting as her climax ripped with sudden violence through her, and pulling her body upright, Heather could do nothing but hold onto the forearm Nathaniel wrapped around her stomach.

Anchored by nothing more than his unyielding hold as he moved powerfully in and out of her body, the wet sound of his ownership pushing Heather higher until her final release hit.

The feel of her inner muscles clenching down hard—the final straw for Nathaniel, who pressed her warm body back down into the soft mattress, pinning her there while he emptied himself into her willing body.

For long moments afterward, they lay like this—Heather's chest cushioned by the mattress, her back slick with sweat and cradled by Nathaniel's wide body as he lay skin-to-skin against her.

His cock still buried intimately deep.

When her inner muscles fluttered once more, Nathaniel groaned and then carefully eased out. Pulling her until she lay on her back, he kissed her fast and sweet.

"Enough. If we do not get out of bed right now, and you don't put some damn clothes on, I'll have you again."

Chuckling, Heather stretched. "Mmm, I'm hungry."

"We have a standing reservation down at the hotel's restaurant," Nathaniel slid unashamed from the bed, his naked body gloriously displayed to Heather's gaze.

"I want to try somewhere else." Heather watched greedily as her husband dressed. Sitting up, she wrapped her arms around her knees.

"Somewhere in particular, *Tesoro*?" Nathaniel buttoned the top of his jeans, dragging his hands through his hair as he considered two well-made but slightly casual button-up shirts.

"Earlier when we were window shopping, I noticed a little pizza place."

Turning at the subtle thread of uncertainty in her tone, Nathaniel moved closer, and reaching out, pulled her lower lip from between her teeth. "Whatever you desire, it is yours. If you want pizza for dinner—pizza it is."

"You don't mind that it's not a restaurant?"

Physically hauling her from the bed, Nathaniel ran his hands down to cup her bottom. "Why would I mind?"

At her silence, Nathaniel moved back slightly until he could search out and hold her gaze. "Why would I mind, *Tesoro*?"

"You're just—I mean, I doubt you'd eat pizza from some small, hole-in-the-wall pizza joint."

Smiling in amusement, Nathaniel asked, "Are you calling me a snob?"

"I don't know," smiling herself now, Heather sent him a look, "if the size twelve, expensive Italian leather shoe fits."

Just for that, Nathaniel tumbled her back into bed, his possession fast and hard and peppered by laughter that turned into gasps.

The cobblestone streets of Venice were quieter now, the bustling energy of the day settling into a calm evening rhythm. The sun had dipped below the horizon, leaving a cool, dusky sky that shimmered with the last hints of pink and lavender.

Nathaniel and Heather walked side by side, hands entwined and their bodies brushing every so often as they strolled along the narrow streets.

The soft murmur of conversation drifted from a nearby café, and the occasional clink of glasses or the gentle hum of a gondola's oars reminded them they were still in the heart of Venice—but the evening had a more intimate, peaceful feel now.

"This place is unreal," Heather said, her voice warm and content as she glanced up at the winding streets and the intricate canals snaking between the buildings.

After a few more turns, they reached a small, unassuming restaurant tucked between two larger buildings.

The warm glow of the sign read *Pizzeria Da Giorgio,* its rustic charm evident in the simple wooden tables and chairs lining the street outside. A few locals sat at the tables, chatting over glasses of wine, and the smell of freshly baked pizza wafted from the open door.

Heather's face lit up. "Here it is! When I spotted it earlier it wasn't this busy, but this is exactly what I imagined it would look like in the evening." She tugged Nathaniel inside, her excitement evident as she led him to an empty table by the window.

The interior was cozy and intimate, with terracotta floors, exposed brick walls, and soft candlelight flickering on the tables.

The atmosphere was casual but welcoming, and a few Italian phrases floated in the air—one in particular sent their way making Nathaniel grin.

The menu was handwritten on chalkboards above the counter, the choices simple but delicious, promising authentic wood-fired pizzas and classic dishes.

Nathaniel took a seat opposite Heather. "This is perfect," he said, leaning back in his chair and looking around. "I think we've found the right place to be tonight."

Heather took a deep breath, savouring the scents that filled the air. "I'm so glad we're doing this. After the last couple of days, I think a simple pizza night is exactly what we needed."

In comfortable silence, they perused the menu, trying to decide between the many tempting options. Heather finally pointed to the pizza she wanted. "I'm going for the Margherita—classic and simple. What about you?"

Nathaniel glanced over the choices before landing on a more daring option. "I think I'll go for the Quattro Stagioni. I'm in the mood for something with a little more variety."

Heather laughed, her eyes twinkling as she handed him her menu. "I like the way you think."

The waiter, a cheerful man with a thick Italian accent and superb English, took their orders and disappeared into the kitchen.

They sat back, enjoying the hum of conversation around them and the rhythmic clinking of glasses.

Outside, the street was bathed in the soft glow of the streetlights, the shadows lengthening as the city embraced the night.

When their pizzas arrived, they were golden—the crusts crispy and steaming with fresh toppings. The conversation between them was unhurried and intimate as they took slow, savouring bites.

The world slipped slowly further into darkness until it was just the two of them, and once the bill was paid, the streets outside were quiet with the unhurried steps of other lovers finishing up their evenings.

Heather looped her arm through Nathaniel's, her head resting against his shoulder as they walked slowly through the streets of Venice, taking in the charm of the night.

The world around them was full of beauty and wonder,

but the greatest part of it was being there together.

'CHAPTER TWENTY'

"Why is there so much paperwork?" Heather moaned, slumped back in her office chair. She chucked her pencil across the room like a petulant toddler.

"That's what happens when you go off gallivanting around the world on your honeymoon," Constance retorted teasingly. Stepping into the room, she closed the door behind her. Bending to pick up the discarded pencil, she eyed it. "Good grief, Heath. What the hell did you do to this poor thing?"

Twisting her face, even as she accepted the gnawed-on pencil back, Heather popped it into the top drawer of her desk and grunted.

Settled comfortably in the chair opposite, Constance ran her gaze curiously over Heather's lazy figure, her hand pressed against the swell of her stomach. "I'd expect after several days in Venice, the most romantic place to honeymoon in the world, one would be returning a little less grumpy. What is it? Did Nate keep you up with lots of hot, Italian sex and now, rather than being refreshed, you're exhausted?"

Smirking, Heather refused to answer. "Seriously though, Connie. Did anyone even step foot in here while I was gone?"

"No."

"No?"

Shaking her head as Constance repeated her answer, she grinned when Heather groaned. "No one comes into your domain, Heath. The juniors are worried you'll be here lurking with more chores for them to do. The older guys don't want to mess up your filing system."

"It's alphabetical! For pity's sake, it's not rocket science —"

"Have you been for a ride on Charlie yet?" Constance interrupted, already knowing what she was implying. Heather frowned.

"That's not the problem. The problem is no one can—"

"I think that's what we should do right now," Constance declared, standing with a soft grunt. She went to the door and threw it open, standing there to glance back at Heather with a raised eyebrow. "Come on, then?"

Grumbling, Heather stood, sulking behind the smaller woman all the way to Charlie's stall. She refused to laugh when he stood already saddled and ready to go.

Holding the stall door open, Constance gestured with her chin for Heather to head in. "Have fun, you two. Heather, I'll see you when you both get back."

Quickly attaching reins to his halter, Heather didn't bother with a bit or anything like that—simply led Charlie past a grinning Constance.

In the laneway leading away from the indoor arena, Heather swung herself up onto Charlie's back, her shoulders loosening as her thighs tightened to grip the saddle.

With familiarity, soon she and Charlie were trotting, moving as one through the long grass across paddocks and through gates, heading towards one of the tracks that connected to the forestry behind Emersons.

In the distance, Heather raised her arm in greeting as she spotted two slender figures on horseback, recognizing Ryan and Mark even from more than five hundred metres away.

When Heather and Charlie finally returned to Emersons, she could admit to feeling more settled— a sense of normalcy falling across her shoulders in a familiar embrace.

By that evening, she had finished the paperwork that had piled up on her desktop, and entering the warm glow of the kitchen, the smile she wore in response to Constance's raised brow was her usual one.

Setting a plate of food she'd kept warm in the oven, Mary slid into the chair at Heather's side, her expression warm. "How did you enjoy Venice?"

Face turning bright, Heather regaled Mary and Constance with stories of her and Nathaniel's experiences—straying far from the hours upon hours they had spent wrapped in each other's arms.

"Sounds like you got the ultimate romantic honeymoon," Mary said with a sigh, collecting Heather's empty plate. "I'm that pleased for you, Heath. Nate absolutely adores you."

Warm, Heather stood and quickly pressed her lips against Mary's, thanking the older woman for dinner. She waved at Constance as she exited to the car park.

Heading back towards Glen Innes and the rooms above the pub that she now considered home, Heather parked in her usual spot and took the stairs upstairs as quickly as she could.

Bypassing the first room Nathaniel had as his office, Heather shrugged out of her coat as she pushed open the door to the kitchen.

"Nate—babe, I'm home—oh."

Freezing at the sight of Nathaniel's mother seated at the breakfast island, Heather felt her stomach sink slightly at the woman's blank expression.

Heather had been too overwhelmed to notice Sofia's absence at the wedding, but now the silent disapproval over their vows had settled in.

Heather knew Sofia didn't like her—had known all those months ago when the woman visited, her words and opinions a whip to feelings surprisingly tender.

"You ignored what I told you then," Sofia's voice, soft but full of glass, settled between them like silent grenades. "I thought I made my opinion very clear when last we spoke."

The memory of a late-night phone call overwhelming her into silence—Heather's heart shattered as Sofia told her in no uncertain terms, "You are not good enough for my son."

"I love him," Heather said, wishing her voice was stronger than it was. "He loves me."

"You are a wet cunt in which he can dip his cock, but you are not good enough for the Feria name. Not worth the children he will plant in your womb—here."

Gaze dropping to the kitchen benchtop, Heather felt herself drawn closer, her hand thankfully steady as she reached out to pluck up the slip of paper Sofia pushed her way.

Heather felt her heart squeeze as she quickly read off the large amount printed neatly on the cheque. "What is this?"

"Incentive."

"Incentive to what?"

"Pack your bags and remove yourself from my son's life. More than enough there to start somewhere else—somewhere far away."

"Leave Nathaniel?"

"Leave Glen Innes."

"What?" Astonished, Heather raised her gaze to Sofia's. "I grew up here—half the people here are related to me by blood. This is my home—"

"As Perth is home to Nathaniel! Perth—where his family blood resides, where he belongs!"

"It's not my fault he doesn't want to live in Perth anymore," Heather said, releasing a shaky breath. She carefully placed the cheque back onto the benchtop and stepped away. "I didn't ask him to move here."

"You tempted him here like the whore that you are—" Sofia hissed, sliding from her stool. She moved around the bench towards Heather, brown eyes so like her son's lacking all warmth or care. "Stupid girl—did you really think he loved you?"

"That's enough." Nathaniel's voice—hard as stone and deep in anger—pulled both Heather's and Sofia's gazes towards the door leading from the office to the landing. In it, they found both Nathaniel and Matteo.

"My boys." Sofia's tone softened, welcoming, as she brushed past Heather, her arms open and her face cleared of the malice it had held—now gentled with love.

"I heard you," Nathaniel said, his expression dark as he stopped Sofia's approach with a firm look. "Matteo and I both heard you, Mamma."

Shrugging, unrepentant, Sofia clasped her hands in front of her. "They are not words I have not already spoken to you, Nathaniel. I told you I did not condone your relationship."

Gasping, Heather pressed a hand to the space above her heart, unaccountably betrayed as she glanced at him with wide eyes. "Nate? Is that true?"

Jaw firming, Nathaniel extended his hand toward her. "Come here, *Tesoro*."

Was he joking? Shaking her head, Heather backed away, glancing deeper into the apartment behind her, hating that the only way out was past Nathaniel and his mother.

"Why the hell did you even marry me?" Heather choked out, withdrawing further. She ignored the expression on Nathaniel's face, her heart seizing in her chest as her throat closed. "Oh my God, I can't breathe."

"Take Mamma," Nathaniel ordered, not bothering to watch as Matteo literally hauled a spluttering Sofia from the room. His whole attention was focused on Heather as she clutched her chest and backed away from him.

"*Tesoro*, you need to breathe."

"Fuck you—"

"Once you can breathe," Nathaniel said carefully, herding Heather toward the bed, "I will indeed fuck you, to within an inch of your life. And you will scream for me, *Tesoro*, as you always scream for me."

"Son of a bitch," Heather felt a second wind hit her, all her anger and hurt convalescing into a ball of rage. "You son of a bitch! I'm not leaving. Glen Innes is *my* home. You and your mother take your filthy money and shove it up your—"

She bit off the rest of her words as Nathaniel moved, striking faster than a brown snake.

He had her flat on her back in the middle of the bed

before she even realised he'd moved, ignoring the way she writhed beneath him—her anger only fanned by how easily he dodged her fists.

"Get off—" she grunted, as each punch or kick was carefully redirected, Nathaniel's hard body above her easily subduing hers.

"No."

When she felt his lips against the fragile shell of her ear, Heather gasped—anger and hurt sliding from her chest to pool low in her stomach. Mortified, Heather felt the space between her legs pulse as it warmed in readiness.

"No—don't!"

"No one is leaving. Glen Innes is ours. But I agree—my mamma can take any money she offered you, and she can shove it up her arse." Deliberately, Nathaniel shoved his hand beneath the waistband of Heather's jeans, ignoring the way she bucked against him to hook his fingers around the gusset of her undies.

Hissing, Heather tried headbutting him but knew it lacked any real intent, her whole body strung tight now with expectation as she felt his fingers feather through the lips of her sex.

Groaning in appreciation at how wet she was, Nathaniel rested his forehead against hers. "Why didn't you tell me how cruel she was being?"

Straining in an effort to move away from those softly seeking fingers, Heather grunted. "Don't—why didn't you tell me it's all things she's said to you before?"

"Because, despite what she may think on the matter, I am a grown man, and I know my own heart and mind." With her twisted up so helplessly beneath him, she was incapable of stopping him as he speared two fingers deep into her wet heat, curling them to rub against that spot within that drove her wild.

Whimpering, Heather turned her face aside, even as she lifted her bottom—meeting the rough glide of his fingers as he pumped them in and out of her welcoming body.

"You are mine," Nathaniel muttered, his lips hot on the long column of her throat. "Mine, mine, mine..."

Refusing to agree with him was her only means of rebellion, his knowledge of her body such that he had her toppling over the edge to climax on another wail.

Limp, save for the way her body trembled at the force of her release, Heather was pliant as she felt him strip her lower body of her boots, jeans, and underwear. Deaf and dumb to everything until he flipped her onto her stomach and then slid in deep, gasping—Heather gripped the bed beneath her, expecting his possession to be fast and rough.

Instead, he forced her fingers to release their grip so he could thread his own through them, pinning her arms to the bed as he stretched the long line of his body over hers like a blanket.

This close, she could feel his heartbeat thundering against her back, could feel the tiny, subtle flex of his hips as he rocked deeper inside her.

"Where were you?" Heather demanded, her voice wet with tears—hating how her heart trembled at the kisses he rained apologetically along her face.

"I have a surprise for you. I had Matteo installing some security for it, and we lost track of time. I didn't know my mother was coming to town, *Tesoro*. I do not leave you alone with her—for that reason alone."

Releasing a single sob as he moved against her in a firm thrust, Heather acknowledged silently that she had noticed his reticence to leave her alone with his mother. Something she had always ignored until now—another way in which Nathaniel was protecting her without her knowing.

"You should have told me what she thought," Heather argued finally, moving to tighten her own fingers in his —her body shifting slightly to meet the movement of his hips.

"You think I didn't see how much you wanted my mamma's love?" Nathaniel grunted, working his body firmly above Heather's. He pressed his lips against her ear. "I wasn't going to break your heart, *Tesoro*. I would have taken her words to the grave. I would have protected you from her opinion, even if that meant burning the world to the ground. Because you deserve nothing less. You are everything, and no one—no one is allowed to make you feel less. Especially my mamma."

The fight drained from her body, and feeling her acquiescence, Nathaniel pulled his glistening cock free, roughly twisting Heather until she lay looking up at him on her back. He hooked the backs of her knees in his hands and pressed them up and out, spreading her completely as he pinned them either side of her ears.

Folded like this, when Nathaniel plunged back into the wet heat of her, the end of his cock kissed her cervix. Heather cried out as the bite of pain instantly triggered her release.

"Yes," Nathaniel hissed, jerking his hips hard and fast as the sheets beneath them became wet with desire. "Such a good fucking girl. Come all over this hard dick— scream my name, *Tesoro*."

So she did.

By the time Nathaniel finally paused in owning her

body, the apex of her thighs was a throbbing, sticky mess she desperately wanted to shower off—but her attempt to leave the bed was once more thwarted.

His arm a band around her waist, Nathaniel dragged her back into the curve of his body. His short denial when she demanded to use the restroom forgotten a moment later.

With her back pressed firmly against his chest, his arms around her body, he locked her in place with his hardened cock buried intimately deep inside her.

"Sleep," Nathaniel demanded—and somehow, she did.

At some point in the night they both came awake. Lying facing each other, Heather had her hands clasped beneath her chin as she studied Nathaniel's shadowed face.

"What are we going to do?" she asked, finally breaking the silence of the room.

Raising one eyebrow, Nathaniel said, "About what? My mamma?" At her silent nod, Nathaniel released a gusty sigh, reaching out to settle a hand on her hip. "Nothing."

"Nothing?"

"Not a damn thing. What she said—those words are hers and hers alone. They do not represent what I feel or think. They have no bearing on our life, nor the life we will create here."

Feeling weepy, Heather sniffed and blinked rapidly. "How can you say that? She's your mum."

"Heather, my relationship isn't like yours was with your mum. It is twisted, and it is complicated, and it is conditional. I meant what I said—I am grown and I have wants and desires, and they all include you. I married you. You have my last name. It's too late now, Heather. I will never let you go. You're mine."

Moving almost before he'd finished speaking, Heather pressed her lips to his, opening her mouth automatically to accept the tongue he pushed past her teeth.

The rest of the night was a blur of passion and possession—whether it was Nathaniel taking her, or Heather astride, riding him to completion.

**

As the sun finally peeked above the horizon, Heather and Nathaniel shared a long shower. Opting to skip breakfast, Nathaniel pressed her into the passenger seat of his car.

"I want to show you my surprise—albeit eight hours or so later than originally planned."

Smiling, Heather reached across the centre console to hold his hand in hers, yawning slightly as she turned her attention to the windscreen to watch as they left Glen Innes and headed out along the highway.

"Better late than never," she muttered, curious as after fifteen minutes they pulled off the highway towards an area she recognised. "Ryan lives out this way."

Making a low noise of assent, Nathaniel squeezed her hand. "Emersons is another fifteen minutes up the road."

"Yes, I know."

"Plus, it's about fifteen minutes from the centre of town and the pub."

Frowning suspiciously, Heather watched as he took a left into a driveway, heading along the gravel dirt road as if familiar with the place.

"Where are we?"

Nathaniel's lips lifted in a smirk. "My surprise."

The long driveway stretched ahead like a ribbon, the

worn gravel crunching beneath the tyres as Nathaniel slowly navigated his way along.

Rolling down her window, Heather inhaled deeply—the air thick with the scent of dry earth and eucalyptus, mingled with the subtle, comforting fragrance of distant wildflowers.

On either side, the land rolled gently, the initial scrubby grassland and ancient eucalyptus trees giving way to paddocks, delineated by simple wooden posts strung with four strands of tight wire.

In the early morning sun, the landscape was bathed in soft gold, the distant hills lit in silhouettes of muted green.

After what seemed forever, Heather spied the end— loving the thick stand of towering trees that framed the end of the driveway as the car rattled over a cattle grid. And there, at the crest of a small rise, stood the house— a beautifully renovated old colonial.

Its whitewashed timber exterior gleamed, and the grand, wraparound veranda stood out, inviting you into the calm, timeless charm of the home.

Tall and proud, with a wide, sloping roof that extended over the verandas, offering shade and shelter from the harsh Australian sun. Its large, symmetrical windows reflected the warm light of the day, and the black iron railings on the veranda were intricately designed, adding a touch of elegance to the home's rustic charm.

Around the house, the garden was a mix of carefully tended flowerbeds and wild, native plants, the sound of birdsong and cows lowing filling the air.

Breathless with anticipation, Heather glanced at Nathaniel in open shock as he slowly rolled the car to a standstill. "What did you do?"

"I bought you a house," Nathaniel stated as simply as if he were commenting on the weather. "I haven't the skill as your Opa did to build you one, but I listened when you spoke to me of your wants and needs.

A house with space for the family we will one day have. Land enough to breed horses of your own. For Charlie to live never more than an arm's length away. Maybe now I will wake in the mornings to your pretty face still beside me in bed, *Tesoro.*"

Unsnapping her belt, Heather crawled across the tiny space, loving the way Nathaniel's deep, rumbling laughter filled the car's interior as she sat astride him.

Framing his face with her hands, Heather was speechless for a long moment—dragging her gaze over the features of a face she had grown to need as much as she needed air.

"You bought me a house?" Heather whispered, undone by the way his gaze softened, his hands gentle as they wrapped around her waist.

"I would offer you the world, if that's what you wanted," Nathaniel said seriously, wondering if now this beautiful, stubborn, amazing woman would finally understand the depth of his devotion.

"I love it," she breathed. "Show me the rest of it."

Hand in hand they wandered through their new home. Both falling in love with the peaceful stillness— the perfect fusion of old-world charm, new-world conveniences, and the tranquillity of nature.

The previous owners had done a remarkable job renovating the old colonial, and now it stood as both a testament to a bygone era, a nod to the past, while offering the perfect foundations for a future Heather and Nathaniel both dreamed of.

'CHAPTER TWENTY-ONE'

Heather should have realised it was all too good to be true. The last three months after her marriage to Nathaniel and his surprise of a house—it was only a matter of time until her happiness was snatched away.

Releasing a shaky breath, Heather pressed her hand against her churning stomach and willed the nausea away, her leg jumping erratically as she hovered just on the edge of the closed toilet lid. It was a rare morning where Nathaniel had already left for the pub, having received a call after the night manager rang about issues with the heating system.

Overnight, apparently, the system—which ran entirely off gas—had stopped working, the guests waking to icy cold rooms. It had been a blessing in disguise. Heather had suspected her "stomach bug" was a little more complex than that.

She'd had the pregnancy test stashed in the guest bathroom the last couple of days, just waiting for an opportunity to do it while Nathaniel was away and she had a moment to herself.

The timer on her phone timed out. Locking her knees, Heather stood and cautiously approached the vanity, swallowing as she glanced down at the face of the rectangular pregnancy test.

Two blue lines.

Stomach dropping, Heather whirled to the toilet, only just managing to get the lid up before she emptied the contents of her stomach.

Flushing long moments later, Heather sank down to her butt and stretched her legs out straight in front of her. "No. Oh God..." Covering her face, she dissolved into the tears that seemed always just a heartbeat away now. So lost in her own cries, it took long moments to notice her phone was ringing.

Heart sinking at the thought it could be Nathaniel checking in on her, she felt her heartbeat stutter back to life when Faith's name flashed across her screen.

Swiping right to accept, Heather held her breath as Faith's bubbly voice came across the line. "Heather! Quick, Jackson and I are arguing about who's hotter— Thor or Captain America."

"Thor!" Jackson's voice came through somewhat muffled, accompanied by him cursing as Faith giggled. In the background, Heather could hear Bastien laughing while Harmony cooed.

Heather opened her mouth to answer with something frivolous, something expected. Instead, she hiccupped, her voice breaking as a fresh wave of tears overtook her.

"Heath?" Jackson's voice was loud and full of demand. "Are you crying?"

"No—" Heather denied, her voice thick with tears. "I can't talk right now—"

"Don't hang up this phone—" Jackson ordered in a lower tone. He could be overheard demanding his phone, Faith presumably giving it to him. "I'm getting Josh to come around—"

"No," this time it was a low, broken moan, and a second later Faith was back in charge.

"I'm coming," Faith said, her voice calm and measured. "Do you hear me, Heather? I'm coming."

Faith was coming.

It was all Heather could hold onto as time distorted. Tucked between the bathtub and the toilet, she squeezed her hands into tight fists and released them systematically.

Faith was coming...

An age later—or perhaps only a heartbeat—Faith was there, pushing her way into Heather's space with wide, worried eyes.

Drawn almost instantly to the pregnancy stick Heather still somehow clutched, Faith released a deep sigh as her face softened in understanding.

"Oh, Heather. Come here."

Folding into her friend's arms, Heather clung hard, her tears hard and ugly and loud. At some point, she noticed Jackson entering with a bottle of cold water and some Panadol. His expression tight and unreadable as he handed them off to Faith, before retreating out of the bathroom and closing the door quietly behind him.

"Is it fear of his reaction?" Faith asked finally, her tone slow and so careful Heather blinked. "Or is it the pregnancy itself?"

"Nate wants kids," Heather managed in a choked whisper. "He'll—he'll be over the moon."

Faith's shoulders loosened as she released a deep sigh. "Okay. So that answers that question... Heather, you adore kids."

Fingers gripping Faith's, she dragged the smaller woman closer, unable to help the crazed glint in her gaze as she whispered, "I can't make them orphans—Faith. There's no one to look after them if I die—who will love them if I—"

"Faith."

Both women turned their gazes to the door, Heather's eyes sliding shut after colliding with her husband's. Of course Jackson had rung him.

Deep down she had expected him before now, the more pragmatic side of her reasoning he'd probably waited until she'd calmed down. Until she'd slipped up and spoken the truth—because Nathaniel was nothing but patient when it came to running roughshod over every anxiety and worry she could think up.

"I'll take it from here." Already stepping into the small bathroom, Nathaniel filled the space with an authority not many could stand against.

For a moment, Faith hovered on the edge of bowing. "It isn't good for her to be this worked up, Nate. I'm happy to stick around in case she needs—"

"C'mon, babe." Materialising at Nathaniel's back, Jackson's soft gaze was tempered with steel. "Let's go grab the kids and head home."

Against two immovable alpha males, Faith had no chance, so Heather didn't hold it against her when she stood, accepting the warm hug the small woman wrapped her in with tight arms.

Waiting until he'd heard the front door close, Nathaniel shrugged his jacket off, draping it over one of the hooks by the door used for towels.

Once he was within arm's length, he extended a hand down to her, waiting patiently until she finally rested her own palm against his.

Hauling her up and into his arms, Nathaniel tucked her

against his chest, heading first to the sink where he helped Heather brush her teeth. He then shuffled her into their bedroom.

Tucking her into the centre of the bed, he wrapped his body around hers, pressing close so that she felt the unhurried beat of his heart against her back.

"Talk me through it."

Eyes filling, Heather sniffed. "Why aren't you mad? You're supposed to be at work, dealing with the heating. Damn Jackson—he didn't need to call you."

"In no reality would you be going through this without me," Nathaniel said, his tone hard. He allowed a tiny bit of annoyance, a tiny glimpse of hurt, to come through his words. "I should have been here with you, waiting to see the results of that test, *Tesoro*."

"I couldn't have you here while I did it," Heather sobbed, "not when I knew it would be positive, when I knew I'd behave like a crazy person..."

Tutting, Nathaniel pulled her tighter in his arms, holding her together even as she broke down into fresh tears. "You are supposed to lean on me when things get hard. I need you to lean on me when things are hard."

Fighting through the urge to just give in and cry herself to sleep, Heather swallowed thickly. "When Mum and Dad died, I had Oma and Oppa. I was still surrounded by love. It was the single worst experience of my life, but I never doubted my place in the world or felt unloved. This baby—" Without thinking, Heather cupped her flat stomach. "Who will they have? Who will surround them in love and safety? I can't leave them motherless, I can't..."

"*Tesoro*, you are planning for a future in which you aren't there—I'm not there. This isn't one set in stone—"

"But that doesn't mean it's off the table completely," Heather argued, turning in his arms until she faced him. She gripped his hands tightly in hers. "There was no possible reason my parents should have been on that particular road, that particular night. But they were. And it cost them their lives—lives I'm sure they never believed would be cut so brutally short. You cannot guarantee me a future in which something terrible doesn't happen to rip us away. Even you, Nathaniel Feria, are not that powerful."

Baring his teeth, Nathaniel dragged her impossibly closer, his lips hot and insistent on hers as he demanded entrance—taking control with a hand around her throat and the other on the swell of her backside.

"You aren't dying, and neither am I. Not until I'm done with you. Which likely will be never," Nathaniel rolled her pliant body beneath his when she would have argued, slowly stripping each article of clothing from her body.

He loved her well into the day, until the evening rays cast long shadows across the room, and exhausted, Heather slept peacefully at his side.

Filled with restless energy, Nathaniel trailed his fingertip gently up and down the length of her side, thinking, planning—three steps ahead.

He hadn't been called away that morning because of a fault with the heating system at the pub. He'd been called by Josh because there had been another package delivered to Heather at Emersons'.

A picture of her in her wedding dress—zoomed in to focus on her face—but her face had been melted, blackened by what Nathaniel imagined was a cigarette lighter.

The words *Enjoy it while it lasts, bitch,* were written in red block letters on the back.

What concerned Nathaniel was the quality of the photograph. He'd needed the morning to chase down Johnny, who, as their photographer for the event, had all the negatives in the darkroom he'd set up at his own property on the edge of town.

Rage—hot and encompassing—had blinded Nathaniel as he listened to Johnny tell him of a break-in, done one weekend when he drove his boys to their mother in the city.

The burglars had made off with all the negatives he had of Nathaniel and Heather's wedding. The fact that he'd told the police—who had then failed to alert Nathaniel —only compounded his fury.

He'd called his brother then, needing Matteo's level-headedness to talk him down off a ledge he wouldn't have been able to come back from.

Nathaniel had been so close to reaching out to his mother's brother—to the uncle who had taken Matteo under his wing and created the darkness that was his little brother.

But to do that would have meant owing that man a favour—one Nathaniel knew came at a price he wasn't willing to pay.

Unbeknownst to him, however, was the fact that Matteo had already been tracking things quietly in the background—had, in fact, concentrated the full force of his private security company into unravelling the question behind Heather's stalker.

What he'd found had left Nathaniel speechless for long minutes.

Manuel Perez.

The man who had lost everything after Heather had reported him to the authorities—his training methods and horsemanship leaving many animals broken after he'd taken their owners for every cent to their names.

There was one other name, one other accomplice that Matteo was still digging to find, but it was clear the main perpetrator was Perez himself.

The man had gone underground, and hadn't been heard from since the month he broke in and vandalised Heather's grandparents' house.

Matteo believed he'd gone to ground because he realised he was being hunted.

"I can feel you thinking." Yawning, Heather snuggled into his chest and pulled him from his thoughts. "Care to share with the class?"

"I don't want to cause you any more stress," Nathaniel revealed after a heavy sigh, "but to keep it from you is wrong."

Feeling her freeze, he loosened his embrace when she pressed her hands against his chest, her gaze bright as she lifted to sit at his side, her perfect breasts swinging heavily as she moved.

Reaching out because he couldn't not touch her, Nathaniel palmed one heavy mound, lifting its weight for a moment before shaping the flesh.

Dragging his thumb over one turgid nipple as it lengthened, he smiled rakishly as she sighed deeply, leaning into his caress even as she frowned at him.

Tone light and teasing, Heather smacked playfully at his chest, the move turning into a slow stroke. "Focus. My eyes are up here."

"Are they?" Nathaniel growled, lifting just enough to take one straining peak into his mouth. He sucked hard, his hands moving to wrap around her waist as Heather went boneless on a moan.

"God, the things you can do with your mouth..." Sucking in a breath as he continued to draw on her nipple, her thighs clenched in response to the gathering moisture. "It should come with a warning label."

Teeth gently clenching the flesh of her nipple, Nathaniel chuckled. Releasing the abused skin moments later, he flopped flat with one arm beneath his head, propping himself up.

"Well?" Heather asked, leaning down to rest her chin on his chest. "Pretty sure my waterworks this morning have dried me all up. Better tell me now before the hormones have a chance to restock."

"Matteo found your stalker." For a moment, Nathaniel wondered if he should have been more tactful in his delivery, as he felt Heather's body draw tight as a bow.

Then slowly, she relaxed, releasing a deep breath as she did so. "Okay. That's good. Who is it?"

"Manuel Perez."

"No shit?" Bolting upright, Heather's mouth dropped open in shock. "That fucker?"

Gaze once more focused on her swinging breasts, Nathaniel reached for a nipple—the flushed peak clearly demanding his attention.

Heather slapped his hand away, crawling out of the bed before Nathaniel had a chance to move. She grabbed his shirt off the floor.

Dragging it on, she haphazardly popped a few buttons in place, then jumped back onto the bed. Coming over him, she pinned his wrists to the bed.

"The fucker that has been making my life a misery —sending creepy fucking packages in the mail and breathing heavy over the phone. The bastard that trashed my grandparents' place—was Manuel Perez?"

Trying to catch a glimpse of her breasts through the gaping holes and neck of his shirt, Nathaniel made a low noise of assent. "The one and only. Matteo's looking for his accomplice. Seems Perez has gone to ground but still has someone doing his dirty work. Coward."

"What the fuck!" Heather screeched, releasing his wrists as she pushed her fingers into her hair, tugging slightly as she tried to calm her breathing.

Worked up as she was, Nathaniel could just make out the dark pink of her areolas beneath the white of his shirt, enthralled by the way the heavy globes swayed and jiggled beneath the material.

Shifting slightly on his back, Nathaniel adjusted the tented front of his black slacks, trying to find a more comfortable position—until finally, he simply unbuttoned the top and lowered the zipper.

Almost instantly, his hard cock sprang free and thumped against his abdomen. Watching as his wife raged, Nathaniel fisted the base and lazily pumped it once, twice—before Heather's attention fixed on him.

Mouth dropping open, Heather swallowed audibly. "Are you—hard right now?"

"Fuck yes, I am."

"Nate—"

"I can see your boobies..." Nathaniel interrupted, his gaze fixed on the nipple that had popped free. He smiled in response to Heather's snort of laughter.

"My boobies? What are you—three?"

Dragging her close, he pushed his hard cock against her stomach. "Does this feel like I'm three?"

That quickly, her thoughts were derailed, and she

moaned as he nibbled along the column of her throat. "No wonder I'm pregnant. Every second of the day you have me naked, spread out or bent over something…"

Growling, Nathaniel dipped his fingers into the warm heat of her. "You love it."

And she did.

Heather woke abruptly and checked the clock. It was just past midnight. She then looked over her shoulder and felt the tension ease her body.

Nathaniel stretched on his back, sheets low on his hips, one hand under his pillow, and the other resting on her hip.

He murmured in his sleep, kicked slightly, and frowned. The sheet slipped lower, giving Heather an unobstructed view of his body.

Even in sleep, he exuded strength and beauty, with each muscle sculpted and flexing with every movement.

His solid chest lifted with slow, even breaths, the pectoral muscles defined and symmetrical. His tapered waist, tight with a visible six-pack Heather knew he maintained in their home gym, framed the sharp cut of his hip bones. At the apex of his thighs, nestled in soft curls the same shade of black as his hair, lay the impressive length of his softened cock.

He was beautiful.

He was hers.

In quiet moments like this one, Heather needed to pinch herself. It was hard to comprehend that if she reached out now—taking the softened length of him into her palm—he would harden and turn into her. He would take her mouth in hungry possession and expect that she give as good as she got.

She had rights to him that no one else on this world did

—just as he had rights to her.

Quietly slipping from the warm sheets, Heather found his discarded shirt and slipped it on, buttoning only the single clasp between her breasts.

Because the air was chilly despite the heating, she also quietly grabbed a pair of fluffy socks from the large walk-in wardrobe, pulling them on as she silently closed the bedroom door behind her.

Leaving the lights off, she wandered toward the spare rooms, poking through each one idly until reaching the one she really wanted.

West-facing, the room had the best view of the sun setting and in the evenings was bathed in the warm, golden hues of the waning light. The walls, a neutral beige, shimmered in shades of soft amber and blush, the room holding onto the day's warmth. The large bay windows drew in the light, spilling it across the polished timber floors like liquid gold, edging the furniture in shadows of deep orange.

This was the room Heather wanted as the nursery—she could picture a comfortable rocking chair over by the large windows, a plush rug underfoot for tummy time.

On soft feet, she padded into the centre of the room, her hands sliding down her body to rest over her abdomen, flaring her fingers wide to fully encompass the soft skin of her stomach.

"What do you think, baby?" Heather whispered. "I think you'll love it. Maybe a nice yellow with clouds and glow-in-the-dark stars on the roof?"

Silence was her response, but Heather nonetheless felt calm—the acceptance of the small life growing inside her a slow tingle in her fingertips and toes. The fears of earlier were overshadowed by the love she already felt.

"I think this is the perfect room," Nathaniel's deep sleep voice surrounded her a second before his arms did. Sighing, she leaned back heavily into his embrace.

"You were asleep—did I wake you?"

"No, I felt you leave and then I woke up. Figured you were using the loo until you didn't come back."

Turning in his arms, she buried her nose against his collarbone. "Sorry."

His lips on the hairline of her forehead, "Talk to me."

"Something woke me up, and then it just felt like my whole body was too awake to go back to sleep. I was heading towards the kitchen for a midnight snack... then kinda ended up here instead."

Taking in the dark room, Nathaniel considered her earlier words. "I like yellow. That way, over the years, no matter if we have girls or boys, they'll all come home to this room—move onto others when they're older. But I like the thought of rocking them to sleep, the setting sun on their skin."

Arms around his waist, Heather squeezed her agreement—a wordless thing between them. When Nathaniel urged her out and toward the kitchen, she went gladly.

The soft glow of the salt lamp she left on their only source of light, Heather took a seat at the long dining table, pulling her feet up onto the chair and wrapping her arms around her knees.

Feeling unexpectedly drowsy, Heather watched Nathaniel as he navigated the kitchen confidently— retrieving deep mugs from the cupboard, a bar of chocolate, milk from the refrigerator, and cinnamon from the pantry.

Heather, recognising all the ingredients, nodded with

her mouth watering as he lifted the pot and raised an eyebrow in question.

Using a knife, he chopped the chocolate bar into small pieces and transferred them to the saucepan. At the stove, he started a low flame, picked a whisk from the jar next to the stovetop, and placed it within arm's reach.

As the chocolate melted, he added milk and cinnamon, whisking it until, five minutes later, he turned off the flame and poured the mixture into two mugs.

He crossed the kitchen with the two mugs, placed one in front of her, sat beside her, and they clinked their mugs together with smiles.

Heather savoured the first touch of chocolate on her tongue, while Nathaniel watched intently as she licked her bottom lip to catch the melted goodness.

Reaching out, he caught the fingers of her free hand and brought them to his lips. Kissing her silky skin, he held on—resting their tangled hands atop the table.

As the night gave way to early morning, they finished their hot chocolates, rising as one to move through the kitchen and deposit their mugs at the sink.

Heather crawled into bed first, settling comfortably in the centre. The sheets were cool against her skin, and she let out a soft sigh of relief. A few moments later, Nathaniel joined her, his presence steady and warm. He wrapped his strong arms around her, one arm slipping beneath her head as the other rested gently over her stomach, holding her close.

She relaxed against him, feeling the steady rhythm of his breath and the comforting weight of his body pressed against hers.

The room was quiet and bathed in peaceful shadows,

the atmosphere intimate. Wrapped in his embrace, Heather felt safe and content—the rest of the world fading away as they lay together in silence, enjoying the calm of the night until slumber took them both.

'CHAPTER TWENTY-TWO'

"Oliver, seriously, what is up with you at the moment?" Ducking slightly to try and catch sight of Oliver's face as he filed Charlie's hoof, Heather tutted when it felt like he deliberately moved so instead she was looking at his backside. "I thought coming back from seeing Isla, you'd be in a better mood."

Heather leaned against the stall wall, arms crossed, noticing his back tense at her comment.

"Did your visit not go well?" she asked, finally subdued.

"No," Oliver replied, his tone short. "It didn't."

"Do you wanna talk about it?"

"Not really, Heath." Standing tall, Oliver gave her a meaningful look. "Do you want to talk about why everyone shuts up the minute you step into a room?"

Ah, so he's playing dirty then, Heather thought with a deep sigh of annoyance. "I'm pregnant. Didn't handle finding out well."

Mouth dropping open in surprise, Oliver dropped his tools. Advancing despite her warning not to, he wrapped her into a hard hug. "Damn, Heath. I go away two weeks and come home to you fucking cooking a little bean? Congrats, you'll make a great mum."

Just like always, Oliver knew exactly what to say to

make her feel better. Wrapping her own arms around his wide shoulders, Heather loosed a slightly wet laugh. "Thanks. Your turn."

"Seriously, Heath." Oliver warned his tone low, his arms still wrapped tight around Heathers slender body, "I don't want to talk about it."

Trying to push back to get a measure of the expression on his face, Heather gave in when it was clear he wasn't relaxing his hold on her. "But maybe you need to, Ollie. You know whatever you tell me goes into the vault, I'm not gonna go blab to anyone."

Sighing Oliver released his hold on her and for all the money in the world Heather never would have guessed he'd say what he did next.

"She's engaged."

"*What*?" Lowering her voice from the squeak it had been, Heather cleared her throat and tried again. "What?"

"I went to her place, and her mum was there. She answered the door. Looked down her nose at me. Told me not to keep coming around, that Isla was engaged to some...billionaire now. Someone the whole family approved of. Told me I was wasting my time and money, by continuing to *pester her.*"

Anger on behalf of her friend filled her, and Heather was the one pulling him into an embrace this time around. "I'm sorry—Ollie."

"So am I," Oliver grunted. Finally releasing her, he turned away before she could catch his expression, returning to his previous position and picking up one of Charlie's hooves.

"Does – does Connie know?" Heather asked softly, unwilling to believe that she did, because had she known and still let Oliver fly over there…..

"No," Oliver continued picking stones out of Charlie's shoe, "it was weird. Her mum told me to leave, and to keep my mouth shut about Isla's engagement. That the fella she's marrying is hot shit, and they don't need the press knowing until they're ready to make an official announcement."

Something uncomfortably close to a warning slid down Heathers spine, frowning she determined to ask Nathaniel about the engagement later.

Surely as long time family friends, he'd have to have at least heard something about Isla's impending nuptials.

When Ryan turned up minutes later, Heather let him take over helping Oliver with the rest of the horses he had on his list. Heading towards her office, she pushed inside and glanced up with surprise.

Hovering at the edge of her desk, Mark quickly shifted something behind his back, his expression pinched even as he quickly tried to smooth it over.

"Mark, what can I help you with, mate?"

"I—" Seeming lost for a moment, he finally drew out from behind him a familiar paper-wrapped package, and Heather felt her stomach clench. "Sorry, I was supposed to put this on your desk."

"Were you?" Moving cautiously closer, Heather studied the teen, hating the suspicion that filled her. "Do you know who the package is from?"

"No—" Mark quickly shook his head and shoved the package toward her, his denial falling slightly flat but his open expression causing more doubts to swim to the surface.

"Mark, if you know who's sending me these packages, I need you to tell the truth—"

"Honest, I don't! This was by the back door in the kitchen. I thought I was being helpful bringing it out to you, so Mary didn't have to."

The stubborn set to his lips was more familiar than the shifting edginess she'd spotted on his expression. Heather nodded slowly once, then gestured toward the door. "Alright. Thanks, Mark. Go find Ryan for me. Give him a hand. He's helping the farrier with the horses who are getting their feet done today."

Without a word of complaint, Mark disappeared to do as instructed, the sound of her door clicking shut as loud as a gunshot in the sudden silence of her office.

Heather knew she was supposed to call Nathaniel or even Josh if she received another package, but her strong sense of independence demanded she handle it herself.

It was just a package, for pity's sake, from a man who was no longer a faceless threat, but one who Heather knew to be cruel—yet essentially a coward.

She carefully tore open the wrapping paper, mildly exasperated as she discovered an envelope within the box. Anticipating yet another photograph accompanied by threatening remarks in red texter, she proceeded to open the envelope.

Powder—its colour hard to determine—shot into the air, and reflexively, Heather drew in a deep breath, sucking the allergen into her system.

The world shifted as Heather felt her throat tighten. Frowning, her next inhalation felt tight, her breaths shallow as panic rose swiftly. Invisible hands wrapped around her lungs and started to squeeze. Feeling suddenly suffocated, Heather gasped and dropped the envelope back into the box.

Lips tingling, Heather's tongue felt too big for her mouth as her heart rate spiked, thundering in her ears. Dizziness washed over her so quickly that she stumbled. Gaze wide, Heather pushed pens and paper aside, looking for her phone, in her panic forgetting it was still in her back pocket.

The ground beneath her shifted and she felt her legs tremble, a cold sweat breaking out across her skin as shock and panic set in.

Hives formed along her throat and chest—raised welts that itched—chasing the tingling spread through her limbs until she felt weak, the air no longer reaching her lungs.

Heather stopped her frantic search and staggered toward her door, her attempts to open it increasingly jerky as the door inexplicably remained shut.

She couldn't breathe. Why couldn't she breathe?

It felt like something had lodged itself in her throat, her voice a bare whisper as she called out for help.

Why the hell wasn't the door opening?

Raising a trembling fist, she banged on the door's flat surface, her throat now too swollen, her calls unintelligible.

She was choking to death, unable to draw breath—and no one could hear her.

Spots danced in front of her eyes as she went from pounding on the door to clawing her throat, her knees buckling as weakness invaded her limbs and the room spun.

Crawling toward the sofa, Heather braced her arms on the seat's edge, trying to focus on drawing air into lungs that felt too tight.

There was a sound—faint, but unmistakable—and with

what strength remained, she tipped her head to the side and watched as the wood warped, then splintered.

Another resounding crack and then Oliver was there, his face pale, his big body filling her vision as he dropped to his haunches in front of her.

He was speaking, but Heather's focus had narrowed to a single thought—air. She needed air.

One hand wrapped around her throat, Heather reached out and gripped his shirt, trying to drag him closer but lacking the strength. Instead, she sent the plea through her eyes.

Air.

Oliver pulled his phone from his back pocket, punching a number and lifting the device to his ear.

Air.

Never once taking his gaze from hers, he held her wrist as her fingers spasmed against his chest.

Air.

Seconds later, Constance fell into the open doorway, her face almost as pale as Oliver's. She shoved the big man aside, her lips moving as she knelt.

Please. Air.

Constance pulled a cap off something with her teeth, urging Heather down to her side. All Heather could feel was hands pulling at her jeans, then the prick of something sharp in her thigh.

For a long moment, Heather feared whatever Constance did had failed—then suddenly, she took the first real breath she'd had in what felt like forever.

Rapid, shallow breaths slowly eased, becoming deeper and more controlled. Her chest remained tight but less constricted. Relief washed through her, chasing away the lingering tension, while nausea and dizziness kept her sprawled on the floor.

Slowly, the awareness of hands on her body leaked through her panic, and Heather could hear Constance's soft voice.

"You're alright now, Heather. We've got you now—that's it. Nice deep breaths..."

The strange warmth of the adrenaline as it continued to work was far better than the suffocating panic from before, but Heather could still feel her body trembling and the lingering tightness in her throat.

"I called Nate," Oliver's deep, controlled voice pierced the soft melody of Constance's reassurances. "The ambulance is also on the way."

A tiny spike of annoyance made Heather frown. She opened eyes that had slid shut to glare, only to be met with a glare straight back.

"No, you don't," Oliver muttered, his voice hoarse as he knelt at her back, bracing her body in the recovery position with his own. "Not after that scare. You're off to the hospital, and there'll be no arguing."

Heather smiled slightly—unable, even if she wanted to, to argue at this point. Still caught in the aftermath, the world slowly came back into focus. The edges of her vision cleared, her limbs regained strength. With a slow lift, she pointed in the direction of her desk, but gripped a handful of Constance's shirt when the smaller woman would have stood. Without knowing what had been in that envelope, Heather didn't want Connie, or the babe she carried, exposed to it.

A single shake of her head and Constance understood the warning. Instead, she turned slightly and spoke to someone behind her.

"I think whatever caused the reaction is back on her

desk. I think we should probably call Sergeant Reeves and leave him to deal with it."

From the doorway, Josh rumbled his agreement, half his attention focused on Heather while the other kept watch on the open doors to the stables—knowing that at any second, Nathaniel would come barrelling in and need talking down.

On the tail end of that thought, Nathaniel appeared, his olive skin a washed-out grey, his hair sticking on end as his wild gaze locked on Josh's.

Moving quickly, Josh slammed into Nathaniel at speed, grunting at the blow Nathaniel sent into his gut.

"Take a breath. She needs you—the normal, cool, calm, and collected bastard that you always are."

For a minute, it didn't seem like Nathaniel could hear him. Then, suddenly, the tall man went completely still, his chest moving in deep, deliberate inhalations.

"There," Josh murmured, flicking his gaze back toward the open doorway. In the distance, he noticed Graham and Mary as they kept everyone back.

"What happened?" Nathaniel's tone—black and empty —sent a shiver down Josh's spine.

"Don't know. Connie got a call from Oliver. All he said was 'bring the EpiPen.' It wasn't until we got to the stables that we knew it was Heath. Ollie had kicked in her door—said he could hear her banging on it but when he tried to open it, it wouldn't budge."

"Let me past," Nathaniel said, removing Josh's hands from the lapels of his shirt. "I'm in control."

Nodding, Josh followed closely as Nathaniel entered Heather's office. He noticed the way Nathaniel's broad shoulders tightened impossibly beneath the cool silk of his dress shirt. Constance moved aside so Nathaniel could drop into her spot. She tangled her hand with Josh's, letting her husband haul her swollen body up into his arms. As she came to her feet she whispered loud enough for Nathaniel to hear, "Heather motioned toward her desk. I haven't gone near it, but I can see a package."

"*Merda*. Your stubbornness will drive me into an early grave, *Tesoro*." Nathaniel smoothed the pad of his thumbs along her reddened skin, feeling his heart skip as he took in her puffy face and swollen lips. "You were supposed to call me or Josh when you got another package."

Because she didn't have the air to spare on a response, Heather squeezed his fingers in apology, her eyes sliding shut as exhaustion settled like bricks into her skin.

Lifting his attention to the huge man at Heather's back, Nathaniel dipped his head in thanks. "Josh said you kicked the door down."

"The handle was jammed." There was so much unsaid behind Oliver's tone that Nathaniel glanced at the door, noticing Josh was already there, frowning down at the handle as he jiggled it.

He slid his fingers along the cool metal and there was a click. Then, when he tested it again, it moved up and down. Josh lifted his gaze to Nathaniel's.

"It was locked."

Frowning, Nathaniel glanced at Heather, who had her eyes open and locked on his. Without him needing to ask, she shook her head once.

She didn't lock it.

"Who was in here with her?" Nathaniel asked.

Oliver shook his head. "No, she was in here alone."

"Then before?"

Silence. The only person capable of answering lay pale with exhaustion and shock, unable to speak as her eyes slid shut.

Suddenly, paramedics and Sergeant Reeves pushed into the room, and in the chaos and pandemonium, Oliver, Nathaniel, and Josh shared a look.

Then Nathaniel was hot on the heels of the paramedics, following their quick, competent movements with sharp eyes. The hour-long drive was the swiftest Nathaniel had ever travelled the distance.

In short order, Heather was settled into a quiet room, a young nurse checking in periodically with sure hands and soft reassurances. Her calm presence helped Nathaniel's heart rate begin to slow.

It was approaching dawn by the time Heather's lashes fluttered, lifting to reveal murky brown eyes which narrowed in confusion. The pinched expression fell only once Nathaniel moved to take the seat at her side.

"I'm sorry," the first words past her lips were slurred slightly by the continued swelling in her throat and tongue. "Is the baby okay?"

Gripping her fingers tight in his own, Nathaniel lifted her hand and bent his head, pressing his forehead against her cool skin to sigh in relief.

"Baby is doing just fine. Doctors are more concerned with you at the moment—you gave everyone a scare."

Squeezing as much as she could, Heather sniffed. "I know. I'm sorry."

Lifting his gaze, Nathaniel let her see his terror—his helplessness. "No more packages, *Tesoro*. Please. Let someone else open them now."

Nodding, Heather sniffed again, closing her eyes as Nathaniel brushed away the tears that managed to push free.

"No more packages."

"Can you remember anything?"

Swallowing, Heather sorted through her muddled memory, frowning slightly. "I'd been helping Oliver…"

Nathaniel pressed a kiss against the back of her hand. "Yes."

"Then… I went back to my office—paperwork…"

Silent, he waited for her to elaborate, smothering the way his stomach clenched when she frowned harder, frustration pinching her expression as she lifted her gaze to his.

"I—I can't remember. Why can't I remember?"

"The doctors said you might struggle with recall. Your brain's doing what it can to mitigate the stress of the situation."

"There was someone in there," Heather muttered, her frown deepening as a headache built behind her eyes. She lifted her opposite hand and pressed it against her temple. "Someone I know."

Wanting to tell her to relax, Nathaniel swallowed the words back. "Was it someone who's supposed to be in your office?"

Uncertain, Heather whispered, "Yes—yes, I think so…"

"So… an employee?"

Pain, sudden and sharp, cut through her skull like lightning, but with it came clarity. "Mark."

Frowning, Nathaniel found the nurse's call button and hit it, even as he asked, "Mark? The junior?"

"He delivered the package," Heather pushed the discovery out through clenched teeth, the pain radiating across her head in rhythmic pulses. "He closed the door behind him when he left."

Silent, Nathaniel stepped aside as the nurse arrived, her young face creased in empathy as she injected pain relief into Heather's IV.

Stewing, he waited until Heather's eyelids slid shut under the medication's weight, then slipped from the room without a word.

Raising a hand in greeting to the nurse at the station, he offered a distracted smile. Unable to wait for the elevator, he pushed through the emergency stairwell door.

Nathaniel stepped outside into the crisp early morning air and took deep, calming breaths. He wished—again —for a cigarette, a habit he had kicked in his early twenties. Occasionally, though, the craving returned hard and fast.

Exhaling in frustration, he reached for a stick of gum and his phone, thumbing through his contacts before pressing call.

Matteo answered after two rings, voice thick with sleep. "Nate?"

"Mark Carter."

The shift of sheets and a soft feminine sigh made Nathaniel smile slightly despite the situation. "Whose bed do I pull you from tonight, *fratello*?"

"Never you mind, *il mio fratellone*."

"I thought you were set on Hope."

A beat of silence followed, broken only by the soft sound of a door closing. Then Matteo answered seriously. "Nothing's changed. Hope is mine in all the ways that matter."

Surprised, Nathaniel cleared his throat, connecting the dots. "Please tell me the woman in your bed isn't—"

"Who is Mark Carter?" Matteo interrupted, his tone

hollow. Still, Nathaniel heard the underlying warning in his voice and dropped the matter.

"The last person in the room with Heather before she stopped breathing. I almost lost her."

The silence on the other end of the line was cold and sharp.

"I'm sorry—what?"

Nathaniel quickly explained, ending with his current position outside Armidale Hospital, freezing as the first light broke through the clouds.

"I need to know what, if any, involvement Mark has with Heather's stalker. I need it yesterday."

"*Si.* Give my *cognata* a kiss from me when she wakes," Matteo muttered, ringing off without another word.

Nathaniel lingered in the cold, letting it cool his fury, before returning to Heather's side.

He slid back into the stiff hospital chair, stretching long limbs in a bid to relax. Somehow, he managed to fall into a restless doze.

A hand on his jaw pulled him from sleep. Heather's pale face was softened by a small smile.

"Morning."

Shifting with a groan, Nathaniel cupped her neck and leaned in, pressing his lips firmly to hers.

"How did you sleep, *Tesoro*?"

"I'll sleep better in my own bed," Heather mumbled, glancing at the clock. "Doctor'll be doing his rounds soon. I feel well enough to get the hell outta here."

"Be that as it may," Nathaniel said with a grimace as the chair creaked, "we'll wait until the doctor sees you."

Plucking at the sheets in her lap, Heather asked, "Last night, when I remembered Mark delivering the package... what happens with that information now?"

Reaching out, he caught her hands in his and stilled their anxious twisting. "I've got someone looking into it."

"Sergeant Reeves?"

When he stayed silent, she frowned. "You did tell him, didn't you?"

"He can't get me the information I need as quickly as others can—outside the constraints of the law."

"Nate—"

"Relax. I don't want you to worry about anything except feeling better."

Not about to voice her suspicions in case someone was listening, Heather settled, accepting the breakfast tray delivered by a matronly nurse.

When the doctor arrived, Heather was pleased to hear he'd sign off on her release—but shocked by the lab results he carried.

"Mustard powder and nuts?" Nathaniel asked doubtfully. "You can buy that in any grocery store. Are you sure your lab tested everything?"

"I assure you, Mr Feria," said the doctor—mid-forties, tall and pale, his hairline retreating and dark circles carved under his eyes—"there's no mistake."

"I'm allergic to mustard and pine nuts," Heather added, brows pulling low. "Most people who know me know that too."

The doctor raised his eyebrow at Nathaniel before returning his attention to Heather, scribbling something down on her chart.

"I've written a script for an EpiPen. From now on, carry one with you always. No more hospital visits, Mrs Feria, we've seen far too much of you this year. Just take it easy —the baby will appreciate it."

Heather nodded, tightening her grip on Nathaniel's hand as it looked like he might argue. She was glad when he stayed quiet until the doctor had left.

Expelling a loud sigh, Nathaniel rubbed his thumb over her knuckles. "What's challenging is keeping a stubborn woman in check. He should be prescribing *me* something. Anxiety pills. Or tranquilizers."

Rolling her eyes, Heather tugged him close and pressed a kiss to his lips.

"C'mon. Help me get dressed and let's hit that call button. I'm ready to head home."

'CHAPTER TWENTY-THREE'

"That's it, Cooper, keep your weight centred and your heels down, nice!" Sitting on the sidelines watching her junior Polocrosse team practice, Heather motioned towards Cooper and quickly Ryan moved towards the boy.

Under Heather's careful watch, he kept pace with Cooper as he looped lazy figure eights, moving a flag on the end of a long pole from buckets set up at each end. Catching one up, he progressively worked his horse through a walk, trot, and canter until he'd completed the course twice through.

Then, moving to the end of the line, he allowed his two other teammates a turn, Ryan carefully watching and adjusting until they were all able to smoothly transfer their weight from side to side in their saddles.

At the opposite end of the arena, Sascha sat atop a pretty bay mare, her usually soft voice raised easily as she helped the group of three working at her end on their rollbacks.

"That's it, Annabelle," Sascha called, her gaze focused. "Slow Happi down to a trot, collect—that's it, squeeze with your legs. Let him get his back legs underneath himself so he can push off—perfect, that's it!"

Even from a distance, Heather could see Annabelle's jubilant smile, Hudson's crow and enthusiastic clap ringing around the arena.

In the crowd, Heather noticed Johnny clap Ian on the shoulder, the two men sharing a companionable laugh even as their eyes remained fixed on their children in the arena.

"Sascha is a natural coach," Constance murmured, seated next to Heather on a camper chair. She fist-pumped and whooped loudly as Bastien ran his figure-eight course. "She and Ryan have really stepped up while you've been recovering."

"Yeah," sighing gustily, Heather rubbed the flat plane of her stomach. "I'm still hoping Nathaniel will relax soon, and I can get back out there in the thick of things."

"You can't really blame him for being worried," Constance smiled to take the sting out of her tone. "We all are. You've been so incredibly lucky the last few months, but we cannot ignore the lengths it seems Manuel is willing to go to."

Nodding as ice slid down her spine at Constance's words, Heather swallowed carefully as she framed her response. "But keeping me under lock and key, preventing me from doing all the things that make me, *me*... He wins in another way then."

Reaching out, Constance rubbed her arm. "I wish I had a way of fixing this for you, some magical wand I could wave."

Appreciating the sentiment, Heather squeezed Constance's fingers, then focused her attention back on the arena, needing the familiar smell of horse and leather, the dust and manure, to remind her that this wasn't forever.

Half an hour later, Heather waved as Ian and Annabelle led a tired but satisfied Happi towards the front of the stable, part of a long procession of riders and horses who made their way home.

"Well done today, kids," Heather praised, turning back to Ryan and Sascha who hovered at her side, waving goodbye to the students they'd helped coach.

"I love it," Ryan admitted joyfully, his handsome face creased by a large smile. At his side, the smaller, dark Sascha grinned and nodded in agreement.

"Well, you are both extremely talented players and naturals with kids."

"I find it's improving my own Polocrosse," Sascha piped up suddenly, then blushed when Ryan sent her an appraising look. "But that's weird, right?"

"Not at all. When I started coaching, my form and game improved too. Teaching reinforces things in your own mind. You visualize the movements, break them down, slow them up—I completely understand." Heather smiled and patted the girl's shoulder. "Thank you both for your help. I was worried I'd have to cancel classes until I recovered or..."

Sascha interrupted with a smile. "Until you find another coach." Heather had yet to tell everyone she was pregnant, waiting twelve weeks until it was more viable. Those twelve weeks had passed, and she no longer had a reason to stay silent.

"I'm pregnant," Heather said with a small smile, Sascha's squeal and Ryan's dumbfounded expression making her chuckle. "With Nate being the beast he is, I'm likely to need to find a relief coach. I doubt I'll be back out there in a coaching capacity until the little bean is born."

Making a 'well duh' face, Ryan piped up, "You don't need another coach, you have Sascha and me. What we did today worked, and by the time you're ready to pop, we'll be able to manage until you come back."

Nodding, Sascha said, "I've already done a bit of looking into things. I'm not sure what I wanna do next year, if university is where I want to go. I've already had a look at the coaching accreditation framework up on the Polocrosse Australia website. With your mentorship, I think I can have the correct qualifications by the time you're having baby."

Surprised, Heather wrapped an arm around Sascha's shoulder. "I didn't know you were this interested in coaching. Why didn't you say anything?"

Blushing—that in itself was an answer—"Wasn't sure I'd be any good at it…"

Snorting, Ryan had already moved to start packing up. "Don't know what you're talking about, you're good at everything you do!"

Waggling her eyebrows at the young girl, Heather pushed her in Ryan's direction. "Well, I'll leave you to the clean-up then. Sascha, come find me later and I'll help you get started on that training."

Heading to her office, Heather stopped briefly at Charlie's old stall. Feeling a small thrill of nostalgia, she slipped inside.

She didn't notice the dark shadow in the corner, nor the way it gathered.

Instinct raised the hairs on the back of her neck, and with trepidation she glanced towards the darkness— any sound she might have made choked off as suddenly she was surrounded, and darkness swallowed her down.

**

"Strange," Nathaniel murmured, as the second time he tried calling Heather he was sent immediately to voicemail. Seated negligently on the comfortable lounge, Matteo raised his eyebrow.

"What is?"

"Heather isn't answering her phone." Clutching the cold device tightly, Nathaniel glanced out the window to outside, noticing the way the trees' shadows lengthened across the driveway as evening gave way to night.

"Perhaps she's on her way home?"

"No, she'd have messaged me."

"Check her location," Matteo advised, already pulling his laptop from its case by his feet, seeing nothing wrong with invading a woman's privacy for her location.

Opening the app on his phone, Nathaniel grunted in confusion. "It says she's still just in Charlie's stall at Emersons."

Listening to the alarm bells ringing in his mind, the sick slide of instinct that told him she was in trouble, Nathaniel dialled Josh's number.

"Yo, what's up mate?"

"I need you to check up on Heather for me. Her phone tells me she's in Charlie's old stall."

Chuckling, Josh could be heard moving. "Heath know you're creeping on her like a creepy, creeperton?"

"Constance know you keep a pair of her panties in your pocket when we play rugby Saturday mornings for luck?"

A beat of silence before Josh swore. "I won't tell, if you

don't."

More silence before Josh made a low noise in the back of his throat. "There's no one in here, Nate. Are you sure this is the location, whatever stalker app you're using is giving off?"

Face white and his lips bloodless with how firmly he pressed them together, Nathaniel didn't bother disguising the demand. "Look everywhere. It's a GPS chip in her mobile."

"Jesus," Josh muttered, grunting through the phone. "You fucking tagged her?"

Refusing to explain himself, Nathaniel waited—his heart in his throat—the sound of Josh sighing deeply a knife to his gut, and he already knew the other man's response.

"I found it. Her phone. It was in here, buried beneath the straw. Maybe she dropped it."

"You gonna try and tell me that Heather would have gone this long without calling in the cavalry to find her missing phone?"

"No," Josh muttered. "This thing is grafted to her hip while she's here. Everyone is always calling her about something."

"Find her," Nathaniel hissed, hanging up before Josh could reply. He was on his feet and moving to the door. At his side, Matteo was barking orders in rapid-fire Italian into his phone.

"Tell me about Mark," Nathaniel demanded, barely waiting long enough for Matteo to buckle in before he was hitting the accelerator.

Opening the lip of the laptop Matteo had brought with him, he started reading through the information his company had found. "Seventeen. Raised by a single mother in Brisbane. Moved to Glen Innes at the start of the year—"

"Why?" Nathaniel grit his teeth as he merged out onto the highway without looking. "Why did they move to Glen Innes?"

"Mum remarried," Matteo muttered, and after a long moment swore colourfully in Italian. "I'll give you two guesses to who."

"Manuel."

Matteo made a noise like a game show host. "Ten points to Mr Feria, you hit the nail on the head. Caroline Carter remarried to a Manuel Perez, March 17th."

"Mark kept his mother's maiden name," Nathaniel guessed, sliding into the long Emerson driveway without once touching the brakes.

"Looks like it," Matteo said, his tone grim.

Pulling into the first spot he found, Nathaniel was out of the car and inside before Matteo had even unbuckled. Finding Constance first, he curved his body around her protruding stomach and accepted her tight embrace, while his eyes sought Josh in silent demand.

"Who saw her last?" Nathaniel asked, and from behind Josh, a small pale face appeared. Recognizing the young girl as one of Heather's, it took effort for him to gentle his tone. "Sascha? Right? When—when did you see Heather last?"

"After three," Sascha whispered. "She left Ryan and me to clean up after her Polocrosse class."

A young man of seventeen stepped close to Sascha as if to protect her. "We watched her leave the arena. She looked like she stopped in at Charlie's old stall."

"Then?" Nathaniel barked, drawing in a deep breath as Sascha jumped and Ryan shifted slightly in front of the girl. "Did you see her after that?"

"No—" Sascha whispered shakily. "I just—figured she was in her office or had gone home."

Without thought, Nathaniel hurled the glass of whiskey Mary had pressed into his hand at some point. The satisfying smash of glass on stone did nothing to assuage his rage.

For a moment, Nathaniel was deaf and dumb to everything around him, aware only enough to feel the smallest thrill of caution as he turned to Matteo. "Call Uncle Giovanni."

When Matteo made to move, he paused when Constance lifted her hand, the other holding her phone tight against her ear. "Wait."

Close to losing his mind, Nathaniel turned towards her, his mouth open to argue—then he noticed the bewilderment on her expression, and instinct bade him be silent.

Instead, he reached out and took the phone from her limp fingers, hitting speakerphone. The entire room froze as Grace's youthful voice filled the space.

"Connie? Connie, can you hear me? I said I've just accidentally hit someone with my car, and I've found Heather in the boot. What do you want me to do?"

"Hit someone with your car?" Nathaniel demanded, his tone chilling.

For a moment, there was silence, then Grace's voice came carefully through the speaker. "That's right. He startled me and instead of braking, I hit the accelerator. I pinned him between the bonnet and the wall of the Woollies car park."

Nathaniel wasn't the only one struggling to understand what the young woman was saying. "Excuse me, can you—repeat that?"

An annoyed sigh. "I said, I have some random pinned between my car's bonnet and the Woolworths building. Undercover parking, level two. He has Heather in his boot. She's a little worse for wear, but not so bad now that I have her out and she's got a bottle of Gatorade to replace any lost electrolytes."

Matteo's chuckles at his back turned into full-blown gales of laughter. Tossing the phone in Matteo's direction, Nathaniel pointed at his brother as he headed back out to the car park.

"Keep her on the phone, send me the directions, but I'm pretty sure I know where I'm going."

"I'm coming too," Josh yelled, kissing Constance on the cheek and following Nathaniel quickly out the door. He only just managed to close the car door behind him before Nathaniel was peeling out and heading towards town.

**

Heather knew she was in trouble, hadn't in fact been passed out long enough to miss the way Manuel manhandled her out the side door of Charlie's old stall. Aware the whole time he'd had her tucked against his side, the feel of a sharp knife pricking the skin of her lower stomach was enough to quell any desire she had to call for help.

Regardless, she knew there was only Sascha and Ryan within hearing distance—two seventeen-year-olds far too young to deal with Manuel's level of crazy.

"What the hell do you think you're doing?" Heather demanded breathlessly, tripping slightly on the uneven ground as Manuel bulled her across the house paddock. "You've done your dash, mate, give it up."

"Shut up," Manuel hissed, his breath rancid and making her stomach roll. "You stupid, self-entitled bitch. You ruined my life—do you know that?"

"It's no less than you deserved," Heather sneered. "All those families you tricked, those horses whose spirits you broke—and for what? Money? How's that money treating you now?"

"Worthless slut!" Manuel yanked her around until she faced him, ignoring her cry of pain as the action pulled her arm from its socket. "When they did me for animal cruelty, the fines sent me bankrupt! I have no money!"

"Karma," Heather hissed, flinching a second later when Manuel raised his arm as if to strike her. He paused, and Heather cracked her eyelids open slightly to watch the expressions flash across his face.

Uncertainty.

Fear.

Rage.

"You weren't expecting me to step through Charlie's old door, were you?" Heather breathed in sudden understanding. She laughed at her stroke of extreme bad luck.

Face twisting into ugly lines, Manuel pushed Heather's shoulder until she stumbled back into a steady trot towards the car park. "Doesn't matter. This is much better anyway."

"Is it?" Heather asked softly. "Because I have a feeling you never meant to take me. What's your plan, Manuel?"

Refusing to answer, they finally reached a beat-up Ford Focus parked as far back in the car park as space allowed. He hit a button to unlock the vehicle, and Heather noticed the sun-powered daisy sitting on the dashboard before he urged her towards the back.

Lifting the boot lid, Manuel gestured with his chin for her to get in. Glancing at him askance, Heather shook her head. "No way. There's no way I'll fit—"

"Not my problem," Manuel grouched, shoving her towards the small space. He managed to dodge most of her wild punches, grunting when her fists landed their shots.

But Heather was still a woman, and Manuel, despite appearances, was still a strong man. With her legs tucked hard up into her chest, Heather felt her breath stutter in horror, and Manuel glanced down at her.

Both hands holding the trunk, for a moment she could almost swear she saw his gaze flash with indecision. Then his expression shuttered, and he smiled nastily, slamming the boot shut with enough force that Heather felt the metal kiss her shoulder and thigh.

Tears would get her nowhere, but in this moment, as the bumpy road of Emersons' driveway jostled her painfully, Heather found herself helpless in preventing them.

Eventually, Manuel rolled to a stop, and Heather flinched when he smacked the palm of one hand down on the lid of the boot, his hissed warning to keep silent rolling through her system.

How the hell was she going to get out of this mess? Hand moving to press against her stomach, Heather drew in a shaky breath, swallowing down the steady stream of tears with short, hiccupping breaths.

Glancing around, she started looking for a way out, running her fingers along the wall behind her, hoping she'd find a catch that would open a space through into the car's interior.

Nothing.

Turning her attention back to the lid itself, she tested the walls around the rear lights for any sort of weakness, hoping that once Manuel was back and they were moving, she could dislodge one of the lights—stick her arm out or maybe manoeuvre her shirt free, have it streaming along behind them like a flag.

Freezing at the sound of raised voices, Heather listened as she recognized first Manuel's voice, then another—feminine and soft, as familiar as it was hard to place.

A beat of silence before a sudden squeal of rubber on concrete, the sharp crack of metal crumpling, and a very masculine shout of pain.

What the hell was going on out there?

Giving up subtlety, Heather used all her strength to punch the light at eye level out, pressing hard against the hole to try and see what was happening.

But her angle was all wrong, and instead, she moved back enough to squeeze her arm up between her body, shoving the limb out as far as she could to wave it around.

"Help! Someone, anyone—help!"

A gasp—the voice close enough that now Heather recognized it. Grace Bianchi, grasping Heather's hand firmly in hers.

"Heath? What the hell, girl, why are you in this weirdo's boot?"

"He offered me a lift into town," Heather grouched, squeezing Grace's fingers tightly in relief. "Can you please get me the fuck out of here?"

"Okay, okay. You gotta let go for a minute, I'm gonna grab dickheads keys."

For a moment Heather couldn't comply, unable to

release her hold on Grace's fingers for all the gold in King Midas's royal treasury.

Grace leaned in towards the opening with a confident and lively gaze that resembled Faith's, causing Heather to feel at ease.

"Trust me," Grace whispered. "I'll be right back."

Uncurling her fingers one at a time was the hardest thing Heather had ever had to do, but finally she managed it, and swallowing the urge to call Grace back when she disappeared, she settled into the silence and waited.

Minutes, hours—days later, Grace was suddenly throwing open the boot, and Heather felt dizzy at the sudden influx of fresh air, breathing it in deeply as she felt Grace wrap an arm around her shoulders.

"Easy does it," Grace cautioned, helping Heather lift until she was seated. "There we go. Hope—in the backseat is a bottle of watermelon Gatorade. Bring that over, will you?"

Blinking, Heather watched Hope approach with careful steps, her small face completely devoid of emotion as she glanced at the man slumped over her sister's bonnet.

Uncapping the orange lid, Hope pressed the drink into Heather's hand, taking Grace's spot, who stepped away —her phone already at her ear.

"You alright, Heath?"

Laughing, the sound somewhat shrill, Heather studied Hope's blank face. "Am I alright? Are you alright? What —how did he get like—what the hell happened?"

"Accident," Hope said, her voice a monotone. "He came outta nowhere."

But that wasn't what Grace was saying into the phone—

Heather picking up 'accident' and 'pinned him between the bonnet and the wall' as she took small sips of the sugary drink at Hope's insistence.

Grace disconnected the call with a surprising level of cheerfulness for someone who had inadvertently—albeit intentionally—pinned another person against a cement wall with her vehicle. She then proceeded to return to Heather and Hope's side with a wide smile. "Alright, let's get you outta there. It smells like grease and petrol fumes."

With both young women's help, Heather shakily stepped free of the boot. But unable to approach Grace's vehicle, she opted instead to take a seat on the curb.

As soon as she'd settled on the hard cement, Nathaniel was swinging into the spot at her side, Josh exiting the passenger side and hurrying towards Manuel, who was slowly regaining consciousness and groaning.

Hands beneath her jaw lifting her gaze, and Heather fell into deep brown pools of worry and confusion. "*Tesoro*?"

"I'm alright," Heather whispered, meaning it. "He's not. But I'm alright."

Folding into his wide chest, Heather drew in a shaky breath, watching as Sergeant Michael arrived and took over handling Manuel, the ambulance hot on his heels.

Amid the hustle and bustle of paramedics, firefighters, and police officers, Heather watched as Hope gripped Grace's arm, pulling the youngest Bianchi close. Hope's gaze was fixed on those around them, her lips moving rapidly.

Still as a statue, something dark swimming in her eyes, Grace nodded occasionally in response to whatever Hope said. Somehow, Heather knew the two had their stories perfectly in tune.

'CHAPTER TWENTY-FOUR'

The silence in the courtroom was deafening as the judge, an imposing figure of authority and composure, raised her gavel high.

The air was thick with anticipation, every eye in the room focused on the bench. Her black robe, crisp and formal, added depth and gravity to what was already a tense situation.

The soft rustle of papers and the occasional cough from the gallery were the only sounds breaking the stillness, and Heather clasped Nathaniel's fingers hard as they rested in her lap.

With a steady hand, the judge adjusted her glasses, her gaze sharp as she looked down on the defendant, who sat rigid in the dock.

Manuel's expression pale and tense with the weight of what was to come, behind him his wife's pinched look of disapproval, judgement in itself.

In the gallery, the murmurs of spectators hushed as the judge finally spoke, her voice steady and unwavering, filled with the weight of finality.

"After carefully considering all the evidence and the submissions of counsel, it is the judgment of this court that the defendant is guilty of the charges laid before them," the judge declared, her voice ringing clear in the silence.

The words echoed in the room, settling heavily on everyone as a collective breath exhaled in relief, the judge's eyes stern and unblinking as she called on the jury to deliver their judgment.

Unanimously: 'guilty.'

As judgment was passed, Manuel's face seemed to drain of all colour, his shoulders slumping under the weight of the moment. Behind him, his wife stood and wordlessly left, Manuel not even bothering to turn and watch her very public renouncement of him.

Still, the only sound was the subtle click of the court transcriber as he captured every word spoken, the judge outlining the decision behind the verdict, the details of the case, and the gravity of the crime.

The judge settled her gaze on Heather, her fingers tapping the gavel against the surface of the bench contemplatively. "Sentencing will proceed at a later date," the judge said finally, her tone full of authority and a sense of detached empathy. "I am glad this court was able to resolve these matters and hope the victim of Mr Manuel Perez can now rest easy in the knowledge the perpetrator is behind bars. Court is adjourned."

With a final stroke of the gavel, the room exploded into action, the low hum of conversation filling the space. Heather stood with Nathaniel's arm about her waist as Manuel was removed from court, never once looking in her direction or acknowledging her in any way.

The judge remained composed, her face betraying no emotion as she turned to address the next matter on the docket, the finality of her words still hanging in the air, heavy with consequence.

At Nathaniel's urging, Heather allowed him to press her from the row of seats by the front they'd picked, carefully picking their way through the crowd and towards the exit.

In the hallway, they paused and waited for the rest of their family to catch up, Jack Senior plucking the clip-on tie from his neck and unbuttoning the top with a gusty sigh.

"Thank God that mess is all over with."

Murmuring her agreement, Constance accepted Jack's tie, then Josh's, with a wry smile. Tucking both offending garments into her purse, she stared around the group. "Anyone up for some lunch?"

All eyes turned towards Heather, and she took a moment to assess her emotional state as well as her physical one. Then, with a smile, she nodded. "I could eat."

Pumping a fist into the air, Grace bounced a little on her toes. "Oh please, let me show you the best little Korean place in the city. Kimchi fried rice that you will crave the rest of your natural life—I kid you not."

Frowning, Hope sidled slightly away from Matteo, who was steadily pushing his way into her personal space. "There's a nice Indian place not far from here."

Rolling her eyes, Grace sent her older sibling a dead-eyed look. "How you can even think to put that place on the same level—cannot even compare."

Lips tight, Hope sent Grace a dark look. "It's just food, why are you so damn dramatic?"

"We cannot all be robots like you," Grace teased, doing a jerky robot impression and making sure her voice was comically pitched the same as a robot might be.

"I don't know," Heather muttered, tucking her chilled

hands into her coat pockets and sliding closer into Nathaniel's warmth. "Honestly, I've never had Korean before, maybe we could give that a go."

As Grace poked her tongue out at Hope, who merely frowned, everyone bustled towards the cars they'd come in, having driven like a small procession at four a.m. that morning all the way into Sydney for Manuel Perez's trial.

Now that Heather was able to put the whole stalking ordeal behind her, she felt a bone-deep exhaustion, the months of sustained adrenaline and stress hitting her hard.

Curled slightly on her side so that she faced Nathaniel, she watched him smoothly handle the busy traffic of the city, the navigation turned low and punctuating the soft jazz Nathaniel had playing in the background.

"Tired, *Tesoro*?" Nathaniel asked, reaching one hand out to lay it over her jean-clad knee. He sent her a soft smile when she murmured her agreement.

"Let's spend the night in the city," Heather suggested. "After dinner, let's find somewhere close by. I can barely keep my eyes open. I don't want you driving while I'm snoring my head off—you need someone to keep you company."

Because he was tired, Nathaniel nodded. Arriving at their destination twenty minutes later, he sent Heather ahead, taking a moment to have Isla organize a room after sending her his location.

He waited long enough for her message to chime through confirming she'd sorted something else, messaging him the details once it was booked, before he slid from the car and locked it securely behind him.

As he crossed the busy street, Nathaniel admired

the soft glow of lanterns illuminating the narrow entryway, casting a golden hue onto the pavement at his feet, the faint sound of Korean pop music playing softly from within mixing with the hum of the city outside.

Spotting his group in the very centre, two smiling servers hovering around them as they picked seats, Nathaniel smiled and pushed his way inside.

Assailed by the fragrant air—the smell of sizzling BBQ, garlic, and fermented kimchi immediately making his mouth water—Nathaniel carefully picked his way through the cozily dim lighting.

Most of the wooden tables, surrounded by low chairs and cushions, were already patronised by small groups or couples. The intimacy and balance between modern and traditional décor assisted with the cozy atmosphere.

As Nathaniel slid into his seat at Heather's side, he smiled as she glanced up at him, answering the unasked question in her gaze. "I've got Isla onto it."

Eavesdropping, Grace leaned in, asking, "Isla onto what?"

"We're thinking of staying the night in the city," Heather commented softly, reading through the menu. "It's been a hectic last twelve months."

"Girl, that's putting it mildly." Grace snorted, picking a set of chopsticks out for herself, Heather, and Nathaniel. She handed two pairs over with a grin. "If I know my city—which I do—I imagine Isla will book you into the Shangri-La. Overlooking the Opera House, absolutely stunning views, top-notch room service, and their beds—everything on them is Egyptian cotton and goose-down feathers. Absolute heaven."

Feeling their gaze on her, Grace blinked her eyes open

and then shrugged at their raised brows. "Remember what I studied at university? Rory wanted me in hotels. I interned at the Shangri-La."

Attention drawn back to the waitstaff who appeared, dressed in neat uniforms, their smiles warm and welcoming, everyone placed their orders and then sat back to chat in smaller groups.

Fragrant steam rose from the bowls of rice, small dishes of banchan—spicy kimchi and sautéed spinach —arriving to pepper colourful contrast against the dark wooden tabletop.

At the table beside them came the sound of sizzling marinated beef, pork, and chicken as it hit the grill, the smell such that you could almost taste the meat.

With her chopsticks, Grace gestured subtly towards the feast. "That's what I ordered."

In shorter time than Heather could have predicted, the waitstaff returned, their arms laden down as they moved efficiently between them, dispensing meals and more side dishes with quick, deft movements.

Between herself and Nathaniel, Heather had ordered hot stone bowls of kimchi jjigae. Heather fell instantly in love with the spicy, sour, and savoury flavour of the hearty stew, which she washed down with a lemonade, while Nathaniel enjoyed some soju.

Through the large windows, the Sydney skyline—a mix of glass and steel—reflected the last slivers of daylight, while in the shadows left behind by the skyscrapers, the streets darkened into shades of indigo and violet.

Splitting the bill, everyone wished the waitstaff a good evening, congregating outside as the icy wind blew through the multiple layers they all wore.

"Brr!" Faith rubbed her arms briskly and glanced at

Jackson. "Well, better be off. Hope, Grace—do you want a lift back to Mum's?"

"I'm heading to my studio in the city," Grace said quickly and tucked her scarf firmly around her throat. "I've already ordered an Uber."

Everyone's attention turned to Hope, whose expression seemed to freeze. Matteo, her silent shadow that afternoon, stepped into place at her side.

"Actually, my place for the evening is in the same direction as your mum's place, isn't it?" Matteo asked, angling his chin towards Hope, even as his gaze stayed locked on Faith's. "It's the opposite direction you guys need to head, though, to get back onto the highway. I'd be happy to make sure Hope makes it safely to her destination."

Turning her gaze to Hope's closed expression, Faith waited for her sister to argue. Surprised when nothing came, she opened her mouth to speak but bit her tongue as Jackson gently touched her lower back. Glancing at him, Faith nodded slowly and waved to everyone before heading toward the undercover parking garage where they'd left their car.

Saying their own goodbyes, Constance and Josh linked arms, their pace a slow and steady waddle behind Jack Senior, as they followed Faith and Jackson toward the multilevel garage.

Wanting to linger instead, Heather felt Nathaniel press her toward the curb, having already spotted their car parked across the road.

Beneath the lamp, Heather studied Hope's closed expression as Matteo whispered something down into her ear. Grace's attention completely diverted by her phone; a second later, she lifted her hand in a distracted wave, announcing, "Uber's here. See you all on the flip side."

Nestled into the passenger seat once more, Heather watched Hope and Matteo across the street—the way the young woman seemed to thaw now that everyone else had left.

Her arms moved to wrap around her body even as she leaned subtly against Matteo's chest, his arm lifting to wrap around her waist.

"Do you think anyone else sees it?" Heather asked, nodding toward Nathaniel's little brother when he glanced questioningly her way. For a moment, Nathaniel paused, also watching the young couple across the road.

"No," he said finally, turning the engine over. He waited for the smooth growl to settle. "Hope is intensely private, and while my brother is not one to hide his dalliances, in this situation he seems to be taking things at her pace."

"Someone should tell Faith," Heather sighed, nudging Nathaniel. A moment later, he chuckled.

"Why do I get the feeling this 'someone' should be me?"

"Because it's your brother."

"Yeah—and she's your best friend."

Closing her eyes slightly, Heather laughed. "Scissors, paper, rock you for it?"

"I have a better idea," his warm hand landed on her thigh, creeping higher until he cupped her sex. "Whoever comes first loses, and then has to tell Faith."

"That's not fair," Heather gasped, arching slightly to press her heated flesh firmly into his hand. "Pregnancy hormones make me come just by looking at you most days."

Laughing, Nathaniel used a red light to press a heated kiss against Heather's pliant lips. "That sounds like a you problem, *Tesoro*."

Grumbling as he broke the kiss all too soon, Heather wiggled in her seat, content to let the silence and the gentle strings of a bluesy guitar fill the car's interior.

Nathaniel followed the directions Isla had sent to his phone, leaving Heather asleep in the front seat near reception. He entered the brightly lit foyer with his characteristic arrogant elegance, completing the booking Isla started with a wide-eyed young man behind the desk.

Then, heading once more back outside to his car, he carefully swung Heather up into his arms, already having directed the bellboy to grab their shared suitcase from the boot.

Taking the elevator to the top level, Nathaniel followed the bellboy as he delivered their bags right to their room, laying Heather down onto the plush bed and returning to tip the grinning man handsomely before locking the door behind him.

Sighing, he took a moment to take in the clean, crisp modern décor and the large windows overlooking the harbour and the Opera House. Pleased with the state of the room, he moved into the bathroom.

The huge shower, tiled in marble, called his name. Toeing off his shoes, he was naked, head beneath the spray within seconds.

Cool air on his naked back alerted him to the shower doors opening, heat enveloping him once more as the glass snicked softly closed.

Warm hands settled low on his abdomen, soft breasts pressing intimately against the length of his spine.

Nathaniel shifted just enough to pull his head free of the spray, using hands he'd braced on the shower wall to push his wet hair from his face.

Heather's hands, warm and soapy from the supplied hotel soap, washed gentle circles over his abdomen. "Mmm, I fell asleep."

"Yes," Nathaniel grunted, his muscles flinching as the blood rapidly rushed into his cock, filling it to half-mast before she'd even touched it. "You are exhausted."

"I am," Heather agreed easily, pressing a hot, open-mouthed kiss against the rippling muscles of his back. She worked the lather lower onto his thighs. "But you, *amore mio,* are also exhausted."

Nathaniel groaned as her fingers finally moved to wrap around his cock, her hold unapologetic and firm as she started at the base, running her grip up and down the hard length of him.

She knew just how firmly he needed her to squeeze, how he went wild at the way she rubbed her thumb over the head of his penis each time.

Her free hand, which had been continuing its massage over his stomach and legs, trailed up his inner thigh to gently cradle his balls. Cupping them lightly, she allowed them to fall through her fingers as she juggled them gently.

Hips flexing in time to the glide of her hand, Nathaniel shuddered when her other hand joined in. She stroked firmly from tip to base one after the other until finally, she gripped the base and dragged one hand back to the tip, circling and rubbing it firmly, spreading his precum and making him shiver.

"Enough." Whirling, he caught Heather off guard, hauling her up with strong hands beneath her armpits.

He pressed her into the cool tiles, sinking into the warmth between her thighs as she wrapped her legs around his waist.

As the shower steamed all around them, Nathaniel slanted his mouth across hers, one hand gripping her wrist to hold it pinned above her head. The other spanning the gentle swell of her abdomen possessively, he notched himself against the wet, heat of her body.

Ripping his lips from hers he released his hold on her wrist, felt her drape her arm lazily across his shoulders, waiting for her lashes to lift to meet his gaze.

Only once he had her doe eyes soft with permission, did he thrust the hard length of his cock into her welcoming body, their mingled gasps the only sound heard above the gentle fall of water.

Afterwards Heather limp and exhausted, her eyes heavy as she fought sleep, she smiled in languid complaint as he slipped from her body.

Not much better, Nathaniel managed to turn the shower off and haul their bodies into the bed after they both towelled off. Tucking close together, they fell into a deep, restorative slumber as the lights of Sydney twinkled outside their hotel room window.

**

Across the city, in a small studio apartment, Grace contemplated the clean white canvas. Her long hair was gathered into a messy top knot, long fingers holding a paintbrush dipped in black.

Tipping her head slightly to the side, she let her mind clear, let the darkness out, and beneath her fingers, the canvas took shape.

With a life of its own, the dark, angry lines became the face of a man grey with sickness, but hinting at the cruelty that once lived in every expression.

Her own personal bogeyman.

Ignorant to the tears leaking slowly down her cheeks, to the exhaustion trembling through her limbs, Grace painted...

**

"I'm not getting into that bed with you," Hope argued, struggling to hold onto her emptiness. She tried hard —and failed—to keep any real inflection from entering her tone.

"Why? We have shared a bed once before," Matteo stretched his arms above his head, gripping the doorframe and blocking her escape from the single room with the king-sized bed he'd requested.

"That was before!" Hope hissed.

"Ah, before this man—this Stephen with whom you are now involved."

"Don't say it like that." Shoving his chest, she moved him only because he let her. She made it a handful of steps before she was swept from her feet and dumped unceremoniously into the centre of the large bed.

Spluttering in indignation, any words she might have said froze as Matteo lowered his heavily muscled body over hers, his expression dark and forbidding but never once stirring the fear Hope so often felt around men.

"Does he kiss you the way you need to be kissed, *Tesoro mio*? Does he excite you with nothing more than his fingers against your bare skin?"

Trying—and failing—to suppress her shiver, Hope revealed more than she wanted to with her next words. "He doesn't kiss me at all."

Immediately, she closed her eyes, calling herself every word for foolish under the sun, even as her body opened beneath Matteo's, his strong hands shredding through every argument and excuse she placed before him...

**

Gaze twinkling, Constance adjusted the angle of the centre mirror in the car, diverting it away from the slumbering image of her grandfather.

"Thank god today's hearing went the way it did," Josh murmured, changing lanes smoothly. He caught Constance check her phone from the corner of his eye. "Would you relax? Leo will be having the time of his life with Mary."

"I know." Angling the phone slightly so that Josh caught a glimpse of their son's rosy face covered in chocolate, she joined his quiet laughter with a soft huff. "Busted. The both of them."

Their hands instinctively met over the console as Constance ran her gaze along the planes of his face, her voice a muted whisper as she said. "I love you."

A moment of silence as Josh's fingers tightened, "I love you too, Connie. So fucking much."

Without letting go of her, he shifted until their joined hands rested on the swell of her pregnant belly. Their child rolled in response, and Josh's lips lifted in a smile as Constance chuckled softly.

**

"God, he's such a granny Mae when he has Connie in the car with him," Jackson huffed, staring into the rearview mirror for the thousandth time, searching for Josh's familiar headlights.

"Hope hasn't messaged me to say she got home," Faith fretted, checking her phone's ringer. "Nor has Grace. Grace at least I know has probably forgotten and is busy painting. But Hope... Hope doesn't forget... Do you think I should call her? Maybe I should ring Nate, grab his brother's number, and try him instead—"

"Or," Jackson interrupted with a smile, "you could take a breath? Hope is an adult. I'm sure she knows what she's doing."

"What is that supposed to mean?" Faith demanded, poking Jackson's side when he was silent too long. "Hmm?"

"C'mon, Faith. You seriously gonna tell me you didn't see the way Matteo and Hope were stuck like glue today? Hell, every time they're within distance of each other, they're like a piece of Velcro and a sock."

Gnawing on her lip, Faith worried—because she hadn't in fact noticed. Her world had narrowed to her tiny family as it grew from three to four with the birth of Harmony.

She hadn't noticed the obvious relationship budding between her quietest sister and her boss's intimidating younger brother. "Shit."

Amused, Jackson squeezed the knee closest to him, chuckling as Faith shouted in laughter and shoved his hand away.

Her glare was all for show, lacking any real heat, and her softly huffed, 'I hate it when you do that!' was a familiar complaint.

"I think the time for worrying has passed," Jackson predicted. "Just be there for her, so that whatever happens in the end, she knows you're there for her."

Muscles liquefying, Faith smiled and let her body relax as she pulled her fluffy car blanket firmly around her shoulders. "When'd you get so wise, Mr Hart?"

"I've always been wise, Mrs Hart," Jackson quibbled, his

smile slow and full of mischief. The fingers he sent seeking that spot that he knew without fail would make her laugh were swatted away...

'END'

K.J MARGARET AUSTIN

PLEASE LEAVE A REVIEW

I hope you enjoyed reading about Nathaniel and Heather.

If you did please leave a review on Amazon, your comments and honest feedback will help me get better!

Go ahead and head over to my website to follow on social media and subscribe to the newsletter!

https://kjmargaretaustin.my.canva.site/

As an Indi-author I rely on my beta-readers to help read and edit my books, but even then things can and do get missed. If you notice anything BIG my helpers and I have missed, please email me. Any and all feedback is always appreciated.

kjmargaretaustin@gmail.com

BOOKS BY THIS AUTHOR

Holding Hart

Constance Wells believed she'd heard the last of the Emerson clan when she was eight years old and her mother died, the Emerson patriarch unaccepting of her parents' relationship a fact well-known. But when her grandfather suffers a crippling accident, he's left with little choice but to turn to his illegitimate granddaughter for help. Seeing the family-run and owned Bed and Breakfast with the attached, internationally recognized horse breeding name, in the hands of anyone other than an Emerson; not something he's about to let happen.

Determined to prove a point to her grandfather...and perhaps herself...Constance is up to the task of taking on the mammoth spread.

But when a spunky, rude, turning-up-uninvited neighbour, Josh Hart, steps into the picture. He proves a greater distraction than Constance first counted on.

Expect the unexpected, and even the best-laid plans will

be thrown out the window. Can the love of a good old country boy, and the support of her new family keep the old demons at bay? Or will her niggling suspicions that she's just not good enough for the Emerson name, drive her away from the one place in the whole world truly hers.

Captivating Faith

Welcome to the second instalment of the Glen Innes Series, fall in love with Jackson Hart as he's 'Captivating Faith.'

Seven years ago Jackson Hart watched the love of his life drive away, now she's back but everything is so much more complicated than when they were seventeen.

Having hidden a son from him all these years Jackson is done waiting, and he's not about to let Faith's fears of the obstacles in their path, get in the way of him claiming his family.

Join us as we revisit the picturesque town of Glen Innes and fall a little bit more in love with the town's citizens.

Tempting Heather

Welcome back to Glen Innes in the third instalment of the series: 'Tempting Heather'

Heather Ross has poured her heart into Emersons, rising from junior stable hand to foreman. Fiercely independent and deeply rooted in her small-town life, she's not easily shaken—until a stalker begins to threaten her peace.

Nathaniel Feria, a hotel tycoon with charm to spare, left Perth for Glen Innes—officially for the quiet life, but everyone knows it's because of Heather. He's patient, persistent, and making headway with her... but his formidable mother, Signora madre Feria, won't have it.

As danger closes in and loyalties are tested, Heather and Nathaniel must decide what—and who—is worth fighting for.

Featuring beloved characters from previous books, 'Tempting Heather' is a heartfelt bush romance where strength, love, and community shine.